W9-CND-305

Queen City
jazz

Kathleen Ann Goonan

Queen City

jazz

TOR

A TOM DOHERTY ASSOCIATES BOOK
NEW YORK

QUEEN CITY JAZZ

Copyright © 1994 by Kathleen Ann Goonan

A Tor Book
Published by Tom Doherty Associates, Inc.
175 Fifth Avenue
New York, N.Y. 10010

Tor ® is a registered trademark of Tom Doherty Associates, Inc.

Design by Lynn Newmark

Library of Congress Cataloging-in-Publication Data

Goonan, Kathleen Ann.
    Queen city jazz   /   Kathleen Ann Goonan.
       p.   cm.
    "A Tom Doherty Associates book."
    ISBN 0-312-85678-4
    1. City and town life—Ohio—Cincinnati—Fiction.
  2. Cincinnati (Ohio)—Fiction.   I. Title.
  PS3557.O628Q4   1994   94-30175
  813'.54—dc20   CIP

First edition: November 1994

Printed in the United States of America

0 9 8 7 6 5 4 3 2 1

For Joseph

Thanks to my readers: Steve Brown, who believed in the book and named Verity; Wanda Collins, Sage Walker, Pam Noles, and Beverly Suarez-Beard. Thanks also to Virginia Kidd, whose enthusiasm helped me finish this book, and to David Hartwell, whose insights were invaluable.

Special thanks to my husband, Joseph Michael Mansy, for his support, encouragement, and scientific expertise; to Tom Goonan, for historical facts and many important technical suggestions; to John Cramer, for the idea that made it work; to Amy Roberts, who was there; and to Irma, Mary, and Susie Goonan.

Memories of Russell and Vera Goonan, and Clarence and Eva Knott—and their homeplaces—were with me as I wrote this book, as well as the memory of Steve Hibberd.

Strange futures lie open, holding worlds beyond our imagining.

—Eric Drexler,
Engines of Creation

In New Orleans—if you could get to New Orleans—would the music be loud enough?

—Annie Dillard,
An American Childhood

> Sometimes their hand will
> stretch out, and after it
> they run—through
> woods—cross lots—over
> fences, swamps, or
> whatever . . .
>
> —The People Called Shakers

1

○ ○ ○

It's a Gift

One

◇◇◇◇◇◇◇◇◇◇◇◇◇◇◇◇◇◇

True Simplicity

John was blue, steady as the blue light far down the abandoned maglev track; Verity and Cairo had walked down it one spring day when Verity was only ten though she was forbidden by Evangeline. Verity watched the light in wonder, thinking of John. It still received the hidden signal programmed into its chips, activated, John told her, by power stored in its solar battery.

Verity had flipped her straw hat back over her shoulders so that it hung by the string around her neck and watched the light for a long time before Cairo, her dog, grew restless and thrust the picture of home before her relentlessly, several times. It was a plain, white frame house on a low hill protruding from a glittering green sea of soy and corn, five miles from the Great Miami River. Solar power was allowed by the Scriptures, as long as it was not Enlivened, and they had several ancient panels on their roof which John had foraged from far-off Columbus.

Verity had gone with John, when she was little, urging the horse on with pictures of oats, though John thought it was the flick of his whip that moved the beast. The empty, deactivated City scolded them audibly for disconnecting the solar panels. It terrified and fascinated her. She begged to go back, but John had been more spooked than she, and it was several day's journey besides. One wagonload was all they got from Columbus. Cincinnati was closer, but it was still living, and the Scriptures absolutely forbade contact with an Enlivened City. John wasn't too comfortable about Dayton either, although it was only about ten miles away.

And if people were colors then Sare was yellow like warm golden cornmeal after it was ground at the mill on Bear Creek, or the sun just after it rose over the fields and forests of Western Ohio. Evangeline, Sare's twin sister, was hard and green like the emerald ring Verity wore on her right hand. They were both around forty.

Blaze, nineteen, was wild as an orange autumn sunset seen through the black branches of the bare orchard just before storm set in. That wild sound was in him too, of branches rattling furious in wind rushing from the flat plains to the west, crystallizing the sky with rapid frigidity. Verity loved weather, and weather's changes, and how people were like weather. She had once hooked into some old weathersats and eddied through years of the quickened flow of storm systems for several hours before John flung open the door of the evening-darkened library and rudely disconnected her, telling her roughly that she could read all she liked but to stay away from that and that she didn't need to know. That annoyed her. Weather, she told John, is very important to farmers and he said well that weather's a century old, a lot's happened since then.

But she often crept into that corner of the library afterwards and hooked herself in. Russ said it was all right, anyway. Anything in the library was for them all. John was not the boss. He only thought he was sometimes. The tiny bumps behind her ears where she hooked in hadn't been discovered till she'd been cleared, certified, and taken from Edgetown, just outside Cincinnati. At that time Verity was, by their best estimation, three years old.

Sare had told Verity how she had found the nubs, the second day Verity was with them. Sare was braiding Verity's hair when she felt the right nub with her little finger. "I trembled," she said. "Then I pulled back your hair for a better look. I'm not the fainting type, but I almost fainted then." Verity had been certified plague-free by a Certifier—an old man—in Edgetown. Verity didn't remember it, but apparently she was taken inside a small black building for a while and brought out with a nod. The Shakers had no idea what went on inside the building, just knew that they trusted the old man as he had been a friend of a long-dead

Sister. Yet though she was plague-free, the nubs proclaimed her abnormal, and the source and effect of this anomaly was completely unknown to the Shakers and therefore to be feared.

They had called a Meeting immediately. Verity could imagine the arguments, but they loved her already and kept her of course, despite the unknown danger.

The Shakers had not dared venture back to Edgetown since they had added Verity to Shaker Hill, even though four Elders and two Elderesses had died and should have been replaced. They never really talked about it, but Verity knew it was because of her. The nubs behind her ears were proof of some sort of tampering; tampering which might infect the Shakers in some unknown way or even kill them. The Shakers took responsibility for her, but fear of the unknown kept them from returning to Edgetown for more children, and the community had dwindled. Twenty years ago, it had been thriving, with fifty Brethren, mostly very old people. The last of those old ones had died when Verity was a child.

But so far, in all the years of her growing up, Verity had posed no danger. She *seemed* quite normal. She knew she was lucky to be at Shaker Hill; they told her so, and she believed it. Her days and nights were part of a larger Shaker cycle bound to the land, exploiting nothing, using what they needed. They were all going to Heaven when they died, which was a lot like Ohio, all ordered and filled with the living light that Verity felt she saw everyone moving through fairly often, especially in the evening when they were preparing dinner, and sometimes when they all worked to get the hay in. Most of them did not like Cairo much. She had come wagging out of a thicket a few years earlier, and became Verity's dog. They were inseparable.

The rest of her family was a jumble of doors—the private rooms in which the Brothers and Sisters lived—and kind faces, arms that hugged, voices that scolded or more often gently corrected and instructed, a deep and wide community that held her in a hammock of relationships until she was sixteen, and taking in the triticale harvest by herself since Tai Tai was not feeling well that day.

Verity hadn't seen the Flowers since she was a child, but often longed for them with a shortening of breath, an ache in her chest, with a vision that spread out inside her mind like the growing light of day. And she had found it hard to believe that Bees were almost as large as humans (if they even existed at all, that is), but that day of harvest, when she was sixteen, she found that it was so.

Her back ached from bending over with the scythe. Her bike lay on its side a quarter mile away, at the top of the bank above the flood plain where she worked, its rust-flowered blue paint catching the sun. The Great Miami River glittered wide, deep, and olive-green, edged by a steep drop-off at the end of the field. It overflowed its banks each spring, making this fertile ground and worth the fifteen-minute bike ride. The remains of a small, old town, Miamisburg, lay across the river. The earthquake flood had swept much of it away. A few remaining sections of a fallen iron bridge lay tangled in the river below.

Verity's rhythmic swipes slowed as a foreign vibration entered her body even before she could hear it. Cairo, who had been lying in a cool thicket at the edge of the field, leaped up and whined.

Verity turned, shaded her eyes with her hand, and saw against the sun a small black dot which grew steadily larger.

It was following the path of the river.

And it was a Bee.

Sweat burned her eyes as she stared. She was twenty feet from the bluff overlooking the river, and wanted to run, take cover, but couldn't move. Her heart contracted in fear as she gradually realized how large it was.

Her entire body hummed as the Bee halted and hovered near her, over the middle of the river and about thirty feet above in the air. She was caught in the rush of air stirred by its wings, in the loud, lovely tone they gave forth in vibrating, almost as if the strength of the sound could lift her too.

Soft gold and brown bands circled its body and glowed in the sun. Its front was a black complication of shiny parts. The eyes that stared at her reminded her of the heart of a Black-eyed Susan. Pictures hummed in the air between them, and Cairo leaped up, stiff-legged, and began to bark.

A man's face was before her, half torn away and unrecognizable. Spurting blood and gray brains mixed with ivory splinters of bone. The remaining eye stared lifeless and she felt deep horror yet could not look away.

Vision segued insistently to a woman lying *dead* in a white room, her pale face washed by blinking green and blue lights. Deep anguish and inexplicable guilt seized Verity.

The next instant Verity stood on the edge of a high chasm surrounded by tall buildings. Far below flowed rivers of light. Across the chasm an impossibly huge iris moved in the night wind, filling her with deep happiness which switched suddenly to a darkness she fully believed would never, never end.

Her own anguished cry startled her. Her vision cleared. She saw the field, the river, the sky above.

And the Bee.

Faced with the hovering Bee, her hair blown back from her face by the wind from the vibrating wings, Verity knew with stunned and instant certainty that the pictures came from Cincinnati, yet did not know why she saw them, what they meant, or why they tore at her.

But she suddenly realized what would happen next.

"No!" she screamed, as the Bee pivoted, darted high into the blue sky, then plummeted full speed into the Great Miami River with a loud smack as it hit the water.

Verity ran to the bluff and plunged down the steep slope. Rough brush tore at her bare arms and clothing as she half ran, half slid down the hill, raising dust that made her cough.

She dove into the river and the current took her, frightening her: they usually swam upriver in a protected cove. Not here in the open river.

The Bee swirled fifty yards from her downstream, and slowly revolved so that its thin legs protruded upward, and Verity realized that it was dead, killed from impact or water—she did not know which but was saddened.

She trod water for a minute, struggling with the invasion of darkness and blood which filled her mind, feeling the cool, pure pull of the depths of the river, wondering what it would be like to dive deep and never come up, but flow along the bottom in long, powerful surges and never take of air again but breathe only lovely, cool green water.

The Bee's last thought eddied from her and she shivered.

Cairo's frantic barks brought her back. She was flotsam in the river, rushing toward Cincinnati.

With a powerful kick, she oriented herself and angled toward the base of the old maglev bridge, and scrambled ashore on slippery mud, gasping, while Cairo danced around her, licking her face, sending an icon at which she laughed: an empty bowl.

She hugged the dog, taking in the smell of her, the hot furry prickle of short black fur against her bare arms. Cairo closed her jaws gently on Verity's forearm and let go, leaving small white indentations where her teeth had been.

Verity got up. It was a long walk back to the field, and she still had a tenth of an acre to harvest before dark.

At that moment, when she was wringing water from her shirt, the second miraculous thing happened in the day she later called the day of miracles, though the miracles were dark and strange and troubling, but she felt from the Scriptures that that was what a miracle was: something which thrust itself on you that you did not understand, something which frightened you, something which gave direction, something which glowed in the dark of night like the radio stone.

She heard faint singing. It was a still day, near the very end of high summer, and hot, with no breeze, almost stifling. That's why she could hear them out there, the Rafters, not their words really, but their tune, rising and falling.

She stood dripping on the bank, breathing hard, and they swept around the bend that hid Dayton—a good City for foraging things like jars for preserving, and safe too as it had never been Enlivened. Though John was as frightened of it as if it had been.

She counted ten of them, all standing, all staring forward: Norleaners. They must have gotten split off the Old Ohio up toward Steubenville, on the West Virginia line. About sixty years ago during the earthquake the old riverbed of the Ohio, which once flowed crosswise past the south end of the Glacier at the end of the last ice age, had opened. Part of the river filled its old bed again and swelled the Great Miami River. At least that's what Blaze told her, that the ancient sideways Ohio River still flowed close to the surface under the farm, that's why their well pipe only had to go down ten feet, and that's why the gravel of Bear Creek was smooth round moraine stones, because it had been glacier scoured.

John just said that the earthquake, which happened before he was born, had been one of the Signs.

Rafters rarely came this way, though—at least not the informed ones. It was much more hazardous, with raw new cliffs dropping into the river, and islands everywhere. Mostly they ran aground way upriver before they got too far down this new branch.

Verity gazed upriver as the raft approached. There was a wigwam in the middle—all of the rafts had one or more, depending on the size, for shelter.

A woman stood at the till, tall and straight and then leaning hard against it. Maybe she was the one shouting and sobbing.

Verity watched without moving, knowing that something important and vital was unfolding before her. She'd never seen Rafters by herself before, and only twice earlier when she was with Blaze and he grabbed her away roughly saying that was something she oughtn't see and that they had to stay far away from the plaguers.

One of them slumped onto the raft. The steerswoman let go of the stick and shook the person—a woman, Verity thought—but the ghostly singing of the rest continued. The first woman screamed and kicked the second overboard with short, hard kicks, rolling her closer to the edge until she slipped off and was swallowed by the river. The raft swirled in an eddy and Verity watched it all happen again, the distant, dull splash of the second body into the river, the harsh scream of the woman, and the cheerful song of the others who were still aboard.

Cairo flattened her ears and bolted upriver as if she'd caught sight of a fox.

The sun stood bold overhead like a great ball of brilliant silent sound, beating into Verity, as, down by the bridge, she saw a third body shoved into the river.

"You didn't wear your hat today," scolded Evangeline, as Verity wearily pushed open the screen door to the house and let it slam behind her. Evangeline put the back of her hand to Verity's cheek and pulled it away, saying, "It's a burn and you can only survive so many with your fair skin. You've had at least three and you're still only sixteen. Be more careful, girl!" She shook her head and went back to breaking eggs into a bowl on the counter. A cake, Verity hoped.

Verity had hooked into an old pharmacological volume one time and had seen how skin cancer had grown exponentially during the last century, after the brief solar flare that disrupted radio communications. She also knew there had been cures—something to do with genes—that Shakers were forbidden by Scripture to use. Anyway, Evangeline was just being overprotective.

"Sorry," she mumbled, saying nothing about the Bee or the Rafters, her own miracles, though it might be selfish. They would figure out some way to make them vanish, or not miracles, or perhaps they would believe her and become alarmed or angry.

Evening sun filled the western windows, and the curtains Blaze had woven, intricate with tiny turquoise triangles and rose-pink stripes, flared into the large dining hall with each puff of wind, lazy as a turtle's swimmy breath.

Evangeline stirred the pot of triticale, which boiled in great slow spits of filmy liquid, and Verity glanced in and saw orange bits of carrot and wrinkled her nose at the pot of turnips, which she actively disliked. No meat tonight. That was all right with her. She never ate it, though she would hunt for rabbits if they insisted.

Ev raised one black eyebrow at her so that it slanted on her white face like a crow's wing, and Verity sighed and crossed into the dining hall and began to take the chairs down off the wall. Eight, slid in around the generous oak table, and then eight of Blaze's napkins, the splotched ones dyed in beet juice and then striped green, despite John who invariably complained that stripes were expressly forbidden by the Millennial Laws, and maybe the lamp to light because night was coming sooner now.

Verity heard the tramp of feet on the porch. The kitchen door opened and Sare danced in, her face flushed, twirling so her skirt stood out and John followed, much bluer in Verity's opinion than usual, more full of whatever made him so blue though it could not be sex since Shakers were celibate but maybe, she thought, love, which was allowed. A rare smile lit John's face as he stood very still, and watched Sare.

For a moment it was as if no one else was in the room. John took a step toward Sare, holding the basket of apples they had picked as if they were an offering.

Then he turned his head, saw Verity and Evangeline and blinked, as if they had appeared quite suddenly. His smile vanished, and his eyes were tinged with sadness.

"Just about the last of the apples," John said abruptly, and hoisted the heavy basket up on the kitchen counter. Transparent, they were called, one of the genetic patents as was every squirrel, fox, or deer. The animal's copyright stamp generally grew in fur patterns behind the right ear, though sometimes Verity found one between the legs as pigmented skin. She only knew about the apples because Blaze had told her. Not that she believed everything he said.

"Send that dog right back outside," commanded Sare, and Verity tried not to be annoyed. She was lucky to be able to keep Cairo, since it said there right in the Millennial Laws, Section VII: "No Believer is allowed to play with cats or dogs, nor to make unnecessary freedom with any of the beasts of the field, or with any kind of fowl or bird," and also, "No dogs may be kept in any family gathered into order." And also that they may not be called by any Christian name, so Cairo was a place, but Verity didn't see why they bothered with that rule at all seeing as how dogs were forbidden to begin with. Cairo had been the subject of many a Meeting, but they were also forbidden to hurt any animal (as if killing for meat wasn't hurting, and Shakers had always eaten meat) and she refused to leave, so they finally accepted her. Verity had never told anyone that they shared pictures in their minds— that would have been it. If they believed her.

She yanked open a drawer to get out the silverware, but pulled it too hard, so that the whole drawer crashed onto the floor, because an odd feeling surged in her seeing John and Sare so happy together.

She stood looking at the mess on the floor and without thinking said, "I saw a Bee today."

Everyone in the kitchen—John, Sare, Evangeline, and now Blaze, just coming in the door—said, "Where?"

Ev asked the Blessing—"We give thanks, O Lord, for this gift of life pure, untainted and human," and after they all held hands and listened to the curtains flap during the Moment of Silence they all started in on Verity again.

"I could not have fished it out, I didn't even *touch* it" said Verity for what seemed like the hundredth time, wondering why she was supposed to avoid such things and why at the same time there was this devouring curiosity. She resolved for sure not to tell them about the Rafters, and most especially not the way some of them had been pushed off the raft.

Blaze was hurt and angry that she had not told him immediately. John was concerned and asked careful, precise questions about what it looked like and how high it had flown and things she couldn't really remember or report to his satisfaction though he asked again and again.

Verity could see that Sare was itching for dinner to be over so that she could run to her room and put something down in her Book, full of neat words and numbers, where she measured flower petals, counted how many carrots you could expect from a single seed after four generations, and wrote down the results of her plague screens, which she got from a little machine which hummed and sat away from the main buildings in its own little house, the only thing allowed here from the Years of the Flowers. Because otherwise they might all die, or worse, be made so strange that they couldn't get to Heaven.

Tai Tai looked severe, as usual, thin and tough as a bramble vine and most concerned about purity and the Olden Ways. She knew the most about the Years of the Flowers, and she also said the least. "It's best forgotten," she would say.

Ev had told Verity that Tai Tai's entire family had been trapped and eaten right near the Eastern Seam of Cincinnati, when the Conversion had surged out of control, and how when they had found her as a girl, those old Shakers who had passed over, she wouldn't speak. They observed her for a week before they made their decision: a thin girl of ten who each morning took a stick of incense to the Seam, which was a rather rough part of Edgetown and not fit for little girls. While the morning light brushed the smooth wall, high as the skyscrapers within because of course it was the half-formed embryo of new ones, she burned the incense, glared at the wall, then left to do her scavenging. She kept herself neat and clean and her hair braided, and the Shakers were impressed and rescued her. Since childhood she had kept a journal of numbers and symbols which Verity had once peeked at, wondered at: brackets, dots, numbers, letters, all jumbled together crazy and tight.

It was she who had admitted to Verity when Verity was young and waking up from nightmares and jumping trembling and crying into her bed each night that the Flowers on tops of the buildings—Verity's nightmares—were real. Real, and living, as alive as the hydrangea bushes which crowded around the house. "Ah, those evil Flowers—why do you ask me such things?" She had hugged Verity tight, her nightgown crisp white in the moonlight that poured through the window and brushed the green and yellow quilt with dim color. "They are genetically engineered. Huge. When they raised their heads from the buildings, when they bloomed, we were all so frightened, we ran . . . horrible that such huge Flowers could be alive . . . nan is evil, a *sin* against God and humanity." Verity remembered nothing after that except crying, and that Tai Tai had refused to talk about them ever again, but strangely enough Verity could sleep after that, and her dreams of the Flowers were happier. Yes, Tai Tai said nothing at this news about the Bee, but she didn't eat much, and stared out the window. Her thin ebony face was drawn and her lips were tight.

And Russ, the old man, whom Verity loved, joked a lot, his round bald head glowing gently after they lit the lantern. He said, "Well, Verity, there was your chance to get away from us old folks. Why didn't you just jump on its back and ride away?"

Tai Tai glared at him.

Russ turned to Tai Tai and said, "I guess you want her to be just like you, old woman. You've never had a man in your bed and all these years I've been so willing," with a wink round the table while Tai Tai's mouth tightened even more. She threw down her napkin and huffed off.

"You shouldn't tease her like that, Russ," said John, but it wouldn't make any difference. This was Russ's house, and he'd grown up in it as a boy, before his parents had turned it into a Shaker Community. He made no secret of the fact that he'd had sex and thought it wonderful.

"It doesn't have to involve reproduction," he'd told Verity once, when she was little and standing next to him while he pruned the apple trees. Her job was to run off with the fallen sticks and pile them for kindling. "But these lily-livered souls are afraid it might, and I don't blame them. There are dangers—I don't deny it. Maybe I was just lucky. And you never know what might come out, nosiree—ha! Might be a clutch of dragons, or a woman so all-fired smart that she puts the sun to shame, like Tai Tai. Not that that's bad, but Tai Tai seems to think it is. Poor thing. Or people who see things different than they do. That's the problem, now that the genes are all mixed so strange, people are just afraid of what might happen, that's all—at least these people." He sighed, and clipped, then said, "Well, they definitely got the population under control," as if he was talking to himself, but then said, "Verity, when you get older, keep in mind that you don't have to stay here forever. These are the best folks on the earth, but they ain't the whole of it, and you strike me as a girl who might want to know more."

Verity had wondered about the dragons for a long time, and when she finally asked Ev about them, she snorted and said, "Don't listen to everything that silly old man says." So when Russ told her about the Bees, even though the Shakers all seemed to agree that such Bees really existed, Verity took it as just one more story. One of Russ's grand and casual exaggerations, like the dragons.

Until now.

Evening was the time of day which most seemed as if it might be like Heaven, when they cleaned up. They all moved around the farm kitchen in motion harmonious as dance. Blaze sat down at his hammered dulcimer ("Trying to slither out of work again?" asked Russ) and picked out some tune that he made up as he went along, then did a little Bach, and started in on a Rafter song. He could slip them past Sare if he didn't sing the words—she hated them.

> I've got a mule and her name is Sal
> Fifteen miles on the Erie Canal
> She's a good old worker and a good old pal
> Fifteen miles on the Erie Canal.

Only, of course, since they were all around listening he just played the tune, and Verity thought the words as he winked at her, thinking about the other horrible thing she had seen today and wondering why she didn't tell them about it too.

Blaze had taken Verity over near Miamisburg one spring day when she was thirteen, and showed her the old canal bed. "Two hundred years old," he said. "Look." He knelt and picked up some sticky crumbly black stuff. "Asphalt. There was a little airport here too—you know the Wright brothers lived over in Dayton, don't you? Russ's great great great—well, something like that—some far-back grandfather used to be one of their customers. They had a bike shop. I believe this railroad line was in use at the same time. Four means of transportation running side by side."

"How do you know all that?" she asked, staring at the shallow indentation. "It just looks like a ditch. I can barely see it. It's not very deep."

"Didn't have to be," he said. "Couldn't be. It was a lot of work to dig the things. They hardly had any machines then. It was a lot like now. The bottoms of the boats were flat. Mules pulled them. Read it in a history book in the library."

He claimed an old steam railroad had run right through the southeast corner of the yard by the house, too, and that he could see the ghost train, but that it never stopped even when he tried to flag it down. Verity had poked around trying to find a trace of tracks, but never had. Blaze was crazy about trains. After the cities had become allergic to each other, the maglev tunnels that crisscrossed North America had all been blown up, to keep the contagion from spreading, but Blaze was constantly trying to find out if they'd ever surfaced in Dayton, and if so, where.

"Show me the exact book—the exact *page*—where it tells about the canal," she told him. It was best to check his references. She jumped down into what he was calling a canal bed, landed on her feet in tall dry grass, and thrashed around some to scare possible snakes. She caught him out, sometimes—he made a lot of stuff up, and she'd believed all of it when she was little and felt silly about it now. He was always talking about going to the train station in Cincinnati too, which was clearly impossible.

"Maybe I will, Demon," he said, and grabbed her by her thin shoulders and squeezed hard, stared into her eyes with wide green eyes that didn't blink, then jumped away. "Race you home," he said, his voice catching in a funny way, and of course he won. Blaze's Gifts were baseball, music, caring for the three plow horses and the five sleek swift riding horses, and running very fast. A lot of Gifts, really, when the only one she had was Dance.

Verity wiped dishes and looked out the window over the sink, at the night sky sprinkled with new-evening stars delicate like they were at this time and not blazing and strong like on a winter midnight. Everyone else had finished and was getting the other room ready for Evening Meditation. Russ said that all this drudgery stuff was taken care of by nan in Cincinnati, because of Enlivenment. "But you never know what them things might be up to next," he'd said with a smile and a wink, just as if the biggest fear of everyone else was another jolly joke to him, who once went all the way to Denver on the maglev in the golden days of the end of the Years of the Flowers. Blaze's Book was full of Russ's stories, scribbled in a wild hand she could barely read.

And her own Book?

She wiped the last dish and put it on the shelf, wiped down the counter, and put the drain board away under the sink. Everything was clean. She turned the lamp down and stood in the dark for a moment, listening to night sounds through the open window—the orchard soughing in the light breeze, and dying crickets singing. She thought of what she had to add to her Book now.

The Bee hovering above her, of course, but how would she show how it had measured her with those strange and wondrous eyes?

Her Book was full of pictures, which made it hard to show some things—but easier, maybe, to show others. That was what always came out. Just pictures. Sometimes she wondered why. Why didn't she use words, like Blaze, or numbers, like Sare and Tai Tai?

She heard Blaze play a few chords on the pump organ, then they began:

> Of the Mother's love begotten,
> Ere the worlds began to be,
> She is Alpha and Omega,
> She the source, the ending She
> Of the things that are, that have been
> And that future years shall see
> Evermore and evermore.

Verity hung up her towel and went in to join them at the second verse.

They sat still on their benches in the Meeting Hall, quiet after the hymn.

Verity felt the Great Blessing echo through her body, unfolding like a flower of light which drew brilliance from the air around her straight into her body, and then it gathered into the center of her bones, concentrated, bright, and rushed upward through her spine until it flowered somewhere above the top of her head.

She began to jerk, but paid little attention to it—the way her head snapped forward on the end of her spine, so that her hair brushed her cheeks. She jerked like this about five minutes, and the light within her grew more bold and warm, and if she opened her eyes she knew that all would be bathed in the light, and when she looked at the faces of those around her it would be as if this had all happened a million times before.

The light pulled her from her seat, and she walked to the middle of the floor, straight, yet fluid, as she felt the Dance form and then propel her.

She whirled, as if on ice skates on Bear Creek. She spun, then stopped suddenly, held out her hands, palms upraised, and began a complicated, repetitive step.

She heard Blaze begin to play once more, as if from far away, a melody which hummed like a swarm of bees, then burst like bright flowers within her vision, and she heard the shuffling steps of others as, one by one, they joined her. She opened her eyes and watched as she and they scattered, re-formed, swirled, and finally stopped, all in the same moment, as if they had practiced but they had not: this Dance, this manifestation of her Gift, was new.

Later that night, she wrote the Dance into her book, in her usual way, with circles, x's, and arrows. This Dance was done in five parts, easily remembered, but this way she could pass it out to the others and they could add it to their collection. Not that it seemed really necessary. She just liked to do it.

They had found that they were of one mind about her Dances. Sometimes, during Meeting, one of them would rise, and dance a few steps, and the others, remembering exactly, would join in, and for a time they would be part of something larger. Dancing had been a big part of what the Old Shakers had done, and until Verity, the New Shakers had just imitated old pictures and descriptions.

She closed her Book. It had been a very good day. First the miracles, and then her Gift had visited her. How could she want anything more?

She put on her nightclothes and turned down the lamp. She lay down, with the window open, then reached under her pillow and touched on the radio stone.

Tonight, it worked.

Two

○○○○○○○○○○○○○○○○○○

It Tolls for Thee

The next month was filled with harvest activity: pickling and canning and drying. Finally, they were able to relax into the season of dark snugness, and it was early on in those days that Verity woke one morning hearing the Bell.

No, she told it, as a dream of scent and color dissolved. The Bell meant danger but it also meant something beyond the danger. She stirred and stretched and *no* changed to *yes.* It always did.

The darkness inside her eyelids was not veined red but black; she opened her eyes and the clean white plaster walls were dull. Without turning over to look out the window she knew the sky was heavy and gray, and that if it wasn't raining now it would before noon.

She dressed.

Verity felt bad stealing one of the loaves of bread John had set out to cool, a bit later, but it was only one, she told herself, and there were lots more lined up, brown and fragrant and just a bit warm. The top of the loaf was smooth and soft because he'd just gone down the row and smeared each one with soybean oil.

She had laced on her good hiking boots too, the ones with heavy lug soles with something embossed in Korean on the bottom. John had doubtfully examined them when she took them out of a Dayton store last year, a neat and tidy store where on the counter still lay a yellowed invoice next to the computer's dead eyescreen. John told her the eyescreen had been able to feel the weight of a stare as he shuddered at the dead simplicity of it all. He hated Dayton because gangs of wild children lived there. Verity wondered where they came from because they didn't live to get old, he said. So where did the new ones come from? And they had never run across any. But John got the sullen look he always had when he didn't know the answer and she stopped pestering him, though she didn't stop thinking.

Yes he examined the boots carefully, looking for a little glowing spot with an "n" in it even though Dayton had never been Enlivened because, as he said, "You never know how the devilish things might spread, and there's no guarantee," then shrugged and handed them to her.

Beneath the bread in her bright yellow and red woven pack were several apples, half a measure of dried bean curd chips, and a jar she could fill with water and soak them in as she walked. Not a lot; she didn't plan to be gone for long.

She heard footsteps in the dining room and whirled and ran out the door and through the cathedral branches of the apple trees, their leaves reddening in autumn's chill.

She looked at the sun and thought she would have to trot to get there by afternoon. It was pleasantly cool, now, but she wanted to be inside as soon as possible.

Hearing skittering behind her in the dry grass she turned, and saw the grasses part and there was Cairo.

"I thought I locked you up!" she scolded. "I didn't bring anything for you to eat."

A movement caught her eye across the field and she froze, then decided that it must have been the wind, or perhaps a small animal. She sighed.

"All right, come on."

It took her half an hour to cross out of Shaker Territory. There was no path, for they usually took the road to Dayton, through a few miles of Rededicated Farmland the Ohio Party had wrested from the Goddamned Government (what Russ always called it). Then it had all failed (no wonder, Russ said, anything having anything to do with the Goddamned Government is bound to fail sooner or later). But she didn't want to be on the road; that was the first place John would look, if he bothered, with a bike or a horse. She felt bad not telling him, she always did, but he would ask too many questions. Besides, she had the right to go wherever she pleased and the answers always came so much more easily afterwards than before.

She tramped through rustly leaves which the wind picked up and spun in tight quick swirls. The sky was clearing. The patches of clear deep blue let the Bell shimmer into the sky and double back into her so they were one, and when she reached the out-streets of Dayton it shifted to the sound of delicate chimes which led her onto a tiny back alley, lined with empty ruined buildings. She stopped and closed her eyes.

The Bell came only once a year. In a way, she was afraid that one year it might not come, but it always did.

She had to veer back onto the solar road to cross the twisted bridge. The roadway had fallen into the shrunken Dayton River, now not much more than a creek, but the walkway had repaired itself and though narrow it had a railing on one side. The old riverbed had grown up in trees and weeds, but Verity saw the glint of glass which was the windshield of an old, rusted bus down below where once there flowed deep water. She and Blaze had hacked their way down one day and picnicked on a large flat rock next to it. The main river now flanked the east side of Dayton, having changed course several miles to the northeast in a great, sudden wrench which heaved up multicolored layers of rock and toppled many of the buildings in downtown Dayton. As she crossed, Verity gazed down on the tops of the trees, where a few yellow, orange, and red leaves still clung to feathery gray branches.

Once she was in the deserted city, the distance between her and the library was a set of discrete distances and turns which led her forward unerringly, a blend of light and sound and scent which she did not question. Sometimes a pile of rubble might block her path, but she could correct her course easily.

It was a bit after noon, she judged, when she dropped, sweating, onto the wide stone steps of the library. They chilled her through her thin brown pants. Ev hadn't unpacked the winter stuff yet, the lovely woolly scarves itchy and warm, the leather Bean gloves all in a very large size, the thinsuits that Evangeline, her long brown hair falling forward over the multicolored heap, said were made of silk, and they even said so in the label. But they were laced with glittering filaments that said something to Verity, like aren't these Forbidden by Scripture, but she realized that they were so very warm and light that the filaments were ignored.

When she asked John about them he frowned and sighed and said that she was right, there was tech there but he was positive that it was not Enlivened tech but just something that wouldn't work at all without a lot of other things around to help it out, the way the computers had died in Dayton without electricity.

But what he didn't know, she thought, grinning at Cairo and splitting off a quarter of the loaf for her, which the dog gobbled in chopping gulps, was that everything in the library, all the computers and everything, seemed to be solar powered. She was sure it wasn't Enlivened power, because otherwise, if any of that was around, they would never go into Dayton, not in a million years, because that stuff never died. It lived, she thought, in its own Heaven, different, perhaps, from Shaker Heaven, but as far as she was concerned it fit all the parameters. Everlasting stuff, and smart enough to know it.

There was a story about the Old Shakers she liked, the ones who had come to the Ohio Frontier in the seventeen hundreds. When they had begun to establish their communities, they had been badly persecuted. People felt antagonistic toward celibates, even if they worked hard and traded fair. Lebanon, a little bit southeast of here, had been the source of particularly violent opposition, while the people of Dayton, at that time the same size as Lebanon, had been kind and helpful.

God told them to curse Lebanon and bless Dayton, so a Shaker rode through Lebanon shouting "Woe, woe, woe," and then traveled through Dayton calling out "Bless this town."

Dayton had prospered. Lebanon never grew.

The Old Shakers apparently had a lot more power than the New ones.

Cairo growled, and the back of Verity's neck prickled. What was that at the end of the street? One of the gangs of children so feared by John, that she'd never seen? She gazed with interest, but saw nothing.

Wind skittering leaves, perhaps; the streets were full of thick trees sprouting right through the center of the concrete and the street signs were often wrapped tightly by obscuring vines, the only reason John ever brought her to Dayton in the first place. "You seem to have a memory for places," he had admitted, and indeed she did. Anywhere she had been before she could find her way again. To *and* from, as if a map was laid down in her mind, and John got lost very easily, and when he did he panicked.

Besides, one of the first times the Bell had called her here, a huge screen inside the library had shimmered and given her a map of Dayton, and had then eagerly piled map upon map: American Waterways, 2032; The Great Democracy of China; The Population of South America in 2023 by colors. That was how she knew where Tokyo, the only station the radio stone would pick up, maybe once a month, was. She had remembered them all. But she couldn't remember any map showing the old canals that had laced the United States in the 1800s. Maybe she'd look for one of those.

She rose and brushed crumbs from her lap. The clouds had returned and it was starting to rain. It slanted down on her and the wind whipped the drops so they were hard as arrows against her face.

She rushed up the library steps and put her palm on the print. The double doors slid open. She didn't know why it worked for her but it did. Perhaps it was somehow lonely for touch, begging for use. She turned in the doorway, stuck her fingers in her mouth, and gave a sharp whistle for Cairo, who had vanished.

She didn't come. Verity whistled again, opened her mouth to call her, and was suddenly afraid.

The branches of the street trees shuddered in the wind. Maybe a storm from the plains was on the way. It could turn from rain to sleet in an hour this time of year. Her loose black hair whipped out behind her. She couldn't leave Cairo out here.

Someone grabbed her arm and she turned, fist raised.

It was Blaze.

He stood there, looking lost and afraid, not like him at all. His face was pale and beneath his red hair all his freckles stood out like someone had painted them on. His hunting rifle was slung over his shoulder on a strap. "Verity, what are you *doing* here?" he asked.

"I don't follow you everywhere you go," she said, as Cairo came panting around the corner. "Look at you, you're soaked," she said. She looked up and said to Blaze, "It's the Bell. I had to come."

"Let me come too," he begged.

"No," she said, but she could see that she couldn't leave him out there in the rain while she was inside. "They'll wonder where you are."

"I told them I was going hunting," he said. "And I was. What did you tell them?"

She looked down at the smooth marble floor, veined with gold. Inside the library stretched long shadows. She pulled Blaze by the sleeve and Cairo trotted after him; the door slid shut behind them and Blaze caught his breath in the dark.

"Don't worry," said Verity, and walked over and touched the wall.

The library filled with soft light.

"What's the Bell?" asked Blaze.

She led him up some stairs which lit in front of them as they climbed, then darkened behind them. "Very smart place," said Blaze, but his voice was shaky. "We shouldn't be here, Verity, come home with me. We can be back by dark if we take the road. Come on. Let's go. This is dangerous."

"Forbidden," she said, because he would not. The Bell was getting louder but it didn't really have to because she knew exactly where it was telling her to go.

It was a small room with four couches. Each was molded in the shape of a human body and reminded Verity of cocoons whenever she saw them, curling up and over in a delicate, fluted curve.

"What is this place?" asked Blaze, and she could see he was trembling next to her.

She turned and put her arms around him, held him close until she felt something in him relax and he took a deep breath. She opened her eyes and stepped away.

The room was a place of flowers, flowers which stood out from the walls. Blaze stepped over a bank of glowing tiny bluebells in a spring glade. He raised his hand, hesitated.

"Go ahead," said Verity. "It's all right."

He passed his hand through them. "Holograms," he whispered. "Tech."

"I told you that you shouldn't come in."

Cairo was lying on the floor, flat on her side, napping already. A tall stand of daisies surrounded her.

Verity stepped toward a couch, and as she moved, the woodland vista changed to meadowland, then filled with beckoning prairie flowers whose names she did not know. They glowed with a razor light, called her like the radio stone. Excited now, she slipped into the couch, which moved to fit her, curved softly around her head. A transparent screen was held over each couch by a steel arm; the Bell told her where to touch it, like it always did.

First, a quick flash:

The advertisements were always different. There was a suppress command, but she preferred to watch. She was fascinated. This time she saw luxurious rooms in the Geo Space Hotel. Something about Chinese clothing software you could use at home, displayed by capering models. They flashed past, compressed, and took less than a minute.

"You try one," she told Blaze, but her voice was faint from bliss and she wasn't sure that he could even hear her. That was a surprise, but she'd never tried talking to anyone before while here.

The last thing she saw as the glow rose around her was Blaze leaning back and slowly sliding down one of the walls, slicing through the holos, patterned with them with his head in his hands, and he began to sing as if he was praying:

> Some rows up
> But we floats down
> Way down to Shawneetown on the Ohio

The glow grew stronger, pulled her inside, stronger than memories and deeper than light.

* {AD.795} *"I WISH YOU WOULDN'T do things like this." A woman's voice, taut with anger and irritation.

Cincinnati, spread out before him, ablaze with Enlivenment, was stunningly beautiful. He could never get over how wondrous it was. Even at night, some of the Flowers were out, petals waving gently in the cooling night wind. "It's just an exercise," he told her. "Just for fun. To explore the possibilities. I've got to keep my hand in, you know."

"It's irresponsible, Durancy," the woman rejoined. She was

behind him, and her angry face was reflected on the glass window, transparent and studded with the lights of Iris across the street. She held a sphere in her hand about an inch in diameter. He wished again that she wouldn't fool with his work. She was only a student, even though she was his latest lover. It served her right if she got upset.

"You've structured this so that it could actually happen," she said, her voice low and trembling. "And what if it did? What if it really happened?"

"Don't be silly. That's impossible." He laughed without telling her of the personal safeguards he'd programmed into every one of his City-seeds, then involuntarily began to imagine.

What if? What if it really did happen?

What if it really happened?

What if—* {**AD.795**} *

She woke screaming.

Verity felt herself being shaken and opened her eyes, gasping.

Blaze stood over her, eyes angry and fierce. "You get out of there, Verity," he said.

"I'm okay," she said, wondering where she had been and why it had made her scream. "I'm all right." She smiled at him. "Really." She pushed his hands away.

Already she was drifting off. Moving toward a large white hydrangea. She sampled a bit of the pollen she collected. It told her that it was to go to Tulip, three miles across town. The information the pollen carried had to do with a shipment of farm shrimp coming in on the Silver Streak this afternoon from Seattle, and which shops were to get it and how much they would pay. The thriving neighborhoods of Cincinnati fluoresced beneath her, bee-yellow and bee-blue, glowing. Her eyes polarized the sunlight, orienting her precisely.

No one had known how honeybees could fly. It was physically impossible, but they had done it. So did she, but her genetically engineered body was lightened with pockets of hydrogen and the various plates of her body were an ultralight nan/bio-synthesis.

Without warning, her surroundings changed.

She was herself, walking through a vast hall with an arched roof of glass for windows, the panes held in a green spidery fret-

work of metal. Rain coursed down the pale green sides. *Beaux arts,*
whispered a man's voice. *Controversial, at the time. Some said it set
architecture in America back fifty years.*

"Verity! Wake up!"

The space shrank to a corridor of anonymous doors.

I want to, she thought, and opened the first door.

There was nothing inside but a lot of books. She touched the
spine of *O Pioneers!* and was enveloped by wild prairie which
smelled sweet beneath the wide blue sky. Tiny daisies punctuated
tall green grass. Emotions surged through her as if she were living
each page of the book quickly, intensely, as if all the characters
formed a single matrix of being which resolved like a chord of
music and she turned as the pictures leaped around and through
her—

"Verity! Please!"

The voice was dear and she longed to follow it. Feeling her
way through prairie, through time, through lives thick and flowing as the New Ohio River, she grasped a doorknob she could not
see and turned it. "I'm coming!" she said. "Wait! Please wait!"
She frantically pushed open a door and rushed forward.

And found herself in the corridor once again.

But the voice had ceased.

Feeling abandoned, she advanced down the corridor. It was
long. She feared each door until she tired of fear and did not know
how long that took, and then the building seemed to be set on an
upward spiral and each door became a painting. *Edward Hopper.
Rothko. Killed himself. Look at those black paintings! But then—the yellow—Oh, here's O'Keeffe, I bet you'll like her,* whispered the voice,
and she gathered each picture into herself until she came to the
end of the corridor, and a door that sliced off the end, which she
both feared and desired to open.

On it was a picture of a very large flower, one which she did
not recognize. O'Keeffe again, apparently quite popular here. She
hesitated. *"Verity! Please!"*

Where *was* the voice coming from? It was different than the
informative voice, it was frightened, filled with anguish, and she
needed to return to it. She turned from the flower and began to
run down the ramp, thinking No, as if arguing with herself, I'll
not go *there,* haven't I been there before? and bleak failure filled
her. She gasped at the way it hit her, just like a blow to her chest.
She paused, hearing once again *"Verity Verity Verity"* in a voice

angry yet fringed with tears but where was it coming from? Beyond the flower door? Or somewhere else? And then she saw before her

Herself.

Verity stopped and stared, feeling the woman's physical presence, her utter reality. Long black hair was gathered at the nape of the neck. She was slim and wore a simple flowing garment of many colors but the chief color was yellow. Verity knew that she was almost-herself, and yet different.

The panel the woman was regarding changed to music that Verity could hear as if it played within her head. *Take the 'A' Train* said the man's voice. In an amused tone he added, *I strongly suggest you take it NOW.*

The other Verity—but Verity knew that was not her name and that name was about to dawn within her mind in a way that might splinter even this strange spiral she climbed, shift it unbearably, far away from the voice that called even now *"Verity!"* and as the woman took a step upon which to pivot and then *see* her, Verity turned and ran back up the ramp, to the Flower at the end of the hall.

She pushed open the door and then grabbed the frame, terrified by the brilliant white glow like sun through fog. She saw nothing, but now the voice called her onward. No! She would not jump from the end of this damned height—without wings—

She turned—

And stared straight into her own eyes.

Her own mouth opened. "You must," said the woman, her eyes infinitely sad. "I should have."

"What's there?" asked Verity. "What?"

"I don't know," the woman said. "But in here is only death."

And then the Bee-picture was back. The one from the river.

Verity gasped, staring into the bloody mess which once had been a face.

"Change this, *please,"* said the woman, and tears flowed down her face, scrunched with pain. "Go!"

Verity felt cool fog at her back, smelled spring. She turned, ran, and—leaped. Screaming.

And was borne forward with a jolt.

* {QC.98325} *SHE OPENED her newspaper. *The Cincinnati Times-Star.* It rattled as she folded it to the editorials. Rich do-gooders

trying to get the stupid Irish educated again. The cable car climbed a steep hill, and she—

No, *he*—

Touched his plain steel-gray lunch pail, which held a baloney sandwich Stell had packed, and soon the pigs would be squealing just before he slit their necks as they dangled from one leg on chains. "Porkopolis," they called Cincinnati, but Chicago was fighting hard for the title. Well, let them fight. He refolded his paper. It crackled as he creased it, gave it a straightening shake. Damned Irish. His own mother, from Oberammergau, had seen to it that he learned to speak and read English, though she still did neither. It was the responsibility of the individual, not the City! Why should *he* have to pay?

It was raining outside, and the tenements were bleak. The streets swarmed with people, and

Verity leaned back on the hard wooden seat.

Staring, staring. *Realizing* . . .

The paper dropped to the floor.

The car stopped, and the woman sitting in front of her stood. She wore a green wool dress tight at the waist then flaring out, quite long, and a tiny black hat with a net which veiled her face, and lily-of-the-valley scent. She walked to the end of the car and debarked into the street. The feet of the other passengers shuffling to seats filled the air, then with a clang and a jolt the car continued its climb.

Come, whispered that other voice. *Please come.*

The sun emerged briefly, and the city shone below her. And that great, broad river beyond.* {QC.98325} *

Verity opened her eyes the next morning and saw Blaze chewing on some bean curd he had fished out of the jar. He must have found water. Her bladder ached, and she rolled out of the couch and ran for the bathroom, just down the hall.

Looking into the mirror, she brushed her hand across the front of the sink and water flowed. The first time it had frightened her like everything in the library, but she had gotten used to it. She filled her hands with cold water and splashed it onto her face. As always after being in the cocoon, her entire body was filled with something she could only think of as *aliveness;* everything looked intense and quite beautiful, even the sink, the diamond-shaped turquoise tiles set in the white wall—

Blaze pushed open the door and stood there. She saw tears glittering in his eyes.

"What's wrong?"

He shook his head, then said, "I couldn't wake you, Verity. I'm afraid you're not going to get to Heaven."

She didn't know why she felt it didn't matter, except that always, afterward, she felt as if she was expanding very quickly, like a flower unfolding in fast motion, and nothing frightened or bothered her for weeks. She was filled with something that made everything and everyone she saw glow with a soft inner light, as if she already was in Heaven. That was when she could see the colors of people most clearly, when John's blue, Evangeline's green, Blaze's orange, flashed out from them in gentle curlicue eruptions. And she always came back with new Dances. The Dances were her Gift.

Blaze continued to stare at her obliquely. She wiped her hands on her pants. "Nothing happened," he said.

"What do you mean?"

"I tried a couch. Nothing happened."

"Did you touch the screen?"

"I watched you. I did everything you did." He seemed sullen, not like himself.

"Maybe the one you tried was broken."

"Nothing is broken in here, Verity," he said, in the ironic tone she loved. "I don't know how long all this has been here, but it's from the Years of the Flowers."

"Everything is," she said.

He shook his head. "No," he said, and his voice was hoarse. "We always thought that Dayton had never been Enlivened. But I think that it was. How else does this library work, Verity?"

"Solar batteries," she said. "Do you think I'd come here if I thought there was Enlivenment?" Anger edged her voice. "Russ said it wasn't. Russ lived here all his life. Russ saw the beginning and the end of the Years of the Flowers. Don't you believe him?"

Blaze looked at her steadily. "I know what Russ says. I write it all in my Book, remember? This all has to do with something different. It's more than Scripture, Verity, more than the Millennial Laws, more than blessings and more than Heaven even. There's a reason and a history of the Shakers, and Russ told it all to me."

She felt slightly jealous. "Oh?"

"This library is incredibly huge," he said. "It must be a thousand times bigger than ours." Russ's parents had been immensely educated, and tried to store as much as they could, scavenged from Dayton, until fear made them declare their project complete. "Verity, I'm not going back."

"You can't stay here!"

"Why not?"

"What will you eat?"

"I can hunt. And the stores are still full of food."

She didn't say anything. He knew that food was one of the ways the plague could get into you, at least that's what the Shakers thought and that's why they carefully grew everything themselves, and took wild animals they'd killed into Sare's special room where the machine she called Plague Radar, because that was what was written on its side, checked it for plague. It sat in its own little house, away from the main hall.

"Please come back," Verity said.

He took her arm and pulled her out into the large hallway. "Every door you see is a room filled with books," he said. She counted ten slants of light before the window at the end of the hall. "There are fifteen floors," he said. "They're not all full of books—but it's all information. It's better than the radio stone, Verity." She let him borrow the radio stone sometimes, if she was feeling generous, which was not often. He complained that she always gave it to him when it didn't work, which was not at all true. *She* had no way of telling when that might be. The radio stone was one of their secrets.

Blaze continued. "I fell asleep on the fifth floor after staying up most of the night. I didn't know where to start. Is that all you do every time you come here? Sleep in that couch?" His look was one of exasperation. "They have little wafers here, clear little wafers on the fifth floor the size of—oh, one of those old quarters we found buried in the orchard. Then the tech thing has a little indentation and you set the wafer inside."

"I've seen it," she said. "Don't you think I wanted to try all these things out? But what I do is more important . . . somehow." She wondered how to explain the imperative energy that pulled her into the couch. And it would be embarrassing to admit that she didn't really remember anything that happened while she was here if she tried, but only that she thought bits and pieces came to her from time to time. "I didn't want to stay too long. Everybody would worry."

"Just take one book. *Huckleberry Finn.* You've read that, haven't you? Well, on one wafer, I found something that read it to you. Or you could go into another mode and it was all like a hologram play that you could watch, like you were there, and you could make it real tiny so that it would fit onto your hand or real big so that Jim's bare foot filled up the whole room. You could drift right down the Mississippi River in a raft with a wigwam on it just like the goddamned Rafters."

Blaze was looking flushed. She put her hand on his forehead. He pushed it away.

"Verity, there are things here that I never even imagined existed. Things even Russ never told me about. How long have you known about this?"

She shrugged. "Maybe six years."

He was silent, and she felt bad. She usually told them she had gone on a retreat, over toward Franklin, that she had to be alone and think. All of them did that from time to time.

"What happens to you when you're in that couch?"

She didn't say anything.

"There's *history* here. The history of the *world.* Don't you ever wonder about all the things that ever happened? I mean, not just here but the whole world. There's old baseball games. The Cincinnati Red Stockings. There are *answers* here, Verity. Don't you *care?* How did the plague happen? What is Enlivenment, anyway? What did the Flowers do? What did the Bees do? Why are we supposed to be so *afraid* of all of this?"

She whirled and ran down the stairs. Blaze frightened her. She had never seen him so demanding. Yes—yes, they *should* know these things. He was right, and yet—

She panicked, and did not know why. The front door slid open for her as she ran through the huge, echoing foyer. She stopped suddenly as the cold air hit her.

The streets and trees were all coated with glittering ice. Cairo ran outside and howled as she slid sideways and bumped down the steps. Blaze followed her out and she quickly turned and palmed the door shut.

"Why did you do that?" he yelled.

"You have to come home. This is all my fault."

"I don't *have* to do anything!"

"What about Heaven?" she demanded, and was surprised when he said, "If you don't care, why should I?"

"You're the hunter," she said.

"Sare's a better hunter than me, and you know it. She just likes to measure and count and plan crops more than hunt, that's all. They can do without me."

But I can't, she thought, and started to ease down the steps, holding onto the railing.

Blaze turned and palmed the door. It didn't open.

"I don't care then," he said. "I'll find a way to get in. Rocks, or something. There has to be another way into this place. I have work to do." He turned to her and his face was pleading. "Verity, the train stations are in there, on one of the wafers. It was like I was walking around *inside* them. Union Station in Washington, D.C. Penn Station." He spoke as if she knew what he was talking about. "I've only read about them before," he said. "I've only seen pictures. It wasn't like *this.* Come back in. I'll show you the Cincinnati station. It was a Union Station too. That meant that all the train lines went to a central station. It's not far from here, you know? Only about fifty miles. I wonder if it's still there. It's a big arch, Verity, like a section cut out of a sphere. I saw it just after it was built, in 1933. I walked around inside and a voice told me about where I was—the News Reel Theater, Cooled by Air in the summer, and the toy store for kids and the lunch counters, and everything in these beautiful long curves, everything was curved back then. And during the Years of the Flowers, it was Enlivened, and they made it just the same as it was when it was new because it was so beautiful, and you could go anywhere in North America on the maglev. In just *hours.* It isn't hard to work these things. A voice tells you everything to do. I bet I could even use that hypertext thing to get on a train and go to all those places, all those places that are gone and dead—"

He burst out crying then, his face crunched up like she'd only seen it once before, years ago, when one of the horses died. She tried to hug him but he shrugged it off, and she pulled out her handkerchief and shook it out and handed it to him. "It's clean," she said. He never had one. He glared at her, then took it and blew his nose and wiped his eyes.

Cairo gamboled on the icy street. The jeweled trees clattered in the wind, which smelled sharp and clean. A picture opened in her mind and it was of tall seamless buildings speckled with windows in a decorative pattern. As if she could see inside, she knew the windows were that way because the levels of the rooms inside could rearrange themselves, become private or public, divide with ramps, elevators, or stairs, or isolate with lofts. There were many of these buildings, in dull, lovely hues, some turquoise, some pale pink like tea roses, distant and stern, and at the top of them were flowers. Not many small flowers, but one large Flower, each tier of the building with its own, with heavy petals waving in the wind as slowly as the plants beneath the crystal surface of Bear Creek. She'd seen them last night, she realized, and was surprised because it was the first time she'd really remembered anything that clearly and she felt a bit afraid.

She turned and looked up, but she was close and the library above was an infinite wall.

It couldn't be, she thought. Dayton was never Enlivened, according to Russ. Wouldn't he tell us?

Of course he would have, and besides, she would have noticed from a distance long before if any of the buildings were like that. Or someone else would have. Her sigh was both relief and regret.

"How come *you* can get in?" asked Blaze, an angry, frustrated edge to his voice. "I'm just going to stay here until I get in."

Why did her body ache, suddenly, thinking of being apart from him? But he ought to be able to know about the trains, if that was what he really wanted. She wouldn't feel right to keep him from them just out of selfishness, and that was what it was.

"I'll make a deal with you," she said.

"What?"

"If I make it so that you can get in whenever you want, will you come home? Then you won't need me. You can come back from time to time." She tried not to think about what this extra secrecy might cost. She already had the Norleaners.

"How could you do that?"

She palmed the door open again.

Across the foyer was a small door that said OFFICE. She opened the door and went inside, and the room lit at their entrance.

She sat in the nubby beige chair behind a large white desk of smooth seamless material. A clear screen slanted upward when she touched a yellow spot on the desk's edge. She touched the screen again and again until she got to the right place.

"What are you doing?" asked Blaze.

She didn't say anything. She didn't know. But she knew it would work. "There," she said, after a minute. "Put your palm there."

He superimposed his hand on the hand glowing blue on the screen and it beeped. He pulled his hand away as if it had been burned and she pushed back the chair and stood up. "Let's go try it," she said.

When they got back outside, they found that it worked.

Blaze was jubilant.

But Verity didn't have much to say during the long hike back to Shaker Hill. They took the solar road, Route Four, all the way because it was always dry, except for a quarter mile in front of Shaker Hill, where one of the early Eldresses had done her best to disable the solar cells, which she claimed were Enlivenment. Verity had seen only one solar car on the road, years ago, a tiny thing that coasted to a halt over the bad patch. A woman had stepped out, looking around nervously, as Verity watched her from behind a veil of leaves in a tree she'd climbed. The car had been light enough to push until it started to move again and the woman hurried and jumped inside. Her clothes had been ragged. Verity had begged John for a solar car, told him that they could probably find one pretty easily right over in Dayton, but he just shook his head and said they had to stick to bikes and horses.

Verity turned back to see if the library had a Flower top when they were about ten blocks away, and turned and walked backwards several times once they were out of the City, but she saw none. Not surprising. She never had before. Next time, she thought, wondering how to get out on the roof.

Maybe she would return this time before she heard the Bell again.

About a mile from Shaker Hill, they rounded a tree-lined banked curve and saw John, running, a hundred yards ahead. He paused and looked into the woods. Then he turned and saw them.

"Where have you been?" he yelled. His breath puffed out in the cold air. The sky was crystal blue above them. He quickly closed the gap between them.

"I've been out half the night looking for you two!" he said. His eyes were narrow and angry. His head was wrapped in a black scarf, reminding Verity that her ears ached with cold.

"What for?" asked Blaze, surprising Verity with his boldness.

"That's what Russ said," John said. His face was red. "Russ

said not to worry, that you two could take care of yourselves."
Verity thought that had either of them been out by themselves, as
sometimes happened, John would not have been this perturbed.
With blizzards that came up so sudden, and the time they spent
hunting, Russ had worked since they were young to train them to
survive in the wilderness Ohio had become.

"We did," said Blaze. "We're fine. Sorry you were worried.
We got caught in the ice storm and stayed in Dayton."

"*Dayton!*" John's voice was edged with alarm. Verity saw the
fear in his face and remembered how wary he was of Dayton,
how, when he had to go, he flitted in and out of the deserted
shops, looking nervously over his shoulder all the while.

"It's all right, John," Verity said. "I'm sorry too. I should have
paid more attention to the weather. Let's get back now, all right?"

John looked hard at Blaze, and then her. His look made Verity
angry, but she said nothing. She stuck her hands deep in her
pockets and began to walk. Blaze came with her. After a moment,
she heard John's footsteps behind them. With an effort, she
turned and waited for him. The three of them walked back to
Shaker Hill together, without speaking, though Blaze brought
down two pheasants that flew startled from high golden weeds
on the outskirts of Shaker Hill.

Three

○○○○○○○○○○○○○○○○○○○○

The Road Less Traveled

The branches of the orchard laced above Verity like a sheltering being, a passageway which she always thought of as leading her to a wider world. The few leaves left fluttered in the wind, a rough, dry flurry that made her think of winter. The tang of woodsmoke hung low this morning and that meant rain. Or, if it was cold enough, snow.

High leather boots laced snug, she left the orchard and entered the field which bordered the creek, stripping dry seeds from the tall grass and scattering them as she went.

The first trap was empty, though it had been sprung. A fox, most likely. She semi-knelt taking care to keep her knees out of the damp, rich dirt of the creekbank, and pried open the trap. Weak sunlight gleamed on the brand name of the trap, holo'd below the teeth in some language she didn't know—Chinese, perhaps; she'd read much about China's manufacturing decades, maybe eighty years ago, just before the Cities had emerged. John had found a crate of them, carefully oiled, when they had foraged through Franklin three years ago.

The third trap was on the creek's edge, in a hollow lined with smooth, ellipsoidal stones in tones of gray, light brown, and glowing white. Verity paused, listening.

A frail skin of ice surrounded some of the rocks near the shore. The creek was shallow and wide. The ruins of an ancient steel bridge blocked passage by raft a hundred yards below. When she was small, Blaze used to tease her by telling her he saw the ghost of an Indian living there. She'd run shrieking for the house one day when she saw the ruins of a smoldering campfire, with an arrow lying next to it, and that afternoon had heard Evangeline scolding Blaze.

She stood and whirled at a sound: like a deer hoof on rock. She scanned the edge of the narrow band of woods which lay between her and the fields, and then the house: nothing.

Then she heard it—a sob, or a moan. Straightening, she walked toward it.

The woman was lying in a copse of bushes on a bed of grass.

Her eyes were dark in a pale face framed with black hair that was filled with bits of dried leaves and branches. She hugged herself, and Verity could see shivers run through her. Suddenly she understood the empty traps of late, and why the last of the late apples had vanished.

But the strangest thing was the faint gold burnish on the woman's face, a slight glow almost like the tech glitter filaments inside the Bean thinsuits.

Verity struggled to breathe for a moment, then said, forcing her voice out, "Are you an angel?"

The woman laughed, though her face looked sad as she did so and her voice was a dry croak ragged as a crow's.

"No," she said. "I have the plague." Her chin lifted almost as if she were proud of it, and the slightest of smiles touched her thin face.

Verity stepped back.

"Come," said the woman. "Getting the plague is the most wonderful thing that could ever happen to you. Plague!" She laughed, and Verity was terrified, for an instant, at the wildness of the laugh. "That's a terrible word for what happens. It's more like a *cure*. A *change*."

"You're sick," said Verity. "I'll go for help." Then she understood. "The raft," she said. "Last summer." Three months ago.

The woman nodded. Her face became fierce. "I need another raft, that's all. I've been afraid to come close to the house. Theo—they killed him up near Detroit. But you're a sweet young girl. Not like—yes, *you'll* help me."

"It seems that if this was plague, you would have died by now," said Verity. "I heard—I heard that it takes you quickly."

"No," she said. "The plague makes you truly alive." Verity didn't understand.

"I'll bring blankets and food," Verity said. She started to turn away and then turned back. "What would you do with a raft?"

"I'm on my way to Norleans," she said, then burrowed beneath the leaves so that her head rested on a tree root. She put her hands beneath her head and closed her eyes. "Hurry, girl," she said. The glow of her face increased for a moment. Verity blinked. So beautiful, so bright.

"I'll be right back," Verity said, and turned and ran for the house.

Branches stung her face as she pushed through the woods, and she stumbled once in the furrows of the soybean field, filled with dry, ragged stalks, then dashed across the softball field, where Blaze had them out pitching and batting and running with special rules for their abbreviated teams as often as he could talk all of them into it.

She slammed open the door of the work hall, the closest building, a place that had space and tools for anyone's projects.

She paused inside, panting. It was huge, eighty feet by thirty. At one time fifty Shakers had lived at Shaker Hill, and Russ had told her how the work hall had buzzed with industry.

Now it dwarfed Tai Tai, the only person inside. She was holding a welding torch, which meant something special. She rarely used her precious fuel canisters.

"Verity, shut the door, would you?" Tai Tai yelled across the room. When Verity just stood there she rose from her welding torch, pushed up her goggles, stomped over, and slammed it. She marched back, lowered her goggles, and made the flame long and blue with a twist of a knob. She bent over whatever she was doing, and her face relaxed with satisfaction. Verity came closer and saw a strange, graceful structure of old metal shapes.

"That's beautiful," said Verity.

Tai Tai looked embarrassed, and Verity became annoyed. "Beauty has a purpose too," she said, because she knew that Tai Tai took the old ways so seriously. Everything had to be useful, have a function. "Where's John?" Verity asked, looking around. Three looms, with half-finished cloth warped, were silent.

Above, heavy beams into which were burned the legend THREE SISTERS, words that always filled Verity with strange longing, framed the support for the roofboards. Verity had heard that when those Sister beams had been winched up, the ten by tens they were bolted to had bent so far beneath the weight it was a wonder they hadn't snapped.

Tai Tai had a fire going in the black Warm Morning stove.

John opened the door opposite them, stepped inside, and deposited a pile of lumber. It clattered as he let it down.

"There's a woman," Verity began, and was surprised when he looked up and froze. His blue eyes, brilliant in a face mostly hidden by curly black beard, clung to hers, and she said, "You *knew!*"

Tai Tai glanced up, but Verity knew she couldn't hear anything over the roar of her torch.

John stood in the open doorway and Tai Tai pulled her goggles from her eyes and threw them at him. She slid from her stool, turned off the flame with a sharp twist of her wrist, and stalked over to the door. "What's the matter with everyone today?" she demanded, and pulled John inside and slammed the door behind him. "Haven't we split enough wood?"

"There's a woman down by the creek," said Verity. "We have to have a Meeting."

"No," said John.

"What are you talking about?" Verity asked. "We have to figure out how to take care of her."

"I haven't been able to bring myself to do it," he said, and tears came to his eyes. "I thought—if I left her—"

"He's right, Verity," said Tai Tai, tall and thin as a cornstalk, her white hair cropped very short so that it stood out like a halo around her dark face.

"What are you talking about?" Verity demanded. "Do you know too?"

"How close did you get?" demanded John. Verity wondered at the look on John's face. His usual sternness was mixed with something she had never seen before, but she wasn't sure what it was.

Verity said, "How about you?" and then she felt many things at once as she understood.

Her life fell away from her with frightening suddenness.

"I thought we were supposed to be different," she said. "I thought we were supposed to help others."

"Theologically, we're different," John said. "Biologically, we can die, Verity, just as easy as that woman out there." Verity resented him talking down to her. "Much more easily," he continued, "since we've taken such care to isolate ourselves." He frowned and looked away.

"How did you know that I didn't have the plague when you took me from Cincinnati?" she demanded.

"You were certified," said Tai Tai.

"Certified by who? By what? What did that old man *do?* Where can we take *her* to be certified? Maybe she's really okay. Maybe she's not contagious anymore. She's already lived a long time. She fell off the raft last—"

She stopped. John was looking at her keenly.

"You saw a raft."

"Last August. They were singing. A woman pushed three of them overboard. I thought they were dead. I thought they'd just float downriver."

"Well, you're a fine one to talk about telling everyone," John said. "Do you think Sare would be able to stay away from her? Or Blaze, to ask her questions?"

She was amazed when Tai Tai shook her head.

"How long do you think you can put it off?" Verity asked. "Until this evening? What if she just has a fever? You—*We*—will have murdered her."

"You—and I—and everyone here were certified using devices that they have in Edgetown," said Tai Tai. "Devices which detect plague. Apparently many assemblers have some sort of detectable magnetic or electric resonance, extremely minute. Though many others have none. That's worse. Verity, they're all *different—frightful—*"

"Can't we use Sare's machine?"

"You have no idea what you're talking about," said Tai Tai, and her voice was pained, yet gentle. She shuddered. "Someone would have to *touch* her to get her to the machine. You were lucky enough to come here as a toddler. I was ten when the Shakers chose me. I know what can happen."

"And I was seven," said John.

"It doesn't matter," said Verity. "This is the kind of thing that Meetings are for. Isn't it? Maybe you're afraid that everyone else might disagree with you. Russ would."

"Russ might," John agreed. "Russ is a foolish old man."

Verity left, and slammed the door behind herself, but not before she heard John yell, "Don't *tell* anyone, Verity!" in his most commanding voice.

She started toward the house quickly, then walked more slowly.

What if they were right? What if everyone rushed out to take care of her, and then they all died?

She wondered again when John had seen the woman, and from how far away. Why hadn't *he* said anything? Had he thought she was an angel at first too?

Verity hugged her coat to herself, and realized that the temperature was dropping very quickly. Along with the barometric pressure, she saw, because the woodsmoke lay in a long, low stratum which stretched north, unable to rise.

A bad storm would be here. Most likely in a few hours. Even before everyone could be called together for a Meeting.

When Verity had gathered everything she could carry—blankets, hats, a pair of gloves, some rabbit jerky, bread, and more apples, and went back to the woods, she approached from upwind. Already the trees were roaring in the rising wind.

She saw the dark shape in the copse thirty yards away. She shouted and waved.

The woman raised her head.

She set the package on the shore of Bear Creek, saw the woman rise on her elbow. She motioned Verity to come closer.

Verity paused, turned, and walked away, her hands stuck deep in her pockets, her shoulders hunched.

The Seam came to her that night in a dream so vivid that she woke sweating.

She lay in bed with moonlight blazing across one sliver of the bed. The clouds must have cleared for a moment. Through a crack she'd left at the bottom of the window rushed icy wind. Verity pulled her blankets closer, sat up, and stared out the window at the ghostly fields. But what she was seeing was where Cincinnati—clean and smooth and tall—stopped, and the old, worn streets of Edgetown suddenly began.

Shaking, she rose, lit a candle, and stared at the flame.

Finally, she got out her Book and drew it. That always soothed her. They got me from Edgetown, she told herself. It's only natural that I remember some of it. Her hand drew buildings, tall buildings, with gentle, curving lines, and then she sketched a Flower atop one—a flat lotus like those that choked the pond in summer. She wrote "yellow" on one petal, then yanked the page out, crumpled it, and threw it on the floor.

Maybe she was just remembering things that Tai Tai had told her, or Russ. A heavy place of blackness grew in the center of her chest and burning tears rose to her eyes; she dropped the pen and tears blurred the careful ink of a new cluster of buildings.

Snow was falling again when she woke that morning, thick and hard. Finally she dressed, and stepped into the hallway.

Blaze was there, at the other end, almost as if he had been waiting for her.

He walked toward her. It was cold; they only kept a fire downstairs, and she could see his breath.

He didn't say anything, only looked at her with his wide green eyes.

"What is it?" she asked.

Then he touched her neck with one finger, through her heavy sweater, at the place where her collarbones met. He spread his fingers, and let his hand lie against her chest, between her breasts.

Throat tight, she stared at him, ducked her head, and he dropped his hand, looking confused. He opened his mouth to say something, then didn't and walked away without a word.

Verity stood in the hall, trembling. She wanted to run after him, hold him close. Do *it*, everything, have *sex*, whatever that was; she'd looked at the pictures and Sare and Evangeline had tried to explain and also had told her why Shakers didn't have sex, so they would all be equal, and so there wouldn't be any monsters, but she didn't *care* about equal, and why would sex make you not equal anyway, and how could you really know anything from those silly pictures of what the inside of your body looked like? Everything cross-referenced *sex* had been pulled from the library, and when she had told Russ years ago when she had first been interested, his face had gone red and he had gone right to John, Verity rushing along behind, and demanded to know what he had done with everything, and John had said Mother Ann had told him about the filth there and that he had to burn it all. "Not Henry Miller too!" Russ yelled, and she feared for John. But Russ's rage passed quickly, and he just stood shaking his head, a thin wry smile crossing his face briefly.

She watched Blaze's back as he went downstairs, then whirled, ran inside her room, and slammed the door.

"Verity, are you sick?" asked Evangeline from the hallway when she didn't come down for lunch.

"No," said Verity, but her voice was muffled, and Evangeline rattled the knob. "Open the door, dear," she said, but Verity said, "Just leave me alone."

"I'll bring you some soup. You should come downstairs where it's warm."

"I'm all *right*," said Verity, and heard Evangeline go back down the stairs.

The snow fell, harder and harder, and Verity thought about the woman lying out by the edge of Bear Creek.

She's dead, she told herself, staring into the thick white cold where the orchard was just barely visible before everything vanished. A sliver of cold wind puffed in through the crack at the bottom of the window where the warped sash would never close.

How must it feel to travel so far, only to crawl into the woods and die?

Her boots and heavy coat were downstairs, lined up in the cloak room with everyone else's. She couldn't leave without someone seeing her. She thought about bundling up with everything in her drawers, then rejected that thought. There wasn't enough. No sense in being a fool.

Her room felt too small. The white plaster walls with their delicate swirls were like the snow outside, something that kept her in. She reached across her bed and yanked up the covers, smoothing the quilt with its pattern of rings, one of hundreds they'd found in a warehouse in Middletown.

The murmur of conversation came through the floorboards.

Lunch. They were all in the dining room.

She jumped out of bed, pulled on thick wool socks, her silk suit with the filaments, several sweaters.

In her stocking feet, she crept down the back stairs, wincing at each creak. Damn, she thought, I ought to be able to help someone if I want.

How to cross the door to the dining room? she wondered.

She turned and walked into it.

The buffet lamp was lit, and also the one on the table. The room was deeply shadowed.

She saw on the table a large bowl of light green lima beans, and a large basket of rolls, so fragrant that her stomach clenched. Some of those, she thought.

Sare looked up and smiled. "Verity. Feeling better?"

Verity shrugged and walked into the kitchen.

She stopped and looked out the window once again. The bare orchard was beautiful, branches wet-black and topped with an inch of snow. She heard them talking in the dining room, heard the stove door slam and footsteps leave her alone.

This was her family. Tai Tai was right. She had already endangered them. A gust of wind shook the house and the branches of the overhanging oak tree tapped on the window. Nothing could live out there, not even with the blankets she'd left. She should have taken more.

Someone touched her shoulder and she jumped.

It was Tai Tai.

Her thin, small hand closed on Verity's shoulder gently. Her large blue eyes were full of compassion.

"She is one," said Tai Tai. "We are many. Come and eat."

"Just a basket of food," began Verity.

"A basket of food for what?" asked Tai Tai. "So she can live to kill us all? You haven't seen it. You don't know how lucky you are. You were just a baby."

"But I remember."

"Remember what?"

"The Flower buildings," said Verity, and was afraid when Tai Tai's eyes narrowed.

"I thought you'd forgotten those silly dreams," she said.

"I remember you telling me they were real," Verity said.

Tai Tai looked away. "You couldn't remember them anyway," she said. "Even if they were real. You couldn't remember anything. You were so little when we took you."

"Maybe I saw pictures of them somewhere."

"Where?"

Evangeline came into the kitchen. Her long, light brown hair, streaked with gray, fell around her face as she bent to pull some rolls out of the oven. Pale yellow trousers of thin wool were knickered in tight around her ankles to keep heat from escaping, and a beaded belt wound in rainbow stripes around her tiny waist. Verity looked down at her back and longed to draw her fingers down the woman's bony spine, which knobbed through the silk shirt she wore, just before she stood up. The color of the pants was beautiful, glowing here on the verge of what would be a long, white winter. Verity felt it closing around her, and longed, passionately, for summer, and flowers, and color. Sun.

Evangeline turned with the pan of rolls and looked at Verity and Tai Tai. "What's wrong?" she asked.

Tai Tai was silent for a moment. Verity looked out the window. Finally Verity said, "I think it's wrong to let that woman die out there."

"What woman?" asked Ev, setting the edge of the pan down on the stove and adjusting her oven mitt.

"There's a Norleaner out there," said Tai Tai, her arms crossed over her chest. "Verity is feeling sorry for her."

"How long have you known this?" asked Evangeline. Excitement flared in her eyes.

"Not you too!" shouted Tai Tai, and there was a scraping sound in the dining room as chairs were pushed back.

They gathered in the arched doorway, and Blaze, in front, stared at Verity like he had this morning, his eyes burning into her in a way she had never felt before.

She remembered her day of miracles, last summer, when the green thick river had closed over the Bee, before it had bounced back to the surface, dead. Months ago. The woman had been living for months.

"She *can't* have the plague," Verity said. Even though her face glowed so beautifully. That must have just been hunger. She must have imagined it. "She's clean, and you're killing her." She stared at John, and he looked away. Blaze was next to him, and Verity didn't like the way his eyes looked all of a sudden, unfocused, as if he had a high fever. His face was very pale, and two red dots appeared on the white skin over his cheekbones.

"I *saw* it," he said. "The train!"

He smiled, but it was someone else's smile.

Then he fell to the floor with a thud.

Four

◇◇◇◇◇◇◇◇◇◇◇◇◇◇◇◇◇

To Turn, Turn, Shall Be Our Delight . . .

Sare poked a pin into Blaze's finger after they got him onto a bench next to the stove and caught some blood inside a tiny glass tube. They all waited silently while she was gone. John had gone with her; they could just follow the edge of the orchard without getting lost.

Sare got back before John, her face red with cold. She removed a scarf crusted with snow and said, "He's all right," then went back out to put all her things in the cloakroom.

"What if he wasn't?" asked Verity when Sare came back in. She was asking them all. "Then we could just toss him out in the snow, right?"

"Run down to the basement and get me an antibiotic patch, won't you?" asked Sare. "They're green." Her weathered face was still bright pink as she sat on a little stool next to Blaze, and she twisted her hands together to stop them from shaking. John came in, stomping snow from his boots.

"I guess we'd better get dinner cleaned up," said Evangeline, and they all left except Verity and John and Sare.

"It's 5,482 nautical miles downriver to Norleans," said Sare, and Verity lifted her head and stared at her. "What?"

"Oh," said Sare, "I was just thinking, that's all."

"In case we have to go," Verity heard John's blue voice, and turned to look at him.

The white walls seemed to waver in Verity's eyes. The vertical and horizontal lines of door and lintel were a deep, polished brown.

John's hair was black and straight, and his beard was black and curly. It all looked extraordinarily sharp and clear to Verity, as if she were seeing him for the first time.

His eyes were blue, like his voice, and were looking at Sare, not at her, Sare who knelt next to pale sleeping Blaze, and Verity wondered how many times they had had this conversation before.

John stepped past her and knelt beside Sare; he took her hand and put it to his cheek. They looked at Blaze, and Verity saw tears rise in Sare's eyes.

"Your machine says it isn't plague," said Verity, and her voice shook. "He's just got some sort of cold, some sort of sickness. Maybe he stayed out too long yesterday. Maybe he hasn't been eating right."

"Maybe it's a new strain that the machine won't pick up," said Sare. She paused. "Verity. Have you ever seen the machine? Really looked at it? The analysis cells don't last forever, I'm sure. It's really just a joke. A silly joke. Nothing stands between us and the plague, really, Verity. Nothing but luck and care. A nanoplague can sweep across the country on the wind. The tiny assemblers are light as seeds. There are uncountable clever ways for them to get into your body."

"Assemblers?" Verity asked, but they were all kneeling around Blaze and she felt angry about all they wouldn't tell her about sex, about the plague, about everything, but she was more worried about Blaze than anything else and didn't say anything more.

"Has he had any symptoms?" asked John.

Sare shrugged. "Like I said. The symptoms for each plague are different. We only know what was happening fifty years ago." Her voice was dry and bitter. "Information. That's what we've given up here. What mother gave up *for* us." Verity knew the story—the bedraggled mother of the twins had shown up pregnant on the doorstep. She had been quarantined for three months and no one would touch her. Sare had been the one who insisted on finding a machine, because her mother had died giving birth to them; she had forced John to take her to a hospital in Dayton and had rooted it out, and a solar battery too.

"Not that I have any idea of who our mother was," she had told Verity once. "It's just that she must have been interesting. She was a medical doctor, you know. I don't know why she didn't do something more for herself, or stay near Edgetown until we were born. She was apparently terribly frightened of something. Frightened, or tired—but they offered her a solar car to leave Shaker Hill and she refused to take it."

Verity was surprised to hear about the car. "Is the car still here?" she asked.

"They got rid of it," John said, but Verity wondered.

The song was a bit jerky at first, then smoothed and crescendoed in transcendent, minor brilliance.

"It sounds funny on the pump organ," said Verity, rising from where she was curled on a Meeting bench to shove a log into the fire. Inside the cast iron maw, brilliant orange sparks flew up the chimney. Heat washed her face, and the door clanked when she shut and latched it. "Have you tried it on the hammered dulcimer?"

"A man by the name of Scott Joplin wrote it," said Blaze, and his voice was dull. He sagged on the bench, then pulled out all the stops, leaned hard on the keys with his entire arm while he pumped furiously with his feet.

"It was lovely," said Verity, when he lifted his arm and the awful din stopped. She sat down again. "The song, I mean." She had been very gentle with Blaze now that he was up and about.

He was different now, washed through with something that seemed to make him frail, pale, and delicate, and his cheekbones stood out and his eyes were somewhere else and she tried not to see and hoped that no one else did either that his skin was starting to have that slow, faint shine, almost as if his body had been brushed with whatever made lightning bugs glow. Tears gathered in her eyes and she blinked them away.

She helped him about, as she might help an old man, and the current that had been in his hand when he touched her (she remembered, she remembered him touching her, especially at night) was gone.

She had a few more minutes until she went down to the cellar to get the jars of green beans and pickled tomatoes for dinner. She disliked it down there, even though that was childish. The cellar was chilly and dark and sometimes cobwebs feathered her face as she snapped through them.

"I know more," said Blaze, and this time his voice was fierce and angry. He straightened abruptly. "This is called 'Chrysanthe-mum.' "

"I never heard you practice these songs," said Verity, after he played the last chord. "That's really good."

"Oh yes," he said, "It's quite wonderful. It's very remark-able." His voice was angry. "It's just wonderful, the things that I'm starting to know. Verity, I need to *go*—I can't stand this—"

"Shhh," she said. "Wait until you're stronger and I'll go with you." He had been babbling about going to the library in Dayton to find out more about the plague.

Verity stared out the window. There were no curtains in the Meeting room. Across the road were the distant ruins of an old weather-grayed barn, and the concrete foundation of a farmhouse that Russ said the people from Franklin had burned with the fam-ily inside one night, with torches, in a mob with shotguns, sus-pecting that those inside had plague. Their little girl had done very well in school, Russ said, and his voice had been unusually bitter. Soon afterward Russ had left to roam the country. The crazed planes of the fallen roof were half-covered with snow, and a line of bare sycamores a quarter-mile beyond sucked water from cold Bear Creek.

Tai Tai had left the week before. She had been straight and si-lent in Meeting, as usual, but then stood, amazing everyone. It was the first time she had spoken in Meeting in fifty years.

Her voice was muffled at first, but she gained control and said, "I'm very sorry. Forgive me. I have to go to Dayton. I need to find a computer. Or something. Whatever's there. I have work to do. Look!" she finished, screaming.

She tossed her book, which she had clutched to her chest all during the Meeting, into the air. It flashed open and loose papers scattered as it struck the ceiling. One paper landed next to Verity, and she marveled at the taut, tiny hand, the utterly unintelligible symbols she saw there.

Evangeline half-rose from her bench and reached out to put her arm around Tai Tai, but the tall, dignified woman shrugged her off and then crumpled to her seat. Her sobs echoed in the cold, spare room, and Sare said, "Let us pray," and Russ said, "Let us *not,*" and picked Tai Tai up as if he were a young man and she were as light as a child and carried her out the door. That afternoon Tai Tai had left, and Verity had seen Russ, crying, alone in the Meeting room late that night.

Now, Blaze slammed the lid of the organ and stalked out of the room.

Just this morning they had been out in the orchard. He had been asking her what she would do if it was the bottom of the ninth and the score was tied and there was one man on second and the ball was coming at her, the batter, and she knew that she could hit a long fly that might be caught or a fast bunt out to left field and she was just about ready to tell him to quit asking her all these baseball questions when his face lit up as she'd never seen it, shone with a happiness so strong that she knew that whatever was happening came from some deep core within him. Thought made him glow like that, she told herself, not plague.

He took her by the shoulders and whirled her around. "There it is, Demon," he said. "Right on time. Twelve noon. It's never late. Never." He waved frantically at the empty air and said to her, "There's the brakeman. Wave! He's looking straight at you."

And while her chest ached and tears burned behind her eyes, she had waved, timidly at first, and then as hard as she could. Then she had run to the end of the orchard, leaned against a gnarled tree, and stared out at the golden field. It was all her fault. She had brought them all the plague.

Sitting in the Meeting hall after Blaze had left, Verity told herself she could wait another five minutes before going downstairs. In fact, she might never go down in the cellar again. No one would notice. No one would care.

Evangeline came in, sat, folded her hands on her lap, and closed her eyes. Verity could feel energy emanating from her, almost as strong as the unhearable current that had stirred her when she saw the Bee.

Evangeline opened her eyes and looked right at Verity, with eyes so washed, so translucent and wild, that Verity was filled with odd certainty, as if she knew exactly what Evangeline was going to say.

She did.

"I wonder how long we have?" she asked.

* * *

"I will give a concert," said Blaze, with immense magnanimity, at dinner. "Everyone's invited."

No one seemed to find it odd.

Sare had posted cards everywhere, each with a single fact. "The Highest Point in Florida Is 345 Feet," said a little card over the stove. Florida, pictured Verity's interior map for her, the penis of North America. She thought it was underwater now but didn't want to argue with Sare. "The population of Andorra in 1979 was 20,000," said a card next to her plate right now. Even as Blaze spoke, Sare had pushed her plate away and was scribbling another card.

"Guess what?" she said.

"Who cares!" said Evangeline, and reached over and tore the card in half. She threw the pieces over her shoulder. They fluttered to the wooden floor. Sare shrugged and started to write on the next one on the stack.

"Stop it!" screamed Evangeline. "I can't stand this nonsense anymore." She stood up, grabbed the cards, and threw them across the room.

"It's not nonsense," said Sare, looking hurt.

"If I want to know any of that, all I have to do is go look in the encyclopedia," said Evangeline, and grabbed some plates from the table and started for the kitchen.

"*I* don't," said Sare.

"I'm not done with that," said Russ, and pulled his plate gently from her. He looked around. Everyone was staring at him. "Whose turn is it to help in the kitchen?" he asked. "Blaze? Planning to give your concert while everyone else washes up, I suppose?"

Blaze slammed the glass of water he had been drinking down on the table, pushed his chair back, and took the bowl of green beans.

"It's only 5,283 nautical miles," said Sare. Snow pinged the windows. Was that the same distance as before? It was dark outside. The woman is dead, dead, dead, thought Verity. Dead or gone, but she didn't dare check.

"I've drawn up plans for a raft," John said.

"No need," said Russ. He scooped cold mashed potatoes onto his plate, poured gravy over them.

"We just can't stay here," said John.

Russ looked at him, his eyes like two dull green olives. "Never said anything about that," he said, and his voice sounded old. "My parents built a perfectly good boat for just that reason. You could stick it out, if you wanted. They did. You won't necessarily die. Fifty per cent, I think that was the statistic back then. Plague takes half. Wasn't quite perfected, you know—otherwise, they wouldn't have called it a plague. They'd have called it a god-damned miracle instead. There were constant mutations. Who knows. Could be completely different now."

"I've never seen any boat," said John.

"More of a raft, really," said Russ. "We built it over on the river of course, down by Franklin. It even has the wigwams. Just like in the book. *Huckleberry Finn.* Don't know why the plaguers want it like that, but they do. There used to be a lot more people on the river, you know. There used to be a lot more people every-where. I check the raft near about every year. It's still good. It's yours, if you want it. If you think you really need to go." Sare squeezed behind Russ's chair, picking up the last of her cards.

"Maybe we can fight it," said John.

"We've got a heck of a head start," said Sare, shuffling her cards into a pile again and straightening them by tapping them against the table. "I mean, what if we lived clear up in Canada? Let's see. How many nautical miles from Toronto?"

Five

◌◌◌◌◌◌◌◌◌◌◌◌◌◌◌◌◌

Last Train to Glory

Two days later, most of the snow melted off in a brief, sudden thaw, and Blaze disappeared.

Fear grew in the pit of Verity's stomach, because John disappeared too.

He could only be tracking Blaze.

And Blaze could only have gone to the Dayton Library.

She puttered around in the kitchen. She pulled out some bowls and started to make bread, but Evangeline looked at the flour and yeast and shortening she had on the counter and chased her out, saying that they had plenty of bread already and more would go to waste. But it was just because Evangeline was being greedy about the cooking and wanted to do it all herself now. When Verity left she was crumbling the yeast into warm water and honey, humming.

Verity went up to her room and stared at the blank pages of her Book, then went downstairs and put on her outdoor clothes.

She walked through the fruit room and selected five apples. No one could complain about five apples. She walked over to a wheel of half-cut cheese, peeled the paper down, opened her pocket knife and hacked off a chunk. No one could complain about a little cheese.

The wind was oddly warm, but she knew that it would change direction, maybe during the night, and that winter would return twice as strong. She hoped that Blaze would be back by then, and wished she had been brave enough to just go to the library and fetch him. Or live there with him. She could lock him up until it passed, like Russ said that it might.

Now that wasn't such a bad idea. She had no desire to ride a raft down the Ohio River. No one even knew if Norleans even existed anymore. It had to be underwater, unless they'd moved it, or unless it was afloat.

The desolation of knowing herself immune was overwhelming. Russ seemed okay. But it was her fault that the others would die, or change, or listen to whatever new thing was growing in their brain that told them to raft down the river to Norleans. Everything was gone. Everything. But now that the worst had happened, the woman shouldn't die of exposure, if she still lived. And if there was a raft, she might as well get on too.

Verity walked out across the corn field, struggling with each step against thick, sucking, black mud. She heard Bear Creek before she reached it, and started cautiously downstream, keeping to the trees.

Cairo snuffed along behind her, flushing birds and whining anxiously. The dog pictured cheese, and Verity smiled. ''Not for you,'' she said, and reached down and patted her. ''At least I have you.'' Cairo leaped around her, wagging her tail.

Verity reached the woman, stared, then vomited.

There was a small hole in the middle of her skull, and her eyes stared straight ahead. The wind pulled at her ragged clothes. The skin still on her face was blue and yellow, swollen and mottled. The package Verity had left was next to her, unopened. Some animal had chewed open one side.

Verity began to breathe harder, then turned and ran.

She was crying as she ran across the field, and her throat burned.

She ran upstairs, then stood in the middle of the room, wondering what to do.

She pulled out the drawers of her dresser, pawed wildly through her clothes, throwing them out on the floor. What was important? The warmest things, she thought, but her hands were shaking as she stuffed anything and everything into her pack so that soon it was full. She dumped it all back out on the bed, her breath coming in little sobs. The radio stone. Her favorite thing.

She pulled it from under her pillow and slipped it into her coat pocket.

Then she heard voices outside, and looked out.

Blaze was stumbling into the yard, pushed by the butt of John's rifle. Verity yanked her window up, and John must have heard it, but he didn't look up, because Russ had just come out the back door.

"We have to have a trial," said John, and his voice was John's, but different.

"Oh?" said Russ, and his voice was calm. He put his hands on his hips.

"He's been inside the library. The University Library. In Dayton. The forbidden place."

"Forbidden by who?" asked Russ. "Put that rifle down."

But John just pointed it at Russ. "Forbidden by Scripture, that's what," he said.

Russ shrugged. "The Scripture that I recall says that anyone can leave at any time, if they like, and that furthermore we must return them all the property they brought with them. Which in Blaze's case consists, I believe, in the softball and glove that were his only property when we found him. Since we've long since worn them to a frazzle, we have to settle on their fair value and give that to him instead. Do you have any suggestions?"

John's voice was rough. "This isn't a joke. He's endangered us, every one of us. And so has Verity. She's in on this too. Things are entirely too loose around here."

"That's not for you to say," said Russ.

"You think you own everything," said John. He was standing straight and stiff and his face was red. Verity couldn't tell if it was beginning to glow like Blaze's.

"Obviously, I do not," said Russ. "But it's absurd to quote Scripture to me. I was here when it was written."

Everyone was down there now except Verity, standing in a circle around John, about ten feet away.

"Don't blaspheme!" shouted John, and shot his gun into the air.

"Oh, but I'm not," said Russ. Everyone else stepped back, but he stood his ground. "Fifty percent, I think that was the statistic back then. I told you. They had fever, they raved, they *built*. My folks were builders, always, and farmers. Kind of like you, John.

They built. By themselves, with winches and saws. Built the barns, this house, the library. Drove to Dayton a hundred times in their gasoline truck. They were mad. Absolutely mad. Took them two years. They were weak a lot. Took a hell of a lot of energy *not* to give in and raft down the river. Shaker Hill, they called it, made it all up out of their heads."

"The Shakers are real, you damned old man," screamed John. Sare put a cautioning hand on Russ's shoulder, and John swung the rifle toward her. "You're not supposed to touch men," he shouted, and Sare turned pale and dropped her hand.

"It's true though," said Russ, going on gently. "My mother was crazy. She believed that she was the manifestation of Mother Ann, sent to purify the human race. When people were dropping like flies. It was pretty bad then. She had a right to think what she wanted. Oh, sure, it was all twisted up with this being right near Shaker Swamp, one of the original settlements way back when. The Indians still lived here when the real Shakers first came. Do you know that? It was all forest. And it was what she saw at the end, I think. The old days, again. That was how it was with her. The plague takes everybody different. Makes them *learn,* you know? Does something to the brain. Supposed to enhance things. Make everyone superhuman. Genetic modification of things that happen in the brain. Only problem is, it got out and spread like wildfire before it was perfected. In fact, a lot of nanplagues did. Just from people who should have known better fooling around. No controls. No telling what might happen to any given person. Apparently there's a lot more to being human than meets the eye.

"Ma got a lot of Shakerism out of the library, sure. A copy of the Millennial Laws, the ones they made up after the real Mother Ann died. Ma gathered in the countryfolk and mimicked the early Meetings, all the rolling on the floor and talking in tongues and the wildness. It fit in with the times. That's what Mother Ann did too, and her cohorts, when they came from England. They made it all up. They devised the laws. They thought they'd reshape human nature to fit their own ideas of what it ought to be. A utopia, in their eyes. Mother Ann sacrificed herself for that. She was beaten and thrown in prison more times than you could count, and died thirty years younger than she ought to have, probably from all those injuries. Sure, she believed that her sacrifice was worth it—she had a vision of the first society where men and women were on equal footing from the start, and they thought the only way to do that was to do away with sex. I'm not sure why my mother thought that she needed to include that too, but she went pretty much by the old rules, I guess. Some sort of fascination that they held for her. Something completely different. Something safe. Something controlled. Not like Cities and the world going crazy around you like it was back then.

"There's been a generation between you and then, John. A generation of Shakers here, and sure, I let them be. They were my family, as you are. You're like a son to me. Remember when I got you out of the Ruins, there in Dayton, over by Wright-Patterson, where the bunch of you was living in hangers—"

"Stop!" screamed John, and there was such anguish in his voice that Verity was chilled.

"No," continued Russ, gently, "Those were hard times for you and I can't blame you for not remembering. You took right to things here, remember Elderess Viola—"

"Stop," said John, sobbing. "Stop, stop, she's in Heaven, don't talk about her, don't *talk* about her."

"It's made up out of whole cloth, every ding-dang routine all of you think is so holy and immutable," said Russ. "I was twenty, I helped them as much as I could. What else could I do? And it worked. It was the one safe haven for miles around. I've been proud of it. My mother did well, I think. It's just like any religion with lots of rules—a rational plan to help folks survive through hard times—"

"Be quiet, Russ," said Evangeline. "Don't you see you're just disturbing him more?"

"What do you think?" continued Russ, in his cool, quiet voice. "That Mother Ann appeared on the edge of Bear Creek in a pioneer dress with angel wings and handed that stuff over? Hell, no! Ma put it together in a frenzy, one fine summer just after she was infected. She was taking a lot of drugs, that was the treatment then. Sometimes it worked. How she sang! In the morning, she'd work on the philosophy. Then when she couldn't hold out any longer, round about two in the afternoon, she'd have to take another dose. The drugs were flat out addictive, you know, and she'd go to the organ and go over all the hymns, sing, write them up. It was ecstasy, all right. It worked. Just like a lot of religions. I didn't tell anyone about it. It's made a lot of people happy."

"You're saying that our lives have been your experiment," said John, his voice flat. "I don't believe it. You're a liar! I've seen

Her down there on Bear Creek. Early in the morning, when the mist is rising. Wearing a fine white dress. In the moonlight . . .'' His voice was high. He was raving.

Verity stepped back from the window. Run downstairs, get a gun off the rack . . .

Blaze started to stammer, his words garbled and slow. They all turned to look at him. "He raped her," he said. "The woman out by the creek. John. I saw him do it. Should have said something—"

"It was before I *knew!*" screamed John. "I thought it would be all right. She wasn't one of us. She wasn't a Shaker. And I didn't rape her. She *wanted* me to. And Mother Ann told me that it would be all right. Her voice was telling me that, and the woman did too. I thought she was an angel, the way she was glowing. Mother Ann sent the woman here for *me!* And I loved her! Her face was . . . was beautiful . . . so beautiful . . .''

He moved one swift step and aimed toward Evangeline, as she raised her hand for some reason, then jerked it sideways and shot Cairo instead. Blood spattered briefly, glittering in the sunlight as Cairo was spun around by the force of the bullet. Then she lay still.

"Against the Scripture," John roared. "Dogs!"

Verity screamed, and John raised his gun and aimed straight at her.

As she stared into John's blue, blue eyes, Blaze raised his arm and grabbed John by the collar. John shook him off, stepped back, and shot Blaze in the middle of the chest.

They all rushed toward him then, and he raised the rifle again.

Verity's hand found the radio stone, cool and sharp and hard, in her pocket, and her hand and arm and eye remembered all that Blaze had taught her on those long green summer afternoons and she crouched and pitched, hard and straight through the open window, so that it caught John in the center of his forehead and he slumped forward and the only music in it, from Tokyo, streamed from the stone loud and mixed with wild high fluxes of sound and static as blood gushed from the hole it made in the center of his forehead. Then a woman's tiny voice said, "This is WWL, your clear-signal station straight from Norleans."

Sare flung herself down, crushing her cheek against John's. Blaze lay silent on the ground, and Russ looked up at Verity, and said "Bless you child," then looked out over the orchard as the

radio stone played "The Erie Canal" and Verity knew that everything in the past was over for good.

As she looked out over the bare orchard to the silver line of
Bear Creek, her whole life seemed to flash through her.

No matter what John had done, no matter what Russ said, it
had been good and true, and still was, no matter where she went,
and right now that was like an open window, the only place without grief: somewhere, anywhere else.

Relief was like a shock of lightning, knowing that the plague
and what it brought hadn't been her fault, but John's, and without
Blaze having said what he did she knew she always would have
carried blackness with her forever. She thanked him with all her
heart. She could not stop crying.

Then she saw them, for the first time.

How could she ever have missed the tracks?

They shone, straight down the middle of the two rows of trees
that formed the orchard. The black engine was enormous. It
dwarfed them all. The steam whistle blew three times, deep and
beautiful, like a song in many parts all played at once.

She thought, it must be noon.

The train pulled around the corner of the house, just below
her, where the track curved past the well. It blocked the old
wagon that she and Blaze used to play in when they were little,
running from one end to the other, shrieking with laughter as it
tipped on its single axle like a huge seesaw and came down with a
thud that shook their teeth.

The train stopped.

Blaze got on.

2

○ ○ ○

Lighting Out

The technology underlying cell repair systems will allow people to change their bodies in ways that range from the trivial to the amazing to the bizarre. Such changes have few obvious limits. Some people may shed human form as a caterpillar transforms itself to take to the air; others may bring plain humanity to a new perfection. Some people will simply cure their warts, ignore the new butterflies, and go fishing.

—Eric Drexler,
Engines of Creation

"Then I set out a line to catch a fish for breakfast."

—Huck Finn

Six

◇◇◇◇◇◇◇◇◇◇◇◇◇◇◇◇◇◇

Bid Me to Live

Verity walked down the back stairs very carefully, because the stairs did not seem the correct distance from one another. She carefully walked through the dining room. The kitchen was hot because of the stove, and the windows were steamed up.

Blaze had gotten on the train.

Yet she could still see him through the windows, a vague wavery figure lying next to John. She pulled all the coats off the pegs as she walked by, leaving them littered on the floor, and then began to run.

The cool outdoor air woke her. Sare was already leaning hard on a piece of cloth pressed against Blaze's chest, and it was red with blood. Russ was gone. Blaze's face was white. She didn't even look at John, but dropped on her knees and found her hands didn't know what to do. Blaze was very still. She felt no pulse in his neck. Everyone was crying.

She turned at a thump and Russ was hauling a round-topped trunk by a handle on one end of it.

Evangeline jumped to help and he waved her back. A few snowflakes began drifting down. "It's not heavy," he said, and knelt in front of it, and lifted the lid.

Inside were sheets of—stuff. Clear, mostly, but within the shimmering middle of the stuff, which was about a quarter of an inch thick, were a lot of tiny geometric shapes. There were yards and yards of the stuff inside the trunk, and it glimmered in the gray light as Russ unpiled it all distractedly, heaping it on the ground, until he got to the bottom and stopped.

Verity couldn't tell if it was ferny pale green moss, dried out, or maybe tiny wires, but Russ scooped up a wad of it, motioned Sare to move the bloody cloth, and stuffed it into the big gory hole in Blaze's chest. Verity, dazed by the immensity of what had just happened, could not look away.

"What are you doing?" demanded Evangeline. "He's dead. We have to bury them." Her voice was high and odd and Sare grasped her sister's arm with both hands and said, "Wait."

Russ spread out a big sheet of the clear stuff, which felt silky-smooth when Verity picked up one end and set it next to Blaze, following Russ's lead. All the time something like the Bell was ringing within her or maybe she was just sick and dizzy. But Russ nodded and she felt like maybe something was happening rather than nothing, which would be what putting Blaze into the ground would be. Something. Something.

Sare ran into the orchard and leaned against an apple tree, vomiting. A few crows flew past in the chill gray sky, and the snow began to come down harder.

"Take his feet," said Russ, and together they shifted Blaze onto the sheet. "Evangeline, fold in that bottom part. Sare," he shouted, "could you help us out just for a minute?"

Sare walked back slowly, straight and pale. She was trembling. "You fold in that top part," he told her, and then they rolled Blaze up inside the sheet, until he was blurry with layers.

Somehow it stuck to itself, and melded into a single entity, and Verity saw a tiny yellow light flash inside, and then a green one answered, where the moss was, and Russ stood up, looking satisfied.

"Now John," he said.

"What is this?" asked Evangeline.

"Not sure," said Russ, pulling out another wad of moss.

"Tech," said Sare. "What does it do?"

"We don't have that much time," said Russ. "Maybe forty minutes or so."

"Does that mean that John will live again?" asked Evangeline.

"Maybe," said Russ, "Maybe not." He spread out a sheet next to John.

"He just killed Blaze," said Evangeline. "I think he would have killed all of us. I don't think that this is a good idea."

Russ's eyes were very sad, and Verity felt that he was pulling Evangeline's soul out by the roots and trying to get a closer look. Finally he said, "Who are we to judge?"

"We're alive only because of an accident," said Sare, staring down at John. "Only because Verity could throw hard. It's true, Russ." She started to cry, her hands over her face, and Verity watched tears run down her fingers as Russ gathered her close and hugged her. "Why don't you two go in and have a hot bath?" he asked. "Verity and I can finish up here. Let's do this first. We can talk about it later."

Evangeline led Sare into the house, and Verity bent over with Russ and picked up John.

She remembered John, blue, always trying to do the right thing, always trying to be perfect and correct and follow the rules. "What does this do?" she asked, as they grunted and rolled John onto the sheet. John was much heavier than Blaze.

"Don't know," Russ said. "It's old. Probably doesn't do what it was supposed to anymore anyway. It just occurred to me, that's all. None of the old Shakers wanted it, of course. Live in the corrupt body anymore after death when they were going to Heaven? Somehow it preserves the systems. That's all I know."

"Well, then, will they wake up in a little while? A couple days?"

"No," said Russ, and stood up. He was sweating in the cold air. "This is about all I know. This stuff came from Cincinnati."

"How do you know they don't wake up?"

"Show you later," he said. "But it seems to me that if a person went to Cincinnati, there might be some sort of chance of figuring this out. Who knows. They might be stacked up like cordwood in Cincinnati. Maybe they never knew what to do once they were wrapped up."

"Well, how do you know what to do with it?"

"Seen it done," he said, "By someone who knew how. When I was a kid, in Denver. Wasn't really a kid, probably about your age, and there'd been an accident of some sort and I came upon it just about the same time as the ambulance. They wrapped the guy up just like that, applied that curly stuff where he was bleeding. Then they hurried him away. I tried to ask some of the people about it but they just acted like I was a stupid hick, which I was, out among the golden Cities in the Years of the Flowers, though of course we didn't know then that they'd soon be over, at least all of the good parts of them, when we all felt like anything was possible for humans—space flight, unlimited food and clothing, education. The plague is education gone wild, did you know that? It makes everything you know that much stronger. Or everything you think you know, which in John's case drove him crazy, since what he knew was that he had to deny himself so much of what he really wanted—split himself apart. Anyway, I had a chance to buy this trunk of stuff off a woman in Edgetown forty years ago, and I would have paid ten times what I did, but it went cheap so maybe," he looked down at them, "maybe it's not much good anyway."

"Well, what if someone had a heart attack, or a stroke, or cancer? Or plague?"

"Must not have worked for plague," Russ said.

"We have to do Cairo too," she said, and so they did.

The glass was square and was not even made for drinking, of thick green glass with bubbles in it. Verity realized that straight lines do not fit the mouth.

Still, she took another drink of the fiery stuff Russ called cognac as she sat in the darkness of the attic, with its hushed corners where the only light came from the Enlivenment Sheet wrapped about young, beautiful Alyssa.

"Puts me in mind of an Egyptian mummy," said Russ, startling her with a hand on her shoulder. She should have heard him making his way through the flotsam of the attic, but the tiny lights, blinking in unpredictable giftlike splendor must have occupied her senses more than she knew.

"The lights of life," she said, feeling like ashes within, like a dim lifeless thing validated only by the tiny, bursting, green, blue, white, yellow, red, and violet lights. One lit Alyssa's sinus from within, for three seconds, then it was dark again.

Alyssa had been twenty-four when Russ wrapped her.

That had been forty years ago.

Her hair was long and black where it splayed across her print dress, and her blurred features were fine and small. A tiny light winked maybe once in a minute, always a different one and always in a different place, and Russ sat on a pile of books and cried. Verity went and held his hand.

"I have to go to Cincinnati," she said.

"It's a fool's errand," he replied.

They sat in silence for a few more moments, watching the lights wink and hearing snow hit the small window at the end of the room with soft, repeating clicks. "But a person has to do something," he said after a while.

In the end, Russ refused to go anywhere. Because of the animals, he said, the horses and the cows.

It took three days total to get Sare and Evangeline off down the river.

One day for all of them to go over to Franklin, on a lonely gray day, Verity riding her bike alongside the wagon. The wagon was full of boxes of food which kept John from sliding out, and Evangeline and Sare sat up front with Russ while the horse pulled them. Verity thought of all the times she'd ridden in that wagon with John, bumping over old roads full of holes, listening to his cautions and fears. She had never thought this would happen, never, that the plague would get him and he'd end up wrapped in blinking sheets of Enlivenment after the plague had driven him mad.

Sare wasn't much better, in her opinion, chattering about the botanical species of practically every tree and dried-up shrub they passed, poked through the snow with dead tips, or the crows or how far it was to the thin wedge of the pale moon in the daylight sky, she just never stopped talking.

Verity wasn't sure if Evangeline had the plague or not. She seemed pretty much normal, but probably just needed to go with Sare and take care of her.

They jolted down Main Street late in the afternoon and went toward the river. Russ pulled the horse to a stop in front of a shed covered with dead vines on the edge of the river. A wooden dock ran from both sides of it into the cold rushing water.

There was a huge lock on the door and Russ got out his keys, searched through them, and unlocked it. He let the padlock dangle on the hasp and pulled wide the tall, rickety doors.

"Oh," said Sare, and ran inside eager as a little girl.

The floor was water and on it floated a raft, bobbing a little in the current which rushed past.

"Big enough for you?" asked Russ, but his voice was a bit choked. "Shouldn't have mentioned it," he muttered. "Shouldn't have said a word."

Sare went inside the wigwam and exclaimed, "It's just right, just the way it's supposed to be. A platform for the fire. Come inside, Vange, you've gotta see this. It's beautiful."

Evangeline stepped on, her heavy boots clomping on the wide deck.

"Why are all the rafts the same?" asked Verity.

Russ shrugged. "Something to do with the plague. They all wanted the same, this identical raft. And they all have to go down the Mississippi to Norleans. It puts me in mind of the way every normal child learns to walk and learns to talk. Everybody with this plague puts together one of these rafts, like they're seeing it in their mind, getting directions. There's more than one plague, mind you, it's just that this one seemed to supersede all the others once it got hold of a person. Used to be a couple of rafts would pass Miamisburg every day. When there were a lot of us there was always somebody keeping guard down at the river, with rifles. If they ever used them they never told anyone, but I don't doubt that they did. There was some talk that the Territory plague had been invented by some folks down in Norleans, which was never converted. They wanted to draw people down there, where they'd be safe from the dangers of the Cities, and thought this was the best way. I tell you, Verity, people were really strange in those days. I guess nothing's really changed."

He walked over to the wagon and picked up a box. "Might as well start loading it up," he said.

They set them loose down the river early the next morning, and waved until the current swept them around the bend, with John tied inside one of the storage benches.

Verity felt empty as she watched them vanish.

"I kind of hate to let you go to Cincinnati all alone," said Russ, as the horse pulled them back to Shaker Hill through small dead towns. The countryside was more than half forest now, full of weasels and foxes and raccoons, and they often drove beneath a canopy of branches and over bumps where roots were devouring what remained of the asphalt. The solar road was the only dependable one—it healed itself. Yet it couldn't prevent the encroachment of determined forest.

The temperature was dropping, and Verity wrapped her scarf tightly around her face. Snow had dusted the countryside in the night, but whenever they crested a hill, pale gold fields and mud peeked through, and the bare trees along the creeks were like dark gray puffs of cloud against the sky.

"Then why don't you come?" asked Verity. She was anxious to get back home, anxious to find the solar car and see if it would run; she had not even wanted to take the time to see the twins off. If Blaze could live again, then she shouldn't waste any more time. "You can bring Alyssa," she said.

Alyssa had not been his wife, of course. She had been a devout Shaker with whom he had fallen in love. She had been found dead in bed one morning and no one knew why.

"There's a ferry at Germantown," said Russ. "I think that's the way to go."

The water was thick and green, like a substance heavy enough to braid and its own rush braided it. Verity stood on the bank of the New Ohio River and was dismayed at its breadth and power.

Snow fell lightly on the solar car she'd found after two days of looking, beneath the barn floor, a trapdoor that opened when she began cranking a rusty crank she had to oil and pound with a hammer before it would work. She had a feeling that Russ knew where it was but preferred to see if she could find it herself, so that he could somewhat gauge if she was ready for the rigors of such an undertaking.

But all she knew was that she couldn't stay there and let Blaze become Alyssa's partner.

"Why didn't you try and find out what to do for her?" she asked Russ, as she sorted through clothing.

He sat on her bed, which was tightly made, as usual, looking out the window at the snowy fields. "The times were in an uproar, my girl," he said. "Reviving her seemed the same dream as the dream of Heaven, to me. They were all so crazy that she probably would have hated me if I'd been able to do it. Cheating her out of Heaven, you see. I couldn't bear to put her in the ground. I made the coffin heavy and nailed the lid down, and they buried that." He shrugged and smiled. "No one ever found her in the attic. It was regarded as my territory, I suppose. It's a great surprise to me that she's remained as young as when I wrapped her.

So maybe there's something to it after all. I'd never have done it with Blaze if I hadn't thought so."

Verity had knelt on her bag and laced it up tight.

And now she was here, at the river.

The New Ohio River had never been bridged, at least not for the length they knew. Blaze had told her that the seeds for an infinite number of bridges, with designs that stunned the heart and eye, were hidden somewhere in Cincinnati. "All of civilization lies buried there," he'd said toward the end, eyes flashing, as if he himself wanted to go and activate the seeds, as if they were presents to be opened and passed out.

Standing next to the near-freezing winter as the wind buffeted her back, Verity was pretty sure that she didn't believe him. If all that was there, why didn't people use it? Blaze just said that the things nan could do were as dangerous as they were beautiful, and that was what made it so fascinating. Something about how the very shape of matter could be shifted and changed and used, almost as easily, once it was all set up, as just *thinking* about it, and about how that was so glorious.

Indeed, she thought. We'll see, Blaze. She glanced at the trailer. It was hard to think that he was really there. We'll see. Yes.

She stamped her feet on the frozen ground, to keep her blood circulating, and scanned the river. It was broad, slow-moving, and the sky that arched above it was the constant, uniform gray of winter. She reached out and grabbed the steel cable that crossed it with both hands and leaned backwards, and was rewarded with a sinuous twist that she could see transmitted across the river. What crude bell did the ferryman have over there? She'd been here for two hours. It was a good bet that he'd died.

She glanced back at the car uneasily. Hooked onto the back was a small aluminum trailer with dented sides, a musty green tarp lashed to the top. Beneath her supplies, well wrapped in blankets lashed around them with padding to disguise their shape were Blaze and Cairo, blinking away, the tiny sensors having migrated by now, Russ had said, to the vital places in their bodies, keeping certain processes going, suppressing others. "You see," she heard his voice, "by the time they figured all this stuff out, there were entirely too many people anyway. A lot of questions about the value of keeping the dead around. Especially their bodies. There were other technologies that could just take the information from your brain—nightmares and all, I presume, which seems to me might possibly have been a deadly or delightful mix when it all went into the stewpot—and store it somewhere. The problem with that was that *you* didn't exist anymore. Other people could take advantage of what you'd known and who you'd been, but you'd never know it. These sheets were for the richest folks, I'm thinking."

The sky was still the same gray, but now it was undeniably tinged with the tenor of afternoon.

Verity cursed herself for not taking a horse. But the roads to Cincinnati had been systematically ruined after the last Enlivenment by whoever was left in the countryside, and she imagined that the earthquake hadn't done them much good either. What were her alternatives here? How many other working solar spurs off Route Four were there, leading east to a river crossing? The old maps showed only three east-west solarized roads between here and Cincinnati, and she'd already tried the first one. After a mile, the road turned to forest. She had walked a quarter of a mile, pushing branches aside and keeping a straight course with the Bean compass that dangled from her zipper pull, and found where it picked up again. Only temporarily disabled. Yet it was ruined, for all practical purposes, hurt beyond healing by someone who knew how. The woods were so thick that it would take days to widen a passage enough so that the car could even be pushed through.

She hung from the cable once more and turned a skin the cat. Arms twisted backwards, hands tight, she then let go and staggered backwards. She'd go back. She didn't have any choice. At least the car was easy to drive. You just flipped the on switch and pressed a pedal on the floor for velocity. Maybe if she went west, she'd eventually find a way to the City.

The air around her was stark, defining, and plain. No simple, happy pictures from Cairo, no sarcastic words from Blaze. Only the river, the forest, the gray sky. She felt alone on the continent, the only person alive in a wilderness of forgotten wonders and desperate dead humans stacked and glowing forever, like kindling for a new and warming fire. Only her eyes were exposed to the world, and she wanted to close them, to go back to the Dayton Library, Bell or no Bell, and lie down on the couch forever.

Above her, the cable jerked. She looked at it, disbelieving, but then the tiny jerks regularized and she allowed herself to look down its length and saw: a lumpish shape was moving across the river along its path.

She stood up and watched.

It took ten or fifteen minutes, and when she realized what she was seeing she began to laugh.

A figure covered with a shining orange poncho was *pedaling*.

The hooded figure reached down with one hand as he approached the shore and did something, then stood up to lean on the pedals the final twenty yards, bobbing up and down like a marionette.

The raft rolled onto the two metal tracks which were attached to the landing ramp, and Verity heard a loud click. The pedaler was breathing heavily.

"Sorry," Verity heard from a woman who then threw back her hood to reveal a somewhat crooked nose in an otherwise beautiful face. Large green eyes reminded Verity of Blaze, and blond hair was pulled back tight. A red turtleneck hid her neck, and she yanked a purple hat from her coat pocket and pulled it on.

"Getting chilly," she yelled over the rush of the river. She knelt and unhooked something and pushed the foot-high edge of the raft down with her boot. It fell onto the ramp with a thud.

Verity looked at the weird craft. A different bike faced the opposite shore, so that the raft need not be turned around. "Need help rolling that on?" the woman asked, nodding at the car and the trailer. Together they pushed it onto the ferry.

The car itself was wondrously light for its size, obviously hollow within its plastic double walls except where the battery lay, somewhere under the floor. Transmitting filaments glittered within the clear plastic bubble that was the roof, from the backup solar battery. The two long metal strips underneath, magnets according to Russ, were the heaviest thing about it, and gave it stability. The wagon with the bodies was about the same weight.

The woman's cheeks were bright red. "Going on a pilgrimage, eh?" she asked, her voice hearty and friendly. "Seems like all these parts have emptied out in the past few years. My dad used to have a lot more crossings. Sorry if you had to wait a long time. I was out hunting. I might go a week or more without crossing anyone."

Verity heard a squall—an angry, wailing sound—and the woman shook her head. "Damn the boy," she said. "I thought he was asleep." She bent down and opened a door on the small, chest-high cabin, which was built haphazardly on the deck. It was nothing that John would ever have stood for—crooked, with gaps here and there, and unfinished edges. The woman reached inside and gathered up a screaming bundle.

The woman stood and bounced it a few times, but it didn't stop the horrible sound. All at once Verity understood.

"A baby?" she asked. She had never seen one. She had always been the youngest.

"You bet," said the woman, and sat down on an overturned bench. "Block the wheels with these wedges," she told Verity, kicking a few pieces of wood toward her with one booted foot, "and we'll get going before it gets too dark. Not that it really matters. Matt will have the lantern lit when we make the other side." She started to coo at the baby, but its small face was red and angry. Verity felt a moment's fear and anger, then laughed at herself. She herself was a possible danger to this woman and her child and all whom she met, she and her cargo, not the other way around.

"It's too cold," the woman said, but finally sighed, unzipped her coat, fumbled with her clothing, and put the baby's head to her breast. She looked up at Verity. The river flashed past, green and angry, and the trees roared in the rising wind. "You've never seen a baby, have you?" she asked, and her grin was wicked. "The scourge of the earth, you've been taught? I assure you, that's entirely true." After ten minutes, she laid the baby in the box, strapped him in, and pushed it back inside the cabin. Verity saw her attach some sort of hook to it, then she rose.

She raised the side of the boat which had served as a ramp. Then she unhooked a belt from the first bike and coiled it on the deck. She walked to the bicycle facing the eastern shore, and lifted an identical belt that was attached to a pulley contraption at the top of the front wheel of the bike. The wheel turned by the pedals was not a regular bike wheel, but an old rusty gear with teeth that meshed with the pulley. It dipped beneath the deck through a narrow slit, and Verity assumed that it was attached to some sort of paddlewheel beneath the raft, the floor of which did not rest directly on the water but on heavy beams onto which the platform was nailed.

The belt ran from the front wheel to a large hook that hung from the cable above. The hook was attached to a pulley, which kept them on course by gripping the top of the cable as the woman climbed on the bike and began to pedal. The raft slowly moved away from the shore.

Verity watched nervously. The whole arrangement looked worn and frayed.

And then the ragged belt snapped.

Verity saw it, but could hardly believe it as it happened, the strip whipping out, wild threads astream in the wind and the woman at first continuing to pedal like some mad, unreasoning demon.

The raft tilted and swirled in the current. Water sloshed over the forwardmost edge of the clumsy rectangular craft. The car and trailer slid sideways from the wedges and rolled forward, slamming into the cabin.

Verity leaped to the front of the rounded car, but there was nothing to grasp. The woman pointed to a rope coiled next to Verity's foot, but she didn't pause to help her.

While Verity struggled to lash her vehicle to the hooks and other metal protuberances scattered around the deck, her teeth clacking in the cold, she saw that one of the metal things, a long rod, was actually a lever. The woman slid from the bike seat, and shoved it all the way back, her face intense with effort. Then she jumped back on her bike.

Crouched over it, her legs moved slowly, and Verity felt the raft respond and turn.

Already they were at least half a mile from the road, Verity judged. Deep forest loomed on both sides of the wide river. The woman pedaled and steered, aiming for gaps in the rocks, and Verity grabbed an oar from the deck and stood ready to push them off from any they came close to. The woman looked back and grinned, and Verity felt more afraid at this than anything.

Seven

◇◇◇◇◇◇◇◇◇◇◇◇◇◇◇◇◇◇

Down the Ohio

Oh, the river is up and the channel is deep
The wind is steady and strong
Oh won't we have a jolly good time
As we go sailing along!
Down the river, oh down the river, oh down the river we go.
Down the river, oh down the river, oh down the Ohio.
—American Folk Song

Verity braced herself against the rough edge of the cabin and tensed her arms. The oar she held was about seven feet long and heavy; she didn't want it wrenched from her grasp.

The woman's brilliant long blond hair was afly as they rushed downriver. A jagged rock big as a house split the river ahead, creating a wave that appeared to be forever breaking toward them.

The woman stood on the pedals and pumped hard; Verity could see her mouth was open and she was gasping for air as she turned her head to the side to gauge their direction.

With a burst of energy, she pulled them clear of the current and they swept past the east side of the rock and whirled into a small, calm cove.

The woman bent over the handlebars, her back shaking. Verity carefully set down her stick, and worked her way around the deck.

Once next to her, Verity realized that the woman was laughing. She lifted her face to Verity, and though tears ran down her reddened face, she gasped for air and then began, unmistakably, to laugh again.

Verity looked into the wilderness next to them, darkening with sunset, and was not amused. No solar road here.

But she was alive.

The laugh was infectious. Verity began to laugh too, to laugh as she hadn't laughed in weeks, and tried not to remember what it had been about, for it surely would have had something to do with Blaze.

The woman stood and kicked one leg over the back of the bike, leaned on the seat, and hiccuped a few times. "Damn," she said. "Didn't think we'd make it." She stepped over to the small cabin, unhooked it, and pulled out the box with the sleeping baby. She looked at him a moment, shook her head, and adjusted his blanket.

"What are we going to do now?" asked Verity.

"That's what I was wondering," said the woman. "Look here." She slid a large board like a drawer out from underneath the cabin's roof with a knob Verity hadn't seen before. It was chest high, and Verity saw that a nautical chart was on it, covered with plastic somehow melded to the wood beneath it. The woman studied it in the waning light.

She pointed a finger clothed in a tattered glove at a bend in the river. "I think we're here," she said, and something in Verity's mind said that she was right.

Something also told her that when the sun went down that certainty would disappear. She needed the sun to know.

She'd never been this far from home before, not in these parts. She'd always figured that her knack for knowing where she was came from having been there before.

The strangeness of the realization was a tiny, inward chill; then a small bright burst of truth like a single star in a vast, dark night.

"We've gone about seven miles downriver," said the woman. "We'll have to walk back up through the woods. You'll have to leave your car behind. Whoops. We're drifting." She backed up a few steps and with both hands picked up a big iron doughnut on the end of a thick rope and heaved it into the water. The splash hit Verity's arm and she brushed at it, not wanting to be further chilled. She shook her head. She didn't much care about the car, except that it was pulling Blaze and Cairo.

"I need the car," she said.

The woman opened a little cupboard and pulled out a lightstick. She smacked it on the roof, causing it to give off a yellow glow. She leaned back against the roof and looked at the stars, which were beginning to show. "The solar road is only about two miles from here, but the woods are pretty thick."

"You'd just leave the raft here?" said Verity.

She shrugged. "What's the choice? I can build a new one, I guess, except that it would take a long time and a lot of work, and there's not much call for it anyways, nowadays."

A gust of wind set the trees to roaring, and Verity zipped her jacket up to the very top. She stood with her hands in her pocket and turned to look out at the dark river, hearing it rush past with a deep, steady song. "Why don't I just take it?" Verity asked. "I'm going downriver anyway." Something in her made her want to be alone.

She had planned on shooting squirrel and rabbit on her way to the City, then camping on the outskirts for maybe a day; she wanted to watch the Enlivened City, to see the Flowers she'd so long seen in her mind unfurl before a sky actual and blue, and to view the Bees feeding. Just a day, she'd told Blaze and Cairo in her mind, give me a day and I promise I'll get you there, just a day of seeing my dreams made real, the dreams I've had all my life come alive.

In the small circle of light the woman's eyes narrowed and she drew back imperceptibly. "I didn't take you for—" She didn't say plaguer, but that was what she meant.

"No," said Verity. "I'm well." Of course she was well. Her stomach turned for an instant, though. Could she, if she had been at fault to begin with, still spread the plague? She'd tested clear on Sare's machine. The one Sare was so derisive about. The one that gave Blaze the all clear.

Verity decided not to tell the woman about Shaker Hill. If she was exposed, it was too late and there was nothing much that Verity could do about it. She could hardly avoid other people if she was going to Cincinnati. She was heading into the thick of it, with no idea of what was really there or what she would do or find. Of course, that was where plague came from. Cities. Wasn't it?

And there was no going back now! Something in her rejoiced in the realization, the motion, the momentum. The journey. What had the woman said? The pilgrimage.

The woman tilted her head and gave Verity a look of mixed measuring and shrewdness. "I guess I have some choices too," she said. "I don't have to go back."

"What about—who? Matt?" asked Verity.

"Matt's a dog," she said. "Matt's a dog, and my name is Violet. Matt pushes the solar switch on with his nose when it gets dark, that's all, so I can find my way home if it's dark. But it's true, I'd hate to leave him. What's your name?"

"Verity," she said, questions crowding forward, like, do you talk to Matt with pictures, could there be another Cairo? "Why would you want to go to Cincinnati?" asked Verity.

"Curiosity," said the woman. "To help you—you can pay me with something or other you've got in your trailer, I'm sure. And they have mule paths that connect the canals back to my place, so if I really wanted I could bring the raft back upriver. I've been wanting to buy a mule, anyway. It would be good to grow some things instead of hunting all the time, now that I have the baby."

"We couldn't really raft down," said Verity. "We don't have any control at all."

"That was an emergency situation, my girl," said Violet. "This is more of a craft than you think. Don't want to wake the boy, but I do have an engine. It takes feeding, though. I was pretty stupid about the belt. I'm sorry."

"Feeding? Like gasoline?"

The woman stared at her for a moment. "Gasoline?"

"Well, I don't see any solar panels."

"Where are you from?"

"Up—around Dayton," said Verity, not being able to think of a good lie, because she didn't know why the woman was suddenly curious.

"No, it runs pretty good on leaves." She kicked a toe toward a round plastic plug on the deck floor to which Verity had lashed the car. "Stuff 'em in there."

Enlivenment. Verity felt herself trembling. The woman narrowed her eyes once more. "Of course, it ain't the best thing to go Cincinnati way, not with a baby."

The disadvantages were obvious to Verity, but she asked, "Why not?"

The answer startled her. "Bees," the woman said briefly.

"What about them?"

The woman stared. "They take babies," she said. "Don't you know that?"

"Of course," said Verity, something moving her tongue which she didn't understand, something brand new. "I just thought if you watched close—"

"They're greedy," said the woman.

Verity wanted desperately to know what they were greedy for, but didn't dare ask.

"Where were you planning to sleep tonight?" she asked.

"I've got a tent and sleeping bag," said Verity.

"Well, get 'em out and put em on the deck. There's room for me to squeeze into this cabin, but that's all." Her tone was much shorter now.

Verity felt uncomfortable with the woman's eyes on her while she extracted her bag from beneath a corner of the tarp.

She heard the baby cry again as the woman crawled into the cabin. "Night," she said.

Verity determined to stay awake all night. Something about Violet made her uneasy. She stared at the brilliant constellations overhead, the splash of bright stars across the center of the intensely black night. A satellite flashed by. Blaze had taught her that. John claimed they didn't exist, though it would have been easy for him to see them with his own eyes and she was sure he had, and thought them something else entirely. Russ said they were dead, anyway. Flying around the earth with nothing to do but catch the sun.

It was probably close to freezing. Her bag was pulled up around her face with the drawstring so that only her eyes and nose were uncovered. She'd even worn her boots inside the bag. Things had switched quickly. First the woman had seemed comfortable with her. Then she hadn't. She unzipped the bag enough to pull the collar of her flannel shirt up to her nose and blow it hard, then zipped it up again and, despite her fear, exhaustion won.

Eight

○○○○○○○○○○○○○○○○○○○

Some Rows Up

Some rows up
But we floats down
Way down the Ohio to Shawneetown
—Ohio Flatboat Song

Verity woke with the sky spinning overhead. Light gray sky. Dawn-sky.

She sat, trapped in her bag, and saw that the raft was spinning away from the cove.

Violet stood on the shore watching, swiftly becoming smaller as the raft swept Verity downstream. Violet held the baby on one hip and a rifle in the other hand.

Verity's rifle.

She struggled from her bag, and saw that the tarp had been thrown back to expose Blaze and Cairo, blinking. She saw that Blaze's sheet had been ripped on one corner and she leaped over to it and smoothed it together and the lights blinked slowly, like lightning bugs.

She hoped that Violet's walk home would be damned hard when she saw that the woman had taken the handgun that Russ had insisted on and all the ammo too. Verity's hand went to the Bowie knife she had on her belt. At least that was still there.

She didn't think for too long. The raft swirled and she looked at the plastic plug and thought, leaves?

Leaves, and what else? It sounded absurd to her. What sort of fire did they kindle? What were the parameters of Enlivenment, as Sare used to ask while Tai Tai glowered and spat "not bloody many, that's the problem."

Luckily, the Ohio was smooth and broad here. The bank was

lined with leafless sycamores, Verity's favorite tree, the subtle brown and white and green blotches of their peeling bark something exotic.

Leaves.

Fine.

She jumped on the bike and began to pedal, turning the handlebars toward the west bank. Did they have to be dry, she wondered?

She drifted beneath some overhanging branches and tossed the rope over one, caught the end as it flapped over and put all her weight on it.

The raft began to drift out from under her. She swiftly wrapped the rope around a t-shaped protuberance on the deck and it held.

Trembling, she took stock.

No gun, no hunting. Well, she had plenty of tofu. She pulled back the flap.

Damn the woman! The food bag gone. The guns gone. The greedy fool! Maybe she was lucky that the woman hadn't killed her in her sleep, though, after seeing Blaze and Cairo, especially Blaze with blood still spattered here and there inside the sheet, brown and crusted.

She heard something in the woods, and whirled.

A group of children dressed in thick winter clothing tore through the trees.

They were pretty far away, she judged, at least a quarter of a mile.

She leaned over and scooped leaves onto the deck, an armful and then another.

She heard a gunshot, pulled out her knife and sawed through the rope, leaving as much length as she could.

She grabbed the oar and pushed off, hard, three shoves in shallow water and she was into the current. She flung herself down behind the cabin as they shot at her from the banks of the New Ohio River, the strange children who were such very bad shots.

But maybe, she thought, as the river caught her, they were just trying to scare her off.

What sort of world was she entering? Had John been right about the enmity of it, the fearful darkness, the strangeness? Well, she thought, if the Shakers had known that Alyssa had been mummified in the sheets right over their heads, they would have done something about it. She had been taught by John to fear Enlivenment, but it was keeping Blaze alive—maybe. Those children feared *her*, and she imagined John living with a pack of kids at the air force base, and a younger Russ finding John sick and abandoned, and taking him home to Shaker Hill, trying to heal his crazed heart, but the crack had been deep, so deep—

But these children were younger than her. What could they know?

They were closer to the City, for one thing. She shivered. Would she soon meet people she should try and kill, before they killed her—especially if they saw Blaze, with that smear of blood across his cheeks and staring eyes that Russ, in his hurry, had not closed? (And besides, my girl, you must remember that he's *not* dead, Russ had said grimly when he noticed.) That is, she *might* have tried to kill them if Violet hadn't stolen her guns—

The raft swirled as it was pulled back into the river. Verity staggered as she stood, and she almost fell onto the large plastic plug embedded in the floor of the raft. Tugging, she worked it free and peered inside, but it was simply dark.

She shoved the sycamore leaves inside, and as she picked up the plug she noticed that there were buttons on the bottom. There had once been writing, but it was worn off.

She pressed a green button, and a light came on, a blue light the size of a kernel of corn. Fine. She stomped it back in the hole, but nothing happened. The woman had probably been joking. It didn't make any sense. Why didn't she use the engine to cross the river, then? Maybe it was just more trouble than it was worth. Maybe she didn't know how to turn it off. Maybe she'd never ever used it.

It seemed to Verity that she was moving fairly quickly, but the river was broad and straight and flat ahead and she pulled out the map, glancing up often to see if there was any danger. She felt tense and tight, and hunger twisted her stomach.

At least it wasn't far to Cincinnati according to this map. Maybe twenty miles. A day's ride or less, she judged, depending on the current. She bent closer to the map and studied it.

There were falls, apparently, on the east side of the City, about three miles before the New Ohio joined the Old Ohio. So she had to leave the river before then. She glanced at her car and trailer, and could only hope that the old edges of the City had solar roads.

She felt a shudder surge through the raft and was dismayed. Apparently something had worked.

As the sensation settled into a smooth, low vibration which she felt through her feet, she gazed at the plug, stunned. Blaze had insisted on this. This *strangeness*. And she had laughed.

"You were right, Blaze," she shouted over the constant rush of the river. Matter was fuel. Something consumed those leaves within that compartment like flame consumed logs and changed them into—

She worked her way back and saw, murkily, a propeller turning just beneath the water's surface. Leaves into motion. And motion *swift*, motion *dangerous*—

The raft swirled suddenly, and she lurched back to the cabin and caught hold. How could she control the velocity? She ran to the front of the raft and jumped on the bike. The lever, next to her? Not the one Violet had used to change the belts, but the other one. She pulled back on it and the sound of the propeller became a bit louder, and the raft slowed just a bit. She found that the steering worked much better now, and took a deep breath. She pulled it back farther until she was comfortable with the speed.

The forest was thinning. It was about eleven in the morning.

She saw, to her right, a flat roof, and one floor of windows. The strip of buildings was long, and angled into the river; she realized, with a shock, of course, it was like Miamisburg. The New Ohio had swallowed towns in a roaring instant, searing down the ancient fault line right through the town of Moraine and down on into Eastern Cincinnati. The map showed a large island where Northern Kentucky had been, then the rivers joined into a single river. At least the raft didn't draw much, as far as she could tell, but the propeller or whatever drove it could probably rip the raft in half if it caught on anything. She tried to peer beneath the river's surface but it was an opaque olive green, shimmering flatly in the gray winter light.

She'd seen where she wanted to go on the map. If only she could get there. It was the perfect place.

The raft came around a curve and Verity's breath caught in her throat.

Cincinnati. How had she pictured it so accurately all these years?

The buildings were dull turquoise, yellow, mauve. Their colors seemed to oscillate slowly before her eyes, and she blinked, wondering if it was a trick of light.

She was still at least ten miles away. And it was disappointing, because she saw no Bees.

And no Flowers.

It's cold, she told herself, but there was an empty ache within.

She passed beneath a sign. It was bright green, and said:

SR 75 SOUTH
ENTER "LOCKLAND" FOR EXIT VERIFICATION NOW
NEXT EXIT 2 MI ARLINGTON HTS

Lockland.

There had been some old locks here on one of the canals, she imagined. "You'd like that, Blaze," she said, and the wind bore her words away as she spoke. "We're on Solar Route 75, which ran along an old canal route, and also on the New Ohio River. Three forms of transportation at once."

She wiped away tears, shifted in her seat, and steered toward the western shore, scanning it for a road. Now she was passing the old nubs of ruined houses, ancient factories, the pre-conversion, pre-flare, pre-earthquake suburbs of Cincinnati, Ohio.

She saw no people as she rushed past the empty buildings. She was not surprised, and not disappointed. Flaretime, plague, and earthquake had gotten rid of more than two-thirds of the population of North America.

The clouds parted and the world brightened a few degrees. Verity studied the shore. It seemed to her that the roar from downstream was increasing. She wanted to land near a road; otherwise she had no idea what she would do.

Then she saw one, arcing out of the river.

The Lockland exit.

She steered toward the smooth black ribbon, part of the Enlivened Highway System which had laced the country during the Years of the Flowers. She had to hit it just right, catch the railing which ran along its edge, or else—

How many chances would she get?

The river was running faster and she began to feel afraid. She yanked the velocity lever back as hard as she could but it didn't seem to make any difference. The handlebars fought her and she strained to keep the raft on course.

As she rushed toward the road, she gave the handlebars a wrench, then jumped off the seat, grabbed the rope, and kneeled on the front of the raft.

The guardrail grew large quickly, and she reached out, was able to pass the rope beneath it, and grab the end—

Then it was yanked from her hands with blistering speed, and trailed in the water behind her as the raft swept onward.

Fear squeezed her chest. She got on the bike, pedaled hard, and steered for shore. Anywhere. Anywhere would do. The hell with a road.

Then she saw it.

A four-story red brick building, decayed and partially roof-less, square and imposing. A stairway led up to the front door, flanked by two concrete arms which formed a tiny bay.

A stone lion stood guard on either side.

Her only chance. Beyond it concrete ramparts rose on both sides of the narrowed river, and she didn't know how long they lasted, or whether she would find a place to get to shore beyond.

Hastily she looped the rope around her waist and knotted it.

Standing next to the bike she steered toward the still square of shallow water, hoping she would not have to jump.

The raft swirled, then a corner of it stuck in a crevice.

The current tugged at it. Verity leaped out into knee-deep water and ran up the steps, unknotting the rope.

On the door was a heavy iron circle. She passed the rope through it, leaning all her weight on the rope, pulling the raft as close as she could.

Then she knotted like a crazy woman, again and again and again, trembling with cold and release. She smelled wet bricks, their scent brought out by the water lapping them as they crumbled away, an earthy smell that contrasted with the tang of the water.

She felt, uneasily, that she was being watched. She looked up and saw engraved in the concrete above the massive door: Lockland High School.

The river was just below the level of the entrance, and she saw that the door stood open a crack. If she could get both doors open, perhaps she could roll the car inside and rest.

She pulled, and the door swung open. The ring the raft was tied to was on the other door, and she stepped inside and leaned upon it, and it too swung open.

Gasping with the effort, wishing that Violet had carried a winch on the raft, she gradually pulled the raft toward her until it bounced against the concrete. She glanced behind at the darkness of the hall, not daring yet to untie the rope. She saw a shadowy stairway, and backed inside the building until she could loop the rope around the metal post. She pulled on the post as hard as she could, and it didn't budge. Satisfied, she went back to the raft and unhooked the ramp, let it settle with a thud. Panting, she got out her knife and cut the car loose where she'd lashed it, and pushed it into the hallway.

There she collapsed, promising herself that she would get up in a minute, just one short minute to rest.

Then she remembered the children with the guns.

Every muscle aching, she stood up.

She pushed open the door nearest her cautiously. It was light inside. She saw tall windows opposite in the high-ceilinged room.

She looked around the door and choked.

Five Bees were there.

Dead, they looked dry and brittle in the pale winter light. Each had been mangled. The legs had been cut off and she could see that the heads had been partially chopped from the bodies.

"Not a pretty sight, is it?"

She jumped, and turned around slowly.

A boy a few years younger than Blaze stood there, looking proudly at the Bees. "Tricked 'em," he said. "Used a doll and a net. They're not all that smart, seems to me. Don't know why people think they are. Maybe their eyes are bad."

He was dressed in a skin-tight dark green suit that glittered with tech. Black boots came to his knees, and around his waist was a belt with a knife and a gun. He wore a yellow hat and his face was pale, almost white. Light brown freckles stood out on his cheeks.

"Cheyenne," he said, and held out his hand.

She shook it. "Verity," she said.

"Good job you did there," he said. "Thought you were over the falls for sure. River takes a sharp curve to the east half a mile down and meets up with the Old Ohio. Most rafters don't seem to know. Just shoot right over. Really just a long string of rapids. Pretty wild, pretty rough, pretty fast. Hungry?"

She nodded.

His eyes were pale blue. She didn't want to ask why he killed the Bees. She didn't want him to see Blaze and Cairo.

But she was hungry. Damned hungry.

On the third floor he had a fortress. She leaned out the window and gazed at the City, colors oscillating in the pale noonday sun.

"Pretty nice day," he said. "How do you like noodles? Yeah, noodles and sausage." His face lit. "Sometimes I get down to the market and get me some sausage. Ever been to Edgetown? Nah. If you had, why would you be coming down the river?" He chattered and fed kindling into a small grill he had next to the window. Smoke drifted out onto the gray air, and the river roared outside. He opened a cupboard, got out a frying pan, then reached around on the windowsill and pulled in a package wrapped in crinkly plastic. "Edgetown's over there, between the river and the Seam." He gestured out the window, toward an uneven cluster of brick and wooden buildings, which looked to be about eight stories at their tallest, jumbled together just below the hundred-foot-high edge of pale, smooth, gleaming Cincinnati— the *Seam,* thought Verity, catching her breath as she saw that fearful, legendary wall. Where the Conversion, the Surge, had halted. The conversion was a nan process Tai Tai had described as *eating*—matter trembling and surging and *changing* as she had scrambled ahead of it, caught up with the mob that rushed screaming from the gastly, devouring wave.

Cheyenne unwrapped a large sausage and cut off about a foot, sliced it into the frying pan, bent over it, and took a deep breath. He put a pot of water next to it on the grill and stood looking at Verity, holding a handful of dried noodles.

"Where you from?" he asked.

"Dayton," she said, mainly to see if he'd react like the ferry woman.

"Not far," he said. "I don't actually get to talk to many rafters, you understand, but most of them come from way up north. What there are of them." He dropped the noodles in the water and stood next to Verity as she looked out at the City.

"It's an awful thing to look at, isn't it?" he asked. "We're lucky it's so cold. Ten more degrees and them flowers would be opening up. This is the best time of year. They're all closed up tight."

"Are they so—mean?" she asked. "I don't know that much about Bees. We didn't have them in Dayton."

"Amazing," he said. "Guess it didn't surge up there. Lucky. Here, nobody gets into the City, and nobody gets out. Not that we should care, I guess, but some people had relatives inside who all went crazy, and the ones who got out weren't much better from what I hear. Fifty-sixty years ago. That was the first time, the main surge. Guess my grandparents were in there, too old to run or too crazy to want to, least that's what I've heard." Verity, watching the side of his face, saw him blink swiftly a few times before he started talking again. "Anyways, Edgetown folks are still mad about it, and afraid. Anybody who ever gets out, gets away from Cincinnati, is purely nuts. The Bees have been their whole life, you know. Weird old woman down at the Market preaches about them, everlasting hell and damnation, and there's a few organizations to try and get rid of the Bees but nothing really works." He grinned and stirred the noodles with his knife. " 'Cept me, I do a pretty good job." He pulled a plastic plate off a shelf and heaped it with fried sausages and steaming noodles after he poured most of the water out the window.

"What kind of sausage is this?" she asked, and he looked at her blankly. "I mean, pig of course, but . . . you know—blood or brain or—"

"Huh," he said, and handed her some chopsticks. "Comes from the market. They got—you know, a sausage machine. She's a rich woman, the sausage queen. I get a bounty on the Bees, and then I stock up." He sat in one of the desks scattered around. Each had a little screen set in it.

"Do these work?" she asked.

"Hope not," he said. "Yeah, sometimes one might come on, but if it does I smash it. Most of them are smashed. Hate the damned things talking to me. When I first walked into the building a year ago they chattered away to beat the band. I thought if I kept them out of direct sun they wouldn't work, but they don't need a lot of light to get going."

"Who pays the bounty on the Bees?" she asked.

"Oh, an old lady down by the tracks," Cheyenne said, slurping up his noodles.

"But why?" she asked.

"Well," he said, "gives people an incentive to kill them, I guess."

"Does anybody else pay besides her?" asked Verity.

"Why? Planning to go into competition?" He grinned, but Verity could see he was wondering why she asked so many questions.

"No," she said. "I've just never been here, that's all. I'm curious. What's Edgetown like?" She knew that it was right outside the Seam, and little else.

His eyes brightened as he brought a bite of sausage to his mouth with chopsticks. Mouth full, he said, "Grand. Just grand. Exciting! Music. Lots of people."

"So why don't you live there?" she asked.

He shrugged. "You need money, or something to trade. People grow things on roofs or have little vegetable patches where houses burned. They make things that other people need, or know how to fix things—stuff like that. But this place is mine, see? Because I found it first. I don't have to pay anybody for it. Not many folks live this far out. I got plenty of room. I don't like to be around them all the time. It's like—it's like they're pressing in on you all the time, you know? Out here I can still hunt, rabbits at least. I can do without Edgetown if I have to. But if anything happened to the people there, they wouldn't know anything about staying alive. Not like I do. Don't want to lose that."

"Who's in charge?"

"Well," he said, "I'm not too sure. It's like they have certain rules that everybody knows. As far as I can tell they don't like the idea of anybody in particular being in charge. That would be too much like the Bees. I think they just try to be happy, try to keep from getting the plague. I try not to spend too much time there. The City might surge again sometime. Eat Edgetown."

There it was again. "Surge?" she asked, wondering what it meant to him. She finished the last of her sausage and noodles and set the bowl and chopsticks down.

"What the Bees do," he said. "They change everything all of a sudden when they take a mind to it. Wipe it all clean. If you're there you don't remember anything. That is if you survive. The buildings and everything all go weird."

"Have you ever seen it?" asked Verity.

He was silent for a moment, then turned toward her. She thought for a moment that he might rise and strike her or cry but he took a deep breath and said, "Sure," his voice rising. "At least I think so. A few years ago." His voice was jerky as he continued, and he seemed short of breath.

"It was late at night. I was living a little closer in. That's when I moved out here, after that. I woke all of a sudden, like I could *feel* something. The moon was full, it seemed almost bright as day. It was the middle of summer. The Flowers were all open. The Bees were flying around like crazy. I didn't know there were so many. Guess they were all out at once, flying from Flower to Flower, and then it almost made me feel like throwing up the way the buildings started to flash and flash, and then there was a big glow, just for a minute—real, oh, it wasn't just pretty, it was *gorgeous*, and then it was kind of like a ripple on water when you throw in a stone. The whole City just seemed to shiver, once. Then it went dark. And quiet. Terrible quiet. Before that I never realized that the City made any sound but I guess it does. I just sat and watched. I should have run but I didn't. After a few hours it started to light up again, just one building at a time. And when I went into town the next day—never seen so many folks running the other way but it seemed like it was *over* and I wasn't afraid— the street where I used to get noodles was *gone*. Just a big wall there." He set his bowl down with a thump. His hand was shaking.

"It's really nice of you to feed me," Verity said, in a low voice she hoped was soothing.

He took a deep breath. "Sorry I got so upset," he said. He stood and started gathering up the pots and bowls. "Anyway, I want a favor too. You got a car, and it'd be a heck of a lot easier if you'd unload that trailer and we could take the Bees downtown in it. I got a cart, but I have to pull it myself. Them there cars are rare. Used to have one, but somebody took it. I figured they needed it worse than me. That's old, you know, must be pre-earthquake 'cause the factories were ruined after that and during the plague. People smashed them up, what was left after the quake."

They say the Cities have the Seeds for all sorts of consumer goods," Blaze's voice whispered.

How lucky she had been. How unlucky this boy was, she thought. How unlucky they all seemed, if they were like him.

"Tell you what," she said. "You think my car will pull your trailer if we add it on?"

He scowled. "It'd be mighty slow," he said. "But it would probably work."

"Is it far to the train station?" she asked. By the map it had looked to be about five or six miles.

"The Rainbow?" he asked. "Why you want to go there?" He shivered. "It's a bad place. Who knows what's down in them tunnels. It's as bad as the City. You don't want to go there. I've heard it connects right into the City."

"Is where you want to go on the way?" she asked.

He shrugged. "Could be, I guess. We could work it that way. But you ought to go straight to Norwood."

"What about Edgetown?" she asked.

"Norwood is the main part of Edgetown," he told her. "It's an old neighborhood. Just happened to be on the edge of the surge, and right on the other side is the New Ohio. The falls are just below it. Kind of boxed in there, squeezed on two sides, river on the north and the Seam to the south, and it can't be more than a mile north to south and two miles east to west. Want to help me wash up?"

They carried the plates and frying pan downstairs, knelt on the front step where she saw the other stairs descending into a submerged schoolyard. Beyond the raft, she saw metal tubes, welded together, just breaking the surface.

"What you got there?" he asked, nodding toward the trailer.

"Supplies."

The clouds had parted to reveal a pale blue wintry sky. When Verity was finished with the dishes she continued to crouch, but lifted her eyes to the City.

"Look!" she said.

One of the Flowers was beginning to open, curling back a pale exterior to reveal a vibrant purple petal. Bright yellow stamen, which must have been fifty feet high, peeped out, tipped with the weight of what must be pollen.

"Won't last long," he said. "Too cold. But who knows. Freeze—thaw—freeze—it happens so damned quick some winters. The crazy lady at the market says the worst part of winter's to come but she was wrong about the fall so I don't know. They say that if we only had a real cold summer, like there was after the earthquake, they'd die off, but they didn't then, so why should they now? They just sleep, that's all." He stood.

They went inside to the car and trailer.

He looked at them for a minute, thinking, then said, "If we go down the main hall, we can get out the back door pretty easily. Not all these roads work anymore, but I know the good ones."

"Look," he said, after another minute, "we could leave your trailer here and go get the bounty. Then we can hook your trailer up and you'll be ready to go. You can have some of it, too. A little."

It sounded sensible, but she didn't want to take any chances. She didn't want to be separated from Blaze.

"No," she said. She could use some of whatever money they used here—in her bag had been some ancient yen Russ had dug up, complaining that most monetary exchanges had been either outmoded or electronic or they'd be up to their ears in worthless currency, living on the outskirts of such a big city.

Cheyenne lay down on his back on the floor and slid his hand beneath the car and felt around. He looked up at her as he lay on the floor and said, "Your capacitors are big enough to take us all, I guess."

He got up and looked at her some more.

"Look," he said, "you know, it's better living out here. Don't know why they all crowd together over there by the Seam. They're all idiots, that's all there is to it. You seem pretty normal."

"Thanks," she said. For a moment she wished that she was normal, that she didn't carry her sad freight and didn't have nubs behind her ears and had never been to the Dayton Library. As if he were a younger brother, she suddenly wanted to stay and protect Cheyenne, silly as that seemed since he knew so much more than she did about living here. "I just want to see what it's like. I've never been there."

He shrugged. "You can always come back. Gets kind of lonely. Scary too, sometimes. You never know who's going to show up."

She followed him through a dark doorway into a room that felt enormous, in the dark. A light came on overhead, maybe thirty feet up, and she saw that the floor was hard and glossy wood with lines painted on it and that the room was huge, as large as their workplace at Shaker Hill.

Cheyenne went over to a jumble of dark shapes. "Give me a hand," he said.

She helped him move things around until he had liberated a

small trailer. "Got my bike hooked up to another one, but this will do fine."

The Bees were surprisingly light for their size. Their furry hairlike bands were rather stiff, but pliable enough so that they didn't draw blood.

"Lookit that there," said Cheyenne, as they put the second one on the trailer. "Pretty bad stinger."

She was surprised. "Do they sting people?"

He laughed. "Sure. How do you think they keep everybody scurrying around?"

"Have you ever seen them sting anyone?"

"No," he said, beginning to sound irritated.

"Well, what happens when they do? Do they die?"

"Not exactly," he said. "But they're good as dead."

"But what happens?"

"Let's just say you don't want it to happen to you," he said. "You'd be crazier than the downtown lady, shouting in the middle of the street. You might be crazy enough to do anything. Run back into the city. Or give your baby to the Bees." He stopped for a minute and looked at her. "All right," he said. "I never *have* seen them sting anybody. But that's what the bounty lady says happens."

"Well, she must know," said Verity.

Or at least she wants people to think that's so.

She looked up and down the street. It was empty of people. The frame houses with broad porches were completely dilapidated; some of them were open to the sky. The forest hadn't taken over the streets as badly as in Dayton, though, so she assumed they saw some traffic. The sky above was still blue, though the sun was moving toward the horizon. She figured they had another two hours of light. The air was clear and cold, but she saw a wide dark band of clouds in the east, and knew that it might rain or sleet after nightfall.

Their tiny haphazard caravan, with its strange cargo, was pointed toward the City. Her car, which reminded her of a smooth shiny beetle with doors for wings, was followed by her aluminum trailer, the tarp covering Blaze and Cairo dark in places from water. Cheyenne had some sort of chain rigged up to attach his vehicle; it was a flat wagon about three by five feet with foot-high lattice sides; he had roped the Bees down rather casually, since they wouldn't get going too fast. Out on the big SRs, the Solar Routes, nan had caught each vehicle and propelled it along with enormous, yet controlled, velocity, without the need of attention from the driver save to tell the car its destination. That panel, in Verity's car, had apparently been damaged by some sort of blunt instrument. Russ had smiled when it was finally liberated and told her she was lucky the damned thing worked at all.

Verity looked at Cheyenne, bent over the trailer as he tied down the last Bee. "Where are your parents?" she asked.

Then she gasped at the sudden onslaught of pictures around her, transparent but powerful, swift and painful, filled with his memories which resonated within her, so much more complex and deep than Cairo's simple thoughts.

A woman with very short blond hair wearing a long blue dress sat on a wooden chair. Her face was half hidden by shadow and she held a violin to her chin. Her feet rested on a rug with large yellow roses and green leaves intertwined. Next to her was a white sink where dishes stood upright on the drainboard. The curtains puffed in the wind and a streetlight came on just outside the window. A man standing next to her turned pages of music as she played. Verity felt deep joy, and peace. This took but a second.

Then they were on a raft with others, plunging away from shore in rough water. The man and woman were there, the woman wearing a light green scarf and a short black jacket. Everyone was singing, with rapt looks on their faces, and Verity lived young Cheyenne's terror at their strangeness, his fear and resolve as he jumped from the raft and struck out for shore as the people he no longer knew called for him, until the raft disappeared down the river.

How long ago? she wondered. She wiped sweat from her forehead. This had never happened before with a human, only with Cairo.

Cheyenne turned; there were tears on his face and he dashed them away angrily. "Where are yours?" he asked. "Come on, let's get going. Let me drive. I can do it."

"I'm sorry I asked," she said. "Maybe later, okay?"

Shaken and limp, she climbed inside the car.

There was only room for two people in the tiny car, and it moved slowly when she pulled the lever back to expose the magnets beneath the car. Slowly, she relaxed. Apparently he was unaware of what had happened.

He told her where to turn, and she became more and more excited and eager. Gradually, the old houses around her showed signs of life—curtains, chairs on porches, boxes piled in yards, an occasional horse, bike, and a very occasional car. Cheyenne waved at a white-bearded man sitting on a porch, and he waved back but stared at Verity. She was glad when they turned a corner. "These people are like me," Cheyenne said. "Maybe one family on a block, if that. That old guy taught me how to hunt rabbits. They live underground. You beat the tunnel opening with a stick, then run around to their back entrance and shoot them when they run out. He raises them in hutches and sells them in Edgetown, but that seems like a lot of work to me."

They went beneath a viaduct and around a park with a statue of a man in the center, but his neck was a rough stump. Several blocks in a row were filled with charred rubble. "Do you believe it?" Cheyenne said. "Years ago they had people who would come and put out fires for you. I think this must have happened during the earthquake, but with buildings this close together if your chimney's mortar isn't too good you can set fire to a whole block. That's another good thing about my place. It's brick."

They trundled around a curve and down a steep hill. In the hollow at the bottom was a long flat-roofed wooden building with a few patches of blue paint. "Stop there," Cheyenne said.

An old woman with workpants pulled up over a green flannel shirt to just below her large breasts came out of a door on the end to meet them. She had long grayish-blond braids, a weathered face, and bright blue eyes. "What you got, kid?" she asked.

He stepped back and bowed from the waist. "Anybody ever have as big a haul as me?" he asked.

"What do you do with them?" asked Verity.

The woman glanced at her as if seeing her for the first time. "Who's that?" she asked.

"Her name's Verity," said the boy, and Verity expected him to continue but he did not, and she liked him better for it.

"Well. You could call it recycling." She reached into her back pocket and pulled out a flat wallet. Inside were tucked coins in rows, brass-looking, about an inch in diameter. She pulled out five of them and handed them to Cheyenne. The center of each seemed transparent, but tilted to the sun as Cheyenne accepted them, they revealed a hologram of a tiny bee. The red scarf the woman was wearing around her head, made of thin, slippery stuff, slid forward as she bent down to examine the Bees. The woman absently pushed it back, and Verity just barely kept from gasping.

Behind her ears were the same nubs Verity had covered by her hair. She looked at Cheyenne, but his hat covered any that he might have. She shivered and looked toward the City. It glimmered, mysterious.

"Why don't we go back, and you can leave tomorrow?" suggested Cheyenne. "That way we can drop off my cart."

"Can we leave it here?" asked Verity. She didn't say that she doubted that she'd be back, but this way it wouldn't be so far from home for him. She felt renewed urgency. She didn't know what was happening to Blaze and Cairo inside their sheets, but the sooner they got out of them the better. Russ had warned her against really hoping for anything, and seemed to regret his actions, but she had to do the best she could to help them live again.

Cheyenne shrugged, and she was relieved. "Wouldn't mind going into Edgetown tonight," he said, "now that I've got some money."

"Good," she said, and they untied his cart and pulled it behind the woman's brick building. Verity felt the woman's eyes on her as she got into the cab, but she didn't look up. If this was her long-lost mother, she felt as if she'd be better off not knowing. There was something hard and suspicious about her; something unpleasant and predatory, like a weasel.

They passed corroded buildings which Verity recognized as factories. One was roofless, the walls blackened by fire. Dry vines rattled in the wind and enormous trees grew in the rich ash-fed soil within, a bristle of bare branches. "They say that was a nan factory," said Cheyenne.

"Oh?" she asked. "What did they make there?"

"Just about anything, they say. They tell me in Norwood. I can never tell if they're joking," he said, and she felt quick sympathy. "Apparently you could just send them your plan and they'd make it up. Anything. Cars. Robots. Prefab houses."

"Isn't that what it's like in the City now?" she asked.

"That's what the wild woman says," he told her.

They were moving fairly slowly, about as fast as a horse could trot. The sun was sinking lower. Cheyenne began to look apprehensive. "Can you go any faster?" he asked. "I don't want to be at the Rainbow after dark."

"Why not?" she asked.

"There's ghosts there," he said.

Every minute brought them closer to the City. The New Ohio shone a mile or so to the west, and the Old Ohio was straight ahead. To the left, only half a mile away, the energy of the City caught and held her, humming in her bones as the Bee had. They trundled along, and a readout told her that they were going fifteen miles an hour.

"Do you believe in ghosts?" she asked.

He nodded. "That way," he said, and pointed to a road that peeled off to the right.

Nine

○○○○○○○○○○○○○○○○○

"When Night Shadows the Plaza and the Front of the Great Edifice Becomes a Radiant Disc of Light"

—The Cincinnati Union Terminal 1933

Winter sunset shimmered the wide sky orange behind the station.

Verity had never seen anything so beautiful as this massive, welcoming arch of concrete and glass.

Spellbound, she stopped the car at the entrance of one of the curving ramps and Cheyenne said no, we gotta go, hurry, it's getting late, but she just gazed.

Nine glass columns caught the sun's light. The tallest, in the middle, was over a hundred feet high, according to Blaze. The glass was indented behind massive columns of concrete, sandy beige pinkened by sunset. An enormous clock, like a huge eye, was set just below the arc's apogee. Cincinnati was reflected, pastel and slanted, cut by thin lines, in the glass. Russ said Cincinnati was self-healing. She wondered if the station was too. It was outside the Seam, but maybe it was. Hadn't Blaze said that it had been reconstructed with Enlivenment?

"We can't go there," said Cheyenne. He was practically whining. "Go back."

She lifted the lever and the car started to move again.

"What do you want here?" he asked.

She knew she was right. She was starting to hear the Bell.

A few pale stars shone in the east when she drove up the ramp at the front. "I need to take something inside," she said, and Cheyenne shrank back in his seat.

"I'm not going in there," he said, shaking his head.

"Just help me to the door then." She got out, and pulled back the tarp. They got Cairo out okay, a squarish bundle tied with ropes, and put her next to the door.

Verity had rewrapped Blaze where the woman had ripped the blanket from him. She grabbed one end and slid him out from the trailer bed. "Don't let it fall," she said.

The boy caught the end and staggered. "What is this?" he asked. He lowered his end and the blanket fell back, revealing the left half of Blaze's face, a tiny violet light blinking at his cheekbone, his eye open and staring.

Cheyenne gasped. "Why didn't you tell me?" he demanded. "I've been carting a *dead body* around. You must be nuts. And this blinking stuff is from the City. No telling what it will do. No telling! You shouldn't ever *touch* something like this. You shouldn't get *near* it." He backed up slowly, edging toward the car.

"It won't hurt you," said Verity.

"The hell you say," he said. "You don't know. Or do you?" His face was very pale. "Why do you think I live so far out? To keep away from stuff like that."

"Just help me take him inside," said Verity. "Please."

"You're crazy," said Cheyenne. His eyes were accusing. "Where are you from really? Are you from the City? You must be. Trying to infect me. Trying to infect us all!"

He turned abruptly and rushed to the car.

"Wait," yelled Verity. "You're wrong. I'm not—"

But he jumped into the driver's seat. She ran over and reached for the other door, but it was too late. He lifted the lever and without a backward look took off at top speed down the ramp.

Verity ran a few steps, then stopped. It was no use. These people were terrified of Enlivenment, just as terrified as the Shakers. Maybe even more so. Perhaps she ought to be, too.

Alone above the City, she took a deep breath.

And watched.

Cincinnati was slowly lighting up. Against dusk, it glowed like a lightstick, all different colors. The tightly furled Flowers were lit from beneath and sheathed in shadow, and tiny lights that were windows blinked on, building by building, until the entire City was glowing, madly, challenging the stars.

And all the time there was the Bell, sonorous. She didn't know where it was coming from. She hadn't expected to ever hear it except at home.

She looked around. A neat row of wheeled carts stood next to the door, and next to them three low flat carts.

Verity was sweating by the time she managed to get Blaze onto one of the carts. Though he was stiff, swaddled in the tarp and tied (not because he's *dead*, she told herself), he was heavy and she had to pivot him around, straining, catching her breath after each shove. There was room on the end of the cart for Cairo. She was easier. Now what?

Verity leaned back and yanked on the cart's handle, and it moved. Once she got it going, it rolled more easily. She pushed it toward the door so she could see inside.

It swung open.

She ran back and grabbed another cart. Pushing the loaded cart ahead of her, she pulled the empty one behind and left it in the doorway. The door swung shut behind her, crashing against the cart lightly, so that it remained open.

Verity stared.

Cincinnati Union Station was stupendous, so huge and so dark that her eyes could not decipher it. There was just enough light to see a row of counters, far to the right, and large blank signs overhead, and shapes she couldn't make out. But she had a feeling of vast, enclosed space, and wondered if something as abstract as the shape of a space could organize and focus thought, and pull forth this feeling of glad expectation toward an unknown, exciting future.

Verity knew that Blaze would like it here, stashed to one side of the cavernous arch spacious as time and endless as the section of the sphere from which it was sliced, something which wheeled invisibly but fully formed through space—above her in steel and stone, beneath her in idea, arcing through the earth.

If he wakened here, and of course he must, he must, she could see him sitting up, rubbing his green eyes a bit grainy with death and seeing with astonishment the main Midwest maglev terminal. Maybe he would go to the News Reel Room.

She could feel the Enlivenment of the terminal ripple through her, and was not afraid. The feeling of empowerment was so strong she felt that she might never be afraid again. It seemed as if she belonged here, as if she were being welcomed.

The moon shone through the glass at the top of the arch above her, and light spread across the marble floor in a pattern of strut-ted shadows, making crazy angles on the gold-intersticed floors.

The whole building hummed. Verity realized that the North American Maglev System (NAMS, said the massive letters over the door, and the signs she'd followed for the last twenty miles) was not dead, not at all. At least, not this station.

Maybe this wasn't the best time to store Blaze, in the dark, when she was exhausted.

But she didn't want to spend the night here. Or maybe it would be the best place to stay, but she should at least hide.

She leaned into the heavy cart and finally got it going. She pushed it toward a long dark counter off to one side. She tried not to wonder what she'd do. Cheyenne could have at least left her one of the coins. Now she had no car; nothing. It was just starting to hit her. But the place's emptiness, its hauntedness, its *aliveness*, convinced her that this was the right place to leave Blaze and Cairo. They were less likely to be disturbed if everyone feared the place.

She wheeled to the back of the counter. Yes. In the near-dark she saw long cabinets that opened with sliding doors. She slid one back and was able to drag and push Blaze into it; she put Cairo into another.

Panting, her arms aching, she sank to the floor, her back to the wall.

Somewhere inside the City, she knew there was something that could make Blaze and Cairo live again. There *had* to be.

And the station itself was waiting, like Blaze. This place was meant for him. The confluence of the most glorious trains in his-tory. Swift and true they had flown beneath the earth.

One of Blaze's favorite songs shimmered through her mind for a moment, and her throat contracted. "It sounds an echo in my soul—how can I keep from singing?" she whispered.

But no—it was *not* in her mind.

Sound splashed from the graceful arch and shimmered down upon them.

The notes were at first slow; searching, then the intensity changed and they pecked down upon her like precise directions to a place she had never been. "How Can I Keep from Singing" vanished into some strange permutation and was transformed by rhythms she had never heard before.

Standing in the dark, the empty, pulling dark which spoke still of enclosure, spoke of crowds and milling and millions passing through and vibrant life and beauty . . .

The sounds came again.

She shivered.

As she listened, the music sparked a picture in her mind: a gray heron on the edge of Bear Creek, patient, dignified, in misty light. As the notes rose he leaped into flight, multiplied into a vortex of birds, in exodus from all purpose, unreigned, a hush of gray on gray.

She took slow and careful steps on the utterly smooth floor, where faint thin curves of gold glinted and then were lost as the moon appeared, then was again swallowed by clouds.

In that moment, she had seen a shadow, moving in rhythm with the music, small and halfway across the terminal.

Did he have a weapon? What was his purpose here?

Her breath caught for a moment.

But his music beckoned and cajoled, threw itself wailing at glimpses of moon and dropped back sobbing when it left. It moved like white clouds across the night sky, like ice floes in the river, and then became more measured. It repeated itself in odd ways, so that she recognized the thread of a tune though it might be transposed up a fifth, or swallow itself in an alternate harmony.

Ah, she thought, if only Blaze could hear this! What is this music called?

All the time she had been working her way around the side, then slipping across to the dark shapes which littered the station like islands.

The music stopped. She heard the sound of breath hissing through something with a grainy squawk. Then, so close to her that she jumped, a smooth voice came from the dark:

"May I be of service?"

He touched on a light and shone it at her.

His face was dark, like Tai Tai's, and his nose cast a shadow that covered the upper part of his face, which was round. His head sprouted curls that reminded her of asparagus ferns on one side, surrounded by patches of geometrical, shining baldness. A crescent that pointed toward his left eye grew large and swept around the back of his head, and was filled with golden, faintly glowing patterns.

He smiled. "Didn't expect to see anyone here. Never have.

People are afraid. The acoustics are so enchanting here, don't you think?''

She saw him move his foot to the right, and several spotlights beamed serene and single from the ceiling, placing them in a pool of light.

"Wynton Sphere Byrd at your service, young one," he said, and made a slight bow. "You may call me Sphere."

She had no idea how old he might be. The gold eyeglasses he wore surprised her, so near to Enlivenment, which was supposed to cure sight problems, and his eyes were large and deep brown. He was thin but not bony. He wore beige pants pulled in tight around his ankles, and beautifully shined black boots that laced and caught the pants at the bottom. His purple scarf looked like it was made of wool, as did his purple hat, a funny, flat affair.

"What's that?" she asked, pointing at his instrument.

"An alto sax, my dear. Most versatile, most passionate, most beautiful instrument ever invented by humans. Some people might argue the piano, but they are utterly wrong. Nothing comes close. Nothing."

He knelt, and opened a gray case. It was lined with dark blue velvet. He took out a piece of cloth and reverently wiped the thing to a silver sheen. He shook the mouthpiece and blew into it once or twice, then took some pieces of wood from it, wiped them, and put them into a small tube. While he did this, he talked.

"I saw you come in, and I caught a glimpse of your face. Pure white, with the purity of a saint. That solid black hair, shining. And so young. I could tell right away by the way you move that you're not from Edgetown. You have no wariness at all. No fear. And so I played for you. Did you like it?"

She nodded, then, aware that his back was turned as he bent over his case tending to his instrument, said, "Yes. It was beautiful."

He clicked his case shut and stood. "Mind telling me what you're doing here?" he asked. "Like I said, most people are afraid of the station."

"Why?"

"Superstition. The nan detectors would go wild here, of course." He swept his arm in a semicircle. His intake of breath was deep and satisfied. "But I find the station absolutely lovely. I hope for the return of the Great Trains. I hope for the return of Civilization. Are you hungry?"

She hesitated. Blaze and Cairo were as well-concealed as was possible, she supposed—beneath a long counter behind wooden doors. Her whole body ached.

"Where are you from?" he asked.

"Dayton," she said, and his eyes narrowed.

"Nobody lives there," he said. "At least that's what I hear."

She shrugged. She didn't know him. She wasn't going to tell him about Shaker Hill. Russ, at least, still lived there. Alone.

"What are you doing here?"

"Everyone's dead," she said, then stopped.

"I see," he said. "No wonder you left. What happened?"

For a moment she actually wanted to tell him, tell him about the plague, about how she killed John, about the rafter woman, all the horrible things that had happened so quickly that she'd barely had time to think about it. But she couldn't. She opened her mouth, but she just couldn't.

"It's all right," he said gently, after a moment. He picked up the case with the saxophone inside.

"Come on," he said.

"Where are we going?" she asked.

"Edgetown," he said.

"Oh," she said, a bit disappointed. "Is there a way into the City from here?" They were standing in a large concourse, surrounded by many arched doors, which once, she supposed, led to train lines.

"Don't think so," he said, and she thought she saw him shudder. "There used to be, of course, but they got twisted up in the quake."

"Have you tried any?" she asked.

"One or two," he said. He looked as if he were going to say more, then stopped. "Come on, it's late."

She hesitated for a moment. Edgetown was closer to the City. And that was where she wanted to go.

She followed him down the steps into a dark tunnel.

"It's not too far," said Sphere.

As they walked, the tunnel lit just ahead. Verity looked back and saw that it was dark behind.

The inside of the tunnel seemed to be made of ceramic tiles. Some of them projected holograms. Advertisements for things inside the City. Hotels in Denver. A Thai restaurant in the Geosyn

Convention Center. They all looked shiny and new in the holos, as if they had been built this very day.

Sphere's footsteps on the hard tiles echoed. He swung his saxophone with one long arm and had an easy stride. "Dayton, huh? How long did it take you to get here?"

"A few days."

"Not by road. There's no road north, at least not on this side." Verity was glad that she hadn't tried it.

"Who's that boy run off with your car?"

"Just someone I met today," she said. "A Bee hunter."

She thought his step faltered for a minute, and she definitely heard him sigh. "Oh."

"He kills them and gets a bounty," she said.

"Very sad, very sad."

"Why do you think it's sad?" she asked, somehow relieved that everyone didn't feel the same way about the Bees.

"I've lived in Edgetown all my life," he said. "There is something quite marvelous about them. Something beautiful and important. It's strange, I think, to want to destroy these exotic creatures without even knowing what they are and what they can do."

"Do you know?"

He laughed. "No. Maybe someday. If I get the courage."

"The courage to do what?"

"To find out," he said.

"But how?"

"Ah—I'm not sure." His tone precluded further questions.

After a while, her legs began to hurt. They had been walking for almost an hour. At least three miles, maybe more. "I thought you said this wouldn't take long."

"A country girl like you shouldn't have a hard time," he said, a grin in his voice.

"How do you know I'm a country girl?"

"Nothing up there but country. But here we are." He pointed. "Turn up this ramp."

They ascended steadily for about five minutes, then he stopped. He opened a small panel on the wall and pushed a few buttons, and the wall next to them slid open. "This is our secret now, hear? It wouldn't do for everybody from Edgetown to go over there. It wouldn't sound half so nice."

They walked down another corridor after the door slid shut behind them, then went up stairs for another two or three minutes, until Verity was sweating, finally emerging into a swirl of light and sound.

She stopped, overwhelmed.

They were standing on a busy street. *Busy!* For a moment there were so many people passing in front of them that she couldn't see the other side of the street; briefly, she felt terror. She had never seen more than the entire population of Shaker Hill at one time. And here, people were walking by, strangers, ignoring her. She heard the rush and hiss of the river, an undertone to other sounds, and remembered Cheyenne telling her that Edgetown was on the river's edge.

"Evening's the best time of day in Edgetown," said Sphere, next to her. "People like to get out and about. Meet their friends. Eat and drink. Pay good money to hear me serenade them, if they have any taste."

Near Verity, a young girl stood next to a small glowing brazier. The air, warm in the tunnel, now bit coldly into Verity's lungs. On the grill above the flames toasted the small, puffy brown shapes of dinosaurs. The wind blew Verity's hair across her face and she saw that clouds had gathered where the moon should have been.

It seemed like the sides of her stomach touched as she looked at the cookie-sized dinosaurs. She realized that she was terribly hungry. Then she looked around again. She blinked at the brilliance of the lights, the people, the constant movement. Half a block away, in the middle of the street, a man at a booth with a green awning was grilling meat. The smell wafted down the street. A group of strolling women stopped and crowded around. The sound of so many feet against pavement was novel, something like the sound of rain on the roof, random yet constant.

There were too many people. Too many *strangers.*

Verity held steady, with great effort, as panic made her want to turn and run back down the tunnel, to drag Blaze and Cairo back, back upriver, back—

Where Blaze could sleep forever in the sheets.

Sphere's hand fell lightly on her shoulder, and she felt steadied, for some reason. "It's all right," he said. "It must be disorienting. I've lived here all my life. Nobody will hurt you. At least not while I'm here, and probably not otherwise. We don't stand for troublemakers."

The things she saw sorted themselves out. All along the streets were small businesses *lit up,* being used. Not deserted places still full of useful, unowned things to be taken if they passed John's strict muster, like Dayton, Columbus, or Franklin.

Small groups of people moved in both directions, walking in the middle of the street, laughing and talking. Streetlights illuminated old corroded limestone buildings. Verity turned and peered down the street, and saw that after a few blocks the buildings became indistinct, enveloped in a fog creeping up from the river; the lit windows of the higher stories glowed faintly, muted rectangles of blurred light. Her heart jumped as someone drew a curtain on the third floor across from her. There were people, unknown people inside.

Verity looked up, and beyond the light's glare saw no stars. A cold hard sleet began to beat down, the clatter of it on streets obscuring the faint music of street musicians she couldn't see.

Then she looked the other way. One block away, through the sleet, she saw it.

A massive, neat wall. Smooth and pale. Towering over the end of the street, which simply *stopped.* Above, partly visible in the mist, she was surprised to see that it was punctuated by some sort of ornate curl of cement or whatever the stuff was made out of—stuff transformed by nan—which furled gracefully toward them. So it wasn't entirely smooth. She leaned back, but she couldn't see the top. It was too close, and too high. It vanished into the darkness.

It could only be the Seam.

The place where the nan conversion had halted, suddenly. Right at the point where it had devoured half of the building it was Seamed to. I was all finished eating right here, it seemed to say. No longer hungry. Thank you. Verity wondered how quickly it had happened, if the people inside had had time to leave, or take their things, or if they were processed and were now part of the wall too.

She shivered.

"Hungry?"

Sphere was grinning, eyes narrow behind glasses flecked with raindrops. He held out three small dinosaur cookies—two triceratops and a brontosaurus. "It's not the same everywhere," he said, nodding at the Seam. "Depends on what was there to begin with. I guess because it didn't have a chance to finish its job."

She grabbed the food. "Careful, don't burn your tongue," Sphere told her, but she did anyway. "Maybe you'd like something more substantial. There's a little place around the corner that makes good soup."

She shook her head, her mouth full of the doughnutlike sweet.

"These are traditional on this corner," he said. "Dinosaur fiatches. That girl's father believed that dinosaurs were still alive and lived out in Oregon. And who knows, during the time of the Flower Cities, that might have been true. Why not?"

"Oregon," she said, finished with the triceratops. "That's on the West Coast, right? By the Pacific Ocean."

Sphere looked at her with admiration. "I knew that you were different," he said. "Come on," he said, and started toward the Seam.

"No," she said, afraid of the enormity of what she approached. The artifact of something that had almost devoured the Earth. If you could believe the Scriptures. "No," she whispered.

He stopped, looked at her, and started to laugh. "Oh, I forgot. It's dead, don't worry. I mean, it's bounded, stopped, it won't start up again. What we need is the stuff stuck inside."

But Verity was shaking and he had to take her arm and pull her along. *It's why I could talk to Cairo. Why we shared pictures.*

Verity noticed that almost everybody who passed Sphere greeted him. She relaxed. "What stuff?" she asked.

"Like, how to heal people. How to stop the plagues. And most of all, we need the minds of the scientists—"

"What?" she said, and pulled her elbow away from him. "What are you talking about?"

He turned and looked at her. "You really don't know anything, do you?" he asked. "Well, this is Edgetown. Maybe that's good, I don't know. You'll learn."

They passed three women singing on the streetcorner. Their voices were sweet and harmonious, and Verity paused to watch them, getting soaked.

"Pseudo-Norleaners," said Sphere, with a laugh. "They'd like to get the plague—they think. It's kind of like a weird religion. He continued walking, but stopped and returned to listen with her.

> Froggie went a-courtin and he did ride,
> Rinktum buddymitchi cambo,
> Sword and buckler by his side,
> Rinktum buddy mitchi cambo
> Caimaneero, down to Cairo
> Caimaneero, Cairo
> Stradaladalada baba ladabadalinktum
> Rinktum buddy mitchi cambo.

One had a stringed instrument, a flat, triangular thing she played with a pick.

Verity's eyes filled with tears.

"Do you know what Cairo is?" Sphere asked, tapping rain from his hat brim. But she couldn't talk.

"It was the jumping-off place for the Pioneers," he told her. "Hundreds of years ago, the ones taking the trails west to the Territory. The wagon trains started up there. It's on the Missouri." He paused. "Well, you'll need a place to stay."

"I don't have any money," she said. "The boy was supposed to give me some for helping with his Bees."

"Ill-gotten gains," said Sphere. "You're better off without it."

Easy for you to say, she thought.

She shrank within her jacket, exhausted, feeling infinitely foolish for having her money stolen, her car stolen, everything, right at first, right off the bat, as Blaze would say; he liked baseball words like they were some sort of holiness. There was no one here that she knew, and maybe this Sphere would turn out to be as strange as the others. Or maybe worse. She was so tired that she could barely see, and there was no Mother anymore and the Mother had always sustained her but Russ said she was all made up. Through a swirl of color and lights and cold sleet she followed Sphere's feet for about ten minutes, trying to keep from slipping on the ice that was forming.

"Come on in." She was being led up concrete steps. Rain hung from the wrought iron railings in heavy glistening drops. He touched a knuckle to a door and then turned the doorknob and opened it.

She paused.

"Come on," he said.

The icy wind bit at her back. She didn't have to stay with him.

She shouldn't. She was used to empty buildings. Hadn't they passed some? . . .

Sphere bent down and peered into her face. He seemed amused. "Don't worry," he said, his voice gentle. "I'm just a normal guy. Well, kind of."

She remembered his music and stepped inside.

They climbed a narrow flight of stairs. "This was a part of town called Norwood," he said. He led her into a room where a fire burned in an iron stove. The warmth felt grand.

She looked around and was startled. The room winked with the light reflected off of thousands of tiny spheres. The size of black walnuts, only crystal or plastic, she didn't know. Like something from the Library. On the floor was a worn red carpet woven with strange patterns, stairs that led nowhere, a curlicue climax of all the lines of it meeting in the center. A soft couch was right across the room. Anyway, it looked soft. Soft enough.

She rushed toward it and collapsed onto it. She heard herself groan and was surprised.

"Help yourself," said Sphere to her closed eyes. She opened them slightly to see him walking down a row of spheres, shaking his head. Then his hand reached out and plucked one from the wall. He turned, holding it, and bent over her. She was too tired to push him away as his torso rested against hers. He pulled a blanket from behind the couch, then stood. "I knew this was somewhere," he said, and covered her with it. The blanket fell gently upon her and she nestled beneath it and drifted off.

The music, when it began, was like nothing she had ever heard before.

Ten

◇◇◇◇◇◇◇◇◇◇◇◇◇◇◇◇◇◇

In the Heart of the City as Verity Sleeps

Ernest Hemingway stood in front of the window that made up one wall of his apartment, hands on his hips, glaring down at the street below. Snow! Just when everything was waking.

A light flashed beseechingly at his right, the interstice which ran like a greedy stripe down the wall about six inches wide. Green, the color of greed. When sated, it would turn pink.

"Screw you," he growled. He turned his back on it.

The damned Surrealists were down below, holding some sort of festival. They'd crept out of their absurd museums where everything was muddled together—bits of pictures, garden tools, utterly twisted visions that made him sick, no matter what Gertrude said. Or was it the Cubists she fawned over? What was the difference! Of course, he had bought a few, as investments. But they were not enjoyable.

Now, they claimed they were creating an exquisite corpse. "Reality Is an Exquisite Corpse," flashed small ads for the event—puffed up glowing letters that floated down upon you in the park should you so much as venture out for some cold oysters and a bottle of wine, then dissolved when they touched the ground.

He didn't know why they were here, anyway. It was all wrong, wrong time-frame for him. They were so inconsiderate. Trying to throw him off! This was all supposed to be so American here, so heart-of-the-heartland, but the Committee had laughed at his complaint.

"Didn't you get your start in Paris, Gen?" asked Ariel, some flibbitygibbit whose name suited her utterly. "And then, as I remember it, you hauled off to Cuba. For *years*. Anyway, all literature and art is one lovely, self-referential microcosm, don't you see?" she asked, and finally, growing angry at what she called his dull brutishness, suggested that he take a bit of a break. "Try some O'Neill," she said. "It might humble you a bit. Or, better yet," she flung at him as he left the office, high above the City on the one-hundred-seventh floor of Carnation, "Ferlinghetti! Loosen up! You can't keep getting stuck on the same old thing. Try some different genes for a change. I can recommend a sequence—" He heard her mumbling something about there ought to be a law as he stepped into the elevator. Damned waste, anyway—almost all the floors below them were empty. Who voted for them, anyway? Things could use a bit of a shaking up around here. They *did* vote on this sort of thing, didn't they? Sometimes he couldn't remember. He put it down to drink. But Nabokov! It was too much, he was really Russian, and Pynchon so damned weird, even though everybody said that he was Pynchon's natural predecessor.

The time-dot in his wrist flashed briefly. It was late. It had been an excellent day. Usually he knocked off at two. But he'd worked clear through till night.

He poured himself some Scotch. When he drank, he could at least remember Spain, and a good war, and not these namby-pamby artists giving each other prizes. He wished he hadn't got his, that was for sure. Ruined him forever.

Haze drove down the main avenue of the Southern town in his high rat-colored car, looking for a theater before which he could preach the Church Without Christ and the new jesus when the show was over and the customers came out. Then he saw him, up ahead: Holy, and his own impostor twin wearing a cheap blue suit and a fierce white hat and looking like his very own future. The man he would have to run over.

He would? Why?

He was puzzled, for a moment, as his decrepit high rat-colored car—a Model T?—no, those were all black—sputtered and slowed, then caught again. These emotions that fueled him were so stark, imbued with dull puzzlement and rage. Why were they so important, so necessary? Why must he go through this? For whose benefit? Why must he suffer? Sometimes he remembered why, and it didn't have anything to do with the Church Without Christ. It had to do with the Bees. He ran consciousness across his mind like the flick of a ragged windshield wiper across a window sheeted with rain. In his bright second of knowing, in the one instant that he could see through the rain, he felt rage.

And envy for those with better roles to play.

Then—he wondered why he had thought that, a non-Haze sort of thought, and even remembered why, and then that was gone too.

He stopped his car, sat across the street from Holy and the man, his impostor twin, and watched the humbug preach.

It seemed imperative that he do so.

Across town, Enoch (who did not think in broad sweeps because his blood did all the work) painted the inside of a cupboard with gilt, knowing he was doing something important but not quite sure what. It would turn out to be the crypt of the new jesus, which he would soon steal from the zoo museum.

He had much better reasons for doing what he did than Hazel. He had wise blood.

He was also enjoying himself much, much more, revelling in the bizarre knife-edge of perception and mission that was the essence of Enoch. Because before *Wise Blood* had started, about a week ago, he had taken a double dose of pheromones. Sometimes, afterwards, if people knew about it (but they never did anymore because he had made the mistake of bragging about it only once) they were angry, and attacked him unfairly in the reviews, saying his performance had been muddy, uncertain, or too wide of the mark. But he knew that could not have been true, that they were just jealous. He just hated waking up in the middle of it all. It spoiled everything. And damn the cold! He shivered. Another false spring. Maybe this would all have to wait.

In a shabby apartment on the Upper East Side, Charlie Parker laid out his spoon, a book of matches with the cover torn off, a small rubber hose, and a syringe.

He wrapped his arm tightly. Damn. Getting so hard to find a

good vein. He shot up, then with a practiced twist, he released the band around his arm with a snap and let the rush mellow into ecstasy.

It was raining tonight in the City. He liked that. He liked that a lot. It soothed his mind, and he needed soothing tonight. His daughter had just died.

Remembering, he buried his head in his hands.

Or was that snow?

He jerked his head up, looked out the window. Snow?

He got up and stared, remembering. Shit.

Light pastel buildings, lit palely with lights that were embedded in the corners in a long strip running from ground to roof, were visible between sheets of snow. The convergence of two rivers down there, shimmering beneath night lights ... where was he now? ... surely that wasn't the Hudson. It looked too wild. Where was the bridge? Oh, there it was. A lot like the Brooklyn Bridge, but somehow a little off ... shouldn't there be *lights* across the river? Lots of lights?

"You forgot your pheromones again, Mr. Parker," said a woman's voice coming from a small panel on the wall next to him. "Please touch the yellow panel."

"Fuck you," he said. He looked around wildly, but all he could see was rickety wooden furniture and an unmade bed. And of course his saxophone, catching the one-bulb overhead light in its opened case. That was out of the question.

"You are the apex of this Program," said the voice sternly. "But the privilege *could* be forfeited—"

He saw the lamp, and reached for it, hefted it. Solid metal.

He smashed it into the panel and it went dull.

He sighed, standing there with the dented lamp dangling from his right hand. His mood was shot, and they were expecting him to go on in ten minutes.

He sat down and shook some more heroin into the spoon.

He thought he heard the panel sputtering, some sort of garble and hiss, and grinned as the Upper East Side appeared once again outside his window.

Now he could go down and play like hell. And not be at *their* mercy.

"Where are the women?"

Ginsburg looked up, puzzled, from the stage of Gallery Six.

He shielded his eyes from the light trained on him. "Go on,"
whispered Kerouac, ten feet away.

Ginsburg cleared his throat and started to read again.

"I said, where are the women?" The loud, insistent female
voice from the audience. "You're reading all this fucking poetry
about freedom and changing society but you're just like everybody else. You're just like the society you're putting down. I don't
see any women up there. What happened to them? Do you think
they don't have anything to say? Don't you think *they* write poetry? Did you cut out their tongues?"

Ginsburg dropped his arms at his side, his papers crumpled in
his sweaty hand, at a complete loss. This seminal, legendary reading at Gallery Six had brought it all together. It was the beginning
of Beat. Everything *always* went smoothly. It was one of the most
popular events of all, the one most appreciated and cheered by
audiences. He felt indignant. It was a *privilege* for her to be here!
This had never happened before.

Had it?

Eleven

○○○○○○○○○○○○○○○○○

A Long Night's Journey
into Day

Verity tossed and turned several times, gradually realizing that she was not in her own bed. She and Blaze had been Bees, flying from mountaintop to mountaintop, pursued by John, who was a human pedaling some weird contraption with a gun attached to the top of it. But they had known that he would not catch them, and as they landed on mountaintops they had jeered at him. Everything had been sharp as a holo, and more intensely colored than the world had ever been, and she and Blaze had not even had to speak about where they would go next, because they thought as one. Every once in a while she wondered where Cairo was.

She pushed her hands outward; a soft wall was in front of her, and she smelled coffee. Real coffee.

She turned over and woke more fully and realized: she was in Edgetown.

She lay there for a few minutes taking it in.

The room itself was shabby. Yellowed wallpaper, covered with faded pink flowers, had peeled here and there in ragged triangles. She was slightly shocked. No one would ever dream of letting things get so out of hand at Shaker Hill. For some reason she had thought that things would be more civilized here. More shiny and perfect. But this was not even as nice as the places that she'd been inside in Dayton.

The glistening rows of spheres were set on long thin strips of wood nailed to the wall, kind of like rails. There was a glittering label beneath each one, but they were too far away for her to read. There were about fifty rows, she thought, and on each row a hundred spheres. No wonder he calls himself Sphere, she thought. He's in love with the things.

They were dull though because the light coming in from the tall front window was muted by the snow swirling outside. She watched it for a moment, then looked around the room. There was a window behind her, but it was completely covered by heavy clear plastic nailed to the frame. Again she was surprised. She had thought that Edgetown would have more sophisticated insulation. That the heat would not come from stoves. That everything would be intricate and beautiful and a part of the Years of the Flowers.

Verity swung her legs off the couch and sat up, pushing her hair back. Aching in every muscle, she got up and stretched.

Suddenly, she was inundated by music. Startled, she looked around and realized that she had interrupted a photoelectric beam. The music was the strange music she had heard last night. The rhythm was not foursquare and direct, as all of Blaze's music had been. It ebbed and flowed. Sometimes it seemed to vanish altogether. The instrument was some sort of horn, she decided. The sounds seem to meld with the falling snow.

She turned and found a dining room around the corner. A shabby green rug lay beneath a chipped table. Five unmatched chairs were scattered throughout the room. Some bread and cheese sat on the table. A pot of coffee was hot on some sort of plate.

Down the hall was a bathroom. Gratefully, she peed, and for ten seconds debated using the bathtub, then turned on the faucet and peeled off her clothes. She even washed her hair; she could dry it in front of the stove.

Feeling better, Verity went back to the dining room and ate a piece of bread and some cheese. The coffee surged through her. They only drank it on special occasions at Shaker Hill because it was so rare and because John insisted that it was intoxicating and against the Millennial Laws, though he never was specific about where it said coffee was bad.

The absence of Sphere disturbed her. She felt completely disoriented. She had no idea what time it was, and couldn't tell the time of day through the translucent covers over the windows.

The music ended. She walked over to the row of spheres and read a label: Jelly Roll Morton. Funny name for a person. Almost as strange as Sphere.

Or Blaze.

She couldn't wait around in here all day. She laced her boots, zipped her coat, and walked down the steps to the street, hoping that she could get back in.

She was shocked to discover it was late afternoon when she stepped out onto the street. Though the sky was overcast, there was an opalescent luminosity where the sun showed the time. Despite the snow, the streets were filled with people going about their business. The smell of wood smoke lingered in the air.

Verity saw no cars and no horses. A few people pulled sleds. The road was covered with snow. She walked down the street and stared through a window. She had seen many places like this in Dayton. But there had never been any people inside. COFFEE SHOP, said the sign. She had no money, so she just stood outside and stared through the steam on the inside of the windows.

How lovely the presence of people made this plain interior. They sat on stools at the counter and at tables. Verity told herself not to be greedy, that she'd already eaten but perhaps those cups were full of real coffee.

A woman's voice startled her and she whirled.

The woman was down at the end of the block. It was a busy corner. Verity shivered, seeing that the Seam was only about a block away.

The woman was shouting. Her gestures were wild and deranged. Her hair was a golden, glowing red-gold, and looked very thick, like a mane.

No. It *was* a mane.

And those weren't gloves. They were *paws*. The woman wore a heavy, blue knee-length coat and boots, but those were definitely paws.

Everyone was ignoring her as they went about their business.

Verity realized that she had never seen so many people in one place. She felt an instant's panic as if moving at a dangerously fast speed, but then she absorbed it, assimilated the situation: this was the way things were, here. The way things *used* to be everywhere.

She walked forward until she could hear what the lion was shouting. From ten feet away, she could see that the woman's face was pale gold flesh, and that her eyes were slanted, yet wide, and very brown.

"There is no Durancy. Durancy is a fraud. Durancy is Satan. I've been to the center of the citadel! There is no one there. Has he risen, like they all say? No! He was never there! You must embrace the One True Light! Embrace the Pheromone Flow! Feel the Hormone Glow!" She ranted on, spittle flying from her mouth. Verity stepped closer, and saw that the mane was some heavy strand that was natural, but unlike fur or hair. Or maybe it was very thick hair. The One True Light sounded familiar as day. "Where did you get that costume?" she asked.

"Costume?" the lion roared, or almost-roared. "Costume, she dares call it! Feel the reality of this most sacred mane!" She reached up and grabbed some within her odd paw—plump, furry fingers with claws instead of fingernails, but still able to grasp, yanked it hard and screamed. "There!" she said. "Satisfied? I'm a victim, I tell you. A victim of an unscrupulous philosophy!"

"Who is Durancy?" asked Verity. The sky was growing more dark, and the wind blew the snow in a stinging swirl about them.

"Durancy! Who is Durancy, she asks? The most heinous sinner of all time, that's who. A trick on the people of Cincinnati! A parasite on the waves of time. He is no savior of mine, that is all I can tell you! No savior of mine!"

Verity felt a hand on her arm, and was whirled around.

It was Sphere, and he was laughing.

"You can't get any sense out of her," he said. "Come on."

They started back down the street toward his apartment. "I was worried when you were gone," he said. She wondered why.

"What's wrong with her?" asked Verity. "Does she have the plague?"

"She escaped from the City. Let's have some coffee." Verity followed him inside the coffee shop, rejoicing. She also felt an impatience, a need to tend to Blaze as soon as possible.

"How did she escape?" she asked.

Sphere shrugged. "Who knows? It was quite a while ago. It's rather unheard-of."

They sat at a table in the window. Verity felt as if she were surrounded by a waltz, where the people moved in time to unseen music, and the snow was the grace notes, and everything was complete. So many people, walking past, going in and out the door, and uncountable people who she didn't even see right now, who she may never see but who formed a sort of conscious mass around her.

She felt Sphere's eyes on her face and looked up. He did not look away, and she could not read his expression except that it was one of intense interest. It made her uncomfortable.

She tried to ignore him by looking around. A curved counter of some solid, green material had stools in front of it, and every one was full. Steam rose, carrying the smell of food sizzling on a grill behind the counter. She wrinkled her nose. Meat?

But the coffee was hot and strong and she drank the whole cup at once. Sphere just watched, and when she was finished stood without speaking, took her empty cup, waited at the counter for a moment, and came back with it full. She wondered how he made money.

After the second cup she felt sated, and very alert. Feelings rushed through her more keenly. She was homesick. She wished Russ had come with her. She wished John was not dead. She wished that Evangeline and Sare had not gone down the river, crazed by the plague. All her life she had been surrounded by people who in a way defined her, told her who she was: Verity, a Shaker, an odd Shaker with nubs behind her ears, one with the Gift of Dance.

She looked up from the white cup and into Sphere's eyes. Kind, it seemed, and also a bit puzzled. He opened his mouth and closed it, looked down at his hands. Then he spoke.

"You want to get into the City," he said.

She felt as if that wasn't what he had first intended to say and wondered what that had been. Sphere seemed nice, but she wasn't sure if she trusted him entirely. "No—" she began.

"You asked about it last night in the Station," he said. "Why?" He gestured toward the people in the shop. "That's the last thing anyone here wants to do, believe me."

She couldn't tell him about Blaze and Cairo. But why not admit that she wanted to get inside? He seemed to know a lot about getting around. "I've dreamed it," she said. "The Flowers. I've dreamed the City all my life."

He shook his head, his brown eyes still on hers. "There's nothing human in there. Everything's different. It's not like out here."

She was quiet a minute and so was he. Then she said, "How do you know?"

He looked out the window.

She wondered why it was so easy for her to read his face. "You've been inside," she guessed.

He slid out of the booth. "It stands to reason that it's different, doesn't it? I mean, think about it. The lion lady is from inside, after all. Let's go. You slept most of the day. Look, it's starting to get dark."

They walked back up his narrow stairs and went back into his apartment. Immediately he went over to the spheres and studied them for a moment, then picked one out. The sphere glittered and swirled, and then the spin of it was just a solid blur.

He sat on a chair across from her. His legs were very long. He was a tall man. His arms were long too. His nose was long as well. It seemed to Verity that he was kind but she wondered if she could really tell, and what she would do if he was not. She felt as if adrift on ice floes in a cold, cold river, and she could not jump off but only ride downriver to wherever they would take her now that she had come here.

Then he said something that didn't surprise her. She just didn't know why he had waited so long to say it—the whole time they were walking down the street and while they came up the stairs and while he did his little music sphere.

"I have been inside."

It was night.

Norwood was pretty, lit by a hundred glowing windows. Verity realized that Edgetown was nowhere near as large as she had imagined from all the talk. About ten blocks on one side and six on the other, curled around the Seam like a crescent moon, it was just a brief smear of life on the plains of the Midwest, like "bacteria" in a page of the encyclopedia. If Sare were here, she could probably sense the population and spit it out to the last baby. Except, Verity couldn't remember seeing any babies, or any children at all. She realized that she had been looking forward to seeing them here, in Edgetown. She had been looking forward to a lot.

Verity and Sphere walked down Vine Street. Sphere carried his saxophone. Their feet crunched deep into the snow, and there were fewer people out tonight than there had been the night before. The sky had cleared and the wind was frigid and the stars were crystals to the north, for behind them was Cincinnati, lit and drowning the stars to the southeast. She moved next to him feeling somehow like an odd twin, as if she could sense some slender bright strand of life within him identical to one within her. It was funny since she had not known him long.

Yet he was vexing as all get out. He would say nothing about inside, no matter how she badgered him. Neither would he agree to take her there. They had spent an unpleasant evening arguing. He seemed to know a lot he wasn't telling her. Fine. She could find out without him.

At any rate, he finally said, he had a gig tonight, and that would help him think about it. Maybe he would take her inside.

Verity choked on the smoky air when they walked down into the place he called the club. It was so dense that she could barely make out the faces in the dim light; she only knew that there were a lot. It was already past midnight, though she wasn't tired since she had slept so late that day. But she marveled at how many people—twenty or thirty, it seemed, engaged in loud conversation—were interested in staying up so late. Sphere took her firmly by her right arm and led her down a narrow aisle to a stage lit by a spotlight. He pulled out a chair for her. He nodded to a tall Chinese woman with long, kinky black hair shadowing a pale lovely face, and to another woman with a black instrument. A fat man in a bright green sweater with hair in two long red braids was standing next to a fiddle as big as he was.

When the musicians were all unpacked and set up and the audience was yelling and Verity was drinking some beer that was not half as good as the beer she and Blaze had secretly made one fall, then went laughing and reeling across the meadow until they threw up, Sphere nodded—once, twice—and they all commenced to play.

Verity was transported. She was in a beautiful, old City. She saw automobiles and throngs of people, more people maybe than were now in all of North America. She walked down those streets, past tall glass buildings that reflected other buildings.

She turned and went into a museum and looked at pictures on the wall which were just circles or squares or a black piece of canvas and knew that she must have heard the music before. She had read the odd titles of the paintings; it was something that had been stored in the library in Dayton. She felt far and alone, small within time and unable forever to help Blaze; she would never again see Cairo's happy face—

Sphere shook her and said, "What's wrong? You've been like

this for the past fifteen minutes." His laugh was sharp and short.
"I know we're not that good, but—"

She pulled her handkerchief out of her jacket pocket and blew
her nose. "I'm all right," she said. "Music does that to me. When
are we going back?" She needed to check on Blaze and Cairo. She
decided that maybe she should just slip out when they started
playing again. She didn't want Sphere to follow and see them.

"Don't worry," he said. "I'm thinking. We still have three
more sets. Maybe you're too tired. Want to go back?"

She shook her head. Well, maybe she should wait and see if he
changed his mind. They're still the same, in their sheets, she told
herself, and there's nothing you can do about them. You have to
get into the City, like Russ said.

During the third set, when she had her eyes closed, she heard
the Bell. It sounded so close, like the library sounded when she
was only a few blocks away.

Verity got up and followed the sound. It called her down the
back of the bar, where the bathrooms were. She passed them and
kept walking. She came to a doorway, passed it, backed up, and
tried the door.

When it didn't open, she braced against the opposite wall and
kicked the knob straight on as hard as she could. The door swung
open, drenching her in cold, dank air.

She stepped inside and halted. It was pitch dark, and there
was a feeling of open space in front of her.

"Are you crazy?"

She turned. Sphere was behind her, his head and shoulders
sticking through the door. She took another step.

"Don't!" he said. "It's past three in the morning, Verity. You
don't know what's down there."

"I have to," she said, though it was difficult for her to talk. To
even open her mouth. To force out the words.

She heard the faint sounds of music behind her. "Go back,"
she told Sphere.

"I must be a fool," he said, and he followed her inside.

"We're lost now," she heard him say, and the winter fields
were austere and gold and she was in such pain that she sagged
against time like a supplicant but time had turned its back and she
blinked in the black tunnel. She wondered where these thoughts
were coming from—the very walls? But they loosened her like

dream so she could follow. Behind her she heard Sphere cursing, then a beam of light sliced through the air from a wall fixture. Those lights blinked on and off fitfully as they walked, often not working. After ten minutes she turned and went up a level and down three and up five and still the Bell rang within her head and she did not have any idea why Sphere was following her and why he had left his saxophone behind. She worried about whether he could get another one. The lights lit in some of the corridors and she saw that the tunnels were bright and sparkling as if they had just been created yesterday and more than once she heard Sphere's sharp intake of breath and a muttering she couldn't understand and she kept walking, and following the Bell.

They walked for another five minutes, then Sphere said, with fear in his voice, "Verity, where *are* you going?"

She didn't want to talk, afraid that it would somehow disturb the call of the Bell.

"I don't think we should do this," he said.

"Then go back," she managed. But still he followed.

She made a few false turns, when the Bell became faint or disappeared, and had to double back.

After several long flights of stairs, one going down and two going up, Sphere wanted her to sit and rest. "You're going to wear yourself out," he said.

"I doubt it," she said, wishing she had some cold water to splash on her face. But she sat, and must have dozed. She woke with a jerk. In dim light from down the tunnel she saw Sphere studying her face.

"Tell me where you're going," he suggested gently.

"I wish I knew," she said, and jumped up. The Bell was strong here, very strong. "How long was I asleep?"

"Oh, about two hours."

"Two *hours!*" She turned and listened intently, found where the Bell was loudest, and began to walk quite briskly. They were on a slight uphill incline.

"Can you find your way back?" he asked from behind.

She paused, but only for a second. It didn't seem to matter. She began to move faster; it seemed louder down at the end of *this* turn, sharp to the right, and then *that* turn, an obtuse angle to the left, and this upper ramp *here*—she heard Sphere, panting, behind her.

She had passed many doors along the way by the time she stopped. This was different from the others, because the Bell told her so, though they all looked the same, bright red metal. She figured that their walking time had been less than an hour. Enough time to get into the center of the City. Or well out into the deserted suburbs, though she was certain that was not where they were.

"*Wait,*" said Sphere, but she pushed the door open.

And stood spellbound.

This was it.

Her slice of vision, which was led down a narrow, faintly lit alley toward a larger street, encompassed buildings shrouded in darkness, an occasional light high up revealing their immense height. Snow lay white and silent, heaped around the mammoth entryway of a building she saw across a very wide park through the empty branches of huge trees.

It seemed old fashioned, what she could see of it. There was texture and depth and form, not the plain, simple towers of Columbus, which were disfigured near the top as if they had dried out and warped. If Columbus ever had colors, they had fled when the City died.

These seemed gray at first glance, but as she watched they were swept with color faint as a blush, which then receded.

Everything seemed so clean, much cleaner than Edgetown, and pure. She breathed the cold, sweet-smelling air and took another step.

Then Sphere pulled her back inside and shut the door quietly. He put his hands on her shoulders and bent his head down close to hers. A light came on, far down the tunnel, when the door clicked shut, revealing amazement on Sphere's face; amazement, and fear. He spoke in a whisper, and his voice shook.

"You've found it," he said. "I can't tell you how many times I . . . well."

"You didn't really know the way," she said, finally released from the Bell to speech. In the light she saw that this part of the tunnel was covered with clean white tiles, and heat was blown on her face from some unknown source.

"Yes," he said. "I found it once, a long, long time ago. It was just an accident, I guess—I was playing around in the tunnels and got lost. Ended up here. Or somewhere nearby. When I was twelve or so. It seems like a dream. I've always wanted to come back. I've tried. Many times. But I could never find the way again. And that other time I was too afraid to explore. Terrified."

"Terrified of what?" she asked.

"For one thing," he said, "it took me two days to find the way back. I was afraid, finally, that I was going to starve to death. Water wasn't a problem; I found plenty of water. None of the doors I found would open for me once I left the City. I ended up way the hell past Edgetown, in a little old deserted suburb called Wyoming. But I suppose the real reason I didn't spend much time inside was because everything is different on the other side of that door. Strangeness is often terrifying. But it's—it's also quite beautiful, Verity. And as I said, quite civilized. Sometimes I think the memory of that beauty and terror are what pulls my music into shape. A yearning for a place that simply can't be real. Yet it is. It's why I go to the Station and play. And of course, I can leave the Station whenever I want."

Verity asked, "Do many people go there? To the Station?"

"No," he said, watching her face closely. "They're afraid. It's Enlivened, of course. The earthquake seems to have crushed the tunnel into the City, but the Enlivenment still flows there."

She had felt it, but asked, "How do you know?"

"When I was a kid," he said, "a big mob formed one day. I was only about eight; I wasn't sure why. But it was exciting. We all marched over to the Station. It was a beautiful fall day. I thought I'd never seen anything so gorgeous; I'd never been there before—only seen it from a distance. There was something about the way it was put together, the lines of it, that made it seem almost perfect, the way I'd like my music to be, if only for a moment."

His face became pensive. Verity shifted on her feet and Sphere continued. "They tried to light fires outside, but it was all glass and steel and concrete and didn't want to catch. So they went inside—they wouldn't have alone, of course, but they were more brave in a group—and managed to set a couple of kiosks on fire with gasoline. I stayed behind, just inside the door with some of them, and watched those fires and felt pain, Verity. When they were satisfied that the fires were going good, they left. It was getting dark. I stayed. The flames leaped up toward the ceiling; ah, it was wonderful and horrible and ghostly. Some sprinklers came on and eventually doused the fire; I'm sure that would have surprised them. I slept there, and left in the morning. That was probably one of the bravest things I've ever done. But the most amazing thing happened the next week."

"What was that?" Verity asked.

"Well, they were disappointed that they hadn't caused more damage. They could see that the Station was still standing. I believe that they made some explosives, or found them, and went back. I hated to see the place destroyed, but I went with them, of course.

"Well, when they went inside the door, they stopped dead. Everything was the same as before. I was as surprised as the rest of them."

"What do you mean?" asked Verity, her heart skipping a beat.

"The Station *healed* itself," said Sphere. Was that pride on his face? "It wouldn't let those petty people destroy it. It's a noble place. I love it. But most people are very much afraid of it, especially since then, and they leave it alone." He looked at her keenly. "Want to tell me anything?" he asked. "Why are you so curious?"

"I just am," she said, still unwilling to entirely trust him. You must, she told herself, maybe he can help you bring Blaze and Cairo here.

But first she ought to find out more. After the way Violet and Cheyenne had reacted, she thought it might be best not to tell Sphere.

The Bell had ceased. Verity felt quite weary. And she, too, was terrified and more than a little angry, but for different reasons than Sphere. If she heard the Bell again, she knew that she would follow it, no matter what.

And why not? What was wrong with that?

It was just too much like a command.

She could still smell the sweet crisp air they had let into the tunnel. There was information on the other side of the door, the information that she'd come to find, the way to resurrect Blaze and Cairo.

"Let's go," she said.

"Verity," Sphere said, "there's something I have to tell you. You don't have to *worry* so much. It's all taken care of. Relax. We just have to wait."

"*What's* all taken care of?" Something in his voice made her turn and stare at him.

"Don't worry. We can spend all the time we need to inside.

They'll be fine. When the process is finished, your friends will be fine."

What process, she said, but the words wouldn't come out. She walked toward him. "*What process?*" she yelled. She felt like shaking Sphere. "You saw me take them into the station?"

"Of course," he said. "I as much as told you so. I asked you about the car, remember?"

"Oh," she said, flustered. "What did you *do* to them?" she asked, trying to keep her voice level and failing. "What *process?*"

He looked at her. "Well—it depends. What exactly was he having done?"

"I have no idea," she said, feeling more and more confused.

"Oh," said Sphere. When he continued, it was in a low, troubled voice. "You were quite interesting, you know. An unusual event—what is that woman dragging into the station? I went back the next morning while you slept. Where did you get the sheets?"

"They're very old," she said. "A—friend of mine got them in Edgetown. Forty years ago." Anger was building in her, and fear.

"I . . . see." He was silent for a moment. "Then all I can tell you is that it's under control of the assemblers, and that they'll complete whatever process he was undergoing. I think."

Sphere sounded so reasonable. Why did she feel as if he had no idea what he was doing? "But what did you *do* with them?" she asked, feeling desperate.

"There's an enclave in the station with spaces for people who are encased like that. Kind of like bunks. Information is transmitted . . . well, from somewhere . . ." His voice faltered, and he looked at Verity with apology in his eyes. "The instructions are printed on the wall, in several languages, and also in icons. I just did what they said to do."

"Go on," she said, beginning to shiver. She pulled her jacket tighter.

"Well, they undergo whatever process was programmed into the sheets. They were very expensive, believe me. The companies that held the patents charged people through the nose, even though I've heard that it hardly cost anything to make them."

"Why didn't you tell me before?" she asked.

"I didn't know we were coming here," he said. "Believe me, I had no idea. I thought we'd go back after the show was over last night and check."

"You might have told me," she said, forcing her voice out.

"I know," he said. "I know that now. I was foolish. But they're quite safe. I'm sure of it. It just takes time."

Verity fought panic. She should be there, with them, watching, waiting for when they woke. "Do you have any idea at all what sorts of processes there are?"

"No." His voice came out in a whisper. "Not really. I mean, I guess there used to be . . . thousands, maybe . . . that's the idea I get, anyway. I've never seen any sheets before. I just heard about them from my grandmother. They used to . . . oh, maybe enhance certain aspects of your intelligence . . . make you more . . . *musical*, perhaps. That would be my choice, of course. Or maybe if you had some sort of terrible emotional problem, you could have it fixed that way. Ah—I think they had all sorts of medical functions too. But . . ." He shrugged, looking very helpless.

He continued in a low voice. "I'm sorry. I thought you knew. I thought that's why you brought them to the station. I wanted to help you. Get it started. I think a lot of people used to use them . . . for instance, if you came on some sort of business, you might order a sheet to be ready to fill you in with very specific information when you got here. I don't think it really took long, but I'm not sure . . . I guess maybe it might have depended on what was being done. Something major might have taken longer . . ."

"You mean," she said, trying to be hopeful, "that he'll be healed now?"

"Healed?" Sphere asked. "He'll be changed."

"Changed into what?"

Sphere looked puzzled. "Into whatever the sheet was programmed to change the user into. I've never really seen it, but . . ."

"What about *Cairo?*" she yelled, unable to speak reasonably any longer. "My dog! What will *she* change into?"

"Oh," he said, looking entirely dumbfounded. "I had no idea. I thought the small package was a child. I guess I was afraid to look too closely. Verity, I'm sorry. I'm so sorry. But I think that I did the right thing. I really do."

Verity shivered.

"We have to bring them here," she said, "and we have to do it now."

"Why?" asked Sphere. "I'll help you," he added quickly. "But I'm not sure that it should be interrupted—"

Verity began to run, back the way they had come. But she had not gone far when she realized that there was a great difference, going the other way. There was no Bell.

She halted suddenly, Sphere at her heels. "What's wrong?" he asked.

"Nothing," she said, beginning to walk. There. She heard the Bell up the corridor to the right. That meant she should go . . . straight . . . or left?

"Verity?"

She felt in her pocket and pulled out something. A smooth stone she had admired this morning as it lay in the street. She bent and put it a foot up from the corner where she had paused.

"You don't know which way to go?" Now Sphere's voice had a touch of panic.

"Don't worry," she said.

"Where have I heard that before?" he asked, his voice wry.

They wandered for half an hour before she gave up. Sphere was becoming more and more distraught, and babbling about his ordeal in the tunnels years ago. "We can come back when we have plenty of food," he kept saying. "Let's just go out and get some food."

Silently she turned and retraced her steps, following the Bell back to the red door.

Sphere was the first one out.

> In physical terms, it is clear enough why advanced assemblers will be able to do more than existing protein machines. They will be programmable like ribosomes, but they will be able to use a wider range of tools than all the enzymes in a cell put together.
>
> —Eric Drexler,
> *Engines of Creation*

> This is harnessed—not worshipped materialism—true mind over matter—on the road from the complete, stony, compressive darkness of selfish materialism to the infinity of lightful, abstract, harmonic unselfishness.
>
> —Buckminister Fuller

3

○ ○ ⬡

Cincinnati, the Queen City

Twelve

◇◇◇◇◇◇◇◇◇◇◇◇◇◇◇◇◇◇

America Is a Poem in Our Eyes

Verity stood in the alley and gazed out at the icy City. She felt entirely bright and aware; her body tingled as before a storm, her weariness and worry washed from her. Almost seven, she thought, judging by the lightening of the eastern sky.

"Well, here we are," said Sphere. He reached into his pocket and pulled out two pieces of gum. Verity looked at them and felt greed. Russ always sought out gum in old supermarkets whenever they went to Franklin or Watervleit, but when she was with John it was always forbidden.

Her heart turned with pain, thinking of John and what he had done. And of what she had done. Killed him with the radio stone.

Sphere held a stick out to her and she unwrapped it.

"It's pretty hard," he said. He looked tired and morose. Her gum crunched to pieces in her mouth and released sharp flavor.

Verity gazed at an empty street. "Maybe they will be all right," she said. Sphere had just been trying to help.

"You can trust the Station," he said. "Really. I've always felt that way." He was as nutty as Blaze about the Station, she thought.

Verity was a bit concerned about how she had become confused in the tunnels. A stubborn darkness in her mind about them bothered her. She had always had such a good memory for routes, so much better than John's. Why had she gotten lost? It was almost as if the Bell had been trying to confuse her. No, she told herself, you were just tired, that's all.

The building next to her was a pattern of rough red brick. Absently she rested one hand against the mortar and pulled it back, startled. The texture was not granular and dry, like brick, but much more melded. She tried to break off a bit of mortar and found that it was hard as steel.

Nan. This was what nan-stuff felt like, or *could* feel like, stuff created and put together molecule by molecule. If you wanted a piece of "wood" in a Flower City, Russ had told her while sweating one summer day over the whining circular saw, you didn't cut crude chunks like this. You just went to your computer and ordered the substance, which was just like wood, every molecule, except that it wasn't really wood . . . yet there was no difference except in how it came into being. And with nan, all you had to do was tell it the exact shape and size and didn't have to do all this work. But it could also look like one thing but be different, the way this building looked like brick but you couldn't rub grainy bits from its surface like you could with real brick.

The surface of the alley looked like worn and pitted asphalt; the building on the other side of the alley, ten feet away, was a smooth sheet, grayish-blue, hard-looking and utterly featureless. She looked up and saw some sort of design indenting it twenty feet above.

Light sliced across a park bare of leaves across from her, and a sense of waiting was in the air.

She walked to the sidewalk and was about to step out onto it when Sphere grabbed her upper arm and yanked her back into the alley.

Cacophony exploded. A wall of sound stunned her.

Old-fashioned gasoline cars, their boxy shape something she'd only seen before in the encyclopedia, appeared on the street in front of her, each with one or more people inside, driving, staring straight ahead. The traffic signals actually worked. She'd seen them hanging dead in the small towns of rural Ohio, though Russ said they hadn't been necessary in the Flower Cities. Exhaust spumed into the cold air, though she only smelled cold clean dawn. Not a foot from her, warmly dressed people streamed past, striding with great purpose, carrying leather pouches.

"Watch," said Sphere, and stepped out into the sidewalk.

The people, like ghosts, walked through him.

He reached past her and waved his hand in front of a lens the size of an eye, which she had not noticed, set into one of the bricks.

The streets were empty again.

Holos.

"Why?" she whispered, throat tight with fear. Not of the grams. Not of how it was done. But of who was—either now or in the past—doing it.

But this was what she had come for, wasn't it?

He shrugged. "Don't know, really."

He reached up and batted it three times, and the people were different, dressed in different clothes. "This is an older time," he said.

Horses pulled wagons, like they had at Shaker Hill. Across the road was a market, and great red sides of beef dangled in the early morning air. She watched as a butcher in a stained white apron hacked off a piece for a woman in a long gown.

Sphere touched the eye again, and Verity recognized people from the Time of the Flowers. She stared, wondering if one of the men might be a young Russ, over to Cincinnati for the day, perhaps buying some of the wondrous things he'd told her about.

Sphere reached into his mouth and pulled out a wad of green gum and stuck it over the tiny lens. The street went empty.

"Not so unsettling," he said, and walked out into the City.

Verity turned and looked at the lens, slipped her fingers into the cavity that surrounded it, and found a small hidden panel, which she pulled shut.

Sphere shrugged and smiled.

"Are there any—real people here?" she whispered.

"Yes," he said. "Kind of. You'll see."

They passed fully stocked storefronts filled with beautifully dressed mannequins, flanked by a bank of small screens on which outfits appeared and vanished after about five seconds. Twice, holographic scenes sprang up across the street from them—once, someone was suddenly giving a speech to a crowd in a park.

"Where are they?" she asked. "And where are the Bees?"

"Too cold," he said.

"What do the Bees do?" she asked.

Sphere turned to face her, staring at her as he strode backward down the sidewalk. She became more and more uncomfortable and said, "I mean, no one would ever talk about it at—at home . . ."

"You mean what do they do? Or what were they *meant* to do?"

"What's the difference?" she asked, and threw her gum onto the street.

"I'm not really sure. Do I smell bread baking?" asked Sphere, stopping suddenly. He walked to an intersection and turned right.

"SCHMIDT'S BAKERY," read a sign overhanging the sidewalk.

Verity didn't know how many "Schmidt's Bakery," "Schmidt's Vat-Beef Shop," or, for that matter, "Schmidt's Authentic Microbrewery" signs she had seen in empty cities, causing her to conclude that there had once been thousands of Schmidts, all of them terribly industrious. None of the establishments had ever held a wink of life.

This one, however, unmistakably emanated delicious scent.

Sphere strode toward it, but Verity didn't budge. "Are you crazy?" she asked.

"No," he said, "I'm hungry."

"But we're not even supposed to be here," she said, surprised to find herself in the company of someone even more reckless than she. "What if they—"

"What if *who what?*" he asked, amusement pouring from his eyes. Being Inside seemed to have wiped his fear away, or perhaps it was just the same excitement that made her concern for Blaze a little more bearable.

"That's my point," she said. "Who? What?"

"Smell that?" he asked. "Coffee."

She saw two people at the end of the street, walking quickly, and was frightened. They went into the bakery.

"There you go," said Sphere.

Her stomach growled. "How would we pay?" she asked.

"With our bodies?" he suggested.

She thought of Tai Tai's family, caught in the Seam, and of Blaze, wrapped in the blinking sheet. Tears filled her eyes. "That's a horrible idea."

"Is it possible you don't understand this most elementary of human jokes?" he asked. He stared up at the sky. "I suppose it is . . ."

"Well, then," she said, feeling a bit huffy, "explain it to me."

"Later, maybe," he said. "Don't worry. We'll figure something out. These Germans can come up with some pretty tempting little things to eat," he said. "Want to wait out here?"

She followed close behind.

Little bells rang as the door closed behind them. Sphere's glasses steamed up; he took them off and started to wipe them with his shirt. Verity gaped.

Behind the counter was a man with a very large nose. It was not exactly a beak, but it was still . . . *large.*

He was portly, and wore a white apron. The fringe of hair surrounding a bald spot was black. Flour frosted one cheek.

Verity hadn't had any good bread in weeks. It reminded her of Sare, and she felt the ache again.

"Well?" asked Sphere, grinning at her.

"Two of those—what are they?" she asked the man.

"Jelly doughnuts," he said, getting them out using little squares of paper and setting them on a white plate. "Anything else?"

"She wants coffee," Sphere said.

It came hissing from a machine and smelled lovely. "Cream?" he asked, and Verity wondered where the cows were but said "Yes."

"Honey?" He dolloped some in and handed it to her.

Sphere got a brioche while she sat at a small round table. Across from her was an empty wire chair, the back of which was shaped like a heart. Sphere slid into the chair and hid the heart.

"How did you pay?" she asked. Of course they had never paid for anything at Shaker Hill, but Russ had talked about the old days of money often enough. But, she reminded herself, those days were before the Flower Cities.

"He didn't ask for any money," Sphere said, and grinned.

A man and a woman a few tables away had glanced up when they came in, but had soon gone back to talking. Verity tried to place their strange clothes, then realized that they were the same kind of clothes people wore in the 1930s. The woman's dress was leaf green and looked like it was made of thin wool. The very long skirt clung tightly, but a slit allowed her to cross her legs as she sat and leaned forward earnestly. The man was wearing a suit, a white shirt, a dark green tie with tiny red dots, and a gray felt hat with a wide band of black ribbon that would do nothing to keep his ears warm. A few more people came in but Verity could still hear the couple's conversation.

"I think it's disgraceful to give any time at all to those neo-postmodern composers," the man said, his small, sharp-looking face (but still with that overlarge nose, she noticed, and the woman as well) contorted in a frown. He had a short black mustache that Verity did not like.

The woman had long, wavy, light brown hair, almost blond, but she had not taken off her hat.

"Why?" she asked. "You're just very old-fashioned, that's all."

"I'm not a radical, if that's what you mean. The cut-off date is the millennium. That's all there is to it."

"That's completely random," she said. "I don't see why everyone thinks it's all right to live completely at the mercy of those—"

The man put his hand over her mouth and jerked his head toward a strip of the wall, four inches wide, which glowed dull yellow. The woman's face became red—from anger, Verity thought—and when the man moved his hand, her mouth was tight and she ate in short quick bites. "Come on, then," she said, pushing back her chair. "I'm through."

Verity could see that he wasn't, but he grabbed his remaining cake doughnuts and followed her out of the store. Verity shivered.

About eight people were in the cafe now. To Verity's relief, they didn't seem to be paying much attention to her and Sphere. But she was getting restless. "Come on," she said. "Let's go."

"Why the hurry?" he asked. "Don't you want to stock up on food here?"

"No," she said. "It makes me nervous."

"The food or the people?"

"Both." She pushed back her chair. Sphere followed her out into the street. She rushed ahead, looking around, not knowing what she was looking for. She paused at a corner. She felt absolutely helpless, and hated it.

Sphere caught up with her. "You have powdered sugar on your face," he said, and brushed her cheek with the side of his hand.

The tall buildings around her glimmered in the sunlight, reflecting their colors on the flat unmarked expanse of snow that filled the park across the street.

Wasn't it better that something was happening to Blaze? Of course not. She had no idea *what* was happening.

"I guess we really *should* get some food from the bakery and go back into the tunnel," she said. "Now."

Sphere nodded, turned, and began to gasp for breath. While Verity watched with growing concern, he sat on the curb and breathed with quick, shallow breaths.

"Are you all right?" she asked. He nodded but said nothing. She watched helplessly and in a few minutes he could speak again.

"Sorry," he said, with a sharp laugh. "You may have to go back by yourself. I didn't realize that I was so afraid. Just the *thought* of those tunnels—"

"You'll be all right," she told him. "You were all right last night, weren't you? Maybe we should go back and get some of that bread?"

Sphere struggled to his feet and looked at her entreatingly. "If you don't mind," he said, "there's something that I've always wanted to do. Just one thing. And then we'll prepare to go back."

Thirteen

○○○○○○○○○○○○○○○○○○○

What a Little Moonlight Can Do

Verity and Sphere had been in the store for two hours. During that time, Sphere had set aside practically every other sphere for himself. When open (and when was that, thought Verity, how long ago?) the store had stocked cases in which to store and carry the spheres. Sphere had filled every counter with open cases and was packing them in an order Verity did not understand.

"Wow. Nanomastered redigitalized Coleman Hawkins." Sphere's voice shook. "This all looks like vintage stuff—genuine premillennium."

"Why does it have to be premillennium?" she asked.

Sphere stopped for a minute and turned to her. He had a John look in his eye.

"Premillennium is when you still had true real artists, that's why. Real jazz. Experimentation. Raw beauty."

"Why?" she asked.

He looked at her in exasperation. "Crossover, that's why. The real jazz musicians couldn't make any money without playing that crossover crap. All drifty stuff with no edge, no passion, no pain. No truth, no soul. No . . ."

"Okay," she said. "I get it. I think."

"And besides," he continued, as if she hadn't said anything, "synthesizers were cheap and music really changed. You didn't *need* soul. You didn't have to dredge it up from somewhere inside. You could just diddle a few bars of stuff and the machines would take care of the rest—rearrange them, repeat them, add other instruments in any other combo you wanted. Shade the horn, even, pianissimo and forte everything just how you told it to. Sure, it sounded real . . . got so that it sounded damned near like it used to. But for a purist, that postmil stuff is shit, pure shit. By the time people realized it, all the old masters were dead. Look at this. Damn!"

He prowled around until he found the player, and beamed when music filled the store. "Miles," he said reverently, but it sounded pretty drifty to her, especially compared to what Blaze used to play.

"I don't know how I'll get these home," he said, his back to her so she could not see the look of glee she was sure was still there.

Sphere had been muttering like this for the past hour.

Verity had closed the eye that had filled the store with browsing customers after watching them for about ten minutes with great interest: so that was what used to happen, in stores. She just thought of them as places to take things from, provided they met John's approval. These holo people didn't pore over everything they picked up—at least not in the same way John had, looking fearfully, suspiciously, for the small glowing "n."

Dim light filtered through the window and she sat on a chair behind a counter and looked out.

"Hey, aren't you going to help?" asked Sphere.

"In a minute," she said, and continued to look.

Where were the Bees?

That was the other part of her journey into the City. She had finally reasoned, battling with anxiety over Blaze and Cairo, that since the sheets had kept Alyssa preserved for forty years, perhaps they were as smart as Sphere said they were. She was anxious to get back, but didn't want to leave Sphere here. And trying to move him, she had discovered, was like trying to convince John to take another trip to Columbus. She hoped he would relax enough to be able to return with her. He couldn't seem to realize that it might not take two days of stumbling around in the tunnels. She'd worked out a plan of marking the walls at each corner, using several lightsticks now in her pocket that she'd taken from the back of the store.

She closed her eyes and saw the Bees flying in cadence to the music, borne up by it, populating the sky over Cincinnati with bright golden-brown beauty, while the great Flowers—larkspurs, perhaps, and gladiola—sprouted hugely from the tops of the buildings.

She opened her eyes, slipped off the counter.

She was *here.*

She restlessly prowled the store, not knowing what she was looking for. But she was here, and not doing a damn thing about it.

She stopped at a glass-topped counter. "What are these radio stones doing here?" she asked.

"Radio stones?" asked Sphere. "I never heard of such a thing." He came over carrying a sphere in each hand.

Beneath the glass were smooth, large crystals about an inch long, of varying pastel tint, each in a unique shape. Verity pushed open the glass, reaching inside to take one out. It nestled in her palm, and her throat ached as she was reminded of Blaze. She pushed away the sudden picture of John, lying flat on the ground, head bloodied by the radio stone.

"Oh," said Sphere. "Those. I've seen them, here and there, in Edgetown. From what I understand, the neutrino bombardment is not constant. It comes in waves. Unpredictable waves. Some radio stations kept transmitting afterwards, and these were one of the receivers that they tried. Each was tuned to a single station. Kind of primitive, I gather, after what broadcasting used to be able to do. Send pictures and holos right through the air."

"Neutrino bombardment?" Verity asked.

"Well," said Sphere, "That's what some people said changed everything. My mom was just a kid when broadcasting went haywire, and she says that it wasn't neutrinos, but that there was some sort of new fast-spinning body in space, kind of like a star, that started sending out erratic radio jets from the center of our galaxy." He paused and frowned, then continued. "A *quasar,* that's right. Whatever that is. And they predicted that these radio jets would become more and more constant depending on how fast this quasar was spinning and what was between us and it— something about ripples in space-time—"

"*Wait,*" said Verity. "I know what a *galaxy* is, I think, but . . ."

Sphere smiled at her a bit sadly. "I don't know much more than that, Verity. It's little more than words to me. The educational resources of Edgetown are just about nonexistent. And it didn't really matter. The whole world became dependent on this new system that they thought up, the Flower Cities. Nan. Changing the human body itself to receive messages so that everything else would change." He chuckled, and looked down at the radio stones. "And change it did."

"I had one of these," she said.

"Oh, did you?" He looked at her sideways. "Did it work?"

"It got Tokyo," she said. "I guess that's in Japan. I couldn't understand anything they said, except that sometimes they said that it was Tokyo in English and that was all. They played music. But I could only hear it good up close. I put it under my pillow." It had been loud enough so that she had to muffle it.

Sphere nodded. He looked impressed. "You needed an amplifier," he said. "And some speakers. Things like this just went back to old tech. The diehards tried to keep things going, from what I can tell. And who can blame them? It must have been magnificent. The whole world depended on radio, Verity. Ships and planes navigated by radio. Everyone got information by broadcasting, and from vast computer nets, which went haywire too because of the magnetic fluctuation. Now, as far as I can tell, nobody knows much of anything." His eyes went distant, and he said, very quietly, "But I think that someone—or *something*—here in the City must know at least a little bit. After all, the Bees still fly."

Verity tried to touch the radio stone on; she brushed the flat oval of slightly rough material on one side the way she had made her own radio stone, the one with which she had killed John, glow. Nothing happened. "Mine got Norleans. Once." She heard again the remote, tinny "Erie Canal" which had flared briefly in frigid air.

She dropped the radio stone back into the case and reached inside and grabbed a handful, let them fall with a soft clatter onto the black velvet beneath, and felt as if her whole life were slipping through her hand as they fell. She watched them glitter, then closed the case with a quick pull of the glass door. It caught with a metallic snap, and she turned away.

"Norleans, eh?" said Sphere. "I didn't know it was still there. I mean, you hear rumors . . . it might not be there, even if something there is broadcasting. There might just be a transmitter someone put on a loop a long time ago, that came on because of some kind of disturbance. You never know."

Then he went back to the other side of the store. She heard the soft clicks of the spheres as they touched one another now and then.

As in the bakery, there were glowing interstices on the back wall, about six inches wide, three of them next to each other. One was yellow, one was green, and one was red.

They drew Verity. She had never seen them anywhere before, dead or alive, and these looked very alive. Standing a foot away from them, she became lost in their glow, and was reminded of Blaze; then she was angry and turned.

"We've got to go," she said, and headed for the door.

Sphere said, "Just fifteen more minutes."

"No," she said, exasperated. "We've been here for hours. There are other things I need to do."

"Like what?" he asked. "Just what do you intend to do?"

"Find out about this place, as long as I'm here" she said. "Like for instance, what are those? Those lights on the wall? What do they do?"

"I don't know," he said. He smiled sadly, as before, with apology in his eyes. "Really, Verity, I'm afraid I don't know much."

"Oh," she said, disappointed, then elated. The City spread out around her, *hers*.

He looked at her anxiously. "You will help me take these back, won't you?"

She looked around and laughed. She had only had bread and coffee all day and was beginning to feel lightheaded. They needed to find some food and be off. "Why are you sorting them out, anyway? You really intend to take every last one, don't you?"

"Well, those are the most important. If I can, I'll come back and get the others later."

"Let's hurry then," she said. "There are only so many that we can carry, you know."

In twenty minutes, festooned with bags, they left the store.

Verity hurried Sphere along as he tarried at store windows, but sent him back to the bakery, where he filled an empty bag with bread and sausage. In half an hour they were back at the place where they had entered.

The door was just an outline in the wall, a barely discernible seam that followed the lines of the bricks.

"There's no knob," said Verity, setting down her heavy load of music with a sigh and rubbing her shoulder where the strap had bit into it. She wondered why she hadn't checked it when she came out—she was used to exploring strange places after all, memorizing the route so she could retrace her steps, making sure the doors were propped open—but she had been upset.

Sphere tried to pry it open with his fingers, but the gap wasn't large enough. They looked at each other.

"It's to get in, but not out," said Verity. She glanced at Sphere, who looked even more nervous, and tried to relax. It wouldn't do for both of them to be upset.

She opened her palms and fitted them swiftly across the door, one row, then another beneath that, hoping that perhaps it would palm open. She looked around for another eye that might somehow trigger the mechanism, but the light was dimming in late afternoon, and hunger pixilated her vision so that the world became a swarm of tiny dots glowing in colors—brick-red, sky-gray. She jumped as the alley lit up, then turned and saw that the City was coming alight. It was dusk. Almost night. She turned, leaned against the bricks, and watched the lights.

Directly across the park was a building whose principal feature was an arch fifteen stories high and perhaps fifty feet wide. On the right side was another, narrower arch, about three windows wide and perhaps eighteen stories; on the left side of the main arch was another narrow arch four windows wide and maybe twenty-two stories high. Most of the windows were slightly squashed circles, fat ellipses echoing the ellipse that was the arch, cut off at the bottom by the street.

On top of each arch, all of which rested against the bulk of the main building, were Flowers. They were furled, just buds, and lit from below. Verity's eye measured them as being perhaps one story high. Not as big as those on top of the buildings. But not real, much larger than what she thought of as real.

She became dimly aware of Sphere behind her, kicking the wall and cursing. She sat on the pavement and gazed at the building. Finally Sphere sat beside her. "I guess we're going to have to think about this," he said. "Hey!"

He shook her shoulder gently and she said without looking at him, "Right."

A fountain erupted on one side of the building in a rainbow of lights, and a holo turned on. Verity watched people, tiny because far away, getting out of automobiles and going into the building. They were dressed in what looked like furs and black suits.

"I guess we can sleep over there," she said. "In that building. Do you think they have anything to eat?"

"Maybe," Sphere said, rising. "We have plenty of sausages."

She got up too, and started away.

"Don't forget your bags," said Sphere.

"Just bring the food. We can leave them here," she said.

"We can't," Sphere said. "What if we don't come back here? What if we find another way out? What if someone takes them?"

"What if we find a machine over there to play them on?" she asked, despite her fears, and he laughed. She opened her bag and fished out four spheres, stuck them in her pocket. "That's all I'm carrying for now."

"Let's at least find a safer place," he said. "Just around the corner, maybe."

She sighed, and hoisted the heavy bags.

Once on the street, they went left, a new direction. "Not more than one block," she said to Sphere, but she needn't have worried. Within half a block they found a door that opened at their touch. Inside was a small shop, empty of people, but filled with blooming flowers—flowers in vases, flowers in baskets, flowers in pots—dim in the evening light. They filled the air with sweetness.

"This is creepy," said Sphere.

"This will do," said Verity. "Put them over here under this table. No one will take them. Why should they?" She raised her eyebrows at Sphere and he shrugged. She dropped her bags and returned the spheres in her pockets to them, and shoved them beneath an oak table decorated with pots shaped like animals.

When they stepped back onto the street, she heard music, a woman's dusky voice, sounding as if coming from all directions, though faint. Sphere began to run.

"Wait," she yelled, but he did not slow.

She saw him duck left and followed, running fast. She came to a place not quite as sleek as the buildings around it. "JAZZ NITELY" read the sign above the door, and next to it a small poster had a picture of a black woman in a glittering blue dress. "BILLIE HOLIDAY," it said.

Verity sighed as she looked at the dark, battered wooden door Sphere was pushing open. She rushed up the steps and followed him inside.

"Sphere," she said, and stopped.

Standing uncertainly in darkness on the landing just inside the door, Verity looked across the small, crowded room below to a slim black woman with a fine, delicate face, half of which was brightly lit. She was the one singing, "Ooo, what a little moonlight can do," while the pianist, half in shadows, rushed ahead of her notes in a very strange way, exhilarating and utterly new. Verity had never heard music like this. Even the things Sphere had played for her didn't quite have the poignancy of the next song, clearly called, "Don't Explain," though Verity didn't quite understand exactly what it was that she didn't want explained.

Behind the woman, who was dressed in a long green gown that hugged her body, a man sat at some drums, brushing them occasionally; an enormous fiddle (*bass,* laughed a voice in her head) and several other instruments—*clarinet, saxophone,* came the whisper once more—leaned unused against metal stands. The next song, "Lady Sings the Blues," because someone in the audience yelled that and they all applauded, brought a stocky woman onstage to play the black instrument, the *clarinet,* twining it around the singer's voice like a morning glory vine. Or maybe, thought Verity, like deadly nightshade, because there was a darkness in the song that was never found in Shaker music, which was straightforward and glowing with God, Mother Ann, and Heaven.

Verity listened to three songs, spellbound. Then the singer smiled and swept offstage, and a man came on and said, "Miss Billie Holiday, ladies and gentlemen. She will be back after a short break," and the lights came on. She saw Sphere push through the small tables and chairs and people who stood up to stretch and rush up the steps to where she stood.

"This is unbelievable," he said, his voice hoarse, his eyes glittering. "Billie. I never realized . . . Verity . . . I don't know if I *will* go back! I don't know if I can . . ."

Verity glared at him. Outrage flared from a place in her she had not known existed. "You have to, Sphere."

"I *will,* Verity, I promise. In just a few minutes. *Please* wait for just a few minutes. I think you have no idea who—"

"You just want to listen to this woman sing! My friends need help!" Verity was quite surprised to find herself screaming, as she had never screamed before, as she hadn't when Blaze was shot right in front of her, or when she threw the radio stone and smashed John's head. It sounded like someone else. "We have to get back to Blaze!" she yelled, and realized that she was sobbing. "We can't stay here another minute."

"Verity," said Sphere, and tried to hold her but she thrashed and struggled and a man came and pried her away, picked her up around the waist while she kicked his shins, and thrust her out the door into the cold.

The heavy door slammed behind her. She tried to open it again, but it was locked. She saw it being rattled from the inside. Sphere! But the knob wouldn't turn and then the rattling stopped and she heard music coming out once more.

She kicked the door, again, and again, and again, until a man came out of a small door at the end of the building and walked toward her menacingly and she decided that perhaps she'd better run and so she did. She ran down the darkened City streets where lights illuminated as she passed, then darkened, changing her shadow as she ran, ran, until her breath was ragged and the sign above her said VINE STREET and she turned down it too tired to run any more.

Fourteen

◯◯◯◯◯◯◯◯◯◯◯◯◯◯◯◯◯

Dinner at Eight

Verity had no idea where she was going.

She huddled inside her jacket, hands deep inside her pockets, wishing she could go inside one of the stores on the street. They were similar to those on one block of Dayton, where mannequins were shielded by enormous panes of glass, those that had not been broken. Life-sized mannequins pirouetted, displaying their wares, including several coats that looked much warmer than what she had on. The mannequins in Dayton had never moved. In Dayton, she most certainly would have found a way inside and taken what she needed. Here, she felt buffeted and alone. Sphere was an idiot.

The wind bit into her as she wandered down streets lit by gas lamps. She saw their gentle mantles glow within glass globes. She passed neighborhood pubs every other block, sometimes glimpsing beyond the neon signs in the window rows of men drinking beer at an ornate carved wooden bar. She was enchanted despite her knowledge that none of it was real.

Or was it?

The spatterings of holo projections bent on some eternally recycled errand grew fewer, until she had been utterly alone for a few blocks. It was starting to snow again, and the flakes were large and lovely as they swirled around the gas lights.

She paused at a brick house with a wide front veranda that

extended across the front of the house and wrapped around one side. An empty wicker chair rocked on the porch, pushed by a gust of wind. Two tall windows on either side of the front door had their curtains pulled back, and the warmth of the scene inside tugged at her. Though she saw no one, it seemed as if someone must *live* here. The furnishings looked heavy and old-fashioned and ornate, examples of unShakerlike frippery. Over the arched doorway, a sconce illuminated the address: 115 Vine Street.

She took a few steps past the house, and thought she saw the faint image of laborers coming back from work in the evening, carrying plain metal lunch boxes. She felt wisps of agony and knew that a factory had exploded, killing hundreds of men. Three hundred and forty-three.

Knowing the number, she stopped walking, shivered once, violently. She felt a headache coming on and reached behind her right ear, absently touching the nub there. She turned sharply and stared into the night, thinking that she heard the Bell mingling with the roar of the high trees in a sudden gust of wind.

But she didn't hear it again.

Yet suddenly the house looked most attractive. Warm, and lit. She was freezing. She shrugged. It couldn't hurt. Could it?

She hesitated, amazed at the impulse she had to enter the house. It *was* a bit like the Bell . . . was that it again? The night was filled with rushing wind. It was hard to tell. Of course, she shouldn't enter this strange house—

Yes. There it was again.

Low and sonorous, almost drowned by the roar of trees in the wind, she heard it. It seemed to come from the house. *This* house, as if she had been heading toward it all her life.

A lifetime of following the imperative Bell changed *no* to *yes* once again.

She turned, and climbed the front steps of the house, touched the brass doorknob. It felt like brass—cold and hard and not holding the alien slickness of nan. She touched the door and chipped off some dark green paint with her fingernail, felt rough wood beneath.

She stood there for a moment, her breath puffing in the cold. Perhaps some parts of the City were real, unconverted. Maybe they had been inoculated somehow. Then she realized how silly that was. Nan could look and feel like anything. If bricks felt slick, that was simply a matter of someone's choice. Maybe it was quicker and easier than absolute duplication.

She shrugged and turned the knob. The door creaked as it opened, and Verity stepped inside.

She was in a small, cozy vestibule. A worn red oriental rug covered dark-varnished floorboards. To her right was a low wooden table. Above it a mirror framed with gilt-painted ornate plaster reflected her cold-reddened face. Below it was a vase of fresh flowers. She shivered, hating for the moment flowers. She remembered Cheyenne and his distaste for flowers with sudden kinship, and smiled.

She felt a sort of peace, and relief. Maybe she could find some sort of refuge here, at least for the night, and recover a bit of herself, maybe try and figure out how to leave this place. She ignored the tug of her heart and mind, an unpleasantly imperative tug, echoing with musts and shoulds, vague but just as stern nonetheless, quite as demanding as the voice of John at his most unpleasant.

On her right, through French doors, Verity saw a fire burning in a fireplace and the back of a brown old-fashioned sofa. Next to it was a deep chair of complexly carved wood; she could make out flowing wood flowers running up the arms in the flickering firelight. The green velvet upholstery looked new and soft. It was not like Shaker furniture.

Emboldened, she walked down the hallway to the side of the stairs, then came to a dining room. The chandelier was gas and gently glowing; she saw that four table leaves had been hastily placed at one side of the room, resting against the wainscotting next to the buffet. There was a fire also in the fireplace at the end of the room, and the drawn-together table had been intimately set for two. Several crystal glasses glimmered at each setting, above an imposing array of silverware on the heavy lace tablecloth.

Good smells emanated from the next room, and she walked into an enormous kitchen. A tiled cookstove took up quite a bit of room. The floury remains of a pie-making spree littered a marble table. Three finished products cooled amid the soft clutter of pie-crust scraps. Apple, she guessed, and cherry, and maybe rhubarb. Her mouth watered.

Thin stalks of new white asparagus were blanketed with yellow sauce and sprinkled with some sort of fresh green herb. She picked one up and crammed it in her mouth, tasting butter and other unknown flavorings, piquant and rich. Hot rolls were in a basket beneath a purple napkin; she took one and stuffed it in her mouth.

"Now, now, dear, don't be in quite so big a hurry," said a voice behind her, and she whirled.

The woman she saw was old. She had never seen an old woman before.

Her breasts, beneath flower-print thin wool, sagged to where a thin belt, embedded with delicate swirls of tiny sparkling stones, circled what once had been a waist. Her dress fell almost to her feet, leaving only thick ankles exposed, and she wore chunky black shoes with low heels.

"I was just changing for dinner," she said, gesturing at a floury apron flung on a turquoise-painted kitchen chair.

In the dim light of the wall sconces, Verity saw a face filled with a million tiny wrinkles. Like Sphere, she wore eyeglasses, and the eyes behind them were rich deep brown. Her gray hair was pulled into a bun at the nape of her neck, and she wore a large glittery brooch over the top button of her dress.

"You look a bit tired and bedraggled," the old woman said, sounding immensely concerned. "Would you like to take a bath first? I'm sure I have something that would fit you."

The rich, old voice pulled on something deep in Verity, and she felt frightened at this, more frightened than she had been by the holos or anything else she had seen today.

"No," she said. "No, thank you."

"The food will keep quite well," she said, and grabbed the railing of the stairs in order to descend the last few steps. Verity saw that the dark stairway, narrow, curved away into darkness, but that each step was filled with stacks of magazines. "But suit yourself."

She hobbled to the stove and picked up the rolls. "We're having roast beef and potatoes tonight, I hope that's all right with you," she said. "Could you take it out of the oven for me? Use those hotpads and just bring it out to the table."

Verity was very hungry. She looked at the pies and the asparagus, then back at the old woman.

"By the way, I am India," she said.

Verity did not feel like telling India her name. But she did. "Verity," she said.

She opened the oven door and grabbed the hot pads.

*   *   *

The meal progressed rapidly, with little conversation, because Verity was ravenous. The red wine was slightly spicy and sweet against the meat, and Verity felt pleasantly tired. She had been walking around all day, she reminded herself, and most of the previous night.

"Did you do all this yourself?" Verity asked, helping herself to more roast beef and mint jelly. She had covertly studied India during the meal. She had no nubs behind her ears, which somehow comforted Verity.

"Heavens, no! Melinda down the street comes in to help me out. She's young and strong. She'll be back tomorrow morning. We don't have to clean a thing."

Verity remembered Russ saying that nan took care of everything in Cincinnati and wondered if Melinda was a fiction to settle her mind, or perhaps some sort of creature not quite human.

"Get me a little glass of sherry, would you?" asked the old woman, as she dolloped large spoonfuls of whipped cream onto Verity's slice of hot rhubarb pie.

Verity pushed back her chair.

The buffet sparkled with cut glass decanters. "Sherry is that round one over to the right," India said, pointing. "Bring it over here and have some with your own pie."

The walls of the dining room above the wainscotting—cherry, Verity guessed—were covered with wallpaper on which was printed peonies. Dark rough-hewn beams crossed the high ceiling above her, and broad dark interstices of wood ran down the wall about every eight feet. The flowers looked so lifelike that Verity felt she could almost smell their rich, full fragrance—Russ's mother had planted peonies all around her house and the bushes had been huge. She felt a pang of homesickness. She wondered how Russ was doing, alone with the animals. She thought of Blaze and of how she was not any closer to figuring out how to wake him and felt sad and melancholy and selfish with her full stomach and glasses of rich dark wine.

"Do you do this every evening?" asked Verity.

"Oh, no," she said. "This is a very special occasion."

"Why is that?"

"Because you are here."

"But how did you know . . ." Then she stopped.

Of course, whoever was here who was human—or, she revised, intelligent, like the Dayton Library—would know she and Sphere had come inside, wouldn't they? She shrugged, then sat up straight, hearing Sare's voice reminding her of Manners. "Thank you," she said. "How did you know that I would come here?"

India's eyes grew serious. "I didn't, exactly. That was merely hope." She smiled, and Verity didn't know why the woman's face looked suddenly quite dear. Confused, she pushed her chair back and picked up some dishes.

"Now, don't bother," said India.

"It's no bother," said Verity. She pushed open the door to the kitchen with her shoulder and it swung shut behind her.

She set the dishes down and stepped to the back door, cracking it open. She had a need of cool, sharp air, and perhaps a glimpse of the stars, except she reminded herself that the sky was cloudy tonight. A few flakes of the snow, just beginning to fall, melted upon her face.

Still, the air steadied her.

As she stepped out onto the back porch, something opened in her mind and she didn't know where it led.

She only knew that she felt quite strongly that she had been here before. But when? How? It seemed impossible. She had just been a toddler when the Shakers found her.

Chilled, momentarily terrified, and then filled with strange deep security, as if nothing could ever harm her, as if the angels in which she no longer believed (else how could the plague ever have destroyed Shaker Hill?) still surrounded her, she let the impressions fall to the deep place within her which matched what seemed like memory to what she saw before her.

The porch was about twenty feet off the ground and square, just a wooden landing with a rail running round it waist-high, and a long flight of open wooden stairs disappearing into the darkness below. The placement of each tree, in the moonlight, was familiar. It fit some map in her mind. Below her, the dark shapes of a large, intricate garden rustled, dry in the winter breeze. She squinted, trying to see better. Tall hedges ran along next to one another, then turned. A maze.

She whirled at a sound behind her, and saw India standing in the doorway. Her face was shadowed, but her hair glowed white, lit by the kitchen sconces.

"Are you my . . . my mother?"

"No," said India. Her smile was a bit sad. "I'm not your mother. But come upstairs with me. I have something to show you."

Verity had plenty of time to glance at the heaps of papers on the stairs as she slowly ascended behind India. She was still surprised by the woman's oldness, by her limp, her wrinkles, her body's general disrepair. Russ had been old, certainly, but this was Cincinnati, an Enlivened City, a remnant of the Years of the Flowers where all was perfect and young and strong.

The papers next to her boots were celestial maps. They were full of suns and moons and arrows and phases and dotted lines, declinations and seasons. At the top right corner of each was a picture of a Bee. It was all rather dim with age. Verity bent down and touched the ragged edge of one. It cracked off the main page and the fragment fell to the step below.

At the top of the stairs was a long hallway carpeted with a thin gray runner patterned with dark green vines and occasional yellow flowers. Verity glanced to the right and within a door glimpsed the foot of an old-fashioned bed covered with a multicolored quilt.

"That's your room," said India, who hobbled ahead until she came to a slightly open door on the right. Pushing it open, she motioned Verity to follow.

Verity stopped just inside the door, surprised. She hadn't really known what to expect, but it hadn't been this.

The room was heaped with clothing. Hatracks were draped with dresses, chairs with shawls, hooks on the walls with scarves that shimmered with all the colors of the rainbow.

There was one small curtainless window next to a dressing table. The wind hurled snow against it with a snicking sound, and Verity heard a low train whistle and shivered. India bent down and pointed; Verity bent also and watched with fear and delight: below, about a hundred yards away, a train streaked past in the night. Lighted windows revealed passengers dining, reading, playing cards.

"The Columbus Limited," India said.

Verity whirled, angry. "I've had about enough of this!" she said. "Nothing is solid. Nothing is real."

"I'm not sure what you expected," India said, "But that's not entirely true. This is a different form of reality than what you are used to, I'm sure. It's very rare that people make their way into the City."

As she spoke, she was transferring heaps of clothing from one chair to another. "Sit down," she said.

Verity was very tired. She wanted nothing more than to go lie in the bed at the end of the hall. But she remained standing, her hands on her hips.

Then she heard footsteps behind her, muffled by the thin runner rug, and turned.

Fifteen

◇◇◇◇◇◇◇◇◇◇◇◇◇◇◇◇◇

Watch Me Pull a Rabbit Out
of the Hat

The man looked quite as startled as Verity felt as they stared at each other. The sound of the train dropped off and it seemed to her somehow that the light-blazing phantom train had cut time in half for her, the way the Shakers taught that spiritual rebirth made one's previous life profane and one's future life holy.

He was wearing a dark green shirt with too many pockets, material stiff-looking, rough and heavy, and the pants tucked into black boots were the same.

His face was long and pale, and his hair was very short and light brown, receding from his forehead in the beginning of baldness.

She stared into his eyes. They were narrow, and scrunched into some weird plea, like apology, so that she could not tell what color they were.

Again, as when she had stood on the porch, Verity felt a shock of familiarity, as if familiarity were a color, something obvious and easily sensed if you had the right apparatus.

Still staring at her, he fumbled in his vest pocket and pulled out a pipe.

"Now, Dennis, don't smoke, you know how I hate that smelly pipe," said India.

He only replied, "You might have told me," and dropped into what must be a chair beneath the piles of clothes. He brought out a tin with a furry beast on the cover and pried it open. The tobacco smelled beautifully aromatic to Verity.

"I couldn't," said India. "You know that."

Carefully, Dennis filled his pipe, picking up the tobacco with a pinch of his fingers and tamping it down with a metal tool he pulled from his pocket. He needed four matches to light it, and tossed each spent stick into a little crystal dish full of bobby pins on India's dressing table. India immediately reached across Verity and picked them out, frowning.

"I—" he paused and glanced at Verity "I did get your message, though. I think you may be right," and Verity wondered how they sent and got messages here and then was confused, feeling as if he meant *her* message, whatever that might be, rather than India's. She began to feel awkward just standing there but didn't want to sit down on top of India's clothes.

"Let's go to the sitting room," said India, and led the way downstairs dragging one foot behind her, making Verity wonder once again what was the good of Enlivenment.

India made a show of serving them tiny glasses of blackberry liqueur, and made Dennis relight the fire in the fireplace. That took up about half an hour, and in the meantime Verity watched Dennis quite carefully because he had nubs behind his ears.

She felt quite alone in the world, as if everything was rushing away from her at a very fast speed, and yet everything—the *stuff* of it—was still there. She clutched the scratchy brown velvet of the broad arm of the couch she sat on, leaned back on the rough white thing pinned to the high back, feeling its lumps press uncomfortably into her neck.

"Don't you have any beer?" asked Dennis, after he'd puffed on the fire and teased it to a blaze, which Verity was sure she could have accomplished in a fraction of the time. His liqueur was untouched. He brushed wood chips off his knees and glanced at India. She frowned at the mess; he shrugged his shoulders, picked up a ridiculously tiny broom that rested against the stone fireplace, and swept the woody debris into the fire.

"Satisfied?" he asked. He scowled, and Verity thought he looked like a spoiled brat, with his small mouth twisted up. She stifled a giggle, and he glared at her.

"Who *are* you?" she asked.

"I'll see about the beer," said India and bustled out of the room.

"If you lived in a decent house, instead of this relic, you'd *know*," Dennis called after her. He dropped into a chair next to Verity, stretched out his long legs, and sighed as if very tired though Verity certainly couldn't see that he had any reason to be.

"What would she know?" asked Verity.

"She'd know if there was any beer without going to the kitchen," said Dennis. "But I'm just kidding her. There's a reason why she doesn't want the house to be very smart, right now. As to who I am, that's a very fair question. But a bit difficult to answer." He smiled and his smile had an odd, sad twist. India came back with a large frosty glass of . . . yes, that must be beer.

Dennis thanked her and took a sip. His eyes lit. "By God, I believe that's real Geswith, am I not right? I take back all I said about your house."

India beamed and began to sit, stopped, and turned to Verity. "How about you? Would you like a beer?"

"Sure," she said. She'd seen so many Geswith signs in her life that it was wonderful to actually come in contact with the ancient reality behind that amazingly popular word.

When India handed it to her she took a sip, then a large gulp.

"That's the spirit," said Dennis, and stared into the fire. Shadows flickered over the flowered wallpaper, and Verity repeated her question.

Dennis looked around helplessly, first at India, who stared at him in a stern way, then at a singularly uninteresting picture over the mantle, and finally at her.

"My name is Dennis Durancy," he said, and she could feel the weight of his stare on her face as the name reverberated through her mind.

"Have another swig," he suggested, and took his own advice, draining the glass. He held it out toward India, who said, "You're not going to get out of this so easily, the way you did last time, young man," even though he did not look by any stretch of her imagination young to Verity.

"Durancy," she whispered, and her head jerked. A bit of beer splashed on her lap, and Dennis said, "You haven't drunk quite enough yet, another gulp, that's it."

"Not everyone is as fond of drink as you," said India, as she rose to take the glass from Verity's hand. Verity, however, clutched the cold glass and resolutely swallowed half of it.

"Maybe you need a little push," Dennis said, setting his glass on the floor. He reached across and took Verity's wrists gently in his hands. "Durancy," he said, looking at her, and then he reached up and lightly pressed the nub behind her right ear, which the Shakers had always carefully avoided touching whenever they brushed her hair as if a touch might send some dreadful current into them, or make her head explode or . . .

Or make her head explode.

"It's *you*, she said, and jumped up, lap soaked with spilled beer and pushed his shoulders back against the chair and stared into his cowering eyes and heard him say "I think she's got it," and then she felt India grab her from behind and she was crying and screaming and despite the fact that she was flailing her arms wildly she felt Dennis grab her, hug her strongly, closely, so that she couldn't move though she still struggled, and to her great surprise he began to rub her lower back with strong, slow circles and she moved from the room into fragments of dream and barely felt them lay her on the sofa, though she did hear Durancy say,

"Well, are you satisfied now? I told you we couldn't rush things, she can't take it all at once. It doesn't work. We tried that before."

And India's reply: "It's not as if we had a lot of time. I feel it in my bones. I wish I could stay longer but I can't—oh, I can't, it's too risky." Her voice took on a desperate tone. "It's coming, it will all just happen again . . ."

"No one should know better than you," said Dennis, voice grim.

"Whose fault is that?" said India's fading voice as Verity heard the door close. Verity's last dim thought was that this exchange had occurred countless times, as if it was one of Sphere's recordings.

Verity woke the next morning to an utterly quiet house.

She stretched amid the lush softness of the bed. Her hands told her that the air was quite chilly and she pulled them beneath the fat, light feather comforter, curled up, and looked out the open window. At first she had no idea where she was.

Then she remembered India and Dennis, and a twist of dark memory that had brightened unbearably before she left them and their voices behind. Had she simply fallen asleep?

She stirred, uneasy now, and sat up. That seemed the most reasonable thing, considering all she had been through the day before. Yet there was something painful about what had happened, something fraught with heaviness.

Snow fell rather lightly, and had piled up to at least six inches on the peaked roof across the street. A thin oriental rug lay on the polished wood floor between the bed and the window. On the bedstand next to her, beneath a lamp, was a book.

She saw that her clothes had been neatly folded and placed on a chair across the room. She looked down, saw that she was wearing a flannel nightgown, and was disturbed. They had thought of everything, hadn't they? Even carried her upstairs and changed her clothes! Well, then, wasn't the lack of a fire an inhospitable lapse? And how about breakfast in bed?

To calm herself, and to put off venturing into the cold, she reached over and picked up the book called, *Cincinnati, The Queen City*.

Verity rubbed her fingers over the embossed Bee on the green cloth cover, then opened the book and read:

Cincinnati is the fourth City in North America to vote for Conversion, on the historic date of October 28, 2032. Since then, a few short years ago, like all the Flower Cities, it has enjoyed a standard of living unparalleled since the beginning of time. Communication has not only been restored, it is conducted at a faster rate and with both a greater accuracy and a wider emotional bandwidth than ever before.

Congratulations on your choice as well as on your acceptance as a provisionary citizen of our beautiful Queen City. For those who are apprehensive about nan, we have provided this book to inform you and set your mind at ease. You are of course free to use any of the various nodes around the City to get the same information, and we hope that once you are more fully informed, you will set this book aside and began to access our great Queen City directly.

Verity flipped to the table of contents.

5. THE HIVE: THE QUEEN, THE WORKERS, THE DRONES
6. INFORMATION GATHERING, PACKING, AND TRANSFER
7. THE PRIVACY BONUS AND HOW IT WORKS
8. CARE OF BUILDINGS AND FLOWERS
9. FAILSAFE FEATURES OF ALL FLOWER CITIES

Verity wanted to read more, but she could no longer put off going to the bathroom, and slid out of the high bed. There were blue slippers neatly set on the floor; she put them on and walked down the hall. Three doors down (the others were empty bedrooms, with unslept-in beds) she found the bathroom.

Shivering, she looked at the large white enamel tub on claw legs and wondered if the hot water worked.

She turned on the knob and steaming water rushed out. She hurried down the hall and returned with her clothes—they were now clean and sweet-smelling, she noticed—while the tub filled.

She did not take long with her bath, more and more uneasy with the silence of the house. Still shivering, she hoped there was a fire downstairs to dry her wet hair. A higher standard of living? There wasn't even any heat! Russ had told her that the buildings in the Flower Cities had always remained the same comfortable temperature inside. And each moment no one showed up made her more and more panicky and sick at heart.

Who were those people she had met last night?

They weren't holo projections—no, she had touched each one.

Durancy. Dennis Durancy. She remembered, looking into the mirror as she rubbed her hair with a towel, that she had been flooded with—what?

Memories. Or were they? Memories of what? Pictures that came into her mind like shards of glass, painful and strong and too much for her. Like reading a book except much more intense. She picked up a brush and tried to work it through the snarls. You don't remember dreams, Tai Tai had told her, because your body isn't doing anything. Children learn by moving, she had said, and that changes the cells in the brain. Verity paused.

Had she ever brushed her hair in front of this mirror? No, of course not! So why did it seem like she had done it before?

"*When?*" she muttered aloud, and flung the brush to the floor, which was patterned in tiny black and white tiles.

She retrieved her boots from the bedroom and descended the

wide staircase, which turned on itself at a wide landing above which rose a window at least twelve feet high.

Relieved to see a fire flickering through the French doors, she set her boots down, rushed across the foyer, and flung open the doors.

The room was empty, but there were some funny-looking rolls piled on a china plate and a silver coffeepot, both on a highly polished table that looked like old walnut. She felt the coffeepot—hot—and flipped open the lid. It was full, and the aroma anchored her.

"Where *are* you?" she yelled.

She felt like kicking the table over and spewing coffee all over the exquisite living room, smashing the dainty glass things inside the china cabinet next to the desk.

She looked more closely at the cabinet. Something caught her eye.

Inside was a photograph in a silver frame. Her heart seemed to stop.

She turned the key, opened the glass door, and took it out.

Beneath a large striped canopy in a summer garden were people she recognized. India, maybe fifteen years younger, sat smiling in a yard chair, but there was an odd, grim look in her eyes. Behind her, a stocky middle-aged man with a pleasant, open face stood with one hand on India's shoulder. Next to them was Dennis, with his arm around a woman with long black hair. Both of them were grinning like fools.

Verity looked at it more closely. Did the woman look like her? Like she would, perhaps, in twenty years? She must be about thirty-five.

Was this woman her mother?

Verity was shaken for a moment. Holding the picture, she looked away from it and gazed into the crackling fire, feeling the heat on her face. She hadn't realized how curious she was about her parents. The Shakers had been so warm and close that she had just accepted that loss. But some deep longing had been ignited, now that she was here. She felt a bit embarrassed at how eagerly she had questioned India and Dennis the night before—as if the first people she met here might be related to her! How silly they must have thought her.

But they had known *something* about her, and they had been expecting her.

She looked at the picture again. Why did she think there was a resemblance? Just because they both had dark hair? Just because—the woman's smile looked a bit like hers? Did it? She held it closer. Did it really? No, of course not.

She turned the picture over and pried out the cardboard backing. Penciled on the back of the picture was "Graduation party for Rose. Ph.D. in City Planning. At last!"

She studied the picture for a moment longer, then put it still disassembled on a table. Enough of this. Where *were* they?

She strode through the rooms, into the kitchen, now improbably sparkling clean though she could tell by the light outside that it was much too early for anyone to have reasonably come by (nan, she thought bitterly, the old woman lied), and there was only one odd thing, a white piece of paper lying on the cold, clean marble table.

She grabbed it up, crumpling the edges.

"Please help us," it said.

She sighed, set the note down, and walked to the back door; stared out its small, high window. "How can I help you?" she said quietly, to no one but herself. "Who are you? Where did you go?"

Then she remembered India's voice of the night before. "It's too risky."

What was too risky? Staying here? Why? Maybe she ought to leave too.

She looked down at the garden and felt more loss. It no longer echoed into her with the familiarity of the night before. It looked prosaic, yet oddly inhabited. Next to the bottom of the porch steps a sled lay half-buried with snow. A hammock dangled between two large bare trees. But she felt no connection to any of it, not overwhelmingly, as she had the night before.

Again, this was how she had always felt after the Dayton Library—as if existence was very plain and stark, immediate, with no past and no future, like the first day she woke lucid after a week of raging fever and hallucinations and Sare sat there smiling with tears in her eyes and she hadn't known who Sare was, just at first.

She was turning to leave, deeply chagrined and increasingly anxious, when she glanced up and saw through another kitchen window a full, perfect view of the City, the downtown part where tall buildings were crowded together. The house was apparently on the crest of a hill, which Verity now recalled climbing the previous evening.

Perhaps a bit more brilliantly because of light reflected from snow, the buildings shimmered with pale colors that passed over them slowly, a collection of wondrously shaped tall towers which she knew were not real glass or stone but nan-stuff, molecules arranged in ways that made them somehow better, easier to change. She saw few harsh, sharp right angles, only enough to form a pleasing contrast to the rounded rooflines that differed by radii and height.

The rootlike interstices were tiny lines from this distance, those lines which seemed to her as if they might feed the Flowers. After all, the buildings *were* growing things.

But now, this time of year, all was still.

Russ had told her that the Cities had been developed to fully function year-round, to magnify energy from the sun and to create a private climate, but that the biological components of the Bees and Flowers had not been firmly set, so over several generations without correction or any intervention they had drifted back to a natural state that echoed their ancient seasonal origins.

She ached to see the Flowers blossom. It was now the end of February, so that could be as long as a month away.

Except that it had so far been a very erratic winter, with wild fluctuations in temperature.

What would it feel like, that massive opening, releasing clouds of scent . . .

She frowned once more as the note caught her eye. Help them? Who *were* they? Who was *she?* How could she help them? Why had they not remained, what had torn them from her? It was Blaze and Cairo who needed help, not them.

Blaze and Cairo. Sphere.

Yes, she was wasting time here. Alyssa had slept in the sheets for forty years, but whatever Sphere had done might have changed the—what had he called it?—the *process,* for them. She didn't even want to think how. She should go back and take them out . . . except Sphere had said something about not interrupting things.

Well, first things first. She needed to figure out how to get out of the City. And if she left armed with information about the sheets, so much the better. After all, that was why she had wanted to come here, wasn't it? She hadn't counted on Blaze and Cairo being meddled with, but after all, she hadn't been able to count on much. And she *had* gotten this far.

Not knowing where she would find food again (and ravenous, she realized, despite the fine dinner of the night before), she went back to the living room. All signs of the previous evening—beer glasses, the tiny liqueur cups—had been cleared away.

Standing, she gulped coffee perfect and delicious as dark wine. The rolls were delicately sweet and quite filling, especially when heaped with butter and honey.

She finished eating quickly and flung a white linen napkin on the table after wiping her hands, then hurried to the coat rack and began to pull on her boots, the ones from Columbus which now, she saw, had suddenly lit with a tiny "n" on the leather over the ankles.

She gasped and then she laughed, laughed until she cried, bending over, laughed to the edge of hysteria, her stomach aching, and then sat there on the floor in the empty house in a flare of pale light that came in through the tall frosted window next to the door. "Are you smart again, house?" she asked. "How smart are you, anyway?" But nothing replied, and she did not feel the menace hinted at by Dennis and India. All she could see was the beauty of a home created for comfort and to delight the eye and heart.

Ah, there was no going back now, was there? Why did everything seem to glow, with a very fine pixilation, as if matter was composed of uncountable, tiny points that only stained the powerful light within them with color? There *was* immense majesty within this City, and she was preparing to meet it head on, and pry out its secrets, and use them to waken Blaze.

More soberly Verity finished tying her boots in the special double knot Russ had shown her, which came undone in a pull; she stood, wrapped the scarf around her neck, and pulled on her faithful golden leather Bean gloves, then stepped out into the snowy street. She pulled the door shut behind her and carefully descended the slick porch steps.

Snow crunched as she headed toward the City with hurried steps.

Then she remembered the book, the one in the bedroom. It had information in it about the City, about what it was and how to use it.

Information that might help her wake Blaze, or fix him if what Sphere had done was damaging rather than healing.

She was only a block away. She turned, followed her footsteps back, rushed up the steps, and tried to turn the doorknob.

The door was locked.

She went to one side of the house, through a wooden gate hanging open, and carefully held the railing as she climbed the tall back steps, then descended to a stone-lined cellar entrance, but both those doors were locked as well.

She paused, panting, and looked for a rock to break the window to get inside, get the book.

But the snow was too deep to find a rock or fallen limb. She spied the sled she had seen from the kitchen, pulled it from the snow, and walked around to the front porch where there were large windows. It was a rather nice sled, she noticed, as she hefted it over her head. The paint had been properly buffed from the runners, which glinted, smooth, metallic, and slick.

Holding it firmly in both hands, she rammed it into the window as hard as she could.

It bounced backwards, and if she hadn't been wearing her gloves, would have torn her skin. She stared at the window, then took the sled and tried again. The same thing happened.

She took off her glove and felt the window.

Smooth as glass and quite as clear. But powerfully strong. Like hitting a brick wall.

She picked up the sled, walked out to the street and held it up in front of her, then took a few steps, flung it down, and landed on top of it.

The snow stung her cheeks as she grabbed the steering bar, and she whooped with delight as she sped downhill, toward the tall buildings, flinging out a spray of dry snow as she skidded around the first corner.

Sixteen

○○○○○○○○○○○○○○○○○

A Little Entertainment

The holos became more frequent as Verity got closer to the taller buildings. She flew past them, and sometimes through them if they happened all of a sudden, and finally she dragged her feet to slow the sled because she was afraid one of them might turn out to be real.

The buildings climbed out of the houses quite suddenly, within the space of a block, high and dazzling on the other side of a wide white park, which was half-hidden by a low building. The snow was already melting beneath the warming sun, and a few green patches were visible.

Verity rose from the sled and brushed snowy crystals from her clothing. This was as good a place as any to start looking for Sphere, and to try and find out all she could about how things worked here.

This close, the skyscrapers were breathtaking. They were not at all simple or predictable; instead, someone had played with form in a way that delighted her eye intensely. The designers seemed to have saved a grand burst of invention for the tops of the buildings, but fine details of repeated motifs were everywhere.

She decided to cut through the park and try that building. She had to start somewhere. As she walked, she became more and more annoyed with Sphere. How could she ever find him? She did not feel entirely comfortable with just leaving him and pursuing her own ends; in some strange way she felt responsible for him. He had seemed oddly helpless at the thought of returning to the tunnels.

When she got past the low building between herself and the park, she stopped, surprised.

In the center of the park, where the grass blazed green in contrast to the snowy roads and buildings around it—though that snow was melting rapidly—was a large stage. It was shaped somewhat like a slice of an ellipsoid, its roof arching up from behind to cover the stage. A shimmering curtain was gathered at the top.

A slight gust of wind blew a piece of paper against Verity's legs, and she bent to pick it up.

It wasn't really paper, but some sort of material thin and impossible to tear, yet with paper's texture.

THE TENTH STREET PLAYERS
PROUDLY PRESENT

A PLAY

BY

TENNESSEE WILLIAMS

THE GLASS MENAGERIE

Strange name, thought Verity. A zoo made out of glass? She took a step closer.

The rows of audience looked comfortable and absorbed, seated in plush chairs. Their clothing was as various as that in the different holo times she had seen. She wondered if they were real, then realized that either possibility made her uncomfortable. She did not feel too happy about having met two real people so far.

A woman stood up from a chair onstage and walked toward a man. Her voice sounded in Verity's ears, not loudly, but quite clearly, and Verity jumped and looked around, alarmed. She was so far from the stage that she could barely make out the expressions of the people on it.

Apparently that was the end of the play, for everyone stood up and applauded. Then all of them flickered out of existence except for about two dozen people, and three of those were on the stage. They immediately convened and began arguing about something, judging from their gesticulations. One rather grumpy-looking older woman wearing boots and an overcoat had been seated at the rear of the audience. She shook her head in disgust and walking directly toward Verity. The few other people remained standing and applauding.

The woman stopped suddenly about ten feet from Verity and looked at her blankly; Verity realized that she was about to walk right through her.

"Oh," the woman said, stopping short. She peered at Verity. Then she said, "Terrible production, really. I don't know what they're all clapping about. Great waste of resources, that, but they keep bringing it out every few years as if it's something entirely new. The Pinkton is much superior, and I'll remind them again in my column. I usually do. Ah, well, next week's an O'Neill, if we don't get a blizzard or something, like last month. The fields didn't do very well, remember? Kept blinking on and off. Most annoying. I think they need some work too." She sighed, and looked even more crabby. "Sometimes it seems as if it's all going bad."

The woman's hair was short, bangs white-streaked and frizzy, cut straight high across her forehead. She wore a turquoise scarf and even though she was wearing a coat Verity could tell she was rather thin.

The woman took Verity's arm and said, "Come, dear, I daresay you have nothing better to do this dreary afternoon than to come to the critic's party. That poor excuse for Laura will be there, but of course it's not her fault. She's just doing what the lines tell her. And don't worry, every winter is hard like this—so dull. The few of us out and about just have to make do. But soon," she said, and her eyes seemed to glow, or intensify, or sharpen," *They'll* be back." She lifted her head and sniffed the air, and Verity thought of Cairo. "See? It's warming already! Even a short thaw would help, and all the signs are right for an early spring. Glorious! The wind has changed—isn't it coming from the south? I smell *stories* in the air! Stories!" She clapped her hands with delight.

"Who'll be back?" asked Verity, "The Bees?" but her question was lost as a group of other people rushed up, chattering. Verity appraised them: they, too, were real. They greeted one another with excitement. And the woman was right. It *was* warming up, quite rapidly. Verity unzipped her jacket and stuffed her hat in the pocket.

Verity allowed herself to be led across the park, excitement growing in her chest so that she felt close to choking. The building she was being led to—not the diamond-windowed one but the one next to it—glimmered in the gray afternoon light, for instants pearl gray itself as if reflecting the sky, and then glowing a pale steel-blue. It appeared to be made of large blocks of stone.

It had been created—grown from seeds as Blaze always claimed—in some style different from most of the buildings in Dayton. It looked very similar to the train station: a vision of matter poised on some new, exciting, and unknowable future. Here and there, in a sort of random stepladder that climbed both sides of the building, were gentle arches of green glass in frames of ornate wrought iron.

She studied it with a growing sense of recognition, like a gathering wave in her mind, and then, as if the wave broke, that excitement, that energy, became words which had always been there but which she could suddenly hear because of what she was seeing, as if vision had made some vital connection and called them forth.

[*Modern*], said a voice in her head, a quiet, male voice. [*Well, Beaux Arts, to be exact.*]

Startled, she stopped while the rest of the group went on ahead and looked around, but she saw no one near who could have said this.

The voice continued. [*Heisenburg's Uncertainty Principle had just been published, in the nineteen-thirties. The underpinnings of matter were just being discovered. What an exciting time it must have been! Everything leaning forward, gathering speed, as it flashed into the future. Matter modeled on thought. I found it very appropriate, quite analogous to what the Flower Cities actually were—matter so very close to thought. Unlimited by old structural boundaries. It was almost like the birth of the skyscraper, the development of the steel web, except of even greater magnitude.*] The voice paused. [*But most of all* (was he slightly pensive now? His voice had shaded into yearning) *I just wanted to reproduce a lot of Old Cincinnati.*]

"Who are *you?*" she asked aloud, but the voice went silent and the pictures, similar to those she had shared with Cairo, vanished.

Evidently it was not a conversation, but a lecture, something like a passage from a book. Almost like a memory, or a phrase of Blaze's music which she might hear all day while picking corn.

After a moment of silence (but not really silence, because the sound of the rapids on the New Ohio River were a dull undertone to everything here, and the voices of real people chattering were random bursts of sound too distant to sort into sense) she followed in the wake of the woman from the park.

The stamp of Enlivenment—form smooth yet lively, surfaces precise and convincing yet shimmering ever so slightly, as if effervescing constantly into the air—was on the building in front of her. Along the high speedy-looking columns stylized tulips about thirty feet high were slightly raised from the surface plane. Incorporated into the vertical lines of the building were thin bright lines that looked as if they might be liquid encased in some sort of membrane, rising to the top of the building.

From high balustrades dangled thick green vines which she thought must be some sort of evergreen. Atop one such ledge, about two hundred feet above her, she saw three thick stalks with unopened buds.

Still too cold yet, Cheyenne had said. But now . . . ?

Melting snow now filled the streets with rivulets, and the trees were shedding wet, heavy snow in chunks. She knew this season well. A burst of summerlike warmth would be followed again by at least a few days of cold, and perhaps a week. And then it would truly be spring.

She wondered how long it would take for those Flowers to bloom, once brushed by warmth.

Her group had vanished into the building, through a glass entrance beneath an ornate overhang.

She approached the building with measured steps.

As she entered the entrance alcove, the interstice next to her glowed subtly.

"Touch please," said a voice.

Verity shrugged and walked over.

The surface was yielding, yet it was membranous, containing whatever was inside, warm and smooth beneath her hand. Small bubbles inside pulsed upward. Her hand tingled pleasantly.

Then there was for her a brief picture of a room full of people, glowing softly on the wall next to the interstice. The tall front door slid open and she stepped inside the Flower building.

All her life, she had wanted to be exactly *here.*

The lobby was surfaced, floor, walls, and ceiling, with dark marble, and gently lit with wall sconces. The door beneath the sign that said ELEVATOR slid open and Verity went inside to be elevated—so quickly she thought she had left her body behind, so silently it reminded her of midnight in her small room at Shaker Hill—and then the door opened and the woman from the park beckoned her inside.

For some reason, after her first deep breath of the sweet, close air, it was suddenly very easy for Verity to believe in Heaven. Spun out in glittering colors were its inhabitants, not the plain winged angels of the Heaven where John—

Was not.

She bowed her head for an instant, then stepped in among the dancers.

Their dress was wildly eclectic, much different from that of the people in the bakery. Verity was reminded of the clothing models that often preceded her descent into cocoon memory lapse. Next to her, a lithe young woman with blond wispy hair and an earnest look on her face chatted with a man. She was wearing a white blouse with many small green buttons; each contained a laser-sharp picture of a Flower that kept changing. Her too-large black calf-length pants were held up by lavender suspenders, and she wore high socks with broad black and horizontal stripes and low black boots. The man she was speaking with wore a white turban and a long, shimmering multicolored cape over a barely glimpsed tight-fitting body sock. Verity turned to look at the rest of the crowd and was unsettled by the fact that the seams of her elevator door appeared to have blended into the wall.

An old man with a white beard handed her a clear, fizzing drink and smiled, then turned away.

The broad, low room clearly echoed an exterior of complex arches supported by black interior beams radiating from a few central points, reminding Verity of tree branches emanating from a trunk. Between the rays were windows. The ceiling slanted almost imperceptibly from the curved interior wall upward toward the light, like an opening eye.

She made her way to the wall of windows.

The high wide view was like standing on a cliff. There was an enormous feeling of naturalness despite the fact that she knew the entire City below her was created. Then she thought, no, it was *grown*.

Twilight gleamed on the wide New Ohio River, rapids brilliant white in the setting sun, and brushed the hills of Kentucky, misted with the light green of early spring. The bridges rushed halfway across the river as if eager to meet someone, then stopped; six of them fanned out like porcupine quills. Two were twisted and ruined, without a roadbed, but one, a stunning structure of steel cables gathered to a high apex at a tall arch, was lighting up. It appeared to be full of people. Festive colored lights winked on.

This was the City for which she had longed all her life.

Lights were beginning to glow here and there, dotting the depths of vast, dark canyons.

It look as if many of the rooftops abandoned their architectural underpinnings and rounded inward toward their apex. Verity caught her breath in awe to see that one Flower, about three blocks away and partly hidden by another building, had begun to open.

The three rows of deep pink petals were spaced by intervening rows of flaming red tongues twisting tendril-like, longer than the blunter petals. Green leaves with serrated edges cupped the three blossoms, which nestled close to the body of the building.

The *building?*

Seen from above, the City looked like a spring garden.

She pressed her hands against the glass, cupped her eyes against the reflections coming from the room behind her. It was as if everything had gone silent and slow.

In the waning light, she spotted other buildings on the verge of blooming.

She turned back to the party.

A dark-haired woman sidled up to her and began to speak.

"The Bees are wonderful! They can do anything! They can even block all plagues, you know? So you don't have to worry again, ever! This is a great free center here, in the ravaged land, free of plagues, free of fear, free of death. I'm telling you this because you're new and I can see you're afraid. Don't be afraid! Don't worry! There is nothing more glorious than living here."

She was drinking some sort of dull orange juice—carrot juice? Lively music came from somewhere. The woman turned and set down the glass with a thump on a low table. She danced away, whirling alone for a few moments like a dandelion seed spinning in the breeze. She danced past again and picked up her glass; Verity wondered what else was in the drink besides carrot juice, but mere alcohol could not cause the odd euphoric intoxication on the woman's face. "You'll never catch me outside the Seam," she said, more loudly, still dancing as she stood next to Verity. "Make no mistake. I know it's there. More of us know about it than you might think, my lovely one from far-off lands."

"How do you know?" asked Verity. The woman seemed amazingly presumptuous, however correct she was.

The woman smiled, tilted her head, and winked. "The patterns, my dear. You give off pheromonal patterns that I—that all of *us*—can sense. For instance—" she held her hand to Verity's cheek for an instant, and her eyes widened for a second.

"What?" asked Verity.

"It's not necessarily so," the woman murmured in such a low voice that Verity could barely hear her. "Only time will tell." Then the music livelied suddenly, and the woman grinned and begin to move to its tempo again. "Your hands are a very important tool," she said, slightly breathless. "But I guess they haven't been fully activated yet. Don't worry. It will come, somehow, probably before too long. We can know so *much* here, you see. We have senses which those outside do not have, senses through which information flows so clearly, so strongly." She reached out and pinched Verity's cheek gently, with an impish smile. Verity frowned and stepped back. "You too have those senses, my dear sister—learn to use them! Then you, like us, will have everything you need, forever, for we can come back again and again—ah, I tell you it is Heaven, it is the Infinite!" and with a last swig of juice she swirled off into the crowd.

Sister?

In the muted light, it seemed to Verity that the walls were faint green. She touched one with her palm, and it yielded slightly, a tough surface, yet not entirely solid. Her hand tingled slightly once again, but nothing else happened.

Verity was starving. She picked a few small round pastries from a passing tray. They were filled with tiny, crunchy black seeds in sweet syrup. Where did these people get their food, she wondered; who cooked it? She looked across the glowing faces filling the room and felt their happiness, realized how complete everything was for them, understood that they never wondered at their fate as she always had. Their complacency was almost as palpable as scent.

Unsettled, she turned back to the window, reached up and grabbed a cold black strut. The City was alight now, as it was almost full night. The great brightly lit boulevards dwindled to darkness in every direction. Abruptly, she turned to leave. She was learning nothing here.

Then the air filled with a fine mist and she felt . . . happy again. Why was she so worried? Blaze would be fine, it would all work out.

But the happiness which seemed to be distilled out of the air around her battled with the deeper unease in her gut. Maybe if she got outside, and stopped breathing this sweet air, she could think straight again.

At one end of the room, she saw a door. Had it been there before? She didn't think so . . .

It gave off a faint pulse of light and the light seemed to call her and she thought of moths and flames but could not seem to help going forward, walking through it into the darkness, the chill and windy spring night, alive with the sound of wind rushing beneath large leaves, rustling as they rubbed against one another.

A narrow brick path before her randomly incorporated gently glowing panels, which threw the wildly various foliage lining the path into deep shadow. The wind was still from the south, and in the western sky a long dark cloud marked the edge of the rapidly moving warm front. The night was alive with the sound of rustling leaves. The roof was overflowing untold varieties of plants, none of which she could recognize in the dark, some of which towered above the others. Perhaps some sort of transparent panel had withdrawn with the warmth, or perhaps the roof itself generated heat that kept them alive during the winter. She knelt and felt damp earth next to the path.

She looked back. The party was colorful and silent behind the glass. The room was full of dancers; it seemed ever more crowded.

As Verity watched, the building seemed to shudder and the people inside became more frenzied. Phosphorescent scarves swirled in the dimming light like the tails of comets and she fell to her knees, terrified, as the building shook once more. She thought she heard muted cheers from the street far below, rising from everywhere in the City, and out over the bridge fireworks burst and she was spellbound watching the huge, shimmering blossoms of light. Then the roof shifted again.

She began to crawl back toward the door, but another tremor tossed her a few feet away, onto her side, wrenching her arm painfully when she landed on her elbow. She heard a tearing, rushing sound, and she realized *it is growing*.

The roof was now slanting slightly away from the stalk of the plant, which Verity could place, about fifty feet away, because it blocked the stars. Looking upward, she saw an enormous, bulbous silhouette with spiky edges, which began to unfurl with slow majesty.

Verity got to her feet. The angle she stood on was not great but she feared another jolt, and looking behind her saw that the roof was edged with some sort of barrier; green and thick in newly lit floodlights, it looked like a hedge. The ground shivered once more and she thought, *doesn't this unnatural Flower know that it's night?* Her hands were caked with dirt and she dusted them off on her pants.

The petals continued the process, sounding like Bear Creek in flood, shot with occasional cracks as if great sheets of ice were breaking—rumbles that made Verity think that perhaps it wasn't the Flower but another earthquake, and then in a sudden gust of wind filled with sweet scent she caught euphoria.

The stars seemed to intensify and pulse above her. Whirling around and running toward the hedge, her fear completely gone, she gazed entranced across the City. Behind her she heard many running feet, music coming from all directions, happy shouts; someone grabbed her shoulders and whirled her around: a young man with a black beard, who said, "Dance with me! What a glorious spring it is! How wonderful to awaken once again." The party had flooded out onto the roof, mad and gay.

She did feel awakened, and she did dance. She danced within a great crowd of dancers and music seemed to come from the earth and from the sky and she did not know how long she danced and she noticed but did not care that the wind was blowing harder, that the drops of rain hissing down became colder and colder, but her partner was long gone and she had been dancing alone when she realized that it was snowing, that the Flower had closed, that the City was dark, and that someone was pulling on her arm.

"Verity!"

It was Sphere.

"Where have you been? I've been looking everywhere for

you!" Verity was surprised at the fine sweat on his forehead, and the odd look in his eyes. "We've got to get out of here."

"Why?" she asked. "How did you find me?"

"She—or *it*—helped me. I'm not sure which," he said. "Don't ask. Just come *with* me. Now! This is not a good place to be."

She wanted to object, yet she knew what he meant. It was fearsome, alien, seductive, insane. She shook off Sphere's hand.

"What happened to you last night?" she asked. But strangely, she didn't really care. Instead, she wanted to continue to explore this roof. She pulled away from him. She was close, so close, to the Flowers! Unfurling, they had seemed to release some kind of information, something that teased the edge of her mind.

"I'm sorry I brought you here," said Sphere, following her. "We should have left immediately."

"I brought *you* here," she said. "Remember?"

"Yes," he said, "But I think—I knew you would."

The pavers she had thought were bricks hadn't broken like bricks would have in the recent upheaval. But—she bent and felt them. Grainy. She was confused. They had healed themselves, reknit . . . or become flexible when it was necessary. Nothing, nothing at all, was what it looked like. The food she ate—what was that, anyway? It was flavorful and good, but she was certain that it was nothing like anything she had ever eaten before—there was a certain underlying similarity to the doughnuts she'd eaten the first day, the rolls she had this morning, the sweet pastries, and even India's feast of the night before.

She felt a tug when she thought about India, and she looked out over the City. Where had that been?

The location filled her bones. Not far. A mile and a half if one took this route. A mile and a quarter by this . . .

Sphere grabbed her shoulders and shook her gently.

"Wake up, Verity. You look like you're going to *swoon*, or something. This is worse than I thought. We have to get out of here before it gets much warmer. If the Flowers continue to open, I have a feeling it will be pretty bad."

"Bad in what way?" she asked. "You've lived within five miles of here for most of your life. I presume." She looked at him. "Right?"

"Yes," he said, "But not *inside*. I—I don't want to be one of them. I want to be *myself*. Do you understand? I don't want to change."

"I wish you'd tell me what you're talking about," she said.

A warm gust of wind blew her hair back. She heard a rushing, tearing sound as the roof shook beneath her feet. She was knocked to her knees and her head hit the side of the building, so hard that it stunned her.

I'm fine, she tried to tell Sphere, but she felt herself lifted and slung over his shoulder. I have to stay. These people know things . . . but her head did ache quite a bit . . .

"Damned City," she heard him say.

I can walk, she thought about saying, but felt a bit sick and dizzy, maybe because his shoulder was pressing into her stomach. He stood next to the door with the glowing outlines, and said, "Open, door!"

Does that work?" she tried to ask.

"Hell," he muttered, and she could feel his panic as he jounced her from one end of the wall to another with his long stride, stopping now and then to yell at the wall.

Then a woman's voice shouted, "Coleman! Over here!"

Sphere whirled and hurried toward the voice. The slim black woman Sphere had been listening to the night before was there.

"Hi, honey," she said in the open doorway. "Why did you run away from me?"

Sphere brushed past her, and said in an undertone, as if to himself, "She isn't real. She's just not *real*."

Verity saw the thin black woman from upside down. She was wearing funny, shiny black shoes that were pointed at the toes and looked enormously uncomfortable. She looked real to Verity. Then her vision clouded over.

"She's bleeding," Verity heard the woman say as if from a great distance. "That's a nasty gash. Let me help you."

"Damn you, Lady, I can help her myself," she heard Sphere say, her ear next to his chest so his voice was deep. Yeah, Verity thought, and tried to move a bit. He can help me.

"I bet you don't even know how to get down from here," the woman said.

The elevator ride did not take long at all.

Verity sat at a plain wooden table drinking hot coffee and rum. Billie gave her a hand mirror.

"See," she said. "All better."

The casement window was open a few inches at the bottom, and an ever-warming breeze stirred the curtains.

"Are we in the same building as before?" asked Verity. Sphere had insisted on carrying her upside down, so of course she had passed out, what with all that blood rushing to her head. It was embarrassing. She'd never tell Blaze about that.

"No," said Sphere. "But close. It's got the same . . . problems."

"What problems?" asked Billie, pulling up a chair. "I know it's not the best place in the world, but the bathroom's just down the hall and I have a hot plate."

Verity didn't say anything, but felt her forehead as she looked into the mirror. Her face was streaked with blood and dirt. Billie handed her a wet towel, and she wiped it clean, then looked again. She should have a bump, a bruise, or a gash. Instead, her skin was smooth and unbroken.

Billie reached over and hugged Sphere around the shoulders with one arm, then let go. "Coleman Hawkins here has been helping me out," she told Verity. "I've scoured this City for new blood night after night for years and in he walks, fresh from his Chicago tour. It's like a miracle." Oddly enough, the enraptured look on her face suggested that she actually believed that Sphere *was* a miracle.

Sphere looked at Verity. "Feeling better?"

She nodded. "I feel fine."

Sphere looked like he was trying to think of what to say for a moment, then he smiled at Billie, and said, "It's been a great honor playing with you, Miss Holiday, but we have to go now."

She slumped back in her chair. Tears gathered beneath her long eyelashes. "I know it's not much, here. I never really seem to get ahead. But I was hoping you would stay. It was pretty brave of me to go up to that white party and get you, you know!" Her chin lifted. "I tried to warn you."

Sphere reached over and patted her hand. "It's great here, Billie, and you've been wonderful. That's not it. I'll try to get back as soon as I can. It's just that my friend here has some important things she has to take care of and we have to be on our way."

She smiled at him. "Don't want to shoot up?" she asked.

"Got to go," said Sphere, and he pushed his chair back and helped Verity get up.

She was wondering where they were going to sleep, since she felt exhausted, but Sphere seemed to have some idea worked out.

"Yes, thank you," Verity told the woman. "And your singing last night was—beautiful. You have the most wonderful voice I've ever heard."

The woman's face lit and she said with great dignity, "I thank you, young woman."

Sphere took Verity's arm and they walked out into a worn, dark hallway lined with scarred doors and peeling wallpaper. They descended two flights of stairs and stepped onto the street.

"What now?" asked Verity. She had to admit that she felt much more clearheaded now than she had while at the party, despite her injury. And even that was as if it never had been. She touched her forehead wonderingly.

"We sleep on these benches," said Sphere. "Away from those . . . *lines* on the buildings. The ones that light up. And those sweet smells inside the buildings. They make me sick."

Verity didn't argue. She fell asleep in five minutes.

She didn't even feel cold.

Seventeen

○○○○○○○○○○○○○○○○○○

Do Nothing Till You Hear from Me

"It's a fine and beautiful sight, isn't it?"

Verity opened her eyes. She felt damp and stiff. The sky was gray and streaked with light.

She sat up on the bench and looked at the man in whose lap she had evidently been resting her head, shrugging off his arm as she sat up.

Sphere was still asleep, snoring on the bench across the sidewalk from them.

Dennis was not looking at her, nor at the buildings around them, but at the river.

She followed his gaze and looked at the ruined bridge.

Large stone towers were still lit up top. The cables were gathered in a beautiful smooth sling that cradled the vast, graceful structure before it ended, suddenly, a shadow precipice against the pinkening sky.

"Roebling designed and built it," he said. "It was the model for a bridge he and his son built later in a city called New York. The boatmen were dead against cluttering up the river, so he couldn't put any piers in the water. Covington had lined up its streets to be a continuation of Cincinnati's, but for some reason Cincinnati didn't like that. They wanted the bridge placed so that the grand trans-state boulevard Roebling envisioned wouldn't work out. The facing's from Dayton. Limestone."

"I've heard of New York," Verity said, feeling more awake. She wasn't going to tell him she was from right around Dayton, though she felt he was trying to get her to. He wasn't telling her much of anything.

"You know," said Dennis, in a light tenor voice that sometimes warbled with emotion, dipped and soared, "I did my best to get him right, but I don't think that I did. Pei, and a woman who came later named Myer—it was part of my training to take them, all of them, but some of us take better than others and I was never really too good at it. I guess I knew it all along." His voice was yearning. He laughed shortly. "Guess that's what made me go bad. Well!" he said, jumping up. "Awake now? Took you long enough. And I think your friend there will sleep till noon."

Verity just sat looking at the huge, ruined structure. "That's not the original bridge anyway, is it?"

He looked at her. "No," he said after a moment. "That's not the original bridge."

"It's all made out of nan, right?"

"That's a science and a process, but that's not what it's made out of. For instance, we mimicked the molecular structure of the Dayton limestone and created it in a factory."

"But a lot of stuff here . . . *looks* like . . ."

He knew right away what she was talking about. He laughed, a short, deep laugh without mirth. "It just got to be fun to do things like that—you know, things not *exactly* as they seemed, perhaps just looking a particular way. Like . . . well, plastic is a good example. And a lot of times people just didn't even remember or particularly care what the original model was. And sometimes it was slightly cheaper that way, in terms of manufacturing time, anyway, not that economy seemed to matter to most people as much as . . . other considerations." He shrugged. The expression on his face was a puzzle to her. "I guess they were right after all. But that really wasn't our fault."

Verity knew who "they" were—people like John.

"What really wasn't your fault?" she asked, feeling a slight chill. "How old are you?"

The park they were in was on top of a small hill that fell away toward the river, with raw Kentucky cliffs across a confluence of rivers that looked more like a rather large lake, though one filled with a hundred slantings of white water and studded with tiny islands, gray in morning mist.

"Covington's completely submerged," he said, then "You might want to try that shop over there for breakfast. The one with the striped awning." He rose and started to walk away from downtown and toward the streets where the tall buildings gave way to dense, old-fashioned neighborhoods.

"I asked you a question," she said, following him. "And I have lots more. Where are you going?" she demanded.

"It looks as if it's going to be a bright sunny day. And rather warm, too, I might add. Spring *will* be early this year."

"So what?"

He said nothing, but just continued to walk. She followed him. He lengthened his stride, and she did too. "You recognized me when you first saw me," she said.

"Not really," he said.

"Don't lie to me," she said. "I could tell. How do you know me? Are you my father?"

"If I were your father," he said, "how in the world could I tell after all these years?" But he smiled for some reason.

"How should I know?" she asked, becoming a bit breathless at his pace. "I'm sure you have your ways. Sare had a machine that—"

"Sare?" he asked, tilting his head as he looked at her, and she was silent. They passed the third corner pub, filled with holos even at this odd hour, or maybe they *had* been filled with patrons so early . . . at one time, she recalled from a book she had read, every man, woman, and child in Cincinnati had drunk sixty gallons of beer a year. Maybe you had to get an early start.

Dennis had stopped grinning. He said in a low voice, "See? That works both ways. No, Verity, I'm not your father." He bowed his head and walked even faster.

"Well, I'm glad of that," she said. "It would be terrible to have you for a father. You're rude and irritating and obfusticating." He glanced at her and raised his eyebrows at that, looking amused, which made Verity say, "And that's just for starters. But there *is* something about me you know."

"I know that I shouldn't have sat next to you all night," he said, "But I wanted to see that you came to no harm."

"Oh, *that's* quite nice of you," she said. "But everyone here has seemed rather harmless so far. Weird, but harmless."

"I assure you, they're *not*," he said.

"Well, I wouldn't be surprised if you're one of those I ought to look out for," she said.

"Snippy," he said, smiling again. "That's a good sign, anyway." He looked oddly pleased, yet concerned. His hands were deep in his pockets. His boots and all his clothes looked brand new.

"You could at least tell me what's going on in this place," she said.

"You would think so, wouldn't you?" he asked. "That does sound reasonable, on the face of it."

"Well?"

He stopped in front of one of the comfortable-looking frame houses lining the street, beneath a huge oak tree whose waving branches were covered with tiny green buds. He looked at her as if considering.

She stared back at him, trying to squeeze meaning from his eyes, which, like the first time she saw him, were filled with apology. "What happened to you and India the other night?" she asked.

That question seemed to bring him to some sort of decision. "I'm going to be as honest as I can, Verity," he said slowly. "And the truth is, for your own good, and for the good of others, I can tell you nothing more right now. It wouldn't help, and it would only hinder."

"Help *what*?" she asked. Her frustration was at the boiling point. "Help *who*? Who am I supposed to be helping?"

He looked around helplessly. "I'm sorry, Verity," he said in a low voice. "This is very difficult for me. I wish that I could just *tell* you these things. But that way doesn't work—see? I don't know everything. I don't know anything of importance. And I've said too much already. Goodbye for now."

He strode off even faster, and she had to trot to keep up with him. "You can't leave," she said. "You haven't told me *any-thing—*"

A loud, shrill sound unlike anything she had ever heard made her adrenalin surge; she leaped behind the trunk of the oak tree and crouched down. She saw it was a car that had screeched to a halt next to her; an acrid smell from the tires filled the air.

The car, black and rounded and much larger and heavier-looking than the small light solar cars, had skidded sideways across the road. The windows were high and small, almost like slits. A door opened and a man in a gray suit and hat leaped out and ran down the sidewalk, then angled toward a wide-porched house. Three men burst from the car and began shooting. The running man stumbled and fell; then the men scrambled back into the car, which roared down the street. Verity looked around wildly for Dennis, but he was gone. She felt an instant's anger, which gave way to stunned darkness when she looked back at the man lying sprawled in the yard.

Just as when John shot Blaze, she could not believe that it had happened. He needed help. She ran over to the man and knelt next to him. He shuddered and cried out once.

Grief exploded in her, though she didn't even know who he was. The back of his jacket was riddled with holes, and blood was staining the gray cloth. She felt a hand on her back, jumped, and whirled.

"Oh, very, *very* good," the woman said. She was wearing a navy blue dress, had wavy blond shoulder-length hair held back on one side by some sort of fastener; Verity noticed with enormous distaste that four small fox heads with beady eyes glaring and sharp white teeth revealed in frozen snarls clustered on her chest, part of a furry wrap.

"He's dead," said Verity, relieved to see other people. Though oddly dressed, they did not seem menacing. "But maybe not. How can we help him? Can we call someone?" she said, thinking of Russ's story of the ambulance in Denver when he had first seen the sheets used. "Do you think we should turn him over?"

The woman laughed, and her male companion smiled. "Come on, Iona," he said. "It's obviously not over yet." He put his arm around the woman's slim waist and steered her away.

"What's not over yet?" yelled Verity.

The woman stopped. "I'm not sure . . ." she said to her companion. "She's not . . . completely . . ." She took five mincing steps on high heels back toward Verity and said, "I really think it's over, honey. I mean, really, this is quite a favorite and this is all there is to it. In fact, it may be the first of the season. What a treat! Oh, what a delight to be *out* again!" She spread her arms wide, threw her head back and laughed, then looked back at Verity. "They'll come for him soon and he'll be put back in the bank and then we can *all* have it whenever we want. Really, you don't have to worry." She took a deep breath and smiled broadly. "My, what a lovely day, isn't it? Just beautiful. I think the sun is really breaking through now, don't you?"

"Come *on*, Iona," said the man, and the woman said, "Bye," and walked away, swaying on her high heels.

So he'd be put back in the bank? *I'd like to see that.*

Verity walked up the steps to the broad porch of the nearest house and sat in one of the wicker chairs scattered about on the narrow, gray-painted boards. She watched the man lying there in the yard out of the corner of her eye. She was sure he was dead. She got up and tried the front door. It was locked. No one seemed to be home. Not surprising. The houses on the street all seemed to leer at her, suddenly—no doubt they *could*, no doubt they could *want to*. She felt very cold.

It really didn't take long.

Within five minutes, a team of two men and two women arrived in a small solar truck. She watched them get out. One of the women, dressed in a smooth purple leotard with a golden stripe up one side, carried a small kit in one hand. They didn't pay a bit of attention to Verity, though she made no effort to hide herself.

They rolled the man over, all smiles. "You hold him up now, Ben, that's it; that makes it a bit easier to get at."

Verity's stomach turned as they made no effort to revive him or tend to him.

Instead the woman opened a small container and set it on the sidewalk. Then she took a scalpel out of the kit like the one Sare's mother had left at Shaker Hill and made a swift cut behind the man's ear. A thin trickle of red zagged down his neck. The woman pushed and something came out, which she put into the container. Then she rose gracefully and went to the other side and repeated the procedure.

They each took a limb and carried him to the back of the truck, opened the double doors, pulled out a sort of drawer, rolled him into it, and he disappeared into the truck.

Verity jumped up and ran down the steps. "Where are you taking him?" she asked, as they all got into the truck. "What did you take out of his head?"

They all turned to stare at her as if they had not noticed her before, but they must have.

The eyes of the man nearest Verity were cold as he stared at her through the open window. His nostrils flared slightly, and then he looked puzzled. "Who *are* you?" he asked, but the woman, who was driving, said, "We've gotta get back, Ben, we're a minute or two behind." She drove away.

Verity watched the truck go down the hill and vanish around a corner. She began to walk very fast, not caring where she went. She did not like this neighborhood.

They had taken something from behind his ears. She reached up and felt her nubs. She pushed the bulges hard. They were the same as always: with just a slight give, not quite as hard as her skull, but she had fallen out of an apple tree once and scraped the skin from it and Evangeline's face had gone pale when she saw it—"Like a bone," she kept muttering, "white, but not really a bone, no, not really," with her teeth clenched and had dabbed anesthetic on it and then sewn it shut. Years ago. The thin, slight scar was a brief ridge beneath her finger. She pulled her hand down and clenched that finger within a sudden fist.

Who were these people? Who—or what—was *she?* She almost wished they'd left the mutilated man so that she could look at the cuts the woman had made behind his ears.

She hurried away and walked head down, thinking, for about fifteen minutes. She headed outward, toward the Seam. Despite all that had happened, it was probably still no later than nine A.M. It was a bit colder now that she was outside the City proper and into the houses. Verity watched her breath puff out in the gray morning.

Then she heard the rattle of metal behind her and whirled.

A small girl was running toward her down the sidewalk. Long blond braids stuck out from beneath a green and white striped hat with a little white fluffy ball on top that bobbed as she ran. She wore a short red skirt that flared out beneath her jacket, but black leggings covered her legs and her shoes were sturdy and not at all feminine. She carried a plain metal lunch box, with something loose inside causing the rattling sound.

Verity breathed cold water vapor, loving the smell, waiting for the girl to run through her.

Instead, she slammed right into Verity and sat down hard, crying. Her lunch box went flying and an apple and sandwich fell out when it crashed against the curb.

Verity recovered her balance, reached down, and set the girl on her feet. "You should watch where you're going," Verity said.

"I thought you were one of the ghosts," said the girl, sounding very cross and wiping her eyes.

Verity stuffed the lunch back inside the box, pushing on the lid to make it close, and clicked the latches. "Here," she said. "Sorry."

The girl took it.

"How old are you?" asked Verity. She had not really expected to see children here. But then where do the adults come from? she wondered.

"Five. And a *half*," said the girl. "My name is Heather, what's yours?" Her eyes were brown and rather serious. Verity was enchanted that someone so small could actually carry on a conversation.

"Verity. Where are you going?"

"School," said the girl, sounding surprised. "I will be very late." She laughed. "I like to be late," she added, and Verity thought her smile looked rather wicked. "It makes Jane really really angry. But she's not supposed to get angry with us, so she gets mad at herself instead. It's kind of like . . . oh, what's that book? Who are you going to be when you change?"

She looked at Verity with wide open eyes and said, "I guess you've changed already, haven't you? I want to be a songwriter, like Patti Smith. Or maybe a painter. Georgia O'Keeffe."

"Who are they?" asked Verity. *What do you mean, change?* The girl began to walk and Verity followed.

"You don't know? Georgia O'Keeffe was the greatest painter in the world. But maybe I'll be a dancer too, like Shirley Temple." Verity was amused as the girl paused and made a few swift steps, which she took to be dancing. Then she started to run again. "Hurry," she said. "I don't want Jane to be *too* angry. Then she's crabby the rest of the day."

Verity trotted alongside her. She turned a corner and Verity saw only more houses, massive, with wide front porches and turrets, like in the books of fairy tales she'd read on winter afternoons in the library.

One had a sign in front that said "Children's House." Heather rushed up the wide steps, pushed the door open, and stepped inside.

The air was warm, and smelled like cinnamon. Four or five children rushed up to Verity all talking at once, then one boy with gray eyes, and freckles all across his nose, said "Where are your manners?"

The other children glanced at one another, giggling, and the boy said, "Please, may I take your coat?"

Verity removed it and watched him step up on a stool next to a row of hooks in the wide, wood-paneled foyer to hang it up.

There was a large room beyond the foyer. Verity saw that the entire back of the building was glass. Pale watery sun was beginning to play across the wooden floor, and busy children were everywhere.

Holoscreens were set here and there on low slanted platforms, but most were blank. Verity saw that many of the children were building things. Two girls were working on what looked like a vast City. Verity heard one say, "I think this building here should be an Iris," and her friend said, "No, it's a Chrysanthemum." The child walked to a low shelf by the window, which was crammed with what looked like a hundred Flowers delineated by type and size, and picked out a yellow Chrysanthemum that settled at the top of one of the buildings.

Verity saw a young woman then, moving among the children, holding a cup in one hand, squatting now and then to look at things closer, standing again. She said to one of the builders, "Do you know why you chose a Chrysanthemum?" and the taller girl said, "Chrysanthemums make engineers. We need balance in our City," and the woman nodded and moved on, glancing at Verity and smiling for a moment before helping another child.

Verity watched, then began to wander around herself.

She touched on one holoscreen and a woman's voice began to speak inside her head. Before her appeared a tiny Flower building, and the interstices—vertical pinstripes of light which looked as if they occurred about every fifty feet—pulsed, as if to get her attention.

"We found the perfect carriers of information re-encoded on DNA to be bacteria. The warm environment of the interstices allows them to flourish. A single strand of DNA, of course, can carry more information than a million old-tech spheres. Once a human is genetically programmed, their own personally generated pheromones are re-assembled into metapheromonal packages capable of precisely echoing the most complex thoughts humanity can achieve. Or the most simple. That package passes through the membrane at a touch, to be carried upward to the Flower via bacterial DNA. There, in a form modeled on pollen, it can be collected and taken wherever needed, deposited and carried downward to the exact target room, and either be directly absorbed by the target or translated to any sort of tangible display. Please place your palm on the indicated space for the next information segment."

A small hand-shaped area glowed, and Verity pressed her own hand on it. There was silence for a moment. Then the woman's voice said, "I am sorry, but you are not cleared for the next segment." Then it was silent.

Verity looked around, hoping that no one had noticed. But everyone was going about their work just as before. It was a pleasant room. The ceilings were high, and a small fire flickered behind a glass door set in the wall.

She sat on the floor at another low, transparent table.

A purple area about two inches square lit and glowed within the transparent plane that slanted in front of her, and next to it were circles: green, red, blue, and yellow, in a column.

"Go ahead and choose," said a woman's voice, which seemed to come from inside her head.

"Green," said Verity, but nothing seemed to happen.

"You have to touch it," said a boy standing next to her, so she touched the green circle briefly with her finger.

"I wouldn't do that if I were you," said another boy at her shoulder. "Jane has to show you first."

"That was Heather's program," said another little girl.

The table said, "You have chosen Shirley Temple."

Verity's face was brushed with a fine mist, and immediately Verity felt quite lovely. The faces of the children around her began to glow.

She heard Jane's voice from across the room. "What's going on over there?"

"She stole Heather's program," said the girl, and Verity just grinned at her as she sat there, even though she breathed what seemed, oddly, the little girl's indignation. The gray sky outside the window seemed very bright. The blue of the wooden rail that ran around the room just below the ceiling was intense and powerful.

Then Heather was standing next to her, her face screwed up and tears pouring down. "She stole my Shirley and I've been working on it for all week! It will take me another whole week to make those meta . . . meta*pheromones* from scratch! Why can't we just *have* them, like Downtown? It's not fair!"

"Stand back everyone," said Jane, and in the space they made, Verity rose and began to dance.

Eighteen

○○○○○○○○○○○○○○○○

On the Good Ship Lollipop

The footlights were very bright, but Verity saw rows and rows of heads, just heads, the first few rows, then blackness.

She glanced to the right and saw Irene, her coach, nodding her head in time to the piano music. Old Ed was playing "The Red Red Robin," leading into her entrance. Her nylon net petticoat was scratchy against her legs and her new, black, shiny tap shoes were stiff and heavy.

She peered into the darkness, wondering if she could see her father and mother there. Her father almost couldn't come, since he was getting ready to go to the War, but finally he got there.

When the intro was over, the dance steps poured into her head, and she began to move.

She barely had to glance at Irene in the wings, dancing in unison with her. Her new shoes made lovely sharp sounds against the wooden stage, and she remembered mother saying something about the movies and someone in the audience tonight. She was the only four-year-old dancing a solo, and tap was so much more fun than dull ballet, where you couldn't even wear real shoes till you were twelve and all the pink scratchy-netted girls were such snots.

The music counted off the double shuffles for her, the intricate steps that flowed and caught her entire body and made it feel light and free. The lights seemed more and more bright, until they were inside her spine, flashing up and down her body as she whirled and Irene vanished and then she was dizzy and vomiting and some woman was leading her across the room and holding her head over the toilet and wiping her forehead with a wet towel and saying, "There, there," and turning around and saying, "You kids leave us alone now. Get back to work."

Verity felt utterly wretched. She leaned back on her knees. "What happened?" she asked.

Jane grinned. "You were just Shirley Temple. A wonderful Shirley, I must say. You are very good at dancing."

Verity took a few deep breaths, sat back on the bathroom floor, and leaned against the tiled wall, wondering if the sparkling cleanliness was because of nan—like Russ used to say.

She realized that she didn't know a thing about nan.

And this woman . . . did she?

And what if she did? Would she tell Verity? If she asked any questions, how would Jane react?

The tiles at her back were cold. She straightened and looked at Jane.

Jane's hair was cut straight at her shoulders, reddish brown and shining. Her eyes were hazel.

"Maybe I ate something," said Verity.

Jane shook her head. "One of the things that Heather had to do was analyze her own pheromonal patterns and develop the insertion mix. It's not the same as yours, so hers made you violently ill. It's not uncommon." She smiled again. "Of course, the Bees do that for us adults, so we never really have to think about it." She looked a bit troubled, and rested her head on the tiled wall. "To tell you the truth," she said, "I wonder if it's going to do these children much good. Everything is so—I mean it's not like it was *meant* to be, I'm sure of it, but I can't quite put my finger on what's wrong." She looked directly at Verity and asked, "Do you know what year it is?"

Verity opened her mouth and Jane waved her hands and said, "Oh, no, I'm sorry, I'm so sorry, forgive me. I do have faith, I really do. It's just that," she lowered her voice and looked around, "it's hard to remember, but it seems as if we are . . . *gone* a lot. I know we have to winter over but I seem to remember . . ." she brushed a hand across her face as if wiping away cobwebs. "I'm just worried about the children, you see. I wonder if they'll ever get to use any of the things that they're learning."

She looked out over her classroom, filled with children, and seemed to become instantly cheery, as if she had put a mask back on. She said brightly, "Most people, like you, probably, never had to go to school. What are you?" she asked. "A writer? An artist?"

"An architect," said Verity, and was rather shocked at herself. Don't tell stories to the woman, she told herself; you'll get in more trouble than if you just say nothing.

Jane looked at her with admiration. "How wonderful. It's not for me to say, but it seems to me that we've had entirely too much of the other type the last few cycles. Well, you probably do all this instinctively. We don't have to think about how to walk anymore, or how to form sounds with our mouth, or how to pick up a spoon. There are millions of commands hardwired into the brain—it's stunning, just dazzling." Jane's face lit, and Verity saw that she was completely enraptured by it all. And rightly so. But what had happened to the other, worried Jane? What had she been talking about—wintering over, and all?

Jane continued, "The children can't hurt themselves, or get sick, like you did. That program was tailored to Heather's pheromonal mix, and to the particular Receptors the Hive gave her when she was created."

Jane got up and reached down for Verity's hand. Verity let Jane pull her up. She felt dizzy. Jane turned Verity's hand palm upward and brushed it lightly with her fingers. She patted Verity's open hand, closed it upon itself, let go, and smiled.

Jane continued. "Look, pheromone molecules come in different sizes. The messages they give are very precise. Of course, you know that, but you probably just give commands when you're designing things, right? You tell the Hive what to do, just by touching an interstice, and she does it. Like we can walk across the room without thinking about it. Anyway, these kids learn how to use the Hive, how to go into all the subroutines. The wrong pheromones—the wrong-sized molecules—can send messages to your individual brain that Heather's brain wouldn't receive. Plus—" she grinned again—a teacher's grin?—and said, "time is also very important. You can send messages which are enacted immediately, or which take several hours and activate lots of different subprograms. The programs that most of the people over there are on—" Jane nodded out the window toward a few Flower buildings just visible out the window through a gap in the houses "—are very, very strong. Not everyone can stand them.

But those that can . . ." a look of yearning came into Jane's eyes and then she rose briskly. "Ah, well, some of us are made for . . . more important tasks," she said, and led Verity back out into the room.

Verity was rather surprised to see all the children, young as they were, still absorbed in their various tasks. The murmur of quiet conversation filled the air. She saw two boys pull on jackets and run outside to a small play yard filled with brightly colored climbing apparatus. Verity thought of Shaker Hill, the ancient unused tractor that had been her and Blaze's toy, the apple trees they climbed, learning every gnarl and handhold, every high branch that made a good seat.

She wondered what was happening to Blaze now, and was filled with a kind of panic.

She needed to find out, she realized, what pheromones were.

She couldn't ask Jane. Maybe that wouldn't be the question that made her suspicious. Maybe Jane wasn't capable of being suspicious. Maybe there was nothing wrong with her being in Cincinnati. But she still didn't want to take any more risks, not right now.

She looked out the large window at the silvery sky, wondering when she would finally see the Bees.

She thanked Jane. As she walked toward the door one of the boys rose from eating lunch, rushed over, and handed her her coat. "Thank you for coming," he said, and Verity stepped out into the afternoon.

Nineteen

○○○○○○○○○○○○○○○○○○

Information Theory

Verity ran along the Seam with a low keening in her throat, which soon changed to harsh, ragged breathing. What are you afraid of, she asked herself, running. Afraid of this stuff? Afraid it's going to reach out and grab you, like it did Tai Tai's parents?

It glittered, it gave off sparks, it flattened itself to dullness; she soon believed that it wavered from time to time, but whenever she stopped and touched it the Seam was hard, and warm, as if the sun was shining on it; but it was not. Despite what Dennis had said, the sun had not come out.

As the gray afternoon wore on Verity slowed to a walk. Sometimes a building had grown out of the Seam, a half-formed building like a chick in an egg broken too soon. Doors and windows sagged, but solidly, and would not open. Finally, discouraged by the Seam's immensity, sweating and exhausted, she sat on a knoll and looked out over the City.

Hugging her knees tight, she tried to relax. This was doing no good, and was wasting time. Despite her fear of the scents, the people, the craziness, she had to go down into the City again. Everything around the Seam looked simply deserted. Verity had not seen another person since she left the school.

It took her another hour to get downtown and find the library, wondering all the while why her maps were closed to her. She finally found a City map on a stand next to a trolley car stop.

Looking around in the waning light she saw that the streets seemed the same, but there was no department store across the street from her, as the map claimed; instead a bright sign proclaimed HOTEL. Still, she would try for the library. Apparently she had been circling it for the last half hour.

A few minutes later, from the shadows of another building, she watched a group of five laughing real people dressed in evening clothes rush up the wide low stairs of the building labeled LIBRARY. They stood in front of the door, then muttered and laughed some more, apparently drunk, then left when the door remained closed to them.

With trepidation and resolve, Verity stepped from the darkness into the spotlights which had come on as the sun set. She climbed the wide, low, granite steps, and looked for a place to palm open the door; to her surprise it opened for her, and warm air enfolded her.

She was in a vast space filled with dark shapes she could not see very well. To her right a row of thin stretchy gray hats hung on hooks. A small green light above the first one in the row blinked for a few minutes, then a voice said, "It is necessary to be initiated in order to use the library. Please put on a matrix initiator for ten seconds. The library will be informed of your optimal learning matrix." The gray hat glittered with tech filaments, but was silky-smooth in Verity's hand.

Gritting her teeth, Verity slipped it over her hair. *Sorry to inconvenience you for so long,* said the quiet, soothing female voice, now much more intimate, as if it were inside her head, *but we run several redundancy checks in order to better serve you.*

After a short pause, *As it appears that you are presently the only visitor, the entire matrix is at your disposal. You may remove the matrix initiator.* Verity pulled off the hat and returned it to its hook.

Then the windows appeared to elongate, the wall sconces to subtly change shape, and the fountain changed to a creek . . . Bear Creek, with the twisted bridge downstream . . .

"No!" she screamed and, chastened, the fountain returned, with a whisper of *Sorry, we did not pick up on that recent pain matrix we are rather out of practice you know . . . look . . .* a whisper of many voices and then, in a more yearning and astonished tone, *It . . . has been . . . so* long. *Has there been another surge?*

"I really don't have much patience left," said Verity. "I don't know what is happening and I need to find out." She strode toward the newly arranged stairway, climbed the first few steps and grabbed the railing when she found that it was bearing her upward, luckily at the same rate as the railing.

We are here to serve you, said the voices anxiously. *Please follow the yellow line,* and the stairs stopped at an open platform that for a moment gave Verity a bit of vertigo until she saw that it was edged with a fence of long thin cylinders of glasslike substance. She stepped out onto the floor, wanting to request that everything take place on ground level, but afraid to even think it too loudly, afraid that the building might comply too quickly. It seemed somewhat clumsy.

Verity was used to old, deserted buildings, though. She swallowed her fears and stepped forward with eager caution, following the golden glimmer until she came to an arched doorway, low, set in what looked like a plaster wall where the plaster swirled in a delicate shell-like pattern.

When she stepped inside she saw Russ, sitting on a low white couch. He looked at her and smiled in the dear way she knew so well.

For a second, her heart fluttered in her chest. Then it was on the tip of her tongue to scold the building once more, but she was so fascinated that she couldn't.

This is your personal archetype of wisdom. We hope you are pleased.

She sat on the couch opposite him and stared.

She wasn't sure what he was made of. Was he a ghost? If he was a bodily thing, how could he have been created so quickly?

"Information theory applies to DNA as well as to all forms of communication," he said. "There is a certain mathematically predictable loss."

"How does that apply to me?" she asked.

"My dear, it applies to everything, for everything is information. But you are experiencing it to a great degree because of . . . because of . . ." He looked at her as if he could not think of what to say next. His voice was a bit different than Russ's. She relaxed.

"Well, then, what *is* happening here?" she asked, to prompt him to continue. Perhaps she could get something she could use out of him.

The construct frowned. "You will need to be a bit more specific."

"Tell me about Cincinnati," she said. "How it works. And,"

she said, greed getting the better of her though something in the back of her mind said *don't confuse it*, "Tell me how to get out."

"You want to get out?" he asked, incredulity in his voice, which for a moment relapsed into a chorus of whispers and she thought ah, there's not too much distance between *him* and *them*; that thought made her feel a bit better, because it was so difficult to sit across from a Russ who was not Russ.

"I just want to know how," she said.

"You are not ready to leave," he said.

"I'm quite ready," she said. "If you're not going to tell me, then I'll find out somewhere else."

"Wait!" he said. "I am authorized to tell you other things." *Other things. Other wonderful things.*

Perhaps she was being foolish. No need to be so impatient. Verity forced herself to listen as the Russ construct continued to talk earnestly in a voice that was very close to Russ's inflections and tone. "As I was saying, I am sure that much of the City's disarray is simply caused by the loss that any form of information transmission suffers. I apologize for the temporary delay in accessing the answers you desire."

Verity folded her hands and bowed her head for a moment, this time trying to carefully frame her question, then looked at him and asked, "If this is disarray, what is *supposed* to be happening? What is the ideal? How can the City return to that?" Her excitement increased, though she tried to force herself to stay calm. Maybe she could find out everything she needed to know right now. As he spoke, she thought about her next question, wondered what it should be—how do the sheets work? A young man and a dog with terrible gunshot wounds are wrapped in sheets in Union Station—how can I make them live?

The construct said, "The Bees have become addicted to the metapheromonal byproducts of human emotion, and very specific combinations at that. Stories. Music. Art. That's why they cause the same things to be relived—recycled—"

Verity was torn between trying to find out more about the City and more about Blaze. She felt despair. There was so much to know, apparently! This was the kind of thing cocoons are for, she told herself, because talking is so very slow. And Information Theory said that this exchange right now had its problems! But of course, then every exchange had the same problem, didn't it?

What was what she was seeing, hearing, touching, *really* like? Old Russ here was saying that it was impossible to know.

But when she thought of a cocoon, the great hall was filled with that same deliciously fogging scent she had breathed at the party. What was it composed of? *90DA,* whispered the voices, *and several other important natural and synthetic pheromones combined with one another!* They finished with an upward lilt, as if they had succeeded at some challenge.

Verity felt slightly disoriented, yet quite intense at the same time. Vision was sharpened and more powerful, as if her normal vision and state of mind was just a vague and discontinuous dream. She felt almost as if she were on the verge of discovering a new Dance, and yearned with all her might for her small family at Meeting as dusk fell in winter and snow tapped on the panes. The ghostly Russ flickered and vanished. She was aggravated for a few seconds, trying to remember what she had been thinking, because it seemed that she could no longer concentrate. The intensity was visual and emotional, she realized, not necessarily cognitive. She stood and looked around wildly, wondering how to get out. But with another burst of scent, she abandoned that thought.

Can one be led by a feeling? she wondered, as she followed her feeling down another hallway and saw at the end a cocoon.

"I don't want to get in," she managed to say, though something pulled her toward it with enormous power; *something* made her want to get in and she hated it.

Tell us why, suggested the voices.

"Because I never remember what happens," she said.

After a moment, the voices said, *we will seek authorization to let you remember this,* and she was angry at this Authorized and Not-Authorized, the Not-Authorized of her past and of all the time she'd spent in the Dayton Library cocoon and of how that library had called Blaze so strongly that he had died for it—

Not died. Please get in and we will show you.

She got in. *Thank you,* said the voices, *This saves quite a bit of energy.*

The cocoon molded to her head and formed some sort of lens over her eyes. Things went bright and then her vision switched to a new way of seeing. At first it felt a bit awkward, something she would have to get used to.

Then she was in another place.

She was walking down a long hall while a young blond woman in peculiar clothes said that she was there to answer questions, but then she faded out. She was quickly assured by apologetic voices that it was not their fault, some sort of strange disarray in the programs, some glitch they were working on that puzzled them, please be patient and enjoy yourself. *Still seeking authorization.*

Tell me about Blaze, she thought, and was surprised to hear her thought echoed all around her, in whatever space this was.

Soon. But let us begin at the beginning.

She watched, through a window, a compartment being flooded with milky liquid.

She was told to hold out her hand and a speck on her palm grew until she saw a device with arms like the arms of an insect, thin and jointed, with claws to clutch. It reached out and grabbed something floating past, a bright green sphere, and then grabbed a blue one, and put them together and they were linked by a black stick (new chemical bond, said the voice) and before she knew it there was another device like the first, with insect arms. *Stage One Assembler Construction* said the voice, and the identical things seemed to whiz through the glass and were there in the milky liquid and then shrank to nothingness and Verity understood she had seen an enlarged picture of some process.

As she watched (*five hundred percent speed,* said the voice) something took shape within the milky liquid; she saw with amazement that it was a solar car. Perfect and new, it was flushed with a deluge of another liquid and her stomach clenched from the far-off place where her real body dozed and she felt like vomiting.

This was early Tech, real and shining, that which had been forbidden and avoided all her life, that which Mother Ann was against, that which Shakers were bound to shun. It could surge out of control, and change the matter of the entire world. They *were* beginning at the beginning.

But it was something, she realized distantly, she would have to embrace, and learn to use.

She lived within it now. She ate it. She could probably wear it. She could *think* it.

Or . . .

Possibly, it could think *her.*

Enough of this. *You promised to tell me about Blaze. Tell me, or I will leave.* There had to be some other way to find things out in the library.

Vision flickered, almost if the library were mocking her, and a deep realization of utter helplessness washed through her.

No. We are helping. That is our duty. We cannot harm you. Your feelings are normal but unnecessary. We shall adjust them. Pay attention, please!

She was in a large, dark chamber in which she could not really see with her eyes, but whose parameters and features she understood with some other sense.

Within hexagonal chambers were beings tended by the other beings who crowded around her. There was an entirely new feeling of mission here, in this place, which in a way reminded her of Shaker Hill but in another way was much more overwhelming and powerful. Volition did not exist here, but it was not really missed, except by her.

She realized that she was in the Hive.

She strove to make visible what some appendage of her body *felt*—was that the edge of the comb? but even flooded with the light she *thought*—at least she had *some* control—everything looked fractured like pictures of Cubist art in the encyclopedia. Her eyes no longer worked right!

Stay calm, she thought, breathe deeply—but even breathing was different in this body and fear forced her outward and then it was not even her own fear, but the fear of someone else, heavy and powerful and rushing toward her at incredible speed. Someone or something that seemed to *know* her, intimately—

She tried to shrink back but didn't know how, in this strange space. Her mind went dark. Contrite voices strove to reassure her that they were working on the synaptic backlash that had just been generated by her limbic system and then something odd that suggested they were not getting enough to eat . . . no, they were really losing power, that was just the way they talked about losing power and, on the edge of consciousness, she realized that the tech voices believed that they were real.

Were they?

One last vision flashed through her, swiftly, as if it were being pulled away from her at great speed and with conscious intent, after she said, *Tell me what I need to know.*

She felt an odd surge of valiant effort from somewhere—within, without; she could not tell. Then she was strolling through a large, fragrant garden; all the flowers were normal-sized. And then, she realized, or maybe they suddenly changed, the garden was full of roses, and only roses.

Beautiful, subtle roses, dusky peach tipped with yellow, brilliant red—even, here and there, for accent, a single black one—

SYNAPTIC DISSONANCE PRECLUDES FURTHER INFORMATION TRANSMISSION, blinked a sign above her, unnecessarily, then added, FURTHER ACCESS DENIED.

Then it shut off as, perhaps, it felt the weight of her stare.

Verity was not sorry. But she was puzzled.

The voices had been right; she did remember what happened this time. She was beginning to feel as if she could gain skill in manipulating the information within the cocoon, if only she had a long enough session. Perhaps she was fooling herself, but that was interesting.

She swung around and tipped herself out of the cocoon and sat crosslegged on the marblelike floor, which shimmered smooth yet was filled with liquidlike fluxes of intertwined shades of violet and green until it stopped abruptly at the window.

Darkness had fallen; the City glowed. Verity was not terrifically hungry, so she gauged that it was still the same day as when she had entered the library.

Was there someone denying her further use of the library? Was there something that someone didn't want her to know? Either that, or there was simply something wrong with the library. She shivered. India had hinted at some possible malevolence. *It's too risky.*

Verity rose and started to wander through the hallways, which no longer changed. There were no books, as there were in Dayton. Everything was apparently completely on this new system.

Her vision had returned to normal, nothing intense, as if matter had assumed its former supporting role rather than being exquisitely tuned to something deep within her mind.

When she palmed touchplates, they did not light or otherwise respond. Everything seemed inert, and she was reminded of Shaker Hill when they all had the plague and did not respond normally, but became tuned to something deep within, as if the world did not matter anymore. The library, which had been awake, had gone back to sleep.

Someone, or something, must be afraid of her.

Why would she be that important?

"Tell me about the Information Wars," she said, recalling a map of that title, which blinked off years quickly in the upper right hand corner while colors surged and receded across the various continents, representing some sort of battles, something to do with why radios and computers no longer worked, or were different. She had been young, and Russ had been startled when she'd asked about them and patted her head. "Viruses," he'd said. "Plagues. Plagues of thought, and plagues that destroy very specific forms of matter. Things a little girl doesn't need to know about."

She asked again, more loudly. "I want to know about the Information Wars." Nothing happened.

Maybe it wasn't me, she thought. Perhaps the library just hasn't been used in a long time. Maybe the power supplies are no longer reliable.

It was full night. Verity sat crosslegged on the floor and looked out over the Seam, a smooth wall, studded with lights, that varied in height depending on the height of the building it had transformed, steel-gray but with opalescent glints, and saw Union Station beyond. Where Blaze and Cairo lay within their blinking Enlivenment Sheets.

She stretched out her hands and tried to feel the tingle of Enlivenment she had sensed in the station. She knew that it was all around her, yet she must have gotten used to it for it no longer seemed to make her skin dance.

Longing and dread made everything seem heavy. If only she could fly over the wall and get to him.

Then what would you do? You left him so easily, to follow Sphere, who is simply smitten with this place and his music. He doesn't care about you or Blaze! Ah, she thought, *Mother Ann was right, John was right, it is sinful to use Tech. It complicates everything.*

Would you rather have Blaze cleanly dead?

Of course not. Of course not.

Whatever he was now, whatever he could become, she prayed that the bright core of Blaze would still exist, his intensity, his passion, his music.

And mostly, she thought, mostly she wanted his love of her to still exist. Was that some sin? Coveting, or greed? To want to keep him fixed in some emotion just so she could be happy? No doubt. But she still wanted it!

She pressed her forehead against the window and saw the powerful, overwhelmingly beautiful arch of Union Station come alight, specially placed spotlights throwing the huge columns into relief.

But the railyards were deserted and beyond them, beyond the dark hills surrounding Cincinnati, were the wide and deserted Great Plains, and legendary Denver, and all the other Flower Cities that had become infected: Seattle, San Francisco, Houston. On the old weathersats they had been constellations of light, like those in Europe and Asia. What had happened to them, she wondered, the Flower Cities on other continents? She remembered Tokyo on the radio stone. And Russ *had* spoken of Information Wars, once: swift and deadly, nan viruses added to one City and then transmitted down the maglines, infecting the others.

Perhaps, like Cincinnati, their electricity still lived, transmitted only to the eyes of Bees and Ghosts. But Columbus had been a Flower City, part of the NN, the Nanotech Network, and it was dead now. The buildings themselves looked like withered husks.

Verity put her palm against the window, and was rewarded with a surge of something.

Happiness? Could a building transmit feelings?

Tai Tai had claimed that anything was possible for nan.

She pushed back and relaxed into that feeling, and felt hope for Blaze and Cairo.

I will save you, she whispered. *You will play baseball again, and most important of all, you will call me Demon.*

Still unhungry, she lay down, one arm bent beneath her head, staring at the City's sparkling lights as if their configuration alone held the answer.

Twenty

○○○○○○○○○○○○○○○○○○

Singin' in the Rain

Verity woke the next morning rather late, for her. The sun was high. Maybe ten.

She pulled on her boots and tied them, then stood, smoothed her long-sleeved T-shirt and tucked it into her long pants, picked up her jacket, and tried to make the library work.

But it was still dead, like the limp unresponding limb of a sleeping person. She descended the stairs to the street.

She was quite glad when the doors slid open for her, and when the air that hit her was balmy.

Small shops lined the street, and to her surprise she saw real people populating the sidewalks. They didn't have that shimmery sharp holo look.

Two teenage boys walked past her. One wore a red baseball cap pulled low that said "The Cincinnati Red Legs." The other wore an opened leather jacket, and his shirttail hung below. The boy closest to her stared at her for an instant as he passed, and she saw his nostrils flare in dislike.

She felt his dislike in some other, deeper way too, some new way that she didn't really understand.

She stood in the doorway for a moment, taken aback.

She was suddenly in a thriving City of strangers. She looked up the street, which turned into a steep hill a block away. Two solar cars were descending slowly, and a streetcar with people leaning out the windows, enjoying the warm spring air. Everything felt abustle and alive. Brightness filled her thoughts for a moment: so *this* was what it was like! The ghost cities and dead towns of her childhood hid within this one for a moment, and she was suddenly afraid that they would trade places, and she would be alone, once again. Just a week ago it had been almost like that here. Where had all these people *come* from?

She smelled approaching rain. At least the weather here was the same. You're part of the same earth, she thought. Part of the same system, no matter how the City contrived to trap her. *You asked for it,* she told herself, then *No, I didn't. I didn't ask for this. I asked to save Blaze.*

And I still shall.

I will beat you, City!

She looked upward, shading her eyes.

Half a block down was a tall, yet stocky building. It was a pale, lovely green, glowing gently. She saw the edge of a large pink petal waving in the breeze, and the darker green leaves around it stood up straight and spearlike. Though stone and concrete were everywhere she smelled the damp earth, mingled with a stunningly sweet scent.

A deep tone filled the air and then, beneath hearing, her very cells.

She knew instantly what it was. She shielded her eyes against the sun and looked up.

A Bee floated above, its furlike body limned against the sun. It did not move swiftly, but still took only a fraction of a minute to cross the street.

Her first! No, her second, she reminded herself, filled with excitement and dread.

A woman passed by with a net bag filled with apples and pears, and Verity wondered *where* she got them as her mouth suddenly watered. The woman stopped as well, and watched.

"Now it'll begin, eh?" she muttered, fully meaning Verity to hear; and Verity said, "I guess so," and the woman then turned and gave Verity a stare that made her shiver. She then walked on, turning once to look at Verity over her shoulder. Verity couldn't tell exactly how the woman felt about the Bee, then *understood* it . . . *smelled* it . . . a complex mixture of fear, excitement, and anticipation.

Verity continued to watch the sky as she hurried down the

street. She turned after a block, to get a better view, and walked down a smaller, less populated street, following the Bee.

She watched the Bee disappear behind a building's edge, then after a moment rise into the sky. The interstices of the building flashed gray, then violet. Verity noticed an open window on about the sixth floor. A young woman leaned out on the sill, stretching upward, searching the sky.

The Bee rose higher, and Verity began to run.

She ran through parks and across narrow cobbled alleys. Her breath came hard and she wished she was Blaze, with the gift of running. Her legs felt like rubber. The Bee stopped at two other buildings, dipping down behind others so that Verity panicked, but it always rose again.

And everywhere she saw people. Sometimes she had to push them aside, and then she heard angry shouts behind her. She ran through what looked like a festival, with bright balloons and a smiling, milling crowd. Then she left them and their happy voices behind and turned down an empty street. Her footsteps pounded in her ears.

Where would it go? What was it getting from the Flowers? she wondered, as sweat slid burning into her eyes. She pounded to a halt in front of an iron gate; above arched a sign: CINCINNATI ZOO- LOGICAL GARDENS.

She watched in wonder as the Bee dipped into the Zoo, some- where behind a jumble of low brick buildings, and vanished. She continued to watch, but it did not re-appear, and then another fol- lowed the first.

The iron gate was locked. Verity shook the bars so hard that the hinges rattled.

The stone wall on both sides was very high, and too smooth for her to get a purchase with her toes, though she ran at it several times and surged toward the top, hoping to be able to grasp the ledge with her fingers and pull herself over. Two stone arches at each side of the main gate also were closed with metal gates.

Panting, she stared through the gate. A small sign said that it didn't open until noon, and that was at least an hour away. She saw a short man pass by inside carrying a bucket; she yelled at him but he ignored her and walked past, down a passageway lined by trees covered by a faint veil of new green. She didn't see a single animal inside, nor hear or smell them either.

Suddenly a boy rushed up to her, wearing plain brown clothing. His face looked odd. She *sensed* a battle of emotions taking place within him, then the turmoil on his face cleared and something clicked for her and all was straight between them.

"I gotta show you something inside," he said. "It's the new jesus. I know you're the one . . . Haze? . . ."

Verity slowly backed away.

The sky was darkening, she noticed. She walked faster, looked over her shoulder, and saw the boy talking to the space where she had stood.

Haze. Haze. New jesus. Hazel . . . *Motes* . . .

"*Wise Blood!*" she shouted, and turned around once again and stood watching the strange boy.

The strange, tortured boy.

She didn't remember the story that well, but it had been one of those that John burned, a real, old book with falling-out pages which the glue no longer held. She must have been ten, and the book had frightened, yet fascinated her. Russ's eyes had lit with a slow smile when she asked him about it—"No, but it was one of my father's favorites."

How Russ must have hated John, if only for a moment, when he saw his parent's library going up in flames. Verity wondered at his control. Verity had taken a run at John and butted her head, hard, right into his stomach, so that he had lost his balance and staggered backward.

A loud thunderclap made her jump, and rain began to spatter the sidewalk. Slate-black clouds looked elastic as they were pulled apart and reassembled by the high winds above, and rain blew through the City in great sheets. Verity, her hair plastered to her head by a deluge of cold rain, turned to look for shelter, and was surprised.

The sun was not out. So why was the green awning of one shop a block away glowing slightly?

She walked closer, cautiously, crossing her arms across her chest tightly and pausing beneath a tree with a few new leaves that did nothing to shelter her. Rain slashed at her face. Yes, the awning really *was* glowing, like quiet neon. Verity crossed the broad, empty boulevard, now thoroughly soaked and shivering, and stood in front of it.

There were thin dark purple lines in it too, arching back toward the building, limned on both sides by glowing white. She stepped beneath it and turned back toward the street.

Wind whipped the trees in the park; their branches flailed wildly. She thought she saw hailstones hitting the puddles in the street and was irrationally relieved that she didn't have to worry about the corn anymore. Then one tore through the awning and hit her cheek.

She heard a voice and turned, her hand against her face.

An old man was holding the door open. A sign suddenly appeared above it: APOTHECARY SHOP, and below it in smaller letters, ASSEMBLERS UNLIMITED.

He was her height, thin, and had a short white beard.

"Come inside," he said, motioning to her. He tilted his head and smiled, and his brown eyes looked very sweet for a moment, as if some happy energy was emanating from them, and his chest expanded with a deep breath.

Several hailstones shredded part of the awning next to Verity, and the man reached out gently, took her wrist, brought her inside. Then he turned and propped the door open so that the sluicing sound filled the air and the silver sheets of falling water seemed brightness itself. Verity choked as she saw the holes left by the hailstones mend themselves. She turned away and looked into the dark building as her eyes adjusted.

"There," he said. "You're cold. You're my first customer of the spring." He laughed, a fuzzy sound deep in his chest, though his face looked sad. "To tell you the truth, now that I think of it, you're my first customer for several cycles." He blinked rapidly several times, then shrugged. "Been kind of deserted around these parts, for some reason. And the ones that did come by seemed unpleasant, you know, and I didn't even bother to open for them at all even when they banged and hollered. I'll get you a blanket or something. Don't go away now."

She watched him vanish into the back of the store.

The shop was a long, dark corridor, perhaps thirty feet wide and twice as deep, lined on both sides with shelves that ran to the ceiling, and rolling ladders on each side.

There was an ornate counter next to her; she rested her hand on it and was fairly sure she felt real wood.

Gaslights (but remember India's house, she told herself, which did not seem nan at first but really was) gently lit rows of small vials.

It looked as if there must be thousands. They glimmered in the faint light like Christmas.

She took a step down the wide floorboards, then another. Moving behind the counter, she stopped next to one of the lights.

Each vial had a vertical holographic strip embedded in the material of the vial, with a lot of multicolored short bars of varying intensity, about a quarter inch wide. Below each was a circle. Presumably some readable label. She reached and took one down.

There was nothing in the circle.

She twisted the vial open and looked inside.

Small golden pellets.

She recognized bee pollen.

She licked her finger, touched the pellets, and sucked them off her finger. Bland.

Then, on the counter, she noticed a palmscreen, with an outline for a hand. She stood on the footprints which suddenly glowed on the floor between a break in the counter and put her hand on the screen, then blinked in the sudden, sharp light that sluiced down from the ceiling, which did not light the room but just her hand and clothing.

Because the light was dim, she immediately noticed when the tiny circle on one of the thousands of vials, several tiers above her head and six feet to her right, lit.

Startled, she removed her hand. The circle went dark.

She palmed the screen again, and the same vial lit, a brilliant green dot. She turned and looked at the rows behind her. Dark, all dark.

She stepped behind the counter and went for the ladder. It was heavier than she thought it would be, even with the rollers. She leaned into it, pushed it to the approximate spot, and climbed up—

So many! All dark now. She would have to climb down, palm it again, try to remember *exactly*—

Footsteps.

Trembling, she backed down the ladder and was rushing unavoidably through the break in the counter with the footprints on the floor just as the old man came back through the doorway, carrying a towel. He stopped short, staring at her.

"My God," he said.

"What?" she asked, glancing at the open door.

He didn't say anything. He handed her the thick yellow towel he was holding. She hesitated, wondering if she should just run, but she wanted that vial. She was probably just as strong as this old man. So what are you going to do, Verity? Knock him down? Why don't you just *ask?*

"Never thought I'd see the day," he said.

"What are you talking about?" Did his eyes have a strange gleam?

"I can see, you know," he said. "My eyes aren't bad for an old man."

"I'm sorry," she said, "I just wondered . . ."

He turned, walked behind the counter, and started moving up the row toward the back, tapping the side of his head with one finger at intervals. He looked back at her. Several times. "Step back over on those footprints, if you please. That's it. Oh, come now, I don't bite."

She had a clear path to the door. Why not. She stepped back onto the footprints, and this time noticed a thin shoot of colored light dancing to her right, a spectrum so intense it looked almost solid.

The vial was lit again. She stepped left and it went dark. She looked at her palm, puzzled. What kind of information was the shop getting from her body?

Though the vial was no longer lit, the old man reached for it unerringly, and Verity held her breath as it looked as if he might fall. But he grasped the ladder with one hand and the vial with the other. He glanced back at her, then at the vial, nodded, and climbed down.

He walked over to her and held it out.

"There," he said. "Take it. I've been in business a long time. A very long time. Never thought I'd have a use for this scan. Thought it just a legend, you see." His face looked more frail, for a moment, a bit like Evangeline's once she had the plague, and his eyes had that wild look like hers.

She looked at the vial, then back at him.

"Don't say where you got it," he said, "and keep it all for yourself. It's been waiting just for you." He sounded more brisk, more businesslike now. "Take it just a teaspoon at a time. You'll know when you need more. It will tell you. But it takes time to work. With this . . . I'm not exactly sure how long."

"What is it?" she asked.

"Ah—of course. Perhaps you wouldn't necessarily know. Activators. Specially made for you. Most of what I have in here works on a broad spectrum (he grinned) of people, though each

one has to be checked out to ensure compatibility. But you are
. . . unique.''

No doubt, thought Verity, not really liking the sound of that.
''What does it activate?''

''Yourself,'' he said. ''They'll focus everything. It's like learning to use a new sense.'' He rubbed the side of his face with his
hand. ''Most people from the outside have a snowball's chance in
hell of getting the hang of anything in our fair Queen City,'' he
said, his voice whispery and filled with a sort of humorous mull-
ing undertone. ''If they do get out, they get out crazed and raving
and never wish to return. They say that if a child blind from birth
has sight restored after a certain age that they can never learn to
make sense of the information. It's kind of like that. But the information is in you. Or should be. If it's not,'' he said, ''I do apologize, because this will make you absolutely insane.''

This sounded like nonsense to her, yet she didn't want to say
so to the man's face. And the bottle . . . *interested* her.

''I . . . I can't pay,'' she said, feeling that perhaps this place of
real wood and odd vials was different from the rest of the City, or
that now that it was all waking up, things might be different.
There was a feeling of oldness here, a feeling of deep time, as if
things had not been rearranged here.

''My dear,'' he said, and his voice was grave and respectful, ''I
never thought I'd see you at all. You have no idea how old I am.
They don't take me back, like they take the others back, no, siree. I
got my ways around that.'' Verity wondered. Could parts of the
City be immune to the surge? Could whatever it was that made
the decision to form the Seam function elsewhere, inside, too?

He waved vaguely at all the vials. ''No need to pay. Now go,''
he said, glancing around. ''Before the rain stops and they see you
coming out.'' The Bees, she assumed.

''How do you know all this?'' Verity asked. She hadn't wanted
to arouse Jane's suspicions, but maybe she should stop being so
cautious. She was in a hurry, after all. If this man and this place
did remain unchanged, perhaps he knew some answers.

He looked surprised, then a touch indignant. ''It's my job,'' he
said. He frowned, then looked at her doubtfully. ''Maybe you're
not the right one.'' He glanced up at the light again, and said, as if
speaking to himself, ''Would *she* ask? Wouldn't she *know*?'' He
squinted once again at Verity and at the narrow beam coming
from the ceiling. ''Still, your pheromonal scan indicates . . .''

He sighed, folded his arms across his chest, and shook his head slowly, looking past her out the window. "Maybe the mechanism is old. It's all too old. Don't care what they say about how wonderful and self-maintaining all this is supposed to be. Things do get old." His voice was tinged with resignation and despair as he maundered. "Just a hopeful old man, that's all. I *think* I'm the same, but how would I really know? It could all change in my sleep, and hell, I wouldn't know. Could just be a trick. Can't let it fall into the wrong hands. Must save it for *her*—"

He raised his head, looked at Verity, and extended his hand. "Here. Give it back then, imposter, and don't try coming here again!" Verity was surprised to hear his voice filled with menace.

As Verity hesitated, he snatched the vial.

Her doubts left her.

She grasped one end of the small, slippery vial, but he held on astonishingly tight for such an old man, and started kicking her shins. "Help!" he yelled. "Robbery!"

She managed to pry it from his hands. The bells on the door jangled as it slammed behind her. She ran down the block as fast as she could, slipping once on the wet sidewalk, then dashed across the street. His indignant cries faded as she turned the corner and ran through the wet, sparkling, sunwashed streets.

There may be two or three
or four steps, according to
the genius of each, but for
every seeing soul there are
two absorbing facts—
I, and the abyss.

—Emerson

There is a third:
Enlivenment.

—Durancy

4

○ ○ ◇

In the Silent Regions of the Gene

Twenty-one

◇◇◇◇◇◇◇◇◇⬡◇◇◇◇◇◇◇

Getting to Know You

In a station of the metro, said a male voice, *The apparition of these faces in the crowd; petals on a wet, black bough.*

And another voice cut across the first and told her not to strut around in the open, bold through the green parks of early spring, and *nonsense,* she said back, *nonsense nonsense nonsense.*

And she walked through the City like she had a million times before. A *million* times. Open. They could see her Patterns from above, and it did not matter to her.

Yes, like before, the voice said, and then they pack you away once more.

Not this time, she thought. *Not this time.*

Who had designed each sparkle of sidewalk? She had! Who had programmed each nuance of joy and pain? She had!

Who put that house there, and who that window?

Who—

Her breath caught in her chest, and blackness and sorrow blossomed from a narrow band within her and then shimmered and spread over the lovely, eternal cityscape so that it was like a barely remembered dream of happiness.

Someone's idea, now shattered, of Heaven.

Who had bent in pain like this and cried? And for how many hours, how many months, how many years? Heart bursting for death after death after death when perfection was all that was planned.

No, Heaven had not been reached. Not here.

Verity felt a weird twist in her mind, almost as if it and vision were a colorful patterned fabric suddenly crumpled by a hand reeling it quickly away from her with a forceful, irresistible, sickening twist. She felt herself falling, felt something as her cheek and palms were torn by concrete, but even that was a distant sensation compared to where she suddenly was.

A number flashed through her mind first, like a night train with lit windows.

And then it was all different.

* {AD.212} *IT IS NOT arrogance, not really.

Durancy looks out the rain-streaked window, and knows that it is not.

He has a way of expanding, in small stages. First his boundaries include simply air, an aura close about him. Then the room, the blue and green striped chair, the particles . . . loose their hold on one another, and dance, he *sees* them dance, and exchange energy with greetings and enormous respect.

Yes this does happen, yes it does, he thinks, staring hard out the window until the grim gray grainy City fills with a billion nuances of thought which he can feel (you are crazy, Abe, crazy, my boy, so he soon learns to tell no one of this, when small. And schizophrenics are slow at thinking, and he is quick like lightning, quick yes I say again like light) and he *does* exchange energy with time and all of the spheres of time, each instant filled with jostling spheres that form and inform matter so he understands its root its source its very air—

"*Abe!*"

How many times—

He stills his trembling hands and turns and forces a smile. "Hello, Millie." His student. His lover. His child, almost. "What's up? Ah, my dear one, don't be afraid. I've put you in here too! You'll be back. We'll both be back *here.* And we won't have to go through those horrible times that we hated this time. *Whatever* they were. The hell with the Puritans! Things will just get *better* and *better* and *better.*"

Why not?

She's heard it before but it's clear now that she never believed him, that she like so many others thought Cincinnati would escape the fate of other Cities caught in the Information Wars (and we *will*, we *will* he thinks exultantly and beautifully too so changed by all that's happened in his strange life) but now she is completely terrified.

He opens his arms and she rushes to them and he holds her close, her head with its smooth, short black hair perfectly centered in that spot in his chest where it all comes from.

"Abe," she says, her voice gasping and dry, "I'm so afraid." Sobs shake her and he holds her close.

"I know," is all he can say, because although it is somewhat his fault and because she will definitely die, as will he, they will also live. He touches the node behind his ear, and where it is hooked in, and knows that even that might be primitive in his next incarnation. He's hoping for DNA storage, like an extra brain, almost . . . things are moving so quickly now, each life like a flash of lightning illuminating a new, bizarre landscape, in this evolution of what Cities were meant to be and he can never escape . . .

But . . . *conversion* . . . He has to admit, he is more rattled at this moment than he thought he would be. More rattled than he ever thought he could be, ever again, after his parents died each so calmly and so horribly . . .

But soon, that memory will be swept away. They will die, but they will also live. Just as he's been telling Millie, soothing her.

Only it is difficult, from this side, to know exactly what that will be like.

"The beauty of the unknown day," he murmurs into her ear. That stray statement, which popped into his head like an errant poem a few years ago, has somehow become his mantra, his litany. For those who centuries before had believed in God, the mystics, it had been God's unknownness, his unknowableness, which held them spellbound, which pulled them on. It was just that holy quality that had infused his quest, his growth toward that which others might think of as death, when what was to come was, put another way, *change*.

There had been horrible darkness, after those two deaths, for a long time, but he had pulled through. And look how beautiful it all was now! Completely beyond what anyone could have even imagined, a few short years ago. Failsafes in place? Though rather dizzy, he checks back in memory: yes. All is well. All manner of things will be well.

Just very, very different.

He sees it below, in the street. A slight sparkle, a wave, a surge, but perhaps he is the same wave and so that's why it stays mostly the same, oscillating in time like such a grand waltz. Only Millie cannot see it, won't turn her head, sobs, cannot . . .

He grasps her tight as he realizes they have only a minute left, as it surges upward and oh, the sun is a lovely glowing point in the west, pink-orange—"*Look*—"

And the future washes through him, bright as sunlight dark as death and then . . .* {**AD.212**} *

Verity pushed herself up from the sidewalk with one arm and felt her chin with the other. Her fingers came away bloody and she laughed wryly and sat up, crosslegged. Her face stung, but just for a moment, then, remembering the night at Billie's, she touched and felt no blood. She reached into her jacket pocket and pulled out the vial. It was still three-quarters full.

She threw it as far as she could.

She looked up and the sleek beautiful buildings slanted away above her.

It sounds an echo in my soul?

No. Not *it* any longer. He.

"Abe Durancy," she said, and pushed herself up. Not Dennis. The other man's name was Abe, not Dennis. She realized that although it had seemed like she had been inside his body, she still had an idea of what he looked like from the outside. Abe looked quite similar to Dennis, but much older and with a long white shock of hair growing on one side of his head. She had not liked being him. He was crazy.

She felt dizzy and sick. She walked across the sidewalk and into the park where delicate pink blossoms studded the tree branches. A warming breeze caused them to bob, and their sweet smell was almost like something Verity could understand in terms of shape, or in terms of Tai Tai's numbers.

She had a lot of information. She sank down on a green bench and pulled her legs up and wrapped her arms around them. Wind from the river blew her hair across her face, and she pulled it around to one side of her neck and held it there.

She could only see a bit of it at a time, as if she were peering through a peephole. That was her limitation. Time.

Well, begin at the beginning. Now that she was herself again she could flip through those memories like she used to flip through picture books in the library.

Abe Durancy's great-grandparents had danced to the Duke Ellington Orchestra when it stopped in Cincinnati on a tour, Duke's private railroad cars with their own generators sitting on a siding so the musicians wouldn't have to endure the humiliation of being turned away at hotels and restaurants. What were the songs the ancient lady remembered, when she came across Duke's autograph one rainy winter afternoon while cleaning the attic with little Abe? "Stompy Jones," that was a lively one. "Let's Fall in Love."

The music swung to and fro in Verity's head, because Abe had taken care of the ancient 78's Grandma handed him, and went downtown to the Cincinnati Museum where they had a place to listen to them, a small booth where the eternally scratched sound came from all around him, and then he asked for whatever else they had . . .

Verity looked up and saw a few Bees scattered here and there in the sky. Ah, how information had become mixed. What were *they* doing with it, those alien creatures whose eyes polarized sunlight; why were they in charge of moving it from building to building, and how did they do it? The Russ construct had said that they were addicted to human emotions—human *stories*, then. Why *were* they packing stories into the pollen baskets on their legs and carrying them to and fro? How had they absorbed so much of what being human was that they craved it?

No, they were not evil. Not any more evil than the smallest child.

They only wanted, just like her, *more*. More information.

Well, now she had it.

She stood in the beautiful green park and looked down the broad avenue that bordered the north side. That looked like a good way to go, as good as any. She felt restless, needed to move and think.

For one afternoon, she would let him bask in the fullness of what he had done.

Then, she'd let him have it!

Where first, Abe?

The Cincinnati Zoo?

She disagreed. No, not this afternoon. Today we shall . . .

Then one side of her vision went white, her knees weakened, and she rushed to a nearby tree and curled between the roots, knowing that, like Blaze's train, it was coming back again and she couldn't stop it.

Twenty-two

◇◇◇◇◇◇◇◇◇◇◇◇◇◇◇◇◇

April in Paris

* {AD.298.1} *Paris . . . so many of them had gone to Paris.

Pound, Stein, Cassat; Man Ray, Charlie Parker, Hemingway, Miller. Even Mark Twain.

Abe agonized over those foreign chunks and how to account for them; how to acknowledge, embed, and use them.

"If only you were Washington, D.C.," he said in a harsh moment and almost felt his City weep—his strong, hardy frontier rivertown. Instantly guilty, he said, "Don't worry, my love. It's not really the Parisian touches we need here, after all. Just a taste, just something that blooms every once in a while, a conjunction of images and atmospheres . . ." and he sifted through *A Movable Feast* once more and got cold oysters, cases of cheap, good wine, and another American, Sylvia Beach.

"Don't worry," he said again, thrilling to the knowledge that the City was an *entity* now; it could *know* and *understand* . . . (ah, let them call him crazy; they would see). "After all," he told her, "you have the Archives, with all those original B. B. King tapes." He was not imagining the way the lights glowed just a touch brighter as he spoke, no, not in the least. He added this overlay to his obsessively endless store of maps. The maps were the basis on which he built his grand edifice of emotion-infused matter.

He could handle blocks of information as if information was a heavy shimmering liquid. He layered and swirled and mixed it, until it coalesced in numbers and specifications as if reflected from some utterly other medium in the back of his mind. Lost in his project, high above the City and all other humans, he had become such a recluse that really, no one knew and no one cared. They were quite happy to have him out of their hair. Had he ranted? He certainly *hoped* he had.

Tears came to his eyes when one day he put the finishing touches on a part of the program, which grew and cross-referenced itself in a stunning way, ready to attach itself to the silent regions of the gene, a reverse RNA that zipped onto the DNA instead of molding itself mirrorlike then peeling away, flinging itself full of directions through the organism. Instead, this stuff cannily sought out places where it could organize, and Abe's hands sometimes felt to him as if they were glowing with some fierce inner energy as he manipulated the biological strands through so many interfaces that he wasn't even sure that what would happen would be anywhere near like what he thought he was doing.

He had been sitting very straight, legs linked in lotus, butt raised by two thin pillows, allowing Paris—not the Paris of Zola or the Paris of Verlaine, but the Paris of Americans, Gershwin and Parker and those who had never come back, like James Baldwin—to take form within the nanobank of architectural images, scents, and sounds. Instantly accessing maps, history, literary references, visual art, and sound, his fingers danced on his biopad and sharpened the swirl to actual seed, to several. He was finally satisfied with a hundred stored Parises, a round number, and then rose.

Just a beginning. It would all multiply, of course. And it was worth any amount of work, after all. It was for *her* . . . He pushed aside the thought of his mother's . . . storage. Because she *wasn't* dead. No!

Tapping the biopad on his interstice panel, he called for the complex mix of Hemingway DNA/pheromones, and allowed them to come on board. Through his fingers, touching the interstice, transdermally. Just Intro, not Deep. Test package, to last several hours only, or to dissipate instantly at any hint of fear or nervousness, which he could well control if he so wished. And he was confident that his core self could never be washed away. It even had an image, so to speak, a sound, or the memory of a sound, as if the self hearing that sound was a moment, pure and shimmering and unadulterable forever, the one true thing.

Smiling, looking out the window as he pulled on his tweed overcoat, he watched his beloved purple Iris bob gently in the wind from off the Indiana plains. Work for the day was done; the sky blended shades of deep pink, orange, and a swiftly lowering serge of intense dark gray.

He shifted to Bee-vision, and Iris glowed with ultraviolet splendor, a deep, powerful blue-purple with a black line that called him into the Flower's heart. Everything was washed with the blueness, though he still retained the red range, unlike real bees.

He stepped out into the vactube and rushed down to the street.

He wasn't sure if it would work. It's only half a block he told himself nervously as he moved swiftly beneath the glittering lights and stars. Hundreds of people were out at this hour, strolling or biking the boulevards, stopping into neighborhood bars for truly fine German beer, attending plays, going to parties. He wove through the crowds feeling like a beneficent father, expansive, with grand presents hidden in his veins for these people he loved.

Already he was changing. It was miraculous. He felt pulled by some mysterious homing force toward the part of the City he'd earlier targeted, the mere half-block with which he'd toyed.

He couldn't actually tell if the pheromones were effervescing from him as he came closer, but imagined that he could, imagined that he could see them spraying forth from his hands like a new kind of radioactivity and lodging in the receptors in his nose, though really they were meant to lodge in the target he was approaching, and send slow and fast information, timed release as well as instant, to the assemblers waiting there. He was led by parts of the City that lit in special ways, which no one else would notice unless they were using Bee-vision as well.

It was a symbiosis, if it worked. An organic unity with his mind and brain the interface, the consciousness which sensed and would enjoy and savor and live something other than himself, a piece of another's life, more delicious than mere reading, or hearing, or seeing, or touching. Art raised to the nth degree, high, fine sensation that he hoped would explode through him, or, on other days, expand to a slow, full, experiential climax of information.

The people became more sparse, and then he was across the street from it, the place mapped within his cells and yes!—there was the pale green interstice circle, glowing, greeting his hand, which he rushed to place upon it . . .

"Hello, Sylvia," he said, as he opened the door of Shakespeare and Company. "Any mail?"

The young woman with the straight-cut black hair turned and smiled in her kindly way. It always made him feel good to realize that she had such faith in his abilities, as if his fame were something predestined and not something he was struggling every day in the small apartment across from the coal factory to forge into something resembling one true sentence.

"Yes, Ernest, as a matter of fact there is." She bent and looked under the counter and pulled out a thin white envelope.

His heart leaped unreasonably when he saw it, before he even turned it over and saw that it was from the United States; carefully, trying to still the trembling in his fingers, he tore it open.

"They bought my story," he said, tears in his eyes, feeling the surge of accomplishment and a momentary stab of joy that for at least a while he could pay for something instead of relying on Hadley's checks. Maybe he was on the right track after all. People did tell him so.

"They bought it," he said again, and looked up to see Sylvia smiling broadly.

Then suddenly it all reeled away, melted. The beautiful rows of books, the warmly lit store, and worst of all, Sylvia. Sylvia faded as the holo program stopped projecting, right on schedule.

Abe Durancy stood looking at a plain piece of paper.

He leaned against the smooth counter made of nanstuff, which so recently had seemed wooden—which, if things advanced as he thought they could, would someday *be* wood— gasped a few times, and burst into tears.

"It worked!" he shouted, and his sobs veered to ragged laughter and quickly back to tears.

How bizarre it had been; how real. How enjoyable.

But would anyone else like it?

All he could think of was making it last longer the next time.

Yes. He knew everything. Or could, if he wanted to. He could live forever.

He could be *anyone,* and then return to himself, like reading a book only immensely more intense.

Yes. He could be . . . *everyone.** {AD.298.1} *

*   *   *

Everyone.

Verity blinked and stirred on the hard slats of the park bench where she had been sitting.

Durancy's memories had absorbed her vision like a reverie or daydream, only much stronger, a portable and ever-present part of herself.

Now, she looked around, to try and reorient herself.

Huge oak trees towered over her, spreading sparse spring shade. A carpet of green fuzzed through brown dead grass under her feet, and brick paths spread snakelike through banks of nodding, brilliant pink and red chrysanthemums.

She had never left the park.

She was puzzled. Apparently she didn't need a cocoon or anything, not a single prop. It wasn't really happening. It was just . . . a dream . . .

Two children ran yelling through the park, followed by a young woman, and Verity watched them curiously, her mind feeling washed and her vision plumping what she saw and softening it, as if it was all rather fluffy, as if she had overslept and everything was out of sync.

Cheyenne had said that the Bees took children. She wondered if that was true. It was possible, of course. And yet . . .

She reached back and felt the nubs behind her ears. They felt fevered, hot, and she couldn't ever remember having had that sensation before. What were these nubs? How did she get them? Did those gay children have them too?

But she was too drained to get up and see, and besides, they were gone, and the woman sitting next to the hot dog stand was reading a book and all was still with only the sound of the wind in the flowers and trees.

Durancy was like riding a dragon. The glimpses were bright yet fractured. Just as when she rose, washed clean from the learning cocoon at the Dayton Library, she didn't feel as if she could really grasp what she had experienced.

Except that this had come from deep within, called somehow by the pollen. If her memories and thoughts about herself were layered like an onion, then somehow, improbably, and most annoyingly, she realized that *he* was at the core, deeper than she had ever gone before.

She shuddered and stood up. The girl at the refreshment stand glanced up from her book, then looked down again. A couple strolled into the park and walked over to the stand. As the girl stood and fixed their hot dogs, they briefly kissed.

Something burned in Verity's chest as she watched them.

She was different than Durancy. Much different. She did not love this City. She hated it. The City was keeping her from Blaze.

She turned and walked out of the park very quickly.

But once on the sidewalk, she stopped. Turned around.

Stop this, she thought, as she searched with her eyes for a bright glimmer of glass. You don't need that stuff.

Once she had eaten an entire cake that Blaze had left out to cool. She just hadn't been able to stop. This reminded her of the cake.

Finally, just when she was beginning to feel weirdly anxious as she crisscrossed the lawn carefully, she saw it.

The small vial of Assemblers. The vial filled with a person. Kind of. Filled with herself, but not-herself. She could not come this far, and throw away the key to mystery. Much as she wanted to. It was just another plague, a very individual plague. She stood over it, staring at it, as it lay in the grass, wanting still to walk away.

She bent and swooped it up. Looked at it.

Opened it.

There were only about three doses left, according to what the old man in the shop had told her.

She looked out toward the river, visible through gaps in the buildings.

This guy Abe knew everything. He was in control. If she knew what *he* knew, she could undoubtedly save Blaze.

Not to mention the whole blinking lot of them here in the City. Something *you* never thought of, she told him, as if he were someone alive, someone who could actually hear what she was thinking. But that was the problem. *He* couldn't be modified by *her*. It was not at all fair. But what was?

She tilted the vial over her mouth. Hesitated.

She remembered looking out her window, down at Blaze, and John, and Russ, the rest of them hanging back, afraid, and then John raising the rifle—

The pollen—but it's *not* pollen, Verity, at least not any pollen you've ever seen before—was pale gold in the sun for a second before she poured it into her mouth.

It was somewhat bitter, and difficult to swallow. She walked over to the hot dog stand; the young woman barely looked up from her book and handed Verity a drink in a can with which she washed down the rest. She trembled a bit when, after the last drop was gone, the can turned to glittering dust that fell with a sparkle from the space between her fingers and opposing thumb and then seemed to be absorbed by the new grass.

Verity shrugged and sat down to wait. The ground was damp. Between the soaring pastel buildings—although on the next block she caught glimpses of an older, stone-gray Cincinnati—the river flashed green and white.

The first thing that happened was a realization that she had the master maps inside her, but that she could not fully access them until a certain crucial chemical pathway in her brain was laid in—just as young children cannot walk until certain biological processes occurred.

And that the laying in of pathways, among other things, was what had been happening in the Dayton Library.

Afraid that movement would jar the progress of her thoughts, which felt as delicate as Russ's ancient game of pick-up-sticks, where withdrawing the wrong stick would bring the whole thing tumbling down, Verity stared at the trees, the drink stand, the shimmering buildings; smelled popcorn and hot dogs; felt the soft new grass beneath her hands, as if all these sensorial stimuli were somehow responsible for converging within her and creating this single point of revelation. Yet she knew that they were not, that it was the pollen in the vial at work, the nanstuff, surging through her mind with lightning speed, *focusing* her, as the old man had said. Or if not exactly *her*, then something inside her, as if all the parts of a vast machine were there and it was being assembled at a very fast speed and fitfully beginning to function.

Verity jumped up, excited, astounded, her lethargy vanished. It was like the sun shining on the water, this realization. She was *supposed* to have had, ideally, several more sessions at the library cocoon, at yearly intervals—

But that still did not answer the question burning in her heart: *Who am I? What am I? Who did this to me?*

She was beginning to sweat and tremble, and felt nauseous. She looked around, feeling unsteady, to see if there was a more sheltered place nearby.

Then everything paled, as if the world was washed of color.

Twenty-three

○○○○○○○○○○○○○○○○○○

White Coral Bells

* {AD.5.326} *HER ROOM was always a wonderland of scent.

Her delicate, pale dresses draped the tops of chairs; hats of all description perched on forms, were stacked in boxes, and layered on the staggered stems of the hatstand and the row of hooks his father had installed one afternoon, the drill making that burnt-wood scent as the pale curls of wainscotting dropped to the floor. She was always wearing hats.

Still poised on the dressing room's threshold, Abe looked each way, but there was no one in the long hall, and the smells from below, wafting up from the kitchen through the vent said peach pie and roast beef, but not until later.

Still, she would be busy.

He walked inside his mother's dressing room and sat down at the table.

In the round mirror he saw himself, a pale boy (you need to get out more and play with the other boys, she would scold, and he would nod, turn the page, and sink deeper into his chair) with light brown hair. Green eyes not so brilliant; often a bit hazel, in fact. Lips thin, nose too long in a too-long face. And why shouldn't he read; the house was full of books, real old books, and the B.E.—the book environment—too, and mother when she wasn't gardening beneath her broad straw hat or teaching at the University was reading too, reading, reading, as if she were thirsty and must ever drink. He knew that feeling. Lately the books he read were about cities, and architecture. Already this month he'd read *The Universe of Cities* and *Paris Past and Future*, letting them swirl and coalesce inside his mind, sparking visions of an utterly new City just out of reach.

He reached over and touched a small vial shaped like a swan, of blue glass amid the clutter of the hair things she used on her long blond hair—wavy elastic cloths and various clips. A bright purple scarf that she often wove through an involuted braid lay carelessly draped over one corner of the table.

He picked up the swan, lifted the glass stopper, and touched the cool, round, rough tip to his nose.

It smelled like her, and she smelled sweet, like lilies of the valley.

He hadn't heard her footsteps so it was a surprise when she appeared in the doorway, then walked in with a swish and swirl of full skirt and bent over and put her arms around his shoulders. She hugged him briefly and rested her chin lightly on the top of his head, smiling at him in the mirror.

Put a little of that on my wrist, she said, her brown eyes smiling at him, strong and merry and knowing as usual, so he put the stopper back in the swan, tilted it upside down and then back up, pulled the stopper, and touched it to her wrist, which she turned toward the mirror for him. She shook him just a bit and kissed the top of his head.

Come then, at least come out and work in the garden with me if you won't go to the pool with Teddy. That's what he wanted this morning when he stopped by, didn't he?

Abe shrugged. He got tired of Teddy and his daring-games. Nothing was ever finished. There had to be a new danger to brave, a higher branch to jump from, a steeper hill to coast down on the bike no feet no hands. I'm reading *Moby-Dick*, he said, and some book about Paris. Besides, I want to see Rosie, but they went to the lake for vacation. She hid something for me again, though. I just found another clue in the garden this morning.

Her eyes darkened for just an instant. That Rose is too flirty; she's older than you, and she should know better.

Then she smiled again, dispelling the sudden anxiety he did not understand. Weed the lettuce with me, she said, and then walk over to the market with me and we'll buy some sausage, and then your father will be home and we'll eat and then you can read. She reached up and grabbed a brown felt Stetson, tilted it over one eye, and winked at him in the mirror.

By then I'll have to go to bed, he said.

Don't think I don't know about your lightstick, she said.

He laughed, relieved that she knew about his secret and didn't care, so he said, all right, let's go.

They hurried down the steps and out into the sunlight at the end of the long dark hall.

Every time he did it he remembered some new detail.

Are you remembering, he asked himself, or are you inventing?

He looked back at his screen, balancing the metapheromone equation, adding a brief fillip based on the holographic chemistry of natural lily of the valley scent that hovered next to him.

He pushed the button to save the last memory, then the air was infused with the new version. And he would see how they differed. It was long, tedious work. But he was on to something. Really on to something.

Excitement fueled him as he returned once again to that day.

This time, her hair was brown . . .* {AD.5.326} *

Twenty-four

◇◇◇◇◇◇◇◇◇◇◇◇◇◇◇◇◇

In the Night Kitchen

Verity woke well into evening, no longer curled between tree roots but lying on a hard bench once again. The sky was intense indigo, with one strong serene star rising. The air was chilly, but when she sat up a light blanket fell from her which someone must have draped over her after carrying her here. Dennis, no doubt.

She flung the blanket aside as she sat up. Below, Roebling's bridge was just beginning to light up, and the dark river reflected shimmering strands. She dropped her aching head to her hands for a moment.

What next?

Behind the darkness of her closed eyes, thoughts were pictures. The life of Durancy—fitful spats now of color and pain—came from golden pollen. Pollen came from bees.

Or Bees.

And the Bees seemed to converge at the Zoo.

She lifted her head abruptly, stared out at the city. The dark park rustled; the breeze touched her face, bringing the scents of early spring.

No. She couldn't go there. The Bees had their guards, of course they must, waiting to detect foreign intruders. She might be killed.

The next picture was Blaze, lying on the ground, covered with blood, next to Cairo, who looked worse.

Tears rose in her eyes, but she stood. *Where does the real power lie?* was a question that had surfaced in her mind, between bouts of Durancy, and to find that, one must go toward that which seems the center of things. She trembled, and tried to push back fear.

At that center, perhaps she would know how to save Blaze. *That* was the information she needed. Not all this other nonsense. Durancy didn't want to help her. He only wanted to help himself, of that she was sure, yet she had no real idea of what his problem was, or how to help him. Besides, she thought, as she straightened her clothes, she wasn't at all sure that she wanted to help him anyway. Help him do what? Why?

The wind off the river swept her hair forward as it pushed on her from the southeast, smelling clean and of Kentucky forest. She began to sweat within her jacket as she climbed the hills, hands in her pockets, but with surprise noticed that she was not tired. The ache in her head was gone. She was—*exhilarated,* as if energy was pouring into her from some new source.

Verity had hoped that the assemblers were finished, but as she turned a corner a new sort of . . . *map,* she supposed you could call it, some kind of graph . . . told her that the nan devices were merely doing some internal adjusting. This was just a lull. She walked faster. She had to take advantage of it.

She should be hungry, since she hadn't eaten in such a long time. But if she was, it didn't register, even though it was quite a long walk, away from the central part of the City, north, toward Edgetown. It would take, one map said, forty-five minutes.

She felt invigorated by the half-moon, the chill, damp air, her complete enclosed aloneness, the silence of the streets punctuated only by the soft sound of her boots on the pavement. Streetlights lit a block ahead of her, blinked out a block behind. She felt, oddly, that she might even be happy, were Cairo at her side. Where was she? Still in Sphere's presto-change-o bin in the train station? Eaten by the sheets? Changed into . . . who knows, a human? She would make a good one! Verity remembered the children at the school and realized: the Shakers had probably been right to be suspicious of Cairo. If the metapheromones could be as precise as that teacher had said, that must be how she had sensed Cairo's pictures—Cairo's DNA had been altered. Or maybe not hers, maybe that of a distant ancestor.

Verity climbed a final hill and stopped.

She was back on Erchenbrecher Street. The Zoo was in front of her, the walls looking like a fortress in the darkness. She found the entrance once again. Though she had been here only this morning, it seemed as if she had been utterly changed by the day, so changed that she might now be in another century altogether.

The guardhouse was the only way into the Zoo, the Cincinnati Zoological Gardens, as the letters spiderwebbed between the rainbow arch of two arcs above the locked gate identified the place, lights coming on and illuminating it as she came close. She brushed the stones of the wall with her fingers: they were damp, and too slick for her to climb even had they been dry.

She hesitated on the empty street and watched lights flash along the ruined bridges. In her mind, those singleminded revelers seemed the least human of all the bizarre creatures in this wild, sad City.

But now it was very dark; even the glow of the buildings was damped and dull within the interstices: did bacteria doze, she wondered? She looked around again, here where the roar of the river seemed ever-present even when she thought she must be too far away to hear it, but the falls were huge and deep and wide and that was what that sound was, and not the snoring hum of Bees. She realized that the falls were quite at odds with Durancy's memories and smiled, pleased. He—the original Durancy—was pre-earthquake. She knew that. She felt as if she were being drawn back in time by him, through the later, outer rings into the central core.

She already knew that place was very sad.

She wiped sweat from her forehead. Reluctance tangled her nerves, giving her the message to leave, and to leave quickly. She was afraid of what lay ahead. She looked out at the City, trying to steady herself, feeling as if *someone, something* was pleading with her to go ahead. Her memories of Blaze? Or something more immediate?

Below was the City which Durancy, that monster within her, loved, the City he'd *created*. Her back against the stones whose natural-looking faces belied their diamond smoothness, she sank down and drew her knees to her chin, linked her hands, and watched it.

Matrices of light blinked on and off throughout the City in

what seemed to be a gently random display that she knew now occurred at night. She loved to watch. The light seemed to flow from one part of the City to the next.

An old memory told her that this was just a cruel fraction of the preconversion City. That the failsafes had *not* failed. Because the Seam contained this static strangeness, this odd repeating magic, this exhilarating Enlivenment, this eternal life. For Durancy lived within her, did he not? The dancing, juice-swigging woman at the party on the roof had said as much: "It is the Infinite!" She, and all of them, lived within the City of his creation.

Mother Ann, she thought, rising and dusting off her pants, would have thoroughly envied Durancy.

One of the dark arches that nestled on the side of the main gate looked open.

Had it been before?

She bolted a few steps, then forced herself to stop.

Taking a deep breath, she searched for a pebble in the light, which gave even the curb a long and menacing shadow, and found none, no fragment of broken pavement to throw into the empty arch and test its reaction.

She pulled off her emerald ring and threw it inside the open arch of the guardhouse instead. It clattered and the narrow place lit up.

She saw that there was truly no barrier. The gate on the other side of the dark arch stood open. She shivered. She could walk right in. Who knew she was coming, and why did they want her inside? Or could it be that the City *had* to open to her now, no matter how reluctant it might be? Durancy had repeatedly envisioned the City as a knowing entity. Considering how often her own impulses seemed at odds with one another, an entity this large could not help being confused, could it? she wondered with some amusement.

She knew of no other way, though, to learn the things she wanted to learn. So far, the assemblers in her own mind had only shown her one selfish man's needs and dreams. She did not know if they had anything to reveal beyond the edges of Durancy's being.

Feeling quite stupid for not seeking out lightsticks from one of the empty stores, and with an outward boldness she did not really feel, Verity stepped inside, grabbing her ring and slipping it back on her finger as she emerged inside the Zoo.

Enlivenment was powerful here. It seemed stronger in some parts of the City than others, as if the slight vagrant charges of dismantled molecules were zinging and singing through the air, through her, the way the negative ionization of the air before a thunderstorm felt. She rather liked feeling alert and sharp, and then she was suddenly truly bold, quite bold indeed, as if the very air was imbued with courage.

She left the pagodalike entrance, walking with long slow steps.

Pale lights lit gently as she walked past eerie, empty cages. The bars cast long shadows across the damp cement. This Zoo, she knew, like so much in Cincinnati, was an older version of itself. It was not the state-of-the-art genebank the Zoo had become just before the conversions. At one time this had been a model Zoo, and then, when real, unpatented animals had become very rare, a place with top international security. The picturing animals like Cairo had lived here, only new and more sophisticated, as yet undamaged by DNA's division among unpicturing old-style beasts, pure and practicing their new and lovely languages.

Perhaps, during the quake, when it was all so wild, some real animals had escaped.

Sure, Verity, escaped where? How long would an elephant live in the woods around Franklin? Or maybe—she smiled at the vision—they all swam the river to the Kentucky forests, eh, all in one group—giraffes, wolves, lions, bears, making for the wilderness. No humans to save them this time.

Her steps became less cautious. She was alone here. Because it was chillier than it had been during the day, she snapped the collar of the thin jacket she was wearing.

Then she turned the corner and saw it.

It was like the Parthenon in the encyclopedia. Isosceles triangle above the massive columns of white marble. Lines and angles saying something true and mathematical about proportion and weight and mass. Tall columns framed an open place which ended suddenly, and there were doors twenty feet high; Verity was going to walk up the steps slowly, cautiously, but found herself running and her chest exploding with odd joy.

What are you hoping, she asked herself, because this was *hope* blossoming in her. She stopped a few steps from the top and turned to look out over the empty zoo and the blacklace branches in the faint moonlight.

Blaze. This reminded her of Blaze, and the Dayton library.

She sank down on the steps, frightened.

Already, she was not herself, or more than herself, or other than herself. Though she always craved whatever had happened at the library, even though she couldn't remember it, she now saw how terrible it was to have parts of yourself you knew nothing of.

What was happening to Blaze? Was *anything* better than *nothing*? What *could* she want for him, if she could choose? She was no longer the same as she had been, and would never be that way again. It was all very frightening and painful. She wanted to toss all this newness away.

But you can't, she told herself. Remember? Blaze was killed. He was truly and entirely dead. That's why you're here. He is still dead, or close to it.

Think about being alive, for a moment, Verity. You look out. You sense things. All your senses reach and consume, or maybe they just sit and wait for the signal to hit, I don't know. But you are the receiver and then it all turns to something called "you" inside. And you act, you decide, you love you play you hope you cry. It all turns to these emotions, nothing would get done without emotions. Who would care? Even mathematics gave humans some sort of feeling, like Tai Tai's endless numbers, some sort of satisfaction, some resonance with pure being.

And Blaze *is* alive. As alive as Russ's Alyssa, which is to say, not-dead. But not alive as you would like him to be, eh? Have you got a better idea? she asked herself. She swallowed hard.

"So *make* him live," she told herself, and stood.

She pulled on the knob, and of course it was not locked; no one but a maniac would ignore the frieze of Bees embedded in the metal nan, and the large cross-section of the Bee-eye like a flower above the door, lit with shimmering pale color now that she had opened that door and a voice said welcome and like so many of the other voices she heard and things she saw now she did not know whether it came from within or without.

In the beginning, on the first floor, was a Museum of the Bees.

This was for visitors, she realized. It would reveal no secrets, and yet she traveled around the entire square, her nanboots quiet on the soft floor.

Here were photomicrographs of pheromones, and the meta-pheromones that *changed* humans, and information on how the receptors worked. The seven hundred floral scents were here, schematically, and those were the simple ones, and then there were all the human pheromones and all the artificial pheromones and the new receptors City humans had, gene splices that enabled them to live optimally in the Flower Cities, for which the original owners had paid a great deal. The DNA helix was referred to as the Stairway to Heaven. Flowery terms for a flowery people. Here were holographic simulations of how the Bee-brain functioned, and she came to the one that explained the Bee-human symbiosis in a measured female voice. She could see every one of these marvels in many different modes. She preferred primitive holographic schematics, understanding as she absorbed them that each person who entered the museum, each person who lived, had an optimal learning style as individual as their DNA. That, of course, could be modified as well. . . .

"Human limbic tissue is integrated into the brain structure of every Bee. A cross-pollination, as it were. This gives them the necessary incentive for the work they must do, and binds them to the City, to humans. In this way they can carry complex emotional information from place to place in the City, information that even the nancomputers cannot translate with full flavor. Biological being to biological being; no more imperfect cyborg go-betweens. This is the great breakthrough of the Bees. They can transmit a new dimension of information dense and individual and vital to the essence of human communication . . . that which cannot be reduced to binary operations—at least not in any reasonable sort of human time frame."

Verity wondered if this had been recently updated. She did not feel as if she was living among beings possessed of a reasonable sort of human time frame.

The display went dark, and Verity whirled, half-expecting to see a dark figure in the shadows, but she saw, and sensed, nothing.

She felt like shouting "Where are you?" but bit her tongue.

Standing as tall as she could and walking with slow dignity, she continued down the hallway.

And then, startling her with its ferocity and suddenness, a map lit in her mind; she turned to the right in a single sharp step and walked through the wall, but it was not a wall.

The diaphanous sheet split and clung to her as she passed, not stickily but snugly. She turned, and the hexagonal-shaped amber skin, a bit taller than her, had healed completely, with no sign of her passing.

She was in the Hive.

In wonder, she forgot her fear. A powerful sweet-sour smell infused the air, and she was stunned by what she saw in the pale green phosphorescent light which limned each hexagon. Looking upward, she could not see the top of the narrow corridor of comb in which she stood. The angle was too tiny, and straight above was darkness. Each hexagonal opening was about three feet across.

She walked along the lower row and tried to peer inside.

A dim cap of milky wax lidded each end. Growing ever more excited, she wished she had some sort of strong light to illuminate whatever was inside, someone to babble to, exclaim with. At the end of the row, which was about a hundred feet long, she paused and turned.

It was very odd.

She had not felt this in so very long.

It was a Dance.

The soft floor in front of her, which suddenly opened up at the end of the corridor of hexagons, was, she realized, worn with many dances, many Bee dances. There was a platform in every honeybee hive where honeybees danced and with each movement conveyed information which their sisters felt as well, as they swarmed over the dancer. The dances advertised the precise location of food in a language the other honeybees could understand; once they felt the dance they knew the distance and direction, were able to fly to the precise spot where nectar had been found.

And what food were the dances that took place here advertising? she wondered. Each dance was an argument, a precise persuasion.

The Dance that Verity felt like doing now was like the cocoon, in its quality of bliss, and even more like, she realized, the plain and constant bliss of Meetings, of a thousand Meetings, and the food she had been advertising at Shaker Hill had been a type of heaven, the heaven within every human brain, which could be reached through kinesis, through particular and repeated motion, sacred, movement as prayer, and she was moving and now the food was simply pure light, and memories of Blaze, of his arms around her one night in the snow when they had been out sledding and the moon was full and they were so very happy with

Bear Creek rushing along beside them. Her face was wet with tears which she ignored.

But it is not only that, she thought, as she allowed the Dance, the movement flowing through her in an odd rhythm so much more pure and focussed and *real* than the dandelion dance of the woman at the party.

This Dance was a message, a message to perhaps just her own cells, a communication within her where information could flow and flower, and it unfolded with the precision of a map, and then she had danced through several rows and she did not know how much time had passed and the Dance was over and she saw . . .

That she bowed at the hexagon of the Virgin Queen.

Verity could sense that this was she, this most powerful of beings, save for the old Queen who may have died over the winter; Verity wondered where *she* was.

At any rate, she had not died, Verity surmised, not in this climate-controlled hive. But what exactly was this creature inside the cell before her? How *conscious* was she?

It was an important question. She would not like Verity being here.

In a hive of regular honeybees, the old queen generally led a swarm when conditions warranted, leaving one or more new queens, already grown within their cells, to awaken. Each new queen who emerged had a choice: lead another swarm, or stay and be queen of the hive in which she was born.

If conditions were right for her to stay—if the Hive was not overcrowded—then the emerged queen called out to the embryo queens with a series of short and long buzzes. The embryos recognized the pattern and replied, revealing their location.

Then, if the queen wished, when they replied, she found and destroyed them. Before they were ever truly born. Before they emerged. The old queen could do this as well, if she did not wish to lead a new swarm. This was her action if she wished to remain with the old hive.

If, however, she wished to lead a new swarm, she would allow the next queen to emerge unharmed, so that the bees left behind would have a leader.

This new Queen before Verity had the same choice to make, even before coming out of her cell. Lead another swarm, or stay and kill my potential rival? She made it by calculating her strength and sampling, without even emerging, the information from the outside world the scouts had brought back to the Hive. Is there a good place for us elsewhere? Are there too many Bees to stay here? She could lead a swarm and be Queen of a new, uncertain Hive or, if the population of the present Hive was low enough, she could stay, and kill her sister backup Queens, who, like her, were waiting to see if they would be used, or wait, or die . . .

When humans had bid the Bees, back when the Flower Cities were new and wholly functional, the Bees had been in service through the winter, of course. But when the City malfunctioned, for whatever reason—the Information Wars, the earthquake, or an unfortunate and unforeseen combination of cataclysms—Bees had reverted to their cell's history and slept during the winter. And sometimes they even swarmed, Verity realized, or tried to, moved by the ancient impulse to split the Hive so that both halves could grow. Scouts went out to find a new, optimal location for a Hive, returned and danced the location. Perhaps the Bee that had dashed itself into the New Ohio River had been a scout Bee, despairing of finding such a wonderful new Hive as this! And then had somehow recognized Verity, and flashed those horrible pictures into her mind . . .

Verity stared at the cell before her. Curious, she put out her hand, fingers outstretched, and pressed it to the soft, yielding cap.

She was horrified when she pulled it back at the faint green imprint that shimmered deep within the golden membrane for a moment before fading.

She stared at the cap, wishing that she could somehow retrieve the touch in even some twisted way, as Blaze had been somehow retrieved from death, at least death as they all had known it. Her hand tingled and she was flooded with certainty: the receptors there were now activated. Not only that, but the Hive had taken information from them, from *her*, and she wasn't at all sure what it was or what would be done with it.

Verity looked in wonder at the growing shadowy embryo, which she could now see, as if her eyes had gained the ability to allow more light in this dim enclave. Her own honeybees had changed from pale larvae grubs in just a few days. The transformation was truly miraculous. What directions were injected into them by the food the workers fed them that would trigger that change from grub to fully formed bee? She had been completely and suddenly astonished when it fully dawned on her one day as a little girl looking at their hive what cells could do, and God was all around her, shining in Her enormous splendor, for how could such a thing happen? It was a miracle.

But this, ah, this, was a greater one.

She could only see a dim, shadowy mass. She would not break this cell open. She would not break any of them open, though her mind screamed you must see if they are human and another part of her mind said so what if they are? And if they are, they will die! What does it matter if they *are* human—live stuff from live stuff, a twist of the DNA? Are you going to stop it singlehandedly, now? How?

And do they start as Bees and become humans, or did it go the other way around? Neither, she hoped. But if so? Could they even metamorph from one form to the other? Perhaps when they flew from building to building sucking up emotions the Bees were at their most human. Maybe that was just one stage of their life, one tier, the way honeybees were nurses, guards, scouts, graduating from one cycle to another.

Verity was shaken. You thought you were so smart, you thought you knew so much but you really knew less than nothing, little girl. Nothing at all. Nada, nada, nada.

But nada can be beautiful too, she told the supreme nadaist who lurked in her mind ready to spring, ready to embrace her, ready to fling her though the City, through stories of his own.

Him, she could control.

She shoved him back, far inside, delighting in the momentary conquest.

She took a deep breath. Information had surfaced during her Dance. Precise biochemical pathways had become kinetically stimulated. Movement gave chemical information to the brains of all developing animals, which fed back into a higher level of growth.

You wanted power, she told herself. Now you must use it. To save Blaze.

Still she hesitated.

Then, as if jumping from a high cliff into cold water, she deliberately pressed her hand once more against the warm comb, in a pattern like the buzzes, short and long, and pressed again. A binary code from deep within her surfaced and focussed in motion, and once more her hand danced upon the cellcap.

A new scent filled the air, laden with information that went directly into her brain through her nose and was translated by her mind into knowledge bringing both dread and fierce exhilaration: she was accepted, and she did not know why.

The scent of acceptance was like the Library cocoon, only much more direct. She was surrounded by information; she sank into it as into a book where she did not ever remember herself, or even that she was reading, but only felt that it all was actually happening, and happening to her, and it was, it truly was.

First, sheets of cells slid plump and glowing over one another and unfurled, and new connections lit, like the lights of the City only many superimposed on one another. So this was how learning occurred. It was like watching what was happening within her own brain at a cellular level.

Learning was the elastic expansion of the universe. Learning was true alchemy, where something new and of utmost value was created out of previously inert matter.

There were senses everywhere, extending into new dimensions, but still she knew the core was there, the sturdy girl out on the edge of golden and infinite prairie as if that slightly rolling ancient sea floor, its yellow promise limned with blue like a medieval manuscript was time and time's promise to her, to her as an individual self—

And yet here she was, *connected* . . .

Never single.

Multiple as her new vision, which gave her much more information than her old vision had. All of them living together, as one, but separate.

Oriented to exact time and season not in the old linear way but in a new way radiating outward from her, telling her what was appropriate to the time at a molecular level.

But mostly, mostly it was, ah, color and scent where wings vibrate and hook, and hers do, and she pauses on the edge of a precipice.

She rises, terrified at first, old heart fading to new and vanishing suddenly as buildings below fall away, their beautiful rounded curves shrinking until, from above, they are a field of hugely petaled color, a universe of scent *more* than scent; it is direction and raw imperative.

It seemed as if she had existed forever.

Humans transmitted themselves indirectly through DNA and she suddenly saw the beauty of that distillation. Each new individual could create anew. While personal memories could not really be communicated with their full flavor, storytelling was immensely streamlined, and reverenced the one who experienced it, who added it to their own layers of self so that each person was unique, like a snowflake. When humans read a story, once in one year, and again the next, each time it could be new for them, have different depths, because of the changed perspective of that ingesting human. And for a moment wave upon wave of what it was like to *be* fully human broke through her, radiated from her, caught her in nostalgia, grief, and longing.

She hated being a Bee.

She fought against the impersonal expansion, struggled against the pull of brilliant color and seductive scent, which were only a cruel disguise for eliciting complete obedience.

As if it were day, and she were actually in the air above Cincinnati, she saw the tiny heads of people below in the City. Holos populated the air with a blizzard of brief action, and she saw how they had a rhythm of their own, appearing and vanishing with the regularity of the pulses within the Hive.

And all the while it was like swimming, this ability to hover, to bumble through the air.

She felt the overwhelming need for certain stories, certain precise emotions, as if they were a sort of vitamin the Bees made sure they got. We need an infusion of Jazz, so below in Bucktown a private train car disgorges Duke Ellington wearing spats, and his famous Orchestra. When they play "Stompy Jones," we feed, we bring that Jazz pollen, that most uniquely American thread, back to the Hive like a precious jewel, and update those old pheromones. We constantly test and examine them. We keep them as precise as Information Theory will allow.

Below, the river ate away at Cincinnati, silty olive-green, and the ancient unrepaired bridges spread out like the rays of the sun, chunks of them gone, discontinuous; dashes that leaped toward the other shore, invisible in places like a sinking creek, sections standing stranded in the river's powerful rush.

Kentucky was a deep green bunched-up land, rugged, each ridge edged with deep black shadow stretching ever wider as the planet rolled beneath her.

Panicked at being unconnected, she then wondered: how far could she fly? Where might she go?

Ah, she realized, deep within each cell, she was entirely rooted to the City.

If she left, her memories would fade, and she would be just a true insect.

She needed the humans below to *be,* to actually exist in any humanly conscious sense.

Their music, *their* art, *their* literature and poetry organized the molecules of their brains into a form that was the highest organization of which humans were capable. These powerful emotions gave off very precise pheromones and were she to come closer . . .

She swooped, and dove closer to the Flowers.

Shimmering neon violet drew her and she entered the vast cup of the Flower.

She remained there only seconds gathering pollen, but it seemed as if time assumed an entirely different shape there.

All her senses were bathed in light, but somehow she knew that it was not the light of the rapidly setting sun, but generated by her own nervous system.

And when she was within this light, she wanted nothing else. Ever. It was all complete in the way Mother Ann was supposed to make it complete, the way dancing and praying and living right and never straying, never fucking, never forgetting an ablution, always struggling with some faction of the mind and now . . .

She felt electrified, light, struck through with nan and a sense of being absolutely direct, all-pervasive. The future, the past, the present, assumed new form. Scenes of her former life were accessible to her; she rose from the Flower and drifted for a moment on the wind, wondering what would come next, seeing her own life, and Durancy's, and Hemingway's, and Gertrude Stein's, and Ultra Violet's, and Kerouac's, and then millions of lives, untold lives laboring in gray rainy midcentury Ohio winter year after year, commuting to factories, drinking at the pubs down there on every corner. The City, as if fickly tossing aside an inappropriate hat, then flashed to trendy bistros, and office cubicles, and then it was all washed to white by the wave of nan so that all was new, and utterly incomprehensible. And there was an edge of memory which she *must* access, while she was here—but why? how?

Then she remembered.

Blaze.

But no—there was someone, something else—so urgent—

Struggling against the multiplicity of images, she tried to focus on the NAMS station, fighting a force that was now pulling her back, back into the Hive, more powerful than any hunger she'd ever felt.

No!

She turned in the air, clumsily. It was night, as suddenly as in a dream. *Remember,* she told herself. It had not truly been day before. This was all taking place in some sort of simulated space, the way reading took place in her mind, except that this was vivid, exact, and her actions *meant* and *did* something, the way a written edict could mobilize an army.

Remember—

Blaze himself was inscribed within her, an infinitely complex being as precisely defined by DNA-determined metascents as she. Somewhere in this Enlivened network, in a cocoon, *he* lay, and Cairo, her warm furry scent coded as well within Verity's memory. They were *there,* below . . . no, *within* . . .

Somewhere in her mind—in *this* Mind—were the directions that would restore them.

But where? How? If she did not find them he might be dead, forever.

She sorted through times frantically, looking for Sheets, for Liberation, for NAMS, for the unknown slot in the station where Sphere had placed them, cool and blinking. She felt as if she were five years old and just learning to throw the huge rough baseball swift and true with a motion copied from Blaze so that it would fly as far; as if she were encased in a clumsy catcher's mitt that she might never master. Her mind screamed with infinite failures, and then a fuzzy picture of him focussed, and then stirred—

Live! she willed. O my love, please wake. Do you remember?

To her anguish she felt enormous jolting *pain* in her chest, saw John's blue eyes stare coldly over the rifle, and then darkness—

No! Before! The orchard! The baseball diamond, cornfields, Russ, Bear Creek.

She felt his eyelids struggle against elastic confines—and, simultaneously, the seed that would repair a way into the City took root, grew tentatively at first, then quickly, working through matter with a crack like thunder—*yes!* It was *working!*

Then a mad swirl of wind hit her, tore her from those cellular moorings. Shrouded in darkness, dazzled by sudden raying lines of light, she heard herself scream—

Her eyes jerked open. She was in the dark Hive. She had never left.

Then she heard a woman's cool voice, rather high-pitched . . . or was it low? It vibrated on many frequencies. A Bee speaking?

IT IS FORBIDDEN BY THE 2048 INTERNATIONAL NAN CONVENTION RULES FOR INDIVIDUAL CONVERSION TO BEGIN UNTIL SUBJECT AGREES TO CONTINUE.

INITIATION SUBJECT AGREES THAT SHE HAS BEEN SHOWN THE INTRO INFORMATION AND THE TEN CAUTIONARY PRECEPTS ARE FULLY UNDERSTOOD.

"What precepts?" asked Verity. "I never heard any precepts." The voice ignored her and continued.

RECEIVED FROM SUBJECT THIS DAY COMPLETE PERMISSION TO CONTINUE WITH INDIVIDUAL CONVERSION.

A soft click sounded everywhere in the close air.

Verity was filled with fear, entirely human again but she had never really changed, not really. She had just been given a terrifying taste. She appeared to be stuck to the waxy walls. Heart thudding, she pulled herself away, relieved when her skin *would* separate from it.

Feeling quite weak, she pulled herself up by grabbing onto the cell walls, which laced in regular angles between the soft, yielding milky caps.

"I don't agree," she yelled, drenched in sweat. I can't give up *myself*—

You have to agree, something whispered, to save Blaze and Cairo.

Did she have to agree, in order to save Blaze? She leaned back against the soft wall, then jumped forward, panting, and looked about wildly for the way out. She couldn't! She couldn't stand it. She would die if she did, she would vanish, change to a Bee forever. Horrible!

Absolute terror kept her from assenting. In the multiplicity of information that would flood her in conversion would be the key to freeing Blaze and Cairo. But that would only be a negligible corner of what she would gain. She might not even care to save them, once conversion was complete. How could she know? But why not do it? What do you have to lose?

Only being human. Any Mother Ann would pay that price, and willingly. Mother Ann sacrificed herself for her vision of a new humanity. Why couldn't she do the same for Blaze, and maybe for the whole City? Why not? Why did it seem as if she had been watching the New Ohio River swell with a single, unbelievably huge wave, which had arched over her, welcoming her with undreamed-of deadly power, roaring down upon her faster than any train?

Was it lighter at that end of the golden corridor? She began to stagger in that direction. Stay, she told herself, stay, but her legs would not obey. *Was* this the way she had come? She begged for maps but her mind would not show her a single one, or even a glimmer of direction. You are giving up control of that too, an implacable, dry voice told her. Wouldn't it be nice to have complete control of the maps? Layer after layer flashed through her. A blueprint of something called the Sears Tower. The London Underground. Australia, 2221. Two square miles of Mars. The Horseshoe Nebula . . . "No!" she yelled. "I don't care!"

Something drew her down a side corridor for a moment; just a feeling, like seeing Shaker Hill from a low rise in the land two miles away; heartfilling and powerful. Is this the way? she wondered, on the verge of panic, as she stumbled in this new direction.

Five steps down the corridor she stopped.

Pushed against one of the cells was her own childhood face, about four years old.

The girl's face brought back early memories of seeing herself in the mirror; the resemblance was unmistakable though blurred through the golden membrane.

Her eyes were closed as if in sleep, and an open hand pushed against the cell end, making a small bump.

Heart beating fast, Verity saw in the next only dark hair, and in the third, half a face but a bit older.

In the rage that swept through her, she felt like pulling these tiny girls forth and leaving them to die—would they die?—on the floor of the Hive. She felt affronted at her very core, astonishingly, since she had never before considered the possibility that she was not unique. This was simply *wrong*.

But after a moment she turned abruptly and retraced her steps to the main corridor. As she trudged in her former direction through the soft, narrow, golden corridor, her initial outrage had become transmuted.

Who did this?

How?

Why?

All the while she was trying to move quickly, but felt as if trapped in a dream. Perhaps she was, she thought, and pushed harder, harder, toward the hexagonal exit where she had come in. Step by step, she made her way through the eerily glowing golden maze, laced with the endless green hexagon lines, forcing herself to *remember* the way, and being human, *remember, remember . . .* for some strong force entreated her *stay, stay, stay, you were born for this! To be at this center!*

At last, she burst out into the cool air of the museum corridor. Staggering across it, gulping air, she slid down the wall opposite the golden hexagon, bowed her head in her hands, and wept.

She was selfish. Too selfish to save those whom she loved. And why else come here? But deep, implacable fear prevented her from even considering returning.

The discovery of her small sisters paled against the wracking pain of having failed Blaze and Cairo. Would Blaze have hesitated?

She had never felt greater grief.

Twenty-five

○○○○○○○○○○○○○○○○○○○○

Bewitched, Bothered, and Bewildered

The next morning Verity woke at the entrance of the Zoo. She must have staggered out here, she thought, before passing out. She was lying on the sidewalk and next to her was the Wise Blood boy, curled beneath a gray blanket, clutching the scrawny, hairy new jesus in his sleep.

She sat up slowly, aching all over.

The sky was slightly overcast and every once in a while a drizzle swept over the City. The sun shone palely through thin clouds, and the Bees were out. Their steady, soothing hum resembled music in Bee-varied harmonies, its half-hidden pauses when several dropped down to feed. Flowers were everywhere, massed in carpets of color and design in rapidly greening parks, in urns and decorating sconces that grew from the sides of buildings in patterns that seemed carefully planned to please the heart and mind. Above, the more dangerous Flowers bloomed, casting slanting shade across nearby buildings.

Verity took no delight in the show of spring the City put on. Enormous disappointment in herself coursed through her.

Then, while she was still not quite awake, standing on a corner while waiting for a silent vehicle to pass, the movement of a young man walking caught her eye.

She could not have said later exactly what peculiarity of motion defined him; it was all of a piece and it was Blaze, three blocks away, casual and apparently unsuspecting that she might be nearby. It was like something happening in a dream.

He was small and sharp and clear, wearing different clothing from that in which John had shot him: the bright yellow shirt, the black pants. Now his pants were pale gray.

She watched down the street canyon for a long minute, not daring to hope that she could possibly be right.

Walking. Breathing. Alive.

"Blaze!" she shouted, and began to run, knees and elbows pumping, wanting to spin the earth beneath her. "Blaze," she yelled again, and wondered why he didn't turn.

She pounded downhill beneath the towering oaks of a park, toward the canyons of Flower buildings, toward the green rushing river; hearing her he turned . . .

She was still a hundred yards away when he started running himself, and he soon pulled away. No wonder. No wonder at all. He had the gift of running. Indeed, it *was* Blaze.

He bolted, and turned a corner. When she got there, he was nowhere to be seen, though she trudged on, her chest burning.

She repeated his name until she came to a halt, all of her aching, feet, legs, chest.

"Cairo!" she screamed, and no one turned to watch her at all, none of the twenty or so people she saw going about whatever business these people engaged themselves in.

She sank down to the sidewalk, drew up her knees, held them tightly to her chest, and gazed with unseeing eyes straight ahead.

Blaze was no more. Because of something she had done last night in the Hive, Blaze was gone, empty, only his form was left, his mind rearranged by something in the damned sheets. Why else would he run from her? But he's *alive*, she told herself, her hands turning to fists. Just not alive as you would like him to be, eh? Killed twice over, first by John, and now by you.

If you could change him back, if you could learn how, how could you even ask him if that's what he wanted to do? Maybe he likes the new way he is.

If the pictures were there, a part of her mind said. If the pictures of who he was before were there, he could choose what he thought would make him happy. He couldn't be happy, now, distant and strange as all the people in this crazed City. He was no longer human, and ah, he had been *so* human.

She stood, entirely drained; hopeless. She was useless. She had failed in all she had planned to do. Darkness settled in her chest and coursed through her mind. At least he's *alive,* said some part of her mind, and she shrugged and thought but it's not him. Someone is alive, but it's certainly not Blaze.

She stuck her hands deep into her jacket pockets.

Then she pulled them out and looked at them.

Had not *something* happened last night?

Barely daring to hope, Verity walked to the nearest building. She ignored its lively, subtle design; more Durancy nonsense, she told herself, and walked straight to the interstice which pulsed, bright green, on one corner of the building.

Will this work? she wondered, holding her breath.

She pressed both hands against it, leaned into it hard, and then did not know exactly what to do. The precise pheromones of Blaze, which she *knew* with the power she had thrown away the night before—was the memory of them still within her? Could she access him? Perhaps by thinking of memories of him?

This one. I want this one. The one who sees the ghost train, the one who loves Union Station.

Nothing. Oh, what was quite specific? *The one who invented a unique, peculiar game of baseball, one that could work with just four people to a team—the one who could play the piano, the hammered dulci-mer*—what was that piece?—*Something by Scott Joplin*—

She remembered, remembered, remembered, pressing into the interstice—

As she clung to the wall, a picture of Blaze's face appeared next to her on the wall, and she shouted, "Yes! Yes!" The City has him, she thought with joy and dread. The City *has Blaze!*

What's left of him.

She let that flow into her, and he was as close as Durancy as long as she touched the warm, pulsing interstice. She drank in Blaze's changed aliveness, unable to pull away despite the torrent of fear and concern that rushed through her, unable to reflect, able only to *know* . . .

Arrested.

But his name was still Blaze.

Blaze . . .

He started as the place where his hand had rested on the counter pulsed, changing from wood-brown to shimmering green. He pulled his hand back and moved down a few stools. But his hand still tingled and the pulse followed him, somehow, so he decided to ignore it.

He sat in a small coffee shop, hunched over steaming coffee, eating some odd sweet roll and he didn't remember, really, where he'd been last. Or where he'd come from. That woman had chased him, frightened him, until, when he finally stopped running, he realized that she knew him. That *was* his name. But on returning to search for her, he had soon become overwhelmed with weariness, as if he just wanted to lie down and sleep, sleep. And he couldn't find her anyway. She had been very slow.

He sat up straight and slapped his face. No sleep. Sleep was worse than anything.

He watched the people going in and out of the shop. People. Sure. He'd known other people, but what were their names? At least he had a name.

Blaze . . .

He tore the roll in half, threw it down on the counter, slid off his stool, and left. He had thought he was hungry but he wasn't.

Why not just lie down and sleep? He shivered even though the spring sun lay on his shoulders as he walked aimlessly down the bizarre streets, staring at everything without understanding.

Arrested. Where had that word come from?

He came to a green park, which seemed very inviting. Beneath the just-greening branches of huge oak trees he sat on a bench and tried to think. It was enormously difficult. The bench pulsed too, like the counter. He was in a fog. As if he was very sick, and certainly he felt weak and perhaps even feverish. He could barely remember waking up this morning. Sharp pains seized his stomach and he gasped; maybe he should go back in and finish that roll.

He hadn't eaten much.

Except at the Station.

It had been horrible, waking. As if he was sick almost to death, but a dog had been tearing at the wrappings that surrounded him, threatened to suffocate him. Sharp teeth had scored his face yet oddly, he saw later in the mirror, left no marks but only served to rouse him.

Rouse him from a dream of quick-running water, dream-green summer fields, trains, dark horrible pain and . . . faces. The water he had remembered was not this mammoth green river running below the hills, between the odd buildings that also seemed like a dream to him but then it all did, it all did, as if he was on the verge of waking but could *not*—

Tears came to his eyes as he remembered that awful awakening. He dashed them away, leaned forward on the bench, put his head in his hand and looked into the blackness. The voices of people walking past, the hushing sound of the wind in the trees, and the roar of the river dimmed.

The dog had worried and whined and he—Blaze—had twisted inside his awful death-cocoon and freed his arms and in the broad daylight streaming through that grand high arch he saw that his shirt was a stiff mass of dried, flaky blood. Blood. *His* blood, and lots of it. From when—

From when—

And *that* was the instant when it all slipped away, swirled back, was sucked somewhere, and he pulled himself out of the soft cushion and tossed away the film of blinking lights, oh, oh, it was all too strange and horrible and something in his chest wrenched and he had cried and cried and cried. The dog lay down and panted on the gold-intersticed floor of the utterly deserted cathedral for trains and at least he knew what that was, for some reason. He looked at the dog and saw that she too was covered with patches of dried blood. The clear stuff still adhered to the side of his own head and he pried it off and flung it on the floor. The stuff blinked, tiny winks of green blue yellow and he almost felt like grinding his foot on it but he wasn't sure why.

He stood then and felt strangely good. All was new and raying out from him like the beams of the great station, and he knew exactly where to go. . . .

Up the curving stairway was the MEN'S LOUNGE, empty and gleaming with seats in an outer lobby and ashtrays and inside urinals and two showers.

Throwing off his stiff clothing from which tiny sheets of dried blood fluttered like leaves, he stared in a mirror at his smooth chest, touched it wonderingly, as if that should mean something to him, as if his hand knew something his mind did not.

He bathed both of them, the dog pushing herself flat against the closed, translucent shower door to get away from the water and when he was done he walked cold and naked back out through the lobby and down until he got to FINE CLOTHING LTD.

That was a bit of a puzzle, actually. When he opened the door, shivering, a man's voice had welcomed him and asked him what he wanted; he ignored it, looking around at a lot of blank screens, and the man asked again, and the third time he yelled, "*Clothes, what do you think?*"

"I only need to know your preferences sir. Step over here," a circle on the floor lit up, "and we'll get your measurements."

Fine. He stood on the circle and was bathed with light; then the voice said, "Here are several initial styles to choose from. Please tell us what you like," and on the screen flashed about ten pictures of men, all dressed differently, one after the other, and then they started again. Blaze watched, astonished, but the third time said "That one" when the seventh came on.

A tone beeped above a long thin door on the wall and a light above said at first 5:00 and then 4:59 and so on down to zero as he watched curiously and then the door slid open and inside were—

Clothes.

A pair of pants of warm, smooth material, gray. They grabbed his calves tightly when he pulled them on and felt quite comfortable. It—but *what? who?*—gave him two shirts and a jacket, shoes that laced up over his ankles, quite sturdy yet lightweight and very pleasing somehow.

And after that there was plenty of food for him and the dog at a smooth gleaming counter where horrible music played as he ate some meat thing that had been in a small alcove on the wall, which attracted him by blinking.

The place made him quite uneasy.

But what was much more painful was some ache in his being when he began to realize that no matter how clean he got or how well he was dressed or how much he ate he was not going to remember who he was or how he got here.

He finished eating and sat at the counter wondering what to do.

He had a throbbing headache.

The dog was flat on her side, sleeping, but the minute his foot touched the floor she jumped up and looked at him with bright, gleaming eyes.

It was then he saw the picture, tall as he was, evidently some sort of decoration but sharp and flickery, as if projected from somewhere. He was halfway across the station though, and paced closer over echoey floors until it became clear.

The picture was of a City, and the buildings of the City were bursting with huge Flowers at the top, moving languorously in the wind as if underwater. WELCOME TO CINCINNATI, THE QUEEN CITY, said the sign.

Cincinnati. Hadn't he—whoever he was—always wanted to come here?

And so he went exploring. This was a train station, was it not?

And trains went somewhere, and the place with Flowers was as good a place to go as any. He wished he would see some other people, but the place felt utterly deserted—long-time deserted—and he knew with a familiar chill that he had been in many places like this, long-time deserted.

A sign in the center of the station said TRAINS. He saw that it was afternoon outside and wanted to go out and explore, but then decided that since it was getting late he ought to hurry. He really didn't want to spend another night here.

He ran down the stairs, the dog at his heels.

He stared at the rows of gleaming tracks below. There were no trains at all. He laughed. "What did you expect?" Still, he was touched by disappointment that seemed much deeper than it ought to be.

He turned and was going to go back up the stairs when a bank of pictures lit as he walked by.

His breath caught in his throat when he realized that *all* of them were pictures of Cities with Flowers atop glimmering pastel buildings, beautiful and weird and thrilling.

He walked closer, hesitantly, as if the pictures might leap out and grab him.

Denver. San Francisco. Seattle. Detroit. New York.

And Cincinnati, The Queen City.

He reached out wonderingly and touched that picture.

"The recently regenerated local Queen City Beeline departs every five minutes from platform three to conveniently serve all NAMS passengers," said a woman's voice, making him jump. "We hope you enjoyed your trip, and that you will ride NAMS again the next time you have travel needs."

He stepped away and saw something blinking down the tunnel.

3, it blinked, 3 3 3, and he walked toward it, beginning to shake, and a train pulled up and it was light purple and the seats inside were green and empty and the lights around the doorway blinked, blinked, blinked, and as they began to slide shut he leaped inside, and the dog too and the train began to move down the dark tunnel and he did not know where he was going but the voice assured him, Vine Street Station in three minutes, passengers please prepare . . .

And at one point in those three minutes he felt a weird surge of energy and jumped out of his seat, so he was ready when the door slid open and he ran out and the dog too.

And with that surge of energy came some information.

He was to perform tonight. And the next night too. He was Entirely Welcome.

Blaze lifted his head from his hands as he sat on the park bench. He remembered all that. He remembered that his hands had tingled as he rode the stairs up into the sunset and he still had not known his name. Now he knew his name, even if he couldn't remember what went before. That was a start.

And he knew he was here, in the Queen City.

But maybe he should go back inside, away from these buildings, and try to eat something again. He knew that, whoever he was, he had never seen anything like these buildings except in pictures. He emerged from the park and stood on the street again.

A cold spring wind rushed through the corridors made by the buildings and ruffled his hair. He lifted a hand to push it back and his fingers ran through unfamiliar length; he forced himself to look upward once again. It could not be true.

But the Flowers were still there. He had not imagined them. He choked back a scream. He stood with his fists clenched against it all while the people passing him did not even give him a glance. The awful Flowers were too enormous for this to be anything other than a dream, a horribly real dream, and he rushed for an alcove lined with doors that led into one of the Flower buildings and sank down, looking outward.

Between the buildings, from his hill, he glimpsed the frighteningly wide river, foaming with rapids and sudden drops that would crush rafts between rocks. Bridges, three of them flung halfway across the river, stopped as if bitten off suddenly, midriver. He thought he saw between the overweaving greenery of the opposite far bank glints that might be windows of another City, the twin of this but ruined by some awful cataclysm that had crumbled and flooded it and made it the victim of the forest.

And then he saw something that made his heart thud even harder.

It could not be.

He stared at the sky, thinking his mind was playing tricks.

The crowd on the sidewalk watched also, and he saw that some of them smiled, while others had looks of worship on their faces, labeled somehow by that part of his brain, and he tried to trace that back to an actual memory but failed as one enormous Bee and then another flew overhead, at the level of the building tops.

He could almost feel the deep tone of their wing's vibration in his bones, and his heart was inexplicably soothed by the feeling.

He did not want it to be so.

He did not want the frightening yearning, the strange affinity that washed through him at that instant. But something had happened to him which made him helpless at its call.

He looked at his hands, trying to break the spell, knowing with absolute certainty that they had once held important information. It was information having to do with time and, yes, with the striking of notes, and . . . with dance, and with a young girl.

He turned and looked at the river. Yes.

The river . . . it was important, somehow. Because it could take him away. Away from this horror, away from this bad dream.

As if he *was* in a dream that he could survive only by force of will, only by thinking quite steadily and staying calm, he took a deep breath, and began walking downhill toward the river, the awful, huge river. Surely, whoever he was, he had never seen any body of water quite so large, so dangerous.

Arrested.

That was what the voice inside his head said. What he heard just before the dog licked his eyes open. Where was the dog now? He remembered. Yes, he remembered that at least. The dog had whined and barked and even snarled when they entered the City, and had hesitated, unwilling to follow him, whimpering no matter how much he called, "Dog, come on dog, it's all right" but even the dog could tell it wasn't and then it acted sick and just curled up and wouldn't budge. He'd had to leave it.

He felt immensely sad and empty and the only thing he could think about was to find an organ or a piano or a . . . a hammered dulcimer . . .

His hands began to tingle once more, and his head filled with music as he rushed through the streets, turning this way and that for no apparent reason, trying to stay in the shadows of the tall buildings so that those terrifying Bees could not see him.

And then he was standing in front of a . . . a DANCE HALL, said a sign, lighting suddenly, mysteriously, obligingly.

Pushing the door open, he went inside.

It was dark, empty, and his footsteps echoed as he walked across the wavy floorboards toward the piano on the stage, climbed the short flight of stairs, and sat down at the piano bench.

But then those pains seized him again and he was drenched in sweat. Gingerly he curled up on the piano bench and watched the beams of light slanting through the empty room from high narrow windows as he gasped, and tears came to his eyes from the pain. Pictures reeled through his head and he knew they had to do with who he was but he couldn't grasp them; they were like an urgent message that he just kept missing.

When it passed he sat up, feeling washed and empty. He played a few bars of music then stopped; played again then stopped.

He remembered his name again: Blaze. He kept forgetting.

Tonight, he had to play here. They were expecting him. He was—yes—Entirely Welcome. Many, many people would come to hear him play. Somehow the thought made him extremely happy. As if it was something he had always wanted. Whoever he was.

The stage curtains were lush, deep green velvet, and trailed across the scarred stage, about ten feet longer than they needed to be. Why were those pulsing lights following him around? Was that a footlight? He knelt and touched it, wonderingly, but it was cool and didn't give off much light. Turning away from it, he pushed the soft material of the trailing curtain into a pile and lay down on it, hoping he would not dream.

Twenty-six

○○○○○○○○○○○○○○○○○○

A Kat, a Brick, an Unseen Door

Blaze's story broke off suddenly, as if the City decided that Verity had had enough of it, and she could not stop the other stories rushing into her, swiftly and insistently, and she had just wanted one, the story of Blaze . . .

It was like dye swirling lazily downward through thick liquid. Verity struggled to keep herself *here*, bright and alert, still a witness.

She pulled away from the interstice but it was too late.

Desperately, Verity imagined herself inside a small, wet stone building in a lush garden, and that worked. There was no glass in the windows and amid the musty smells of old earth-clotted tools she leaned on the sill, taking care not to step on the clawed digging thing, and looked out at the encroaching garden.

Then that fiction vanished, but the place, the idea of that place, was still there except she was in Cocomino.

* {QC.47983} *It was breathtakingly bare of solid features. Night flashed to day suddenly, and trees and rocks flickered equally quickly—

And then it slowed, the emotional calculus, the instant-by-instant framing of bioneurological events within her mind. It was too much to look at each one, and at any rate here came a Mouse with a Brick in his hand.

He was thin and spindly and had odd red hair.

"Who are you?" she asked.

"Dollink," he said, "My name is Ignatz Mouse. You are a 'Kat.' "

"And what is that in your hand?" she asked. "Or is that a 'claw,' or a 'paw'?"

He put the brick behind his back and opened one hand, which was empty. "It's not a claw, that's what birds have. It's not a hand, that's what humans have." His voice was puzzled.

She grabbed and squeezed it while he struggled to pull it from her grip. "It looks like a 'paw,' I suppose," she said, "but it feels exactly like a 'hand.' "

"Well," he said, finally yanking it back from her, "there's not much doubt that this thing in my other hand, paw, claw, or what-have-you, is what is commonly called a 'brick.' " He turned and walked a few steps away from her, then hurled it at her head.

She felt an instant's ecstasy as it approached, and tried hard to duck but something in her fought it.

The brick smashed into the side of her head and she felt herself crumple to the sidewalk. Why am I so happy, she saw herself wonder from her stone citadel. This makes no sense at all!* {QC.47983} *

Verity opened her eyes and was sitting on the bench again. A woman's arm was around her, and she felt the side of her head being wiped with some rough cloth. She gasped, suddenly feeling the pain, completely unsettled at this new direction the City had taken.

The woman had white hair arranged in funny lumpy waves, and her kind eyes were large and gray. She was rather heavy and wore a frumpy dress almost crawling with enormous, shoutingly bright flowers.

"There, there," she said. "I don't know why you're so slow, but you were lying there bleeding for *such* a long time . . . it seems like the bank should have come to pick you up by now but of course it's so wonderfully busy right now. Yes, it looks as though it's healing up nicely." She squinted and watched Verity's forehead for a moment, then nodded as if satisfied.

"What happened to Ignatz?" Verity asked, still a bit dizzy. She sat up anyway. Then she remembered Blaze. Where was he? At some dance hall . . . if only she had continued, last night in the Hive; agreed to the conversion, he might not have been *arrested*. She looked around wildly, but when she tried to stand the world reeled and she sat down suddenly.

The woman helped Verity sit again and looked at her with delight. "You'll feel better in a minute, you lucky thing. Krazy Kat is very pure, isn't it? Complex and at the same time you get this wonderful resolution so quickly!" She frowned. "I'm involved in some sort of muddle, to tell you the truth. I—oh, you know how hard it is to remember when you're not *there*—(Verity nodded when the woman stared at her for a second with hard and curious eyes) but I have to wear a large scarlet 'A' on the front of my dress . . ." She laughed, shortly, and said, "I must say, I *like* the way I look there much better . . ."

She shook her head slightly and stared down at the sidewalk. She took a deep breath and spoke without looking at Verity. "These are really the hardest times, of course, nothing seems very real or very important while you're waiting for new information." She slumped back on the bench, crossed her arms with difficulty across her very large breasts, and stared across the park. "Things have been awful slow this season. Sometimes I worry." She turned her head and stared at Verity again. "Do you worry? Does it somehow seem *different* to you this year? But of course it *is* hard to remember from year to year . . ." She continued to look at Verity, but her eyes had a pleading cast now.

"I think it is different," said Verity very gently, feeling as if the woman was sending pain right into her body through her eyes, and as if that pain was crystallizing something in her joints so that very soon she wouldn't be able to move at all.

She patted the woman's hand gently and got up.

A Bee's deep, throbbing hum filled the air, and the woman pointed. It was dipping down toward a large spear of foxglove on the roof of a building across the park.

"Oh, I *knew* it would come back!" said the woman; she jumped up, and ran with a funny huddling gait toward the building, her arms outstretched. "Wait," she called. "Wait, I'm coming."

She vanished inside the building.

Verity followed her.

The doors slid shut at Verity's approach, and though she pounded on a button, they refused to open. Verity peered into the small, dark lobby, where light fanned out from sconces on the wall. She saw the woman, a dark shape, pacing, looking anxiously at the elevator door.

Then a strip of color lit next to the elevator door.

Verity's breath caught at its shimmering beauty, its depth, its odd *attractiveness*. She caught herself looking for a stone or something to bash the door in, but saw nothing, so she pressed herself against the door and stared.

The woman knew she was there, and turned to grin at Verity over her shoulder.

Then she leaned into the strip of color, which was about six inches wide. She raised one hand and pressed it firmly against the strip, and Verity saw the side of her face relax in what looked like bliss.

A strange hunger flared in Verity, and brief tears of frustration burned her eyes.

Then the elevator door slid open and the woman stepped inside. Though she looked straight out at Verity, she did not seem to actually see her, and the doors shut.

Verity turned away and sat on the steps of the building.

Large urns of flowers flanked the doorway. She rubbed the steps. They were very clean and shiny and looked like marble. She felt her head, remembering the thud of the brick, but felt no evidence of injury. She held her hand out in front of her, and stared at the pale palm, wondering why Blaze seemed so distant and unimportant. She felt thirsty. She rose. Maybe she'd feel better if she had something to drink.

Another woman approached, wending her way down the street, surveying every building, looking around with avid delight and curiosity. The wind lifted her long blond hair. She looked about thirty years old. She looked lovely.

And she looked straight at Verity.

"It's you," she said. "I know who you are, even if you don't."

Verity was not in the mood to play along. "What do you mean, it's me?"

The woman continued to stand. She slipped her hands into the pockets of her dress. "Something is going on here. You have to either accept or deny it."

"What happens if I deny it?" asked Verity. It seemed like an excellent idea. Deny it. Forget that Bees foraged in giant Flowers; forget that everyone was crazier here than the plague could possibly make them. Forget the giant Hive, the Zoo, and Hazel Mote, and the church of the new jesus. Forget the golden plains stretching westward to the other ruined Cities.

In a way, she could actually, like these people, forget by accepting. She had seen how easy it would be. She could feel how much the City wished that she would. But were those forget-me-nots nodding in the urn next to her? Could a City have a sense of humor, and a sick one at that?

The woman shrugged. "It doesn't make any sense if you deny it, that's all. If you accept it—and that's a struggle too, and it's not that you can just decide to do it, accept it that is, but if you decide to then the information gets stronger, and more precise, and it all *means* something again. It's quite a relief, when it means something, because if it means nothing it's just too absurd."

"But maybe it really does mean nothing," said Verity. "Maybe it's broken."

"It doesn't matter. You're thinking of the City." She squinted into the sun. "Of course it might be broken. But that doesn't matter either. That's part of what you have to accept. I've even found by accepting that I can stay awake all winter. Shhh!" She held a finger to her lips and smiled. "Don't tell anybody! But I think I've been awake for many, many seasons. My secret is that I just stick to one area."

"What area?"

"I stick to the area of Pynchon," she said. "I don't have to stay Oedipa Maas. I can be others, too. The Pynchon universe has lots of people in it. But they're really all the same character, trying to see same thing, trying to grasp the code, and trying and trying to make sense—that's often so frustrating but crazy and fun too— and then giving up and—oh, you can't give up until you really give up, you can't just pretend to give up, that doesn't work at all—but then when it happens it's worth it, because light and meaning all flood in and it all makes so much blessed *sense* . . . you do know that we're all quite dead, don't you, dear? The sooner you accept that, the happier you'll be. And I'm not jealous. If you want to try Oedipa, I think there's room for more than one here. No need to be stingy. In fact, I'll tell you a little secret." She leaned forward and whispered in Verity's ear as her dress flapped in the breeze. "I want *everyone* to be me. Or one of us. How glorious that would be, if we *all* knew. I'm sure that something absolutely amazing would happen then." She straightened and frowned.

"That doesn't sound too much like a religion, does it? I think it does." She shook her head and walked away muttering, "That's the only flaw, I just don't like that angle too much, have to think about it a little more . . ."

Then she was out of earshot.

Verity took a deep breath.

She remembered Oedipa Maas. Oedipa Maas was a character in *The Crying of Lot 49*, by Thomas Pynchon. That all fit.

She wondered, sitting there while the breeze pushed the scent of fresh popcorn her way from a vendor in the park, how she knew about this. Had she read it, had it been one of the old classics Russ's parents had stocked in the library John burned? Or had it been dumped into her on one of her trips to the Dayton Library? How many stories were happening around her that she really knew nothing about? She took a breath of clean air, and felt more and more alert.

Who *was* she?

She thought about Russ, Sare, John. (Not Blaze, it was too hard to think about him.) All of the people she'd known had a definite beginning and middle, if not yet an end. And the things they remembered were things they had experienced. The feelings they had were their own.

These people had lives piled upon lives. What had Oedipa said about seasons? Cheyenne, the boy in the old school, had said that the Flowers and Bees were not out in the winter. So spring—now—must be the season she referred to. That made sense. The City had been empty when she and Sphere arrived, pretty much, and now it seemed as if there were many times more people, though it still had an empty feel. It was nothing like cities in centuries past, swarming and teeming with people, overrun with people crowding upward, surging underground, blending and melding and swirling and synergizing.

The inhabitants were stored, of course, in the winter, where her three small sisters slept.

Uneasily, she remembered how quickly her honeybees changed from larvae to real bees, dissolved in a mucus that contained the raw ingredients for the DNA to assemble into bees—and a bee with a particular purpose already programmed at that. It held an uncanny resemblance to the vats of liquid in the nan factories, where a certain plan was injected, a certain program, which from a single seed assembled quickly, in a matter of hours, a thing—a machine, a wardrobe, components of a home. Perhaps the people were not even stored. They could be dissolved. The pheromonal receptors could be programmed to accept only certain scent molecules, which triggered the "memories" within them. Scent was enormously evocative.

None of these people seemed very happy. They all wanted something. They were still partly human.

They wanted themselves, that was all. They just wanted themselves. But they were doomed to go on repeating these stories to please those monstrous Bees.

You do not need to help them, Verity, she told herself with John's stern voice. You can't, you have no idea how. Just find Blaze and leave, somehow, anyhow, before you end up like them. Already it's starting. She wondered how much longer she had.

The sun was angling downward. The wind rushed through the City as it did every evening, and Verity pulled on her jacket and stood up. She tried to remember her last thoughts of Blaze. Something about a piano. Something about a performance. Where?

At first she wasn't sure that it was the Bell she heard, or just the distant revelry beginning on Roebling's Bridge.

And then it focussed and grew stronger, like a knife within her brain.

With frustration, anger, and hope, she began to follow it. The buildings around her began to glow with gentle light, and large windows were filled with people dining and laughing silent behind the glass. She passed a theater where people were lining up to see a Sam Shepard play. She turned the corner there, where the Bell sounded so much sweeter, and began to run.

Twenty-seven

○○○○○○○○○○○○○○○○○

My Funny Valentine

As Verity rushed up the stairs of a high building, her lungs began to burn.

She was only on the fifth floor, with at least thirty more to go. She sagged against the smooth tile wall, checking reflexively first to make sure there was no interstice before doing so.

She had not taken the elevator because of the soothing smooth lights which she was sure distilled the essence given off by her thoughts. At the very least the lights could sense the crude emotions of fear, anxiety, even happiness. She wasn't sure if they could portray more complex thoughts to the Hive in the form of the mix of particular molecules she could not help emitting, by-products of her momentary being, and then perhaps take regulatory steps, invade the elevator air with corrective chemicals, throw her off course with Krazy Kat and Oedipa Maas.

Ah, she shivered, as she forced her reluctant legs to undertake the arduous climb once more, slowly, pacing herself; John was right. There is horror here, horror among the brightness, darkness woven into the open mind because the roots went right to the heart of volition and sense of self.

The Bell sounded again, when she reached the sixteenth floor, and she closed her eyes as she sank down onto the landing. No, she thought, I have to follow the Bell. She tried to stand but could not because the walls around her began to pale.

The air around her seemed to change, to open, with each new tone, and then she was there.

* {**AD.0**} *COOL SPRING AIR eddied around her.

She sat in a large chair, legs drawn up and covered with goose bumps, her penis a flesh rose between her legs. A boy, perhaps seven.

"Abe!" he heard, faintly, and smiled with mischief because he knew the sound came from the other side of the house. "You get in here and get your clothes on right now! We'll be late!"

Abe's mother fell silent, or perhaps his ears switched focus.

Bird calls came rich and deep. Early sun slanted through a green yard intense with deep shadows, filled with cathedral trees and grass still glimmering with dew. A slight breeze brushed the fragile blossoms of the pink, red, and white impatiens, blooming among the mosses of his father's rock garden and edging the tiny mazy hedges his mother had started.

Next to him, suspended from a branch, long green-mottled pipes struck each other with lazy sonorous tones, and he felt something in him expand until he was this place, this most holy of places, this here and now, and the joy he felt was the joy of unasked-for perfection.

The French doors opened and his mother peered out.

"Get in here! What will the neighbors think!"

"They don't care," he laughed.

But he was cold. He rose, rubbed his backside trying to smooth out the diamonds embedded in his flesh by the metal-work of his chair. He scurried inside.* {**AD.0**} *

Verity saw no more.

But she knew that it was there. All there, held like some sort of trust or cancer so deep within her that helpless fury swept through her like a storm across open prairie.

Not her and yet her deepest self, this mischievous boy whose memories controlled her.

She stood suddenly, knowing in the bright afterwash of his re-membering that Cincinnati had been meant to be an immensely kind City.

Struggling against lactic acid to make the top floor, where the Bell still pulled her, most loud, she wondered what had gone wrong. She finally burst out a door onto the roof.

The roof smelled of damp earth mingled with sharp herbs and the scents of the Flowers. Verity pushed aside the joy she could not help feel among the smells and tried to think. Why had she been called here?

A narrow brick path led away from the small roofdome from which she had emerged. The Bell was occasional but intimate.

She took a fork that seemed to curve toward the edge and got to a chest-high wall against which she leaned.

The bridges were just filling up with people. Soon revelry lights would glow on every other block, pulsing with what must be music. She imagined the swirl of thought—of *stories*—occurring below and shivered in the wind's chilling edge. The roadless bridge frame was a necklace of light across the darkening confluence of the New and Old Ohio rivers, where rapids glinted white and pink in the sunset. She fancied she could feel them dancing out on the quarter-mile of solar road that was still intact: the outlaws, who dared the Bees out in the open, laughed at them in the dark, and who went to bed in the City each day exhausted from revelry, never making any actual plans to leave, for the excitement was simply in the dance and the thought and never in the doing, not for them. It was like dancing in the cornfields and daring sharks not to swim through golden rows and bite them. The Bees didn't fly at night.

The roof was terraced, graced with benches, and she could not see the other side for ferns shaded by rocky overhangs. Several fountains murmured and wind rattled through the just-bloomed branches of some sweet tree.

Slowly, the path down which she had walked dissolved, melting to dark earth as she watched, her eyes insisting it was a trick of late afternoon light but her mind knowing better.

Another brick path where none had been before led away to the right, and she knew that the soil was a thin and fluid skin of molecules whose color and density were regulated by—what? Who?

She stomped along the new path half-hoping to hurt it, wanting to close her ears to the Bell which now rung low and deep and resonant in the center of her chest, as if different parts of her traitor body could participate in this auditory torture.

And then it all stopped, as if the hand that had been leading her dropped and left her alone.

Why had the City lured her up here? To tease her? And what

was it doing to Blaze? Changing him, that's what, making him like everyone else, then trapping her here. Taunting her, a cruel City. See, the City told her, I am much more powerful than you. Do not think that you can save even one person from me.

With a silky rustling, the Flowers around her began move slowly as underwater plants in the quickening breeze.

There were three great ones, she saw. One pink, one black, and one white. One translucent pink petal arched over her, after about fifteen minutes, and the scent made her giddy and joyful. Colors intensified and she felt glad to be alive, a feeling that superseded her utterly reasonable pain and confusion.

She heard his voice then, he who had infected her vision with longing for a City not really here. How conscious was he, she wondered? How alive? He seemed to live in that other man— Dennis—in a way. But she sensed that the one within her was somehow different. More pure. He had a story to tell; she could not escape it.

"Go ahead," she said, and sat on a chair beneath the shade of the Flower, looking out over the City.

She was chilled and surprised when the voice began immediately. Things were clearer up here, unmuddied by the other stories the City wished to inflict on her. Maybe that was why she had been called to the roof.

She was back another layer in Durancy, closer to the central madness. It was the speaking that was unusual. She saw with him, as if riding his mind, and at the same time he was explaining everything to her. Kindly, lucidly. There was an odd calm in the telling. A measured recounting.

* {AD.35} *WHEN CINCINNATI VOTED, I went up to the Big Lake. The beach was gratifyingly cold: windy, with distant islands gray smudges like cardboard blips on the knife-edge of the horizon.

I had other knives to think about. Surgical knives, whereby the memory sponge was quickly slipped into the brain's base behind the ears. Completely illegal, of course, since although there were great ramifications for it in the field of education, there were also great ramifications for it in just about every realm of sociological control. They interfaced directly with the brain, and could hold an infinite variety of assemblers and pheromonal analogs. They terrified and exhilarated me. Encyclopedic information flooding into the brain—but *whose* information, and under *whose* control? It would take intensive training just to master these things, it seemed to me. And the next step, of course, the step of terrorists, would be simply to release information assemblers into the atmosphere. The wisdom of the ages? Hardly likely. My bet was political ideologies. Various slave mentalities.

But was I any better than those imagined fascists?

My second morning there, the light coming in the kitchen window was white because of the morning mist. I could see nothing outside except that soothing, unvarying whiteness, like a blanket. The old clay pots in which Mom had grown cilantro and dill when we stayed up here for a month at a time during bright blue summers still held dry dirt and withered stalks. A large mouse with unpleasant beady eyes stared at me with enormous insolence from the light green counter as I walked into the kitchen and I wondered what he had found to eat among those ancient moldering stores in the pantry.

Ghosts were all around me. I took a certain cup from the cupboard—just a typical souvenir mug with a deer on it—and as I did so I remembered, against my will, a day five years earlier.

Rosie, my cousin, had been at the cabin a week when I got my father's letter. She was quite snappish, he wrote in his neat, forward-slanting print, and noted that that was unusual for her. He said that he was trying to stay out of her way.

He knew, of course.

It made sense that she was there. The lake always helped both of us when we were stalled. Rose's parents had died several years back; her mother had been my dad's sister and Rose had inherited their share of the property.

I should have stayed out of her way too, I suppose, but after that day's mail I took the maglev and after that rented a good old-fashioned solar car and drove until the towns got older and then fell away altogether and it was just me, miles of pines, and the brilliant lake in glimpses through the trees. I got there late at night and lay awake, watching the path of the moon on the restless dark water, too aware that Rose was asleep just down the hall.

She had always been a bit jealous of the speed at which I'd progressed through my own advanced degrees, and after her master's in architecture had opted for city planning. She had avoided me for six painful months, but the reason was not professional jealousy; she'd long since developed her own confident approach, much different from mine.

In my room above the kitchen I heard a cupboard door slam and woke from my light doze. The sun was barely up. Hurriedly, I dressed and went downstairs.

She had just started coffee. I watched her from across the still-dark rustic dining room; she didn't know I was there.

Her long dark hair was loose, and straight bangs fringed her eyes. She was tall, slender, and never moved quickly. Her face was a pale Irish face, prone to freckles. She tanned beautifully, and from the glow on her bare arms I knew that she'd been lying nude out in the deserted dunes, probably listening to study tapes. My heart beat faster as I watched her, and I was so surprised. But then, not. It was just new for me.

It had been six months since we had slept together. It had only happened once.

She whirled when I came into the kitchen and said, "Oh, Abe. What are *you* doing here?" Her tone of voice was not welcoming.

She turned and looked back out the window toward the golden dunes and the line of dark green water which met the sky, the line we'd tried to sail to when younger. The window was open and sunlight washed the counter and the cedar cabinets. There was a smell of fresh water, pine trees, and ground coffee. Despite my frantic trip, I had no idea what to say but I tried.

"I came to see you. Is—is everything all right?" I asked.

"Why shouldn't it be?" She turned and looked at me quizzically.

I put my hands on her shoulders and she stiffened; I was filled with sadness. "Rosie," I said, not liking the sound of pleading in my voice.

She said, "I thought you were supposed to be all tied up in Cincinnati this month. Big nanotech doings, I heard. Your presence essential, of course. Otherwise I wouldn't have come." The breeze stirred little tendrils of hair at the sides of her face. "The coffee's ready," she said, and twisted away. "Want some?"

"Dad told me you were here."

"Hmm," she said.

"Well, I hardly need to apologize," I said. "This is my house too, after all. And I didn't think you'd be so wild to be here alone with Mom and Dad anyway."

She got two cups out, the old deer and owl that had miraculously survived our childhood, and poured us coffee. We both drank it black. She looked at me for a minute and something in her relaxed. She laughed a bit. "You know, I always think so well up here. And they're not a bother. We don't interact much. He fishes all day and India reads and I work up in my room. At night we play three-handed spades. Your dad's still a damned pistol at cards. Remember how we used to play every night in the summer out on the screened-in porch?"

I didn't know when I'd get another chance. I stood there afraid to put my coffee down because then I might grab her and she'd probably get angry. "Look, Rosie," I said. "I'm sorry—"

For a moment I had the feeling that she might toss her coffee in my face. "Nothing to be sorry about," she said. But her voice wavered a bit. She took a deep breath. When she spoke again her voice was level.

"You were kind of at loose ends, I guess."

"No," I said, "that's not true at all. I'm sorry I—I didn't call you for a few weeks afterwards—"

"Months," she said. "It's okay. It was a bad idea."

"Maybe a month," I said, and she rolled her eyes.

"It was a *good* idea! It was! It had nothing to do with loose ends or wild oats or anything of the sort, what you said when I finally called. It has to do with *you!* Rose, I—I have such strong feelings about you. I just had to think. I didn't—I *don't* know what to do."

"I don't see what the problem is," she said, though of course she did. She did and it annoyed her tremendously.

"There isn't any, not anymore," I said. "I've been thinking about what to do, a lot. Rose, I love—"

"Good morning, children," said my mother from the doorway, and I froze.

"You were saying, Abe?" asked Rose. She was not being sarcastic. She was not being coy. She ignored India. Her eyes said, *We are adults now. At least, I am. Are you?*

I found that I could not speak. Rose read me, of course, and after a long moment turned away. She stepped onto the veranda and closed the screen door quietly. I felt as if the world was moving away from me and would never return.

If I had known how right I was I would have run after Rose

and shouted at her, shouted what was in my heart. But I didn't know. Something inside her closed forever, then. Now that I think back, I realize that it took years to happen, and that was the final, telling moment.

When I turned around, my mother was smiling innocently. "Well," she said, "I see you made some coffee." She poured herself a cup. "Let me heat up these rolls and we can sit in the dining room. Rose is very busy, you know. You shouldn't bother her."

Right.

I think it would not have been too late to follow Rose. But I was too busy being angry with myself, I guess. And I always hated it when she was right. She was right about me, right down to the very last dotted *i*, and that hurt, and I didn't like her putting me on the spot and calling it right, which it was; oh, Rosie, you were right!

"No thanks," I told India.

"Abe—" she began, and touched my arm and there was apology in her eyes. "I just think—"

"Never mind," I said. "And it's none of your business." I went out on the warped weathered dock, fired up my dad's fishing boat, and took off.

That night Rose was my dad's partner in spades, and India was mine. They trumped us every time. Rose was calm and as usual sharp as a tack. I was frazzled and couldn't pay attention. She packed up and left sometime in the middle of the night. I left the next day. She wouldn't answer my calls. I was busy, truly busy; the Flower-City debate was heating up and as it turned out I was a crucial player. I hadn't really had the time to go up there in the first place.

We had a party when she finally got her diploma. I thought maybe after all that work was over she might relax; have time to think about what we might do. I thought we had all the time in the world but she seemed to have made a decision and we were never as close again. I got her a good job on the Committee; to my surprise she accepted it; she was far and away better qualified than anyone else. We were perfect together in design; we achieved several true breakthroughs. But despite the time we spent together there was a new distance in her now, something I'd never seen and something I couldn't find my way through. She was always cool and professional and dated men whom I imagined were far more interesting than me. I married for less than a year, then divorced. Rose barely seemed to notice. And after she knew too much about the project, she resigned.

Damn.

I put the deer cup down on the counter, hard.

Though the mist retired just a bit, the sky darkened with rain, which spat at me as I labored along the dunes in a scratchy red sweater, a scarf, and a wool hat rummaged from the closet shelf with the sweet tang of cedar which brought back so many memories that my eyes were swimming with tears and I slammed the closet door and hurried outside.

Despite my melancholy, I was very glad I had come, when I realized how much I itched to do something about the Cincinnati vote. Which was today. It's not true that absolute power corrupts absolutely. I was proof. Yet perhaps meddling just then would have been better than what I finally, actually did. Yes, probably.

To tell you the truth, I'm sure of it. I was pretty sure of it at the time. But only if Cincinnati converted could I put my plan into effect. So I wanted it as well, even though that was completely, utterly wrong.

But I wasn't completely twisted. As the waves crashed on the majestic empty shore, how I longed to change, like a truculent child, those years of campaigning for nan. We—the Committee— had done an excellent job. It would pass. How could humans resist the idea of virtually free stuff—clothing, shelter—swiftly concocted? Many of them, like stupid, naive me, at first, didn't understand that their initialization fee, enormous, would be financed at a rather high interest rate carefully calculated to take a good chunk of their lifetime paying off. But they were told that paid for the genetic work that gave them the receptors. And even if they saw that, what a small price to pay for their children's future—and after all, there would be a savings when compared to the old system.

But many of them were voting their gene pool out of existence.

How many of them read the fine print in the act? How many of them could? Icon-sensitized, they of course saw only the glorious taped, not broadcast, not for several dark years now—visions on hv, only a few dark downturns of possibilities, carefully contained and described by announcers with calm, positive verbal inflections and reassuring body language. Yes, now all disease would be cured, they wouldn't even have to feel guilty or be materially deprived if they chose not to work. And communication and commerce would begin once again, after years of radio cessation during which we'd fallen way behind the Cities, the countries, which had converted before that happened. It would all be on an entirely new level.

But the Cities were quite beyond anything that any of them could actually comprehend. Life would be radically different and here I was completely torn at the last minute.

I must have walked two miles up the beach in this funk. I turned back and saw Dad's dead ham radio tower waiting for never. The house was full of radios of all description. Receivers, transformers, dutiful signal transmitters.

So much more precise and direct than humans, because they worked without emotion being a factor.

The Bees did not, which in a way worried me.

I looked at that tower for a long time, thinking about information. The quasar had put a stop to that sort of transmission. The radio jets from that hithertofore undetected quasar at the center of our galaxy had gradually and inexorably washed out frequencies just as predicted, while the world scrambled to create a substitute before the possibility of quick and close worldwide scientific collaboration was completely precluded. Because it was utterly undependable, only a few diehards kept to it, eventually setting up stations that would perpetually transmit. Some Cities even tried to keep transmitting current information, but most gave up and went to endlessly repeated loops.

And despite the heroic initial effort to develop the crucial alternative, everything soon degenerated into secrecy and backstabbing as research foundations competed for funding from governments, and hesitated to share information before it was patented. I had been lucky enough to have the highest access because of my reputation as a nan-architect; one of the prototype Cities designed by Rose and I won the highest award in an international competition. Nan opened up a whole new world of possibility, responsibility, and individual contribution within certain guidelines. Rose had become overwhelmed by the ramifications. How long had it been since I had seen her? Two years?

The Flower Cities which resulted, after much international fervor, were, of course, for the ultimate benefit of the companies who held the patents, the ones whose trademark was dotted on the back of each Bee, organic, grown, just like an eye or a leg. If you invested in a Flower Building—a Plant, as they were called, of course—you had a lot of decisions to review.

You wanted Bees that ran on the same system as everyone else—probably. The options ranged from clunky cyborgs to the more organic Softbees. I envisioned a time not far from now when they would be entirely organic. The only reason we had cyborgs was because more money could be squeezed out of the participants when the technology switched. Private business concerns were one of the great drawbacks to this system, in my opinion. But that was what fueled it all to begin with anyway, and what was the alternative?

Consciousness by committee, that's what. That was the alternative. A dictatorship of direction. A Knowinger Than Thou conglomeration of social scientists, economists, engineers, and a single, somewhat twisted nanoarchitect.

Me.

Which was the real reason Rose had run screaming from the project, I was sure. I missed her input dreadfully. She was older than me. She had known me all her life. She knew me better than I knew myself. All my strengths. All my flaws. And the dreadful pain I fought each day. Harder to do, without her. I'd stopped thinking about all the things I had done wrong, with her, beginning with not understanding what was happening between us in the first place.

Any one of us on the Committee had the ability to step in and subvert the entire plan, though I wasn't sure that anyone else knew this but me. And, I suppose, Rose. I didn't know why; the back door hadn't been all that hard for me to see, and was simply an intrinsic aspect of nan. Those who control the assemblers control humankind. *I* could. *They* could. Anyone at our level could. At other levels, perhaps, the intricate failsafes would hold. But I figured that there was someone like me in every damned City. Had to be. And that's what bothered me. What would *they* do, and when? Things were moving along so damned fast that maybe only someone like me would spare the time to think about this problem. The engineers were all sitting around figuring out how to program the guts of the buildings; the economists were freaking out because you wouldn't need money anymore, and the sociologists were pondering how that would affect human behavior, so deeply based on barter.

The worst part of it was the fact that trouble was brewing, worldwide. What about, what were we fighting for? It was terribly disturbing to finally acknowledge that even at their most subtle, the Cities would be at war—for more! More!

Because of tribalism. We still had tribes. The ancient human division of us and them had to be tracked down at the precise point of the genetic code where it occurred and be switched off.

It may *have* been isolated. It probably *had* been discovered, long ago, by some government or Nobel hopeful, and the information buried and its re-discovery nipped in the bud. It was much too powerful for the warlords. What is a warlord without an enemy toward which to point his weapons, to rally his minions against? Us and them had to be bred out of us. I didn't think it ever would be.

So I dreamed. Just like the warlords. Once I dreamed that space, not space as in out there but the spaces in which we lived, could influence us to be different, really different.

Frank Lloyd Wright said that he could design a house that would make the occupants want to kill each other after living there a very short period of time. Of course, I wanted to do exactly the opposite. In a big way.

The frigid gusting wind blew my bitter laugh up the beach toward Canada. I followed it, running as fast as I could, a slow-mo idiot fighting sand and gravity, a nanoarchitect who would change the world, the Man Who Would Have Been King.

The man who had killed his mother.

No, I thought, falling winded at the end of a very hard mile. The inland sea was gray, silver gray, falling at my feet again and again. I'd wanted to save that deep laughing woman, rewind that immense thought-fire that blazed through her. I thought I was giving her eternity, instead of merely eternalizing her.

Unfortunately, there was an enormous difference. The same sort of difference, the same cognitive dissonance that would be physically realized once the City was Converted.

Ha. I drew up my legs and clasped them tight, shivering as sweat cooled, leaning into the cold, iron-hard dune. No, my boy, you just wanted Mommy Forever, that's all. You didn't give a shit about her and Dad saw that. She was an individual to him, someone who deserved the dignity of death, as he chose. She wasn't an individual to you. She was Mom. You traded on her fear of death.

So what else is new? I'd gone over this a million times. The grooves were worn quite bare. There was no absolution, only a dark and crazy place I avoided touching as much as possible.

So why are you thinking about it now?

The clouds had formed a dark heavy line on the horizon and I thought I smelled snow. Though it was early, that would not be unheard of in these parts, October snow in the U.P.

I went back to the cabin.

Already, by that pivotal day, I was working quite hard on my final, alternate plan, which had rushed around my mind often enough in the previous year like a swift gust of wind. Now I caught its tail and gave it color, as I had so often given form to thought through the medium of organizing space with buildings.

Snow was falling in earnest by late afternoon, and the dashing, howling blizzard only made it all seem that much more imperative. I worked long into the night, even after my dear and bedraggled guest showed up and fell asleep, finally stopping at about five A.M., fielding the caffeine shakes, turning off the light to stare at the snow-blanketed dunes, the slowed and freezing lake with its moonpath, drawing me into the future.

The future of You.

The future of myself.

Some of us, you see, never learn.* {AD.35} *

Twenty-eight

○○○○○○○○○○○○○○○○○

Talk of the Town

Verity waited for a few minutes after Durancy's voice finished, wondering if there was more.

But he had fallen silent, and she heard the first volley of evening fireworks as the streets below began to fill with revelers. The falls roared an undertone to the City's evening sounds and Roebling's Bridge lit, one steel cable after the next, generating light like the strings of a hammered dulcimer vibrated sound.

She took the elevator from the roof, somehow strengthened by Durancy's long-ago thoughts. They filled and steadied her. This was *his* City. She would make it hers then, and truly and finally heal Blaze. She would reach into the workings of the City with all the power at her disposal and wrench Blaze free.

She stepped out onto the street and turned toward the bridge. She longed to be out there, wild and distracted, for perhaps if she disarranged her mind he could break through again. Threesomes and foursomes of gaily laughing people were striding toward the river, and the pubs were filling up with people drinking and eating. She brushed her face as something light bounced off it, then looked down where it rested at her feet. And stopped.

For Blaze's face shone for an instant on the small triangular puff before it dissolved. She looked up.

Hundreds of the small puffs had been released from a high place. They littered the air, floated and danced on the breeze. Another came near; she ran to meet it. "Scott Joplin performs Rag-time at the Old Bucktown Hall," it said, beneath Blaze's pale face fringed with orange hair. "Don't miss it!" She reached out and tried to grab it but it evaporated at her touch.

But as it did a map flashed into her.

The old part of town, the ancient, core Rivertown with streets like dirt (not really, but like dirt, like it), horses (and they seemed real enough) pulling wagonloads of beer just for atmosphere because of course they could have a damned (sorry Evangeline) beer *faucet* if they really wanted to.

She set off running, an easy run, a loping run, down the hills. Only about a mile, nothing was really far here on the Seam-bounded island that she thought of as New Cincinnati. She noticed that many other people were heading the same way. She saw the picture again, here and there, puffed along on slight breeze. Had she heard lilting piano music, too, when she'd touched it, or had that been coming from a nearby pub with open windows?

Someone grabbed her arm and she yanked it away and kept running and he said, "Wait up" and she turned, prancing backward, and saw Sphere.

"Where have you *been?*" he demanded.

"Where have *you* been?" she asked, not slowing down. She was oddly glad to see him, though, despite her need to get to wherever Blaze was. She turned and continued running.

"Busy," said Sphere, "Very busy," but there was awe in his voice. "I never imagined . . . I've met so many of them. Billy Stray-horn. Duke Ellington—it's true, Verity, he has *hundreds* of pairs of shoes. And Miles Davis! He actually sat and talked to me. You know what he said? Listen to this, Verity. I don't know how many times he told me. Like it was some grand rule of the universe. Less is more. Less is more—" Sphere started breathing hard. "Wait up, Verity. It's not him, anyway. You should know that before you go and get disappointed."

"What do you mean?" she asked, slowing to a fast walk and turning a corner where inside a large plate glass window many people were eating and drinking at a long counter. She wished she had time to just *talk* to Sphere, tell him everything that had happened, or try to, but all she could think about was getting to Blaze.

"Well, for one thing, Scott Joplin was black," Sphere said.

"I don't even know who Scott Joplin was, though I think I've heard the name somewhere." she said. "That was Blaze. My friend from the train station."

Sphere stopped dead for just a second. "Are you sure?" he asked, then hurried to catch up.

She didn't reply. "This way, right?" she asked, and made another left turn.

"I'm just following you," he said.

"You don't *know?*" she asked.

"I assumed you were going to the evening's entertainment," he said, "But no, I don't know where the Old Bucktown Hall is. None of those little things said where it was. And slow down, my legs are killing me. We've got at least fifteen minutes."

"Mmmm." True. Verity knew that it would only take eight to get there, walking. She paused for Sphere, took his arm, and said, "You really don't know where it is?"

"No," he said. "I really don't belong here. I never will." His face filled with yearning, resignation, and hunger. "All the greatest music of all time is here, but I can't . . . *swallow* it. I can't *know* it like these holy people can."

Verity felt almost like snorting but did not. She was beginning to wonder what the best way to live really was. There were so many more ways than she had thought possible. She reached up and touched his cheek gently. "Are you sure that's what you want, Sphere? The last time I saw you, you hated it here. What's happened?"

"I—is that so?" He appeared puzzled. "Maybe I'm getting a better idea of what's going on. I mean, they *understand* music in an entirely new way. You don't know what it's like to live for something like that. It consumes you. It's like something you want to *know,* but that you can't really know, not entirely, and so you keep learning, hoping for some sort of climax, some kind of resolution . . . sometimes that did happen, when we were playing. Rarely. Maybe twice." He shrugged. "I'm sorry about your friend, Verity. I thought I was doing him a favor."

"You keep mentioning that," she said. But she could see that he was enormously upset. "Well now," she said, trying to make her voice strong, "we'll find out, won't we." She patted him on the shoulder and then linked her arm through his.

The old Bucktown Hall was crowded. The huge porch was overflowing and Verity had to elbow and kick her way in, dragging Sphere behind.

Everyone was standing, and Blaze was on a low stage way at the front, small, a hundred feet away, formally framed by a shimmering green curtain though behind the piano the stage was heaped with crates. The music he played seemed to come from everywhere and focus in the center of her head.

She felt, rather than heard, Sphere gasp next to her when Blaze was a few bars into his first piece. Perfect, his mouth said, though she could not hear it through all the other sound, and he pushed his way forward through the crowd and she followed in his wake.

Close to the stage people were dancing on the wide dark floorboards and Blaze's face was illuminated not only by the lights but from something within and his eyes were closed in ecstasy.

Verity tried not to think that this was really Blaze. It wasn't, after all. He had run off when he had seen her. Only his outsides were the same, which seemed quite cruel. He could barely think, from what she could tell. Well, she couldn't say that she was much better off.

She watched, wondering what in the world to do. Run up and shake him, try and jar him into recognition of her? But he had run off once already, terrified. She stood in the crowd, torn.

"Gladiolus Rag," shouted Sphere in her ear, as Blaze moved into a new and gentle number without pause.

Verity drank in the vision of Blaze. It was as if the moment of him lying dead and bloody in the orchard had never been and indeed it was easy to think of it as a terrible dream. His eyes were closed as he played, as if he listened to something deep within. It was almost as if she could see some light within his bones. Maybe, she thought, those awful sheets thinned his skull. His brain turned to jelly and rearranged itself according to some goddamned Bee agenda and he sure did know his stuff. There was new depth and majesty in the sudden changes, the Joplin forays into a haunting minor key and then out into the sunlight once again. Unexpected complexity surfaced for bars at a time, then vanished into straightforward beauty. All the while the music rang out strong and without hesitation, fluid, light, and sure.

And yet, it was hideous. She wondered if Blaze still had the plague, or if he had been cured. It seemed not, because this Joplin music was from the plague. Yet the dancing woman had said something about the Bees blocking plagues.

Arrested . . .

He could have risen from the train station whole and truly himself. If only she had agreed to be converted . . .

The room was filled with the scent of spicy pork barbecue and the dull sweet odor of years of spilled beer ground into the floorboards, and sweaty, dancing bodies. Blaze's long fingers which had once entangled themselves in her hair, curling and swirling it round and round, meditatively, while he stared into her eyes and she stared back longing to touch the side of his face, the slight hollow next to his eyes, moved up and down the keyboard in assured strides, though his eyes were still closed and his head thrown back. He looked older. He looked like a man.

Sphere thrust a sandwich at her, strands of sauce-covered meat sticking out from the sides, and she wrinkled her nose— meat, then realized that it wasn't, not really. No matter how it smelled it would probably have the sweet subtle undertones of everything else she'd eaten in Cincinnati and she was quite hungry. She ate it all, wondering what to do. Wait, she thought, until he was finished, until he awoke. He *would* wake, wouldn't he?

Maybe it was best to get close while he was so absorbed. He had run away before, but she wasn't sure it was because he recognized her or because he was just new and afraid at that point.

Oh, how much is *you*, she wondered.

The entire room was dancing, as if dancing were a virus that spread almost instantly at the insistence of the high, triumphant passages of music. As she pushed toward the stage Sphere grabbed her waist with one hand and her shoulder with the other, and as his legs moved, hers did too, and she was amazed to find herself smiling into his eyes while the horribly changed Blaze sat and played the music to which they moved, so perfectly, together, with everyone else in the room.

I have to get to him, she kept thinking, I have to tell Sphere and he'll help me, but she couldn't seem to say it. *The food,* she thought. *The air.*

She was lost in a whirl of dance and time vanished.

The mind of Blaze, whatever Blaze was now, entered his fingers and reached through the air directly into her mind and as she danced she laughed and cried and thought, yes, Blaze, it's you, it's you, my friend, it's really you, and she danced, she danced to Blaze's aliveness, and how happy she was that everyone was dancing with her, dancing to the music that poured from Blaze and only incidentally went through his fingers, as if he radiated a bright and beautiful precision that made them all one entity and then . . .

The music was gone.

She saw oddly that it was just Sphere, sitting on a chair, watching her dance.

She stopped, feeling empty. "Where are they all?" she asked. She was exhausted. "Where's Blaze?"

She walked right up to Sphere and shouted it again in his face. "Where's *Blaze?*"

He looked bewildered. "I don't know. He went out that door. Backstage."

Verity took a few steps and he rose and grabbed her around the waist and said, "Whoa. It was about half an hour ago. He finished up, stood, and thanked us for being such a wonderful audience. Everyone clapped, and you did too, Verity. Don't you remember?"

"No," she said dully.

"Yes," he said. "Everyone clapped so much that he did an encore. A very long one."

"Oh?" she asked, looking around at the huge empty room, smelling the stale beer.

"He said, 'I have a special request for a piece called 'Chrysanthemum,' ' " and he sat down and played it, and Verity, only you danced."

"I did?" she asked. The doorway looked dark and empty. The piano bench was so bare without him. He's alive, she thought, but it did not seem to matter.

"Yes," Sphere said, and his eyes were gleaming and his mouth curved in a smile. "It was a very beautiful dance. I don't think anyone here had seen anything like it, though toward the end people were beginning to imitate you."

"Is that so?" she said. That did not surprise her. That was what the Shakers had done, after all. "And then you just let him go."

"You just kept on dancing after he left," Sphere said. "I tried to stop you—not very hard, I guess, because I was a little bit afraid. Verity. Where are you really from? What are you doing here?''

But she was crying then, and he had to stop asking questions and hold her.

They slept together that night, in a small, pretty place Sphere found just a block from the Dance Hall. The bedroom was neat and the curtains were white and frilly and she undressed in front of him and said, "I want," then paused, not knowing exactly what to say or what it was that she really wanted.

But he did.

And late in the night she woke, entangled in his arms (it might really take a few times before you really enjoy this, he had said anxiously) and oddly happy, thinking that she had heard a dog bark.

I must be dreaming, she thought, but lay awake, listening.

Below the ancient highways, on the river's edge, where trains used to roar and cars zoomed overhead and riverboats steamed beneath the Seven Bridges, a black dog ran, her mind filled with pictures and the picture was of Her, Verity, and the dog ran and sniffed and whined and at last lay down exhausted and slept below old pilings, feeling sick, so sick and alone, twitching as she dreamed of the huge and frightful Bee.

Twenty-nine

◌◌◌◌◌◌◌◌◌◌◌◌◌◌◌◌◌◌

In a White Room

Verity tossed next to Sphere, restless.

Finally she fell into the Bee dream again, herself and Blaze Bees and yet themselves as well, flying from roof to roof through bright clear laser sharpness and color, with motion more fluid than human senses and synapses would allow. First her vision saw in frames, and then the frames came faster and the darkness flickered, then switched to eternal light and deep, rich color.

Her new nose deep in Flowers, she sucked forth stories, stories, stories, they fell off the stamens that weren't stamens and stuck to her legs and she pushed them into pockets and *stored* them there laughing, in her dreams, in the beautiful and perfect greed of this glorious sucking up of pure experience. Other Flowers beckoned, and soon her legs were packed with precisely configured information to return to the Hive.

Her sisters waited on the dance platform as she disgorged her food. The Russians were brilliant in color and pattern and taste, but they disdained that, programmed to other needs. Dance this American stuff, they told her, scenting that and nonscenting Russian, German, Thai, Japanese. Those are so far away, after all, and do not arise from these our native Flowers.

So Verity danced the Dance of America for them, from deep within the flashing maps. Danced the place of Twain, of a White Whale that was so much more than just a whale, danced a Pacific paradise pushed deep with the American places of both those men so that the rest of America, when they could, had to go and fight for those tropical green jungle dots spattering an unbelievably blue sea. We must die for this, as the Polynesians did before us, spoke her Dance, her thin black legs so much more fluid than mere human twos. Here are the pictures that prove this, I can show you kinetically, as skyscrapers are kinetic, swaying and giving beneath the caress of the wind and here let them grow Flowers because of the pure outbursting of the beauty of Information, of Organization, O let us dance to Life's deep Organization and to the Light within it.

And so she danced some more.

Here are more Stories, she told them, Stories of small towns and factory workers and their wives and husbands and children and here also is the compassionate gaze, the way we reconcile life's pain and fear and limitations except now, now, we are not limited! How many stories we can have now! Every story, every story the Land has put forth! Streams of endless stories from television, stories from comics, stories which are only pictures and stories which are only sound.

And the stories shone and coalesced, golden, in the heart of the Flowers, and she and her sisters rose in a group and arrowed straight toward them, and stored them anew and relived within the Hive, food for a new Generation.

When the stars came out, their vision faltered and they slept, warm within the heart of the stories, the power given off by emotions, by emotions made into matter pheromonally, ready for re-transmission, re-infusion into humans. We will always have mammalian truth, they told her, stored with insect cleverness but there is emotion here too, blind striving, a consciousness single yet made of many, a sidepath to you yet something you can put in jars and feed from. We Bees are your happy slaves, we store your Stories, and from them we Feed, we complete a cycle, we merge with you in a way that is entirely new.

The Guard Bees were out, though, at the entrance to the Hive, guarding it from those who would lay waste.

She realized that the City was a storehouse of that which was most dear to the hearts of old America: the poisons as well as the positive parts, unpurged, complete, ready to be transmitted ever and ever again.

Eternal.

I am a part of Eternity, she thought. And I am not sleeping, not at all.

She was awake. This was truly how the Bees saw their mission. And Abe was back, pressing upon her mind.

Sphere was breathing deeply and regularly; moonlight touched his shoulder and made a parallelogram of light on the wallpaper. She turned over and closed her eyes. Go away, she thought, I've had enough. I want to sleep.

But she was drawn into Abe's world more closely and more vividly than ever before. This was, she could tell by the pain preceding it—how terribly close these sessions were coming now!—essential, close to his core.

She stopped trying to push him away.

Yes, she agreed, and there he was. Or there she was.

* {AD.5} *Abe Durancy, half-asleep, shifted his body in the chair. The ancient dark green plastic covering the cushion crackled, wakening Abe fully.

On the hospital bed in front of him, his father's face was bathed in the faint violet light which feathered out from a wall fixture. His breathing was shallow. Abe watched his chest rise and fall. That was usually the first thing he looked at, the chest, to see if life was still there.

Damn the man!

It was still dark outside. Abe had been here for two days. He rose and stepped out into the empty hallway. At one end was the central computer. He saw the woman who was monitoring it take another sip of coffee while staring at the screens, a small, lonely figure.

Abe went the other direction, and stepped into the lounge at the end of the hall. He lit a cigarette. Everyone could smoke with impunity now. Everyone except his father. Damn his hardheadedness! He looked out over the park. The trees were dark irregular blobs six floors below. His City, his new City, which he had designed, was just on the verge of beginning. But the beginning was much more twisted, much more horrible, than he could have ever imagined when he started on this path, ten years ago, at the First International Nan Conference.

The stars were fading. It would soon be dawn.

He thought for the hundredth time about how easy it would be to change his father's directive, that no nan was to be used, absolutely none. In fact, nothing. No technology at all. No feeding, no oxygen. The man definitely wanted to die.

Well, it was not as if he really wanted to die. He just didn't want to be *made* to live. He had no religion, of course, not like his wife, whose flowery Episcopalianism he had tolerated with mild amusement. No, his decision was a very fundamental thing.

Abe felt that his father wanted to hurt *him* with this decision, and was just able to skirt the edges of that abyss. He'd wrestled with his own feelings about it for a long time, and those were all he could bear.

Abe pulled in another breath of smoke and blew it in the direction of the pulsing pre-nan "NO SMOKING, PLEASE" sign which he had spurred to frantic activity. There were only about ten other patients on this floor, and they were in just about the same fix as his dad. No one came here who wasn't.

After what had happened to India, his father had quietly joined the Society For a Natural Death, SFND, as they called it. He had their insignia tattooed just below his left shoulder, where life support teams had to look before they started anything. Abe hadn't really known until they called him from the hospital. He had just visited his father that morning, and the old man had seemed almost translucent to Abe as he sat in the garden, where his City-supplied aide, a man named Janson, had lifted him.

His father had tossed his cigarette on the brick path, a backward motion familiar to Abe as light. Then, he had just a few rasped words for Abe, but those words had propelled Abe from the garden like a shot, blinded by tears.

It was not the first time, but Abe had continued to visit the old man, no longer with any hope that he would change his mind about his only child, but out of some dogged sense of duty.

If only I had taken care of him myself, he thought now. Bathed him, dressed him. I would have seen the damned tattoo, I could have argued with him.

The cigarette was making his chest hurt. He thought of his mother, stored in the Bank, and did not really feel very good about that either. In fact, he felt wretched.

He was sure that India was flawed. The first test had been so utterly painful, especially when she had to be returned to the Bank, that he had simply not tried again.

Perhaps *flaw* wasn't the right word. Maybe she was just more elemental. The personality tests had shown that a very young aspect of her emotional being had been liberated, without the gloss of socialization that modified most adults. That seemed to be missing, though she responded normally enough—that is, in her very high range—to intellectual questions and problems. And maybe everyone would be like that when they got their new bodies—the bodies that some firm, he was sure, was developing at breakneck speed. It was hard to improve on nature, he was finally beginning to believe. Yet it was far too late to turn back now. And after all, weren't humans natural? And therefore all they did?

A rather bitter thought, for him.

The sky had lightened in pearly streaks cut by fluffy violet clouds. The sun blazed suddenly against the tops of the downtown buildings. Abe took out another cigarette, then put it back and turned suddenly, feeling something.

He rushed down the hall and into the room, certain that his father had opened his eyes. Certain that he had one last message. The one Abe had was too difficult to hold forever, *forever,* as his father's last words. What he had yelled that last morning in the garden. "You have made humanity a monster. A monster, like your mother, like yourself."

His father didn't really know the half of it. Hardly anyone did. The fact that a true nanplague had been loosed by someone, somewhere, was absolutely top secret. He had done what he could. To save her.

Unfortunately, he had.

And there she would remain. Saved. Forever.

Forgive me, he longed to say, and cry, as he had when a small boy and his father's arm had come around him in a strong hug, lifting him off the ground, forgiving him before he even knew what it meant, talking things over. How the old man had changed, since . . .

Abe ran through the open door.

His father was still lying in the bed, but his chest no longer moved.

Abe sat in the chair next to the bed and took his hand. It was not yet cold. "Please," he said, and bowed his head, and cried.

The only thing the attendant was empowered to do was close the old man's eyes. She could also, after returning in half an hour and seeing Abe still sobbing, take his hand quite firmly, lead him to a small room with peeling pink paint, and make him drink several cups of coffee before allowing him to go.* {AD.5} *

*   *   *

Verity woke wracked with tears. She opened her eyes and did not realize who or what was holding her in bed so that she couldn't move, then she saw Sphere's arm across her chest, turned her head.

She took a deep breath. She was very glad to be here. She was very glad that she was not Abe Durancy, and that it was morning.

She touched Sphere's nose with hers and his eyelids fluttered and his arms loosened.

Their small room had wallpaper of vines and hydrangeas. The hydrangea blossoms, large and pink, appeared to be flying through the air as if they were in a hurry to get somewhere and do something.

Verity sat up, swung her legs around until her feet touched the bare wood floor. She was surprised to find it warm. She stretched and the covers fell back from her shoulders.

She poured water from a pitcher into a bowl and splashed water on her face, dried it. Much better. She walked over to the double-hung window and struggled to raise it, then noticed a small circle of the wood sill that was not wood glowing. She touched it and the window slid up.

She leaned out into the morning. She was wearing nothing and she didn't care. Everyone would think she was part of some story.

And of course, she was.

The City never ceased to amaze her.

Above, the Flowers were unfurling toward the sun. The hum of Bees seemed to resonate in her bones.

She heard a knock on the door and ignored it. A panel on the wall began to flash and a voice said, "Your breakfast will get cold, Verity."

Her breath caught in her throat. She turned in one motion and dropped into a beetle-green velvet chair, curling up as if she could squeeze herself tight into one point and perhaps vanish. What was she doing here?

She couldn't leave, for one thing. Hadn't she tried?

Sphere sat up. "What was that sound?" He looked around. "Isn't there some way to get some music here?"

"I wouldn't be surprised," said Verity. "Our breakfast is waiting outside the door, I think. Why don't you request something?"

"Why do I sense that you're not in a very good mood?" asked

Sphere. He got out of bed. Verity watched him walk the few steps toward her, marveling at his smooth beauty. He knelt in front of her and took her hand. "Is everything all right? I mean—"

"Oh. Fine. Yes." She threw her head back and laughed. "Yes, all that's wonderful." She took his head in both of her hands and looked at his face. "Thank you," she said.

The voice said, "What music would you like, Sphere?"

Sphere's head, on which her hands still rested lightly, jerked. He rose in one motion and said, "I'll never get used to this." Then he looked back at Verity. "But why do I love it here?"

"The music," she said. "Choose some, why don't you?"

"Let's have a little early Dorsey," he said. "Tommy, that is."

As the music started, he motioned to her to get dressed. They accomplished it quite quickly, and he grabbed and whirled her around as she was opening the door and kissed her once, quite hard. She could hear his heart pounding. Then he let go, nodding his head at the floor.

She had almost stepped on a platter of food.

Many strips of bacon were piled in a crispy heap. She knelt and lifted a silver lid and saw yellow scrambled eggs. "This toast smells wonderful," she said, noticing the tiny white porcelain cup which held orange marmalade.

Sphere shrugged. "Whatever you think, Verity. I guess the food's the same everywhere." He looked back into the room and smiled ruefully. "This is the second night I've slept inside," he said. "I try to avoid the buildings."

"Who did you—" she struggled over what word to use—"*stay* with the first night?" she asked, and smiled when he shot a glance at her and said "None of your business."

They stepped over the food and went down the stairs on new, gray carpeting entwined with honeysuckles and bordered with pink and yellow roses.

Thirty

○○○○○○○○○○○○○○○○○○○

My Father Always Promised Us that We Would Live in France

The street was awash with color, and Verity and Sphere stepped out into it.

With the advent of people as the season had advanced, the hologram realities had withdrawn. Now, Verity saw them only down otherwise-empty streets, in the squares and parks on the edges of the City where people rarely ventured. Then it seemed as if the City longed to fill its loneliness with those shapes made of light.

Trees covered with bright purple blossoms lined the street. Vehicles silently moved past, some empty. A bus with passengers in four or five seats glided by, green, and stopped on the next block, where someone else got in.

The sweet scent of flowers filled the air along with the ever-present scent of water.

Sphere seemed bent on some mission, and she followed, raising her eyes from time to time to look at the Flowers above.

She wasn't sure what she should do next, but felt oddly content.

Until she saw the hologram of Blaze.

She pulled on Sphere's arm, and they stopped.

The holo was bright in the shadow of an overhead awning. Blaze was surrounded by shadow and lit by a spotlight.

He was sitting at a piano, and his arms moved. Moved, she

realized, as they had last night. Her breath caught in her throat. She walked slowly forward and stopped.

There was piano music playing from the figure, which was about a foot high, and beneath it flashed a message: DON'T MISS TONIGHT'S PERFORMANCE.

But the music was garbled. That was not like Blaze. He was so precise, so sure. He instantly invented what he did not know; any lapse of memory became a new variation.

The hands of the holo stumbled and paused, then he looked around blankly.

"Something's wrong," said Verity. "Sphere, do you think—do you think this could actually be happening now, somewhere?" She touched the holo but felt nothing as it colored her hand.

"Anything's possible, Verity," he said. "That's about the only thing I've learned here." His voice was low. "I'm sorry," he added. "It's my fault."

She whirled and shouted, *shouted* at him, surprising herself, and she could tell by his face she surprised him too. "It is *not!* It's *mine!*" Then she grabbed his shoulders and started to shake him very hard, all the time yelling, "It's my fault! It's my fault!" until he finally reached up and touched her wrists with the fingers of each hand, and ran those fingers lightly up and down the backs of her hands, and when she relaxed, he put his arms around her.

"All right, all right," he murmured. "I was only trying to be polite," he said, and she laughed in spite of herself and everything, the whole mad City.

"How can I find him?" she said.

"And more to the point, what will you do when you do?" he asked.

She looked up and said, "Well, I'll—" then stopped.

"You see, Verity, I think there are *parts* of him that are . . . different . . ." his voice trailed off.

"How long were we together?" she asked. "I mean, he could see me last night, right?"

"About as clearly as you could see him, apparently," said Sphere, his voice wry. "You communicated, in a fashion, for about an hour."

"I danced for an hour," she said.

"That's my best estimate."

"I don't remember it," she said, and turned to face the river. Then she looked away. Parts of her seemed to be rushing away quite as rapidly as the river. Watching it made her dizzy. She took a deep breath. Sphere's arm came around her again.

"Look Verity," he said, "I came inside the City for my own reasons, but I'm here to help you now. I want to help you and Blaze. Why don't you tell me about yourself. Just a little bit more, eh? It might help a bit."

She was just starting to when the assemblers surged again inside her brain, taking the color from the world and making her tremble.

"I'm sorry," she said, barely able to talk, "but there's something else I have to do right now." She looked around and as her vision faded she rushed toward a bench she saw but had to lay down on the sidewalk right in front of it as she listened to the damned, level voice begin, accompanied by the fleeting, dream-like pictures he always brought with him when he spoke directly to her. In his more sane beginnings, she had begun to realize, he was most direct.

She felt herself lifted to the bench, Sphere picking up her head, settling it on his lap, and pushing back her hair with one hand, then settling his hand on her waist as she listened again to the person she carried inside.

* {AD.47} *It was hard on the old man when the broadcasting went. He was sick already, and I think it finally did him in.

I mean, it was damned hard on us all. It was the passing of the foundation of the civilized world as we knew it, instant communication, bandwaves bouncing off layers of the atmosphere and satellites, hopscotching around the world, or being the beam that airline pilots followed. The archetypal symbol of those old towers in the newsreels with the lightning bolts coming out of the top, sending the signal, was suddenly as archaic as European cathedrals.

Of course, we were addicted by then to signaling. We just had to find a new medium.

So many people just didn't believe it. I don't believe that any of the military in the entire world believed it, despite the undeniable evidence. It would go away soon.

But it didn't. The quasar changed life as we knew it.

God, I remember, do I remember, how pissed he was when I went to Korea to be a part of the first International Flower-Intelligence Conference. It was one of those private things that the old farts in government—any government—had no intention of being a part of. But who cared? Nan promised to be faster and more powerful in every way. That was not the problem, really. The glitch was . . . how big could the system be?

Citybig. That was the optimal size. And everybody was worried about speed. We were addicted to speed, too. Everything was different then. But we soon realized that it didn't have to be speeded up.

It had to be *slowed down.*

I mean, get this. Everything instantaneous. Information vacuums! We're too *slow* to take full advantage of it. But we could use it, sure, to make clothing, create edibles, all that kind of thing. What a shift that was. Eventually, it made a lot of us into children.

Anyway, there were these hot new ideas at the time about DNA processing and transfer of information—*any* information, don't you see, it's *wild,* DNA can do it all—and there was this other weird contingent promoting these new ideas which I found, to be frank, architecturally stunning. I mean, the *air* will always be there, right? And the Bees were just like a new kind of *radio,* in a way. And who knows, maybe those biowizards who after all held patents on all this stuff and had nothing to lose puffed a lot of feelgood pheromones into the air and we were hooked and there you have it.

Hong Kong was the first City, and it really surged ahead after it was converted. Nobody could compete with it. Practically all you had to do was have human DNA and you instantly had everything you needed. Free. Talk about having time on your hands to think! Talk about education! It was like a beacon to the world. It just took that one City to spread. It swept away Hinduism in Benares in one fell swoop, or rather, it changed it, because your caste was right on your forehead beamed by your DNA, but then people found they could *change* that if they wanted to and the powers that used to be were pretty busy trying to think up some other kinds of comfortable stratification, but the rest of the world had no interest in that particular problem. They just wanted it. Everybody wanted it. Well, I won't say everyone. Always of course the diehards. The luddites, the naysayers, the old farts, the fundamentalists, and the dads. Even when the radios started to falter, even when they had the grand, sad Radio Festivals to mourn their passing and some of them lost the wave right in the middle, quite fitting if you think about it.

And my dad in particular, I think. Didn't want it, I mean. Oddly enough. He was a cynic, a pessimist, from the word go. Always the next depression was just around the corner, keep your gold in the mattress. And on the other hand he was one of the world's foremost unsung innovators in things having to do with thinking up neat, elegant, economical solutions to technoproblems. But it's hard when your whole emotional infrastructure gets kicked out from under you like that—like, what if you don't need gold anymore, what if you have all you want, what if you can fill up your bathtub with Krugerrands? Then what? Of course he didn't want gold—he wanted gloom, he wanted America. That always puzzled me, how flowery and bright European literature was, and how grim and gloomy American literature was like *they threw us out and it's hard* and then when I got older I realized that it was in the blood. Dark, grim, hard, straight, and pure honesty would allow no rewards, no Heaven peering around the corner with blond ringlets, ribbons, and a child's innocent face beckoning. No it was rough and rough was good, goddammit. Mark Twain's Susy died, and another daughter was an epileptic, and his dear Livy died too and after all that there was no more Territory; it was all bleak and dark, and bitterness consumed him. It didn't take other writers quite so long to get to that point. It was a point of departure, not a point of arrival, after that, except the Territory was there, in other ways, as my mother taught me, in early Dos Passos, in early Kerouac, and still glowing in late Ginsburg, and twisted to an entirely new vision throughout O'Connor.

And he worked hard all his life, did my dad. To send his little Abe to the finest schools, for starters, even though he was an unsung government worker. And my mother, well, it's probably pretty easy for you to guess, was an artist. An artist of literature, a weaver of thought. That was her house that you see, with the garden—been in her family for a hundred years, one of the original Vine Street mansions.

Anyway, that's why my father always promised us that we would live in France. Because that's where she wanted to go, and really, she made enough to take us there, or would have if she'd ever given a thought to managing it, but they spent too much money *living,* living well, living beautifully. But there was always tomorrow, and he—

Verity was stunned to hear Durancy's voice break for a moment before he went on.

He was among the last of the humans who chose not to be saved. Mom was . . . saved . . . a few years before it was really perfected, tested and everything. That made me wild, because I knew that it was coming and coming with the speed of a bullet train. And he said all the information he needed to pass on was in me, and that he was afraid to see what might be coming. Afraid of the future.

Long pause.

Now, I can't say as I blame him.

Then his voice came back, with the bright edge Verity was beginning to love despite herself.

But then again, I believe in brightness. I'm different from him, that way. It's the brightness of the unknown day that I believe in. You must too. What do I mean by that?

Does a child know what it will be like to be an adult? Do mystics know who God will turn out to be, though they yearn for Her with all their heart and mind and though Her darkness, Her hiddenness, is really, for them, a form of light? Do you know for sure when you turn the next corner as you walk down a busy street that you won't meet the love of your life? No! Or at least you shouldn't or you're as good as dead and you may as well not keep on going. And if you've met the love of your life, well, isn't it odd that all streets suddenly become not streets but a Person? and that all of time from where you are is transformed, becomes a new medium, a medium that transmits that most vital of all information, the Signal? Unknown future Person, you are like that for me, a street transformed into the Ground of Being, as they used to quaintly call it.

Now his voice was fierce, strong as the New Ohio in rapids.

And you, *he finished, his voice gentle and full of yearning, surely as brilliant and warm to her heart as Flowers were to Bees—*

You, all of you, or one of you. Or maybe none of you. You are my unknown day, my brightness.

You can choose to use my eyes and mind. You can choose to let me flood and infuse you. I give you that choice. You've come this far and that means you can handle choice. *(Another wry laugh.)* Hell, as Dad would say, what do I know.

But you can let me live again or you can use any part of my information that you like.* {AD.47} *

* * *

The voice stopped, and the codes lit up before Verity then. She saw them as clearly as if they were outside her yet knew they were only pictures in her mind, information hardwired by someone whose glory it was to think in that particular way.

Then they swirled away before she could fix on them, though she had a glimpse of the forks in the road of thought she had to take, now, to get there, the references (the Bell, Radio, Dad, and the Childhood Garden) that would direct her to the center of Abe Durancy. It was her choice now, if she wished to find out more. If the assemblers were working correctly, that is—rather an outside possibility, she realized. More information meant more parts of a puzzle. But many pieces were still missing. She did not know if they existed, anymore, in this latter-day City.

She was not ready to choose even if she could, she realized. Being filled with the being of another and infected with some as yet unknown mission seemed to her a form of slavery, to be jettisoned as soon as possible. But Durancy's knowledge held the key to restoring Blaze if anything did, and she was not ready to kill that gentle voice, to kill another human, however lost and gone or hidden within her like some new limb, like some new eye.

She might be the last. Especially if the whole system he had put himself into was breaking down in such a crazy way.

She sighed and stirred and felt hardness beneath her and opened her eyes to find that it was evening, and Sphere was sitting next to her with large, hot cups of coffee, and some sort of sausages covered with sauerkraut.

"I don't know if you like this kind of stuff," he said. "Looks like I planned this just right. It took you *forever* to wake up."

As Verity sat up and took a deep breath, she said, "It seemed to me like it only took a minute."

"You were saying, before you so rudely left me?" he asked.

"It's kind of hard to explain." Visions crowded around her.

"I can imagine," he said.

When we've been there ten
thousand years
Bright shining as the sun
We've no less time to sing
God's praise
Than when we'd first
begun.

—"Amazing Grace,"
Final verse by John Rees

A rose is a rose is a rose.

—Gertrude Stein

5

○ ○ ○

"Miles Always Said Less Is More"

—*Amy Roberts*

Thirty-one

○○○○○○○○○○○○○○○○○○○○

Since Love Is Lord of Heaven and Earth

Azure's kitchen was large and sunny. The wooden table was painted white, and in the middle of a red-checked tablecloth sat a vase of flowers: an iris with electric yellow tracing each petal's center; several carnations, some hot pink and others more pale and mild. One large yellow spider chrysanthemum laced curving tendrils through the other flowers.

The sun was warm on Verity's back, and she relaxed. She closed her eyes and remembered: the green waving cornfield, rolling in rustling waves to the trees which lined the creek, leaves turned up silver against an oncoming storm sweeping in from the plains.

Sphere was off on a search of his own. For two days they had looked for Blaze and not found him. "He's a musician, Verity," said Sphere. "So am I. I'll find him." Verity's hands got only garbled, frightened spurts when she tried to locate Blaze, and she became so upset that Sphere had tried to convince her that perhaps his way was better. Verity felt emotionally exhausted. Maybe that was why she could not find Blaze.

Azure clattered some pots, and Verity opened her eyes.

Azure was difficult to place. Verity watched her as she bustled around the kitchen. A breeze coming through the screen door that opened onto the high back porch moved the edge of the tablecloth.

The tall woman wore intricate drapings of cloth: a long skirt dense with some sort of dull pattern, a teal-green fringed scarf for a belt, a violet blouse with a sheen and large square crystal buttons.

Verity could not really tell her age. Forty? Forty-five? Somehow she was reminded of the twins; perhaps by the slightly gray streaks in the honey-colored hair, which frizzed in riotous curl. Verity saw, holding back one side, a golden clip shaped like a Bee.

On the table by the wall were brass candle holders also shaped like Bees, holding hexagonal honeycomb candles. A small book with a Bee embossed on the cover ruffled in the wind, and Verity reached over and thumbed through it while the sharp deep odor of ground coffee emanated from the small hand grinder on the wall where Azure was finishing her preparations. Water shushed from the tap, a match scratched as Azure lit the gas burner, and Verity gazed at the odd little book with dawning recognition.

"This is a prayer book?" she asked.

Azure pulled a chair next to her and perched on the edge. "Yes, dear, of course." She smelled sweet and clean, almost like a field of corn; green and growing. She bent her head over the book and Verity saw pale freckles on her paler face, the crescent of clear lens over her azure iris, her long, sandy eyelashes lowered.

"But why do you worship the Bees?" asked Verity.

Azure looked at her sideways, and her eyes were fired with something deep and certain. Her words came slowly.

"Out in the world, beyond the Seam, as best I can tell, humans give their children death with life."

Azure rose in a swirl of cloth and opened a cupboard, took out two rose-shaped cups and set them with a thump on the counter. She turned and her eyes were filled with happy calm.

"But there is no death here. There is light. Bright immortality. How can you not love this? When it is time, we merge and blend. Then once again our cells come forth and fill with information. But you know this better than anyone." She pulled the cubic glass pot from where she had stuck it to the wall and poured the coffee. "Honey?" she asked.

Verity shook her head and picked up the book once more.

She had met Azure in the market, where the sun slanted through the open wood beamwork overhead. Verity saw that open place deflect a brief afternoon shower.

Azure had walked right up to her, put her hands together in the center of her chest and bowed her head.

"Holy one," she had said, "I do not know your name, but mine is Azure. Your light is very beautiful. Will you have coffee with me?"

"Why not?" said Verity, ignoring the strange greeting, thinking about how good she was getting at ignoring strangeness here.

Now, holding the book open, she read aloud, "Holy Queen of Information, of Stories, of Time's precise arrangement, we worship thee with sacrifice."

Azure set the cups before her, and a plate of the inevitable sweet cakes covered with small, crunchy seeds.

"Sacrifice which is complete, but which is amply rewarded, don't you see?" she asked, and slid into the chair opposite Verity. "I remember past lives, O indeed, I do. It is true reincarnation. And we do not have to get old. When our bodies begin to creak, when the chemicals of hope wear thin, we can commit our Selves to the Hive once more, and wait for a new body."

Her eyes filled with tears.

"Verity, I know who you are. Why you are here. How can you want to destroy this wonder? This beauty? All of *us*? Don't you see? It can go either way. It is up to you to decide."

Verity didn't ask why Azure thought these things. Everything here was so bizarre. But all she had to do was remember broken Edgetown, the waste matter. Cheyenne, so ignorant. Sphere, finite and yearning.

Yearning for this, she told herself. Yearning for what Azure already is. But were the Bees to blame for this? Blame implied volition, and she had seen little of that here in Cincinnati.

And most of all there was Blaze, enslaved somehow, who must be unriddled.

"Do you live here by yourself?"

Azure's eyes went pensive. "No," she said. "Well . . . yes. Gene is my husband. But he's not here right now."

"Where is he?"

Azure shrugged. Her fingers picked at the edge of her placemat. "He's down in Storyville, I suppose. It makes me a bit angry, to tell you the truth. It's not every life that we get to see each other." She sighed.

Verity leaned forward and put her elbows on the table. She

heard the cries of children playing outside and wondered if the children were real or just some sort of construct the neighborhood thought it needed to be complete. She wondered how hard she could push Azure without coming to the strange blank place she'd found in every person she met here. "So you don't have to be in a story to live here?" she asked.

Azure looked uncomfortable. "No, not really," she said. "But," she fumbled, "It's part of the plan. Someone has to do it," she said. "We all feed Her in our own way."

"Why?" asked Verity. "What are you feeding her?"

"Information," said Azure. "That is what I am giving you now. We do not question the desires of the Holy Queen," she said, looking surprised herself as the words came out, staring very directly at Verity.

Because you can't, thought Verity. "So you don't have a story? Why is this?"

"I can trace my incarnations in a straight line preconversion," said Azure. "It's because of that. I do have a story. But it is my own. I give it freely." She nodded toward the prayer book. "I'm a part of the Hive, a part of the music of the Hive. You cannot imagine how beautiful it is to be a part of that holy music. When We decide, We decide together. We decide everything." Each We she uttered was charged with hushed significance.

Verity could imagine how beautiful it was. That was what worried her. She swallowed. Perhaps she was more Bee than she would like to know.

"Do you have any children?" asked Verity.

"These are very strange questions," said Azure. "I would think that you would know everything. But I suppose that's a function of time, after all. The delicious not-knowing, the chemicals of discovery." She looked out the window. "We did have children. Yes, Gene and I did. Two girls and a boy."

"Where are they now?" asked Verity, seeing that the questions hurt Azure but wanting to know.

"Given," said Azure. "They didn't get back . . . in time. They are everywhere now. I know that Gene can't understand this. He thinks it's his fault. You see, when it . . . it *happened*—"

"The Conversion?" asked Verity.

Azure looked down and nodded. "They were playing and I was at work and he was calling and calling and they laughed and wouldn't come—how many times he's told me this!—and then he *saw.* . . and he became very frightened and ran for the cocoon and left them, but I always tell him that it was Her will. Poor Gene. He needs to have more faith. I think that's why he always goes to Storyville. He thinks maybe he'll see them. Then he despairs, and intoxicates himself with stories, so he can forget. But—I hope you won't hate me for this, or think our sacrifice incomplete—one of them became very angry with me before the Conversion. Yes, she did. We had a terrible quarrel, and she left the City. The boy and the other girl . . . I hope . . . no, I *know*, that some day, I'll see them in the market . . . some life . . . if there's any truth at all to this. But there is!" she said, and covered the prayer book with a strong freckled hand.

"Sitting out here now," Azure continued, "the Hive is a bit like a dream. But I know I'll return. When it's time. When I'm called. When I'm needed. You see, I remember. Most of them, like Gene, choose to forget." She shrugged. "Really, I suppose it doesn't make a whole lot of difference. I prefer to know. Others prefer to be entirely involved in what they're doing. In a way, I suppose, it frightens them. Not all of us were frightened, preconversion. We learned from San Francisco, from Denver. The Way was communicated to us like a flash of light roaring down the train tunnels."

The Information Wars, thought Verity suddenly. This religion is just another form of information that the City has used to its advantage. Maybe that daughter just wasn't affected for some reason. Verity really couldn't know if that was better than living like Azure. The daughter was perhaps an ancient woman in Edgetown now, or maybe had perished on her way down the New Ohio River, or died a lifetime ago in the earthquake. While Azure lived, again and again, this particular part of her life.

"Well," said Verity, swallowing hard, "what happens then, when you're called?"

"Come," said Azure. "I'll show you."

Verity followed Azure up the broad stairway. The woman paused, then held her hand up next to a door and it slid open.

"The room will have no problem accepting you," said Azure, and her voice was shy.

Verity already knew what she would see.

A shimmering cocoon was the only thing in the room, which quietly glowed with Enlivenment.

The room looked just like Azure. It was a place of enormous beauty, filled with pattern, color, and light.

"It's waiting," said Azure, "Because She loves me."

That's love? wondered Verity as the door slid shut. And then the door itself pulsed with light; Verity's breath stopped for a moment when she saw her own picture, faint, on the door, for about three seconds. Then it vanished. It filled Verity with unease.

Azure looked at her once more and said, "I knew I was not mistaken. But all in its good time, I suppose. If we knew everything all at once, how dull it would become." Her face was shining as if she saw one of her children as she looked at Verity.

Verity followed her back down the stairs to the kitchen.

"You said you know who I am," said Verity. "Well, who am I?" Azure seemed quite direct, and unusually harmless, and though Verity could easily see her pulsing information back through the cocoon, it was information that the entire City had access to, if it wanted. But maybe Azure was right. Maybe it was just time that was holding her back. She could only take in so much at a time. She couldn't run before she walked, could she?

"O my Lady," said Azure, and her wide, eyes filled with tears that were not surrounded by the facial musculature of pain, but of awe. She brought her hands together, once again knelt on one knee, then looked up.

"Would it be impure to ask to see them once again, my loved children? Oh, yes, I know it would be, please forgive me. Forgive me. Forgive me." Tears were streaming down her face. "I didn't ask for myself, but for them . . . at least I don't think it was for me. . . ."

"Azure," said Verity gently, though beneath she was filled with rage at the City, at what had happened to this woman—though after all it was not much different from what life had been for humans since time began: pain, separation, loss, grief, mixed if they were lucky with joy and limbic reasons for the continuation of the cycle. "Please get up, Azure. Here, have some coffee. Have you eaten yet today?"

"My Lady, you are the new Queen. Please bless me. I have been faithful through all these lives. Faithful to You."

"No," breathed Verity, though in the instant before Azure spoke she had seemed to feel it coming, inevitable as Blaze's ghostly train. "No," she said. "You are wrong about that."

But Azure gazed with her with eyes that suddenly gained new

depth and definition, as if a part of the iris's function had changed, like John's eyes sometimes had changed from blue to green. Verity could see that the strange woman was seeing very clearly, seeing something that she herself could not see at all, just like the old man in the apothecary shop. A juxtaposition of possibilities, almost like the clash of fencing swords, surfaced briefly far back in her mind, and she felt deep despair and keen, blossoming anger at all she did not know about herself. But she knew that she had no desire to rule these lost people with dancing metapheromones. Yet how could she dare to change matters for them? They were so much different from people outside, like children playing in fields of gold. Azure was the first person she had met whose suffering seemed real. Tears rose to her eyes. Who was she to say that Azure's hope and faith were futile? If she could grant her wish, should she not do so?

Don't be silly, she told herself. You can't even save your dear friend Blaze. You can barely tie your own shoes.

"Azure," she said, "get up!"

Azure rose, and remained standing, still as a statue, still gazing at her with love and adoration.

Then she began to sing: "Changed from glory into glory, Till at last we see her Face." She had a deep, melodious voice of great beauty.

Verity knew the hymn. Blaze had played it often, in the Meeting Room, as snow tapped on the window.

It was a hymn to the Mother. Not to her. Not to her. Never to her.

"Till we cast ourselves before Her, Lost in wonder, love, and praise."

"I'm *human*," Verity yelled, pushing the thought of her sisters, stored in the Hive, far from her, and when Azure would not stop singing, but instead entered a deeper phase of trance, Verity turned and ran out the back door, stumbling on the sill, then recovering, clamoring down the wooden steps (not wood, she thought, like wood, not wood but identical, she finally realized, wood is wood, that's all no matter what its history).

The words were lost by the time she was down the steps and into the back yard, through the hedge, and out into the alley.

But the melody rose and followed her for more than half a block, while her throat began to burn for air. The house itself, with flutes and wild violins, had joined the final verse.

Thirty-two

○○○○○○○○○○○○○○○○○

Die and Live

Only a few hours later Verity was leaning against a nineteenth-century red brick building, eating an apple, when the sky flashed and everything paled, except this time she knew what it meant.

The City seemed suddenly composed of particles that were light and color, but behind them was another vision, another reality.

She trembled, feeling weak and sick. She leaned over and vomited, and knew that no one would care. Wiping her mouth with the back of her hand, she tried to breathe deeply and get to a protected place. She had to settle for crawling to a doorway, and wished she had something to drink. Her mouth was dry and fuzzy. Yes, she told it, following the codes as if they were a knotted rope in darkness.

Evidently it wasn't meshing right this time. The first-activated assemblers ran biochecks and adjusted themselves for accuracy. But the man in the shop had said they were old . . .

She realized now that if anyone else took these particular assemblers they would probably have seizures and die. But because her brain had been specially monitored and initialized when she was very young, these assemblers, saved for her and the others identical to her, the cellular-level adjustments the assemblers made caused her to feel ill for a while. Where were those identical to her—staggered in time? She could not believe that she was the first, though she might be the first to get these assemblers. She and her phantom sisters were helpless preprogrammed emissaries sent forth to do—what?

She shivered as a fine drizzle began drifting down over the City. She tried to rise so that she could at least make it into a building, but her legs would not bear her weight. Though she was shivering, she felt as if she had a fever.

Maybe this would be the episode where she'd find out what she needed to know.

She closed her eyes and suddenly the path was bright and clear, and then he focussed within her.

* {AD.12} *ABE CONSIDERED canceling his customary Wednesday evening dinner with his parents, but decided that it might be best for him if he could maintain some semblance of normalcy. And what could be more normal than this? His parents were so soothing that when he and Katy, a fellow at the Nanotech Center, had divorced amicably after a year-long marriage that simply did not engage, she too continued to dine with them every Wednesday evening whenever she got a chance.

Even though she was immersed in her new Meta-American Arts overview, his mother had hired the perfect housekeeper and cook, David, a middle-aged man who happened to be her culinary clone, so as usual all was absolutely stable there.

It was a dreary Midwest winter day, which darkened well before Abe made his way down to street level to catch a bus, adding to his depression.

As he stepped onto the free, driverless Green Line vehicle, which would take him to within a block of his parents' house, he sat down behind two blond children evidently on their way home from a late school day. No one else was on the small bus, and their chatter formed the background for his pensive musings. For his incredulity. He could not believe that this was happening.

Not many people knew. He wished that he didn't. He wished that his top clearance had not become this two-edged sword, informing him of his culpability and naivete.

When most people worked on a top-secret project, they didn't know much about what the product was going to be. But in this case, he had been suckered into working for the Information Wars department by allowing himself to believe that it was purely to develop a defense against this. He knew, bottom to top and inside out, exactly what he was doing.

He therefore knew that he had failed.

Each and every nan packet, light enough to be windborne, tinier and more deadly than any virus because of its enormous versatility, had easily hacked through anything that might encapsulate it, cancel it, disarm it, transform it. Any designer could generate and incorporate a hundred wicked twists in very little space.

And what might these information nans do?

Ostensibly they had been designed to educate. Cheap and easy brain growth for the masses. Brain growth as we see fit, cleansing the human race, essentially, of those mindframes that need to be left behind. Like criminality, all forms of retardation. Searching and changing the DNA, rendering many people sterile. Certain mindframes already patented and trademarked; buy success for your children. And the rest of you, if we allow you to live at all: be content to labor for us, and do not question your life.

Durancy didn't understand that at all. The sociobiologists charged with this immense responsibility didn't seem to understand that nan, as manifested in *his* meticulously planned Flower City, would bring relief from the age-old problems of food, clothing, and shelter. There would at last be time for people to develop their creative energies. Their *individuality*. His father during one of their many arguments had said, "But Abe, you don't seem to understand that very few people are truly creative. In fact, I find you incredibly naive concerning the energies that inform the lives and concerns of most people. You and your elite crowd."

"But we'll—" Abe had said, then paused.

"But you'll *make* them so, is that it?" He had risen and left the room at that point, and Abe had known that he wouldn't see his father again that night. When Dad got angry enough he didn't shout. He just withdrew, leaving quiet condemnation hanging in the air behind him. Sometimes Abe didn't know how his mother had stood it, but she had always seemed cheerful enough.

He knew now that his father's fuddy-duddy luddite concerns were chillingly on-target. Who in the world was wise enough to see humanity through these wrenching changes?

Certainly, he thought, looking down at his clasped hands, not me. He looked up, and saw that they were passing the old drug store. He would always remember the soda fight he and Rose had there, shaking up the bottles and squirting each other while the old man tried to make them stop.

But even that couldn't make him smile today. It just reminded him of how miserably he had failed with her. Sometimes he wished he could bring himself to be angry with India, but he knew that Rose's take had been right. India was entitled to her opinion, to her feelings—feelings that probably stemmed from old familial struggles that had occurred before he and Rose had even been born. She had simply never liked Rose much, and had never liked Rose's mother much. But it was his responsibility to be true to his own feelings, no matter what his mother thought. She wasn't the one who had wanted to . . . to marry Rose. Yes, marry her. And where was she now? Well, maybe it still wasn't too late.

Abe wrenched his thoughts from the subject of Rose. He wondered, not for the first time, if nan could have killed the radios, killed all broadcasting, saturated a level of the atmosphere somehow, to make way for the Flower Cities and the profits they would bring to a new cadre of careless profiteers . . .

He tried to feel a bit more cheerful as he walked up the familiar front steps and opened the ornate leaded glass door.

Good smells. Roast chicken, potatoes. The burnt-sugar smell of custard. David came into the living room, wiping his hands on his apron, nodded when he saw who it was and disappeared back into the kitchen.

The table was set. Three yellow hothouse tulips, huge, each petal bisected by a pink line, crossed stems in a clear cylindrical vase. Yellow cloth napkins were held down by silverware of a graceful modern design. John Cage was playing—or not playing—and Abe knew his father would switch it to Bach as soon as he became sufficiently unsettled by his wife's musical preference.

It all looked normal. Abe knew it was not. Nothing would ever be normal again. But perhaps in this island of normalcy things could stay the same longer than elsewhere. He prayed that might be the case, and poured himself two fingers of single malt at the buffet, then went off to look for his parents.

His mother was in her office, her bookmaster switched on as usual, projecting small, vibrant holograms with wonderful resolution, a storytelling mode generally used by children.

She was curled up in her deep easy chair, her head thrown back, her eyes closed. She was regal and not too thin, midwest heavy-boned but always in shape with exercise. Her blond hair was loose and flowed over her shoulders. Her face was pale and slack, giving Abe a turn.

At a sound from the corner behind the door he looked around, saw his father gazing at his mother.

"I think she's sick," he said. "She's been like this for about three hours. She can't be tired. She said no sooner did she get in the pool this afternoon than they closed it down for some reason. She was pretty grumpy when she got home—you know she likes to get in at least a mile." In the multicolored light of the holo, as rain streamed down the window behind the generations-old lace curtains, his father lifted his own glass of whiskey and sipped. "Start up the fire, won't you?"

One corner of the tiny room was an angled gas fireplace. Abe turned and pulled a long match from the vase which held them, leaned down, twisted the pilot, and scratched the matchhead across the bricks. A blue flame flared, and he adjusted it.

The walls were lined with bookshelves, all American first editions, many of them signed, the work of a lifetime of collecting. Their faded covers filled the room with color and life and a certain lovely, musty smell. She had a first edition of *For Whom the Bell Tolls,* which had cost ten thousand dollars. Abe was always surprised that though his father didn't understand this passion, he never complained about it. He just commented when she brought it home, "Guess we won't be going to Paris this year either," lit his pipe, and went out to sit in the garden.

Abe went over and felt his mother's flushed forehead. She stirred, and to his surprise, began to sing in a deep, clear voice. "Froggie went a-courtin' and he did ride . . ." Her eyes remained closed as she sang the whole song out, every verse, and started in again. A slight smile touched her lips.

"That's it," said Abe's father. "We're going to the doctor. David," he hollered, and when the man came to the door, he said, "Sorry, but India's sick. Just put dinner on hold, will you, and call us a cab."

Together, Abe and his father got her into her heavy coat, and she cooperated as if heavily drugged, smiling and mumbling bits of song.

"Must have caught some sort of flu at the pool," his father said over and over again in the cab, clutching her hand with his so tightly that his knuckles were white.

Abe was silent and wretched as they sped through the bright City streets.

He knew better.

The doctor winked at Abe as he punched the prescription into the computer on his wrist. "Guess by next year this time we'll have a whole new class of drugs to choose from, right?"

He was referring to the date finally approved by the FDA for the release of the new nan drugs that all the companies were seething to cash in on.

Abe could only nod, sick at heart.

He didn't say anything on the way home. The two of them helped her into bed, taking care not to dislodge the silly, useless antibiotic patch.

Abe spent the night. When the rain turned to snow, the drumming on the roof stopped, and he was able to drift in and out of nightmare-riddled sleep.

But when he got up and went into her room, she was alert and smiling, a bookmaster propped up in front of her.

"Hi," she said, smiling, and took a sip of her Earl Grey tea. "Sorry to upset you guys so much last night. I'm fine. You go on to work and drop by tonight if you have time, all right? No don't kiss me now, I'm sure I'm contagious. Abe," she said, and her face became serious, "have you heard from Rose? I've always been sorry—"

"No," he said. "Haven't heard. But please don't worry, all right?"

Abe's hands were icy when he walked into the Center. He was in another world, not in the cozy old-fashionedness of his parents' house, and not even in the smooth-running present-day Cincinnati.

Here he lived in the future.

Maybe, he thought, it was making him crazy.

Surrounded by prototypes of Flower Cities, small holographic models, he decided that he was most certainly crazy.

He got up and went down the hall to the Transfer Center. The guard waved him through and he sat in the control chair for a long, long time.

There were already many people in the bank. Abe himself was updated every six months, and in the Flower Cities the update would be continuous and effortless. All top secret, of course. He was sure that there were bodies, somewhere, in some other water-tight department. Once the ban was lifted, there were many companies ready to bank anyone's mind. Some people doubted that it would ever be lifted, but he didn't.

Abe had a feeling that it wouldn't be too long before complete broadcasting cessation took place, and then everyone's backs would be to the wall. There had been patchy lapses, when HV platforms went empty and TV screens went dark, but when information resumed, some sort of mass blindness decreed that ignoring it was the best way to deal with it. Maybe it hadn't been real. The scientists had to be wrong. Humans didn't have to change to Flower Cities. They didn't have to submit to DNA tinkering and all the rest.

No, they could go back to the eighteen-hundreds, and rather quickly at that.

Already San Francisco had voted to change, the first City in North America to choose to do so, and massive preparations and intricate failsafes were being put into place right now. He'd heard ugly rumors that what was happening had nothing to do with a quasar, as the media had been telling them for years, but that instead it was all the result of some nasty nan devices that ate fiberoptic cables and transistors. He didn't know what to think anymore. The world was aswirl in newness, in change even more time-compressed than in the twentieth century, where a person could have ridden in buggies when young and watched men walking on the moon when old.

Where was Rose when he needed her? She was always so lev-elheaded. She had seen all this so clearly, and turned her back on it. Said she wouldn't be a party to it.

Katy came in then, cool and professional as always in her white lab coat. Her black hair was smooth and cut straight, and her blue eyes were filled with concern.

She walked over to him and took his hand, and stared at the empty cocoon with him for a long time. Then she said, without looking at him, "Are you sure?"

"I'm sure," he said. "She's not the only one either. They closed down the pool yesterday. I'm not sure what happened. I heard there was some sort of incident before I left work, but I had no idea . . ."

"I heard from Section C that it's under control now," she said.

"For whatever that's worth. They hit several public places, it seems. From the data we've gathered from local hospitals. An art museum. Three restaurants. Two of the people have died, hallucinating. But most of the others are fine right now. In fact, chances are that they'll *continue* to be fine . . ."

"Come on, Katy," he said.

They were silent for a few minutes longer, then Katy sighed. She squeezed his hand and let go. "Are you going to tell her?"

"Of course," he said. "She'll have to decide."

"Are you going to tell your father?"

"That's up to her," he said. "I'm pretty sure he'd be against it."

"I'm sure too," said Katy.

It took five days to evacuate San Francisco, because of those who had to be ferreted out and forcibly removed from their homes. The conversion took forty-eight hours.

The transfer of India to the computer bank took about a day.

Longer than expected. In the middle of the procedure, which was pretty new, they realized they had to do a complete, because her heart had stopped.

They kept it going until the transfer was finished.

Then they had to let her go.

Abe had spent the afternoon begging every branch he could think of for the heart-repair nan that was already complete, that would be on the market in just six months. It was hard for him to believe that they could all turn him down by saying he had to go through the proper channels. There had been no time for that.

"Abe," Katy had said, her face wretched and pale after it was over, "I have to tell you, there was something odd about the redundancy tests. I ran them three times. I'm not sure if the copy is any good. She—she died in the middle of it, you know, and there was some sort of break. Abe? Please say something."

He turned and walked out onto the snowy streets of Cincinnati a completely changed man.

Reporters had ferreted out seven instances of a strange new virus. Authorities were denying any link with nan. The vids were filled with the enormous, enthusiastic party that San Francisco had become, once the Flowers had bloomed and the Bees had begun their work.

Abe was never sure why he chose to live, that night. Maybe it was just some odd, bizarre, sprouting hope. The hope that Katy was wrong.

And the beginnings of the formulation of his Great Plan, wherein Cincinnati *had* to vote for conversion.

Only in that way could his mother live again.* {AD.12} *

Segment over, said the voice. Verity recovered herself, in an instant's dark void, and then opened her eyes. That voice was new. She didn't like it much. It seemed impersonal. Maybe it came from a different time, an early, stiffer time.

She gradually realized that it was late afternoon. She looked down through the City and could see a glimpse of the river several blocks away.

She felt weak, but no longer sick. She rose, hungry, and wondering how many of these memories she would have to endure. Was there an endless supply? She didn't see why not. Memories were layered, each called up another, and that one referenced yet another. The addition of each segment of information was like the growing light of day to her. The more she knew, the better chance she would have of restoring Blaze.

The next one began so soon that she was caught completely off guard, but she managed to get into the lobby of a large, empty hotel and lay down on a couch, panting and feeling quite ill. Get it over with, she thought. Let's have it.

At first she was looking down a very long corridor with frames inside of frames, a tunnel with a small and distant picture at the end and then it was . . .

. . . Bright rushing green, rain on windblown leaves, the sharp spines of some pink flower without a lens so it was crystal clear and without a frame so she did not know the name, flower. But she did.

But I do, she whispered, and where am I now?

Verity reached up for some reason as she lay on the couch, for the same reason perhaps that her fingers had once unerringly reached to the smooth brown skin on the top of her thigh and felt beneath a lump that Sare cut to as she watched, anesthetized and curious, and squeezed out and showed her: a white lump of fat. Now, her fingers reached behind her ear and *pressed* in a particular pattern. Short long long short. She repeated it three times.

And where before through years of bumps and casual pressure nothing had happened, now something did and she was back one frame and saw herself, but close . . . she was inside the child body that had grown to this one and she was running.

* {#23.0} *HER HEART was pounding and a small readout in the upper right part of the picture said 3.11. The path was uneven brick and she tripped and fell and could not stop then from screaming in terror and hurt.

Large hands picked her up, the pretty lady with the long brown hair had her. She kicked, hard. The woman just tucked her beneath her arm, against her hip, casually and easily and said with a grim edge, "Sorry," panting. "It will be . . ." her voice broke . . . "all right."

She felt something smoothed upon her neck and then she could see and feel everything still but felt no rage, only curiosity.

There was a man too in the white place and he said, "Are you sure that she's the best one we've got to work with?" He turned away and opened a small door and white mist frosted the air until he pulled some things out and he closed it.

"Hurry up," she said. "Yes. Why do you think she ran away? She's the brightest one we have, Dennis. Do you want a child who would just sit around like a dummy and let someone do something strange to them? Someone docile? We need someone *different.*"

Verity—but that wasn't her name, was it?—tried to say something but her mouth wouldn't move. She just stared at the man and the woman. Stared hard. Maybe she could get away from them, or hurt them terribly, just by staring *hard.*

"She hates us," said the man. "I'm going to put her out."

"You can't," said the woman. "If you close down those functions we won't be able to check how she's doing. Is sterility one hundred percent yet?"

"Almost. Ninety-two. Ninety-seven. Ninety-seven and holding. There."

Verity felt a strange sensation behind first one ear and then the other, and briefly saw two white roundish shapes in the hands of the woman who had been watching her and playing with her and pretending to make friends with her for the last few weeks in the garden. Now the woman frowned.

"How are we going to make sure that these are activated by the feeds at the right time?" the woman asked. "It's so hard to tell from inside the City—I think that's been the main problem with every one of them."

"A signal," said the man. "This time I've put a signal in these sponges. And of course the maps will be in her. She'll be drawn to the nearest cocoon. That in itself should assure success, at least at one stage. Assuming the network outside is still active. It should be. It's modeled on mycelium. Presumably we will at least know when she's had a new feed. One a year."

"Knitters, please," the woman said, and smeared something cold behind each ear. Then the child saw all kinds of numbers and letters dancing in the air in front of her, and the man and woman turned to watch them.

That part took a long time, and after that it was like a whisper of soft mist brushing her face as the woman said, "All right, little one, now we'll see if this *works.* I pray to God it does."

And many bright pictures, flashing so quickly that they were fragments of color, filled her mind, and she did not know how long it lasted.

They were back in the garden, in the shade of a large violet translucent petal. She still couldn't move very well.

She was tied into the suit by the man and woman. The woman's hands shook and finally the man pushed them aside and sealed and snapped and tied and the woman said, "I think that's the best we can do; now we just have to cross our fingers."

"I hope I disguised those directions adequately," said the man, his voice hoarse. "The last one . . ."

"This one will *work,*" said the woman.

The little girl felt a brief kiss on her cheek and then the hum of the descending Bee began to fill her body, her mind, her being.

She was not afraid when it lifted her. It was all too gloriously beautiful below and they must have given her some drug to take all fear away, to leave her with just the beauty of the flight over Cincinnati, of being lowered onto a soft green field that was quite scratchy actually where a woman rushed from a small house crying and screaming and shaking her fist as the Bee rose and vanished.* {#23.0} *

Verity opened her eyes, wondering what would happen if she somehow removed the bumps from behind her ears now. If she could find someone to remove them for her, if they weren't attached to anything but just sat in sockets like eyes, and could be popped out and thrown into the river. She sat up and watched holographic guests fill the lobby. She lay down and they disappeared. She liked it better that way. She stared at the lovely furniture, the intricate carpet.

Are you any worse off than any of these misfits? she asked herself. The only time people were normal was in the time when they wrote those books that you used to read. But the world hasn't been like that for over a hundred years. You thought you might find that place, didn't you? Maybe in the back of your mind.

She shook her head at her own foolishness. Even though you wanted the Flower Cities you thought that maybe after you saw them you could go on to Normal, to a place where there is no plague.

Well, I've got news for you. This is as normal as it gets.

What do you *want*?

Say Cairo and Blaze were restored, just the same as they used to be, and you could walk out of Cincinnati and go on back to Russ, and Shaker Hill. Would you want to?

The answer both chilled and exhilarated her.

It was *no*.

She thought of the falls, probably shimmering right now in the afternoon light. There was *something* ahead, something that called her. "The Territory," she said, and laughed, remembering Huckleberry Finn and how the rafters could think of nothing else.

Without the plague, she too could take the same trip.

She sat up, ignoring the phantoms that suddenly filled her vision.

What if she couldn't help Blaze?

What if he stayed the same, this strange, unknowing half-human, with skills but no real memory, no real humanness anymore. What was the answer for him? What process had been interrupted? Should she find out, and let it be completed?

What if Blaze had been turning into a Bee?

She turned that possibility over in her mind. After all, where did the Bees come from, anyway? Why did they really exist? What was their function? Had this happened in all the Flower Cities? Or was this some special architectural interface designed by Durancy?

She remembered the heavy, seductive perfume of the Hive,

and the bright, flashing pictures, how the Flowers glowed, the utter joy of complete fusion with a group mind.

Would that be so bad?

She got up and walked about restlessly.

It wouldn't be so bad, perhaps, if he had the choice, if he was able to decide and choose that.

But he didn't have that choice, and she had to make it for him.

"Demon," he whispered in her memory, and it didn't take much thought. She was the one with choice right now, and though it meant that she might lose that most precious capacity if she attempted to restore it to Blaze, it was something she could choose to do. She had to acknowledge and *use* whatever those people had put into her.

And perhaps, if she could, change it. No matter what the cost.

She felt afraid and very much alone. She had no idea what might happen, or, really, exactly *how* to make anything happen, much less any particular thing. She might trigger another Conversion, which would sweep through the City, and perhaps even beyond the Seam, perhaps all the way to Shaker Hill where Russ would see it coming, over the rim of the hills, and chuckle knowing exactly who and why before he was swept into pure Being, something without memory or volition or any humanity whatsoever.

She *did* have choices. She could take the half-Blaze and chance the river. Surely, somewhere, there was a map for even that, a way to shoot through or around the turbulence. Leave them all behind, in their bright and endless suffering, their horrid performances through which they, like Azure, half-glimpsed redemption. That was the safest way, to seek help elsewhere, from some unknown future savior.

A savior who most likely did not exist at all. They would have to save themselves. Mother Ann was dead.

How could she choose to possibly lose herself in this forever? Changed, would she even remember anything, remember Blaze, remember that she had failed?

She stood. The door, far across the lobby, opened for her silently, and she walked out into the City.

Thirty-three

○○○○○○○○○○○○○○○○○○

All the Music of Life Seems to Be

As if in response to her new resolve to do *something*, Verity felt the City change. She did not like the feel of this summons. The mood of this invitation. "Come," the City whispered. "This way."

Its colors were murky and terrifying as they drew her onward down the street, mapping only the next block through with any sort of clarity. Then it all wavered. Shit, she thought—another of Russ's fine words. This never happened before. This was not one of their Stories. This was happening now, in the present.

She felt groggy. The Flowers were furled and there was a feeling of disorganization and weird randomness permeating the City.

As she walked an old holo flashed on and transformed the front of the building she was walking past: an old beergarten, with a sign painted in rustic letters: FREE HOT DOG WITH DRINK. But it flickered as she walked past, then vanished. "Please," said the wall next to her, and she reached over and brushed the rough stalklike surface with one hand, like an absent caress, and the voices kept saying, "Please, please please," until she left that sound behind as well.

She paused at a flat screen that took up an entire plate glass window because the giant woman on the screen in black and white was India, a young India whom Verity recognized from one of the Durancy memories, and as a crowd applauded, the sound like a rush of autumn leaves in Verity's ears, like the distant roar of the river, a crude meter had its arrow pressed hard to the right and the man set a cardboardy crown on India's head and wrapped her with a long cape trimmed in ermine.

"I crown you Queen for a Day," said the man, whom Verity now saw was Durancy himself. He was very young though, barely a teenager, and he said, "What do you want?" and the woman looked a bit flustered then said with a firm voice, "I choose the washing machine" and the crowd went wild.

Verity continued to stare, but the picture vanished. She chose the washing machine that time, thought Verity. What will she choose this time? A City! A whole City! And a flood, just like after the earthquake, but a different sort of flood. Yes, a flood of sorts. An enormous washing clean. Wash them all clean, wash them in blood, wash them in the Blood of the Lamb—that has a respectable history here after all. Quite a precedent it seems.

Verity's thoughts were grumpy and scattered, and meanwhile the dark holographic swirl continued to coalesce before her, leading her on. Groups of two and three people passed her, going the other way, some with looks of grim intent on their faces. From far off she heard a scream and turned, but several people began to run in that direction so she continued on. A man sitting leaning against a building across the street unzipped his pants, pulled out his cock, and began to masturbate, a smile on his face as he stared across the street at her. Verity began to run, not too quickly though, to keep a bit of energy, since she didn't really know, this time, how far she had to go.

She turned a corner of an old, ramshackle factory of some sort, with faded advertisements painted on the side, and wondered from which book of old photographs the City had gleaned it. Streetlights made the drizzle sparkle in cones of illumination which shrank in a row toward the vanishing point. Her mind in fact saw the street suddenly in an exquisite grid, changed to a watercolor rendering, transparent yet impersonal, and she saw too the date, green, on the lower left-hand side beside a stunted tree: CINCINNATI, NILES & CO. FACTORY, 1834.

She realized that she had less time than she thought. The City, the Queen's Queen City, all the old, layered information Durancy had loved, was bleeding into her. Verity was almost afraid to continue down the stark, bare factory front with its tall, dark windows, but half a block away four or five laughing people were entering a door, and she saw they were dressed for a night of entertainment.

She stood there for a moment in the dark night, arms crossed, looking across satin blackness of the slick and sliding river, sliced with wavery colored lights from the half-bridges that were almost up to the roadbed in the New Ohio River. She was close enough to hear faint music, and she saw the dancers, heads bobbing, neon-bright scarves swirling around their heads. Trying to wear out those red slippers, she thought, and turned back to her desolate street.

What was her *choice* here?

"I am being devoured cell by cell," she said aloud, almost as if praying except that Mother Ann had been left far behind, in John's final vision, on the banks of icy Bear Creek. "And there's nothing I can do about it."

"There might be," said a voice, and she jumped. Then relaxed.

"Where are you, Durancy?" she asked, but when he stepped from the shadows she was shocked.

His face was haggard, his cheeks hollow, and his eyes appeared much larger than she had previously noticed.

He wore a plain brown coat beaded with water drops and streaked darkly down his chest with rivulets. His hands were in his pockets. His head was bare and his hair looked black, plastered against his head.

"You look terrible. Why are you following me?" she demanded. "This is all your fault. Just *tell* me what's going on."

"I can't," he said. "I just—can't. It's impossible." He was quiet for a moment, then said, "The best I can do is to tell you that I think that approach has been tried before. It doesn't work. We've come to believe that there's something in the entire cycle which has to unfold at a particular rate. You're our only hope. But *we* can't know what you're going to do."

"The hell with you then," she shouted. "What do you mean, it's been tried before? I've never been here before."

"That's the point," he said.

"Or have I?" she asked, and narrowed her eyes. Why wouldn't he *admit* it? "I was from Edgetown, at least that's what the Shakers told me. If you're not going to help me there's no point, is there? I need to find out how to make my friend Blaze and my dog Cairo better. That's all I want to do. And then I want to get out of this place. I don't care about you, I don't care about

your City, I don't care about whatever your problem is. I just want
to make them better and go home!''

Dennis said quietly, ''I wish that I could help, Verity. How I
wish that I could help.''

''Then why *don't* you?''

His eyes said that he wanted to, wildly. He opened his mouth,
but no sound came out. He looked down at the sidewalk, his face
troubled. Finally, he spoke.

''Humans can learn from experience,'' he said, ''Even humans
as strange as we are, from experience utterly new. Where you
were,'' he asked gently, ''did you have parents?''

''Kind of,'' she said. Two could play his game. Why should she
tell him what she knew about herself, and what she knew about
him? What might he do, then? She couldn't be sure. He might try
and do away with her. She had no idea what his perspective was,
exactly *who* he was, though he was modeled on Abe Durancy.

''But not really?'' he asked. ''Not a couple, like a mother and a
father, or like them?'' Unasked questions filled his face, and she
somehow understood that he wanted desperately to know every
detail about her, almost as a lover might want to know, but with
even more urgency.

''No,'' she said. ''There were people I lived with who were like
parents, who gave me love and the truth of what they knew.
Though the truth was pretty long in coming,'' she added.

His face brightened. ''Exactly,'' he said. ''Well, the truth is
here, don't worry. But this is what happens with parents. They try
and tell you things, important things that they've learned. They
want to help you with all their hearts. But soon they learn that
they can't, not really. They can only give you information that is,
in a way, oblique. Parents—*good* parents—realize that there are
certain things that you have to learn for yourself. It's the act of
incorporation that's important. That's what lays down the synaptic paths, not just *hearing* about something. It's *your* doing, *your*
failing, *your* actions, your own enormously individual kinesthesis
within the world, within matter's confines and matter's release,
within this very strange sea where we swim that causes growth.
Believe me, Verity, I've tried to tell you before.''

''You have not,'' she said, angry. ''You created me, didn't you?
You created me, and dropped me outside the City, and since I've
been here you've never tried to tell me a goddamn thing.'' Amazing how easily Russ's casual epithets came to her mind, and how

much sense they made when they flowed through her mind and out of her mouth. Quite satisfying.

"Well," he said, and she could not read his look, his strange amusement. She was surprised. He ought to look ashamed, or something, but instead he looked radiant. "You're right, of course. Happily so. We have enormous hope, Verity, but don't take it all too much to heart, when you finally find out more. There's always another chance. But there is one thing that I can tell you. It's very important."

"What is that?" she asked, fervently.

"Don't ever go back to India's."

"Why?" she asked, disappointed in the paucity of his advice.

"I can't tell you," he said, a stubborn glint to his eyes. "But I can tell you that I do wonder often where that point was," he said, hands in his pockets, looking directly into her eyes so that she could feel the entirety of his pain; *Abe's* pain. "Where exactly was the place where *I* stopped giving and *she* started taking. Where, you see . . . it's hard to *talk* about . . . I just don't exactly know when that simple and powerful childlike part of *her* that was indelibly, powerfully saved, without any sort of older personality overlay, any kind of maturity, took over. Simply took over the City. When it stopped being pretty pictures I painted for myself, and a matter of me having to step back aghast, unable to—*destroy* her, as I should have. But you see, I had no idea what would happen. No one did." He sighed, and looked down at the wet pavement, where metallic green and bright yellow stripes caught Verity's vision and pulled it toward the suspension bridge. It seemed much more crowded tonight, and from it issued a low, solid din, a sort of static overlay to the rush of the river. She listened to him as she watched. He sounded like Abe to her. No difference. It was odd, to be listening to this voice, to this *life*, outside of herself. Maybe he really *did* want to help her. After all, it seemed that he had *created* her.

"But," he continued, startling her, because she thought he'd finished, "I've gone very far beyond guilt. It's impossible for you to catch me with that."

"I don't think so," she said without giving it a second's thought. It was something she *knew*. "That's the reason I'm here, isn't it? The reason *you* embedded yourself in *me?*" She looked at him quite levelly in the far-cast light of the street lamp and his eyes said of course, and the pictures said help us, and the buildings whispered please, and he reached out quite suddenly and pulled her close, and she realized that he was shaking because he was crying.

"Oh, Verity, not completely. Not completely. I hope not. We're all still quite human, you see," he said, his words rather muffled. "That's the part that needs help."

Her arms went around him and she said nothing, while the river rushed, the partiers reveled, and music erupted from the door down the block.

As she held him she could feel the tension drain out of him, and he took a few enormous gasps and still held her for a bit longer.

"And there's nothing else at all that you can tell me, nothing that might help me?"

He loosened his arms and leaned against the wall, looking desolate. "No," he said, his voice a harsh whisper. "But you do have it all there. It's a bit like a problem of the brain, you see," he said, and she felt her temper rising.

"And what problem is that?" she asked, trying to keep from screaming it at him and succeeding.

"The mind interfaces with matter in strange ways, Verity, and it did even before nan."

"What makes you so smart?" she flung at him, but he just kept on talking, staring at the dark hills of Kentucky.

"People believed in God," he said.

"We did," she replied. "Some of us. So?"

"Yes, well most of those people prayed, and when they prayed, they spoke out loud, and they were actually speaking to other parts of their brain, the parts that interfaced with matter with senses that they really weren't entirely aware of. For instance, a long time ago many things concerning the way vision works and the way taste works and even the way thinking works, in a crude way, were deciphered, and we were able to create what might be called artificial senses, and yet they were never as swift, never as sophisticated, or as conscious, or as lovely, as our original mind.

"And parts of our mind," he continued, and Verity realized that he seemed as if he was talking himself into a trance, he was in a very strange mood indeed tonight but who could blame him, "had a completely different sense of time than the other parts, the parts which planned and spoke and believed that they were living."

"Go on," she said, beginning to feel very damp and wishing that she had some sort of umbrella but not wishing very hard, because she did not want, say, a man to drive by in a car and hand her one with a nod from the window, or for the building next to her to suddenly grow an arm with a detachable umbrella on the end and say, "For you, miss, with our kind regards."

"Time is one way which the mind organizes matter," he said. "We *have* to do it, we can't help it. And . . ."

He drew himself up and grinned wryly. "Sorry," he said. "I've been spouting, and it really makes no difference. Trust yourself, Verity. I believe in you. Others here believe in you, too. Have you met them?"

Azure, she thought, and whoever else wants some sort of savior. Which I am *not*.

"I know that you'll do the right thing," Durancy said. "That's all."

"Because that's how you *programmed* me?" she shouted at him as he turned and walked back down the street.

He turned toward her as he walked backwards and said, in a normal voice, so that she could barely hear him, "No, Verity. Because that's the person that you've grown to be. You've grown beyond anything we could have ever done. It's what we hoped for."

He paused for a moment, then said, with his hands outspread, "If all has gone well, Verity, you can choose not to help us. But please do. Please help us."

"You *would* know the right thing to say," she muttered, turning away and walking very quickly.

"Another thing, Verity," he shouted, and she turned.

"Things are getting . . . rather unbalanced. I don't know . . . I'd better get away from you. . . ." His voice was edged with panic. "Remember! Don't ever go back to India's," he said. "Stay away from her." He turned and ran.

She stared after him, wondering about the change in his voice, which had become harsh and commanding, as he disappeared into the darkness.

She turned back the way she had been going. The dark swirl had turned to a bright glimmer which eagerly, it seemed, drew her up the sidewalk like mica chips sparkling in the sun. Her heart bowed with the weight of that small boy who had roller-skated here, down by the factories where he was absolutely forbidden to go, but he came anyway because of the long, heavenly smoothness of the sidewalk and was often spanked when he got home because it seemed like she always knew.

That boy was in some chamber of her heart, and yet she wished him gone, she wished him gone and when he was gone from her he would be dead forever.

Maybe.

She glanced back at the City once before walking inside the door and felt with a chill that nothing she could do could kill the City.

But maybe she could reach inside its workings and change it, just a bit.

She only needed to figure out how.

Her own wry laugh, identical to Durancy's, was swallowed by the music as she went inside the dark, cavernous room.

And there, on a small stage, illuminated by spotlights, were Sphere and Blaze, and her heart caught in her throat, suddenly far beyond anger and much nearer to dread.

The small round tables that filled the immense warehouse were covered with white tablecloths and each had a candle on it. She saw waiters moving among the tables, bending down to take orders, carrying trays of full glasses among the hushed audience. They wore white shirts and black pants, the men and the women servers. She looked around the room some more, to avoid looking at the stage.

The tables were all full. The room was crowded, and she had a feeling of vast space here because the tables feathered away into darkness, and staring into the darkness she saw only the yellow repeated glow of hundreds of candles, and here and there a glimmer of candlelight on glass as someone lifted a glass and drank. She had a feeling of it all being enormously, completely unbounded, an enormity, in fact, a room without end, amen, and she was afraid because of course a Conversion could sweep right through it, at any minute, in stately, thorough progression, devouring them all like stars devoured themselves, changing the atoms of mind within that brief white ash to something blank and new and waiting for the new fresh rush of information to flower and grow.

A waiter came up to her. He was wearing white gloves. She could *hear* why. Masters were at work up on the stage, and Blaze was already quite new, had moved far beyond anything she had heard him play before; *no*, she thought, the City is playing him—but still she wondered.

His piano was complex, and touched her mind fleetingly to images she simply did not recognize, but only *felt*, as they danced on the edge of vision's possibilities. Sphere wove through those spaces, darted, stood bravely and briefly alone, fled in a flattened flash toward the edges of all sound and all being and then drew it all into one point that glowed in every star in the universe, in every candle flame vanishing into never.

"Never," she whispered, "this never was."

"No," said the waiter, "this *always* was."

"Everyone's a poet these days," she said; he grinned, and she allowed him to lead her to a table near the stage.

How she yearned for Sphere and Blaze to glance down and see her, for eyes to light in recognition, for one to put down his saxophone and the other to fold his hands in his lap, for them both to bound from the stage and say, "It's over. That was a good show. Let's go home."

At the same time, she longed for them never to stop.

This was beauty's apex and humanity's core: to create, to listen, to die and live and then create again. For meaning to flow forever into a vacuum, and then for them to give it ears and finally, perhaps, a heart.

But she knew that the heart of this City was hollow and vengeful and troubled and roaring with vacuum and pain, and that all these people would be sucked into that pain and turned to ash as surely as those on that vapor bridge that spanned the river that at one time flowed through the Hiroshima of the encyclopedia. This was no different.

She wept as she listened, wept for all of them, all the lost generations, and wondered why Durancy had made her this way. Why did she have to divert people from this odd and elegant sideways life, no matter that it ended, every time, in chaos and fear, because they would always live again. What was *wrong* with stored minds flowing into new bodies, bodies programmed to accept the stories of others—beautiful stories? Why not stay here with them?

Soaring within a sudden turn of the notes she realized:

She had to stay here. Of course.

She had no choice.

The grim gray streets of the present City rayed out around her, holy and constant and calling her surely as any god might call his goddess.

She pushed aside all the thoughts of idolatry and sin and pride and thought it, no, *realized* it, again.

It was so simple.

It was so very simple.

Freedom was better, though it led to death and pain, and she did not know why but thought that maybe that was the one thought of value Dennis had given her, distilled from lifetimes of pain. She could take it or leave it, she realized. It might *not* be true.

She had it within her to free them all. She wasn't exactly sure how. Don't go back to India's? I will meet the Beast, she thought, though fire and brimstone—or a nan conversion—consume me! But she didn't want to think about it right now. Not just yet. She wasn't quite ready.

Because now it was time to dance.

"Play something dancy," she said out loud, "This is a request from a very special member of the audience," and without missing a beat, Sphere and Blaze swung into something lovely— maybe even something *theirs,* she wanted to believe, though she knew that was not possible—and everyone pushed back their chairs. The waiters rushed in to pick up the tables and the candle flames bent sideways as they were whisked aside, making Verity feel as if the walls had vanished and they were traveling through the stars very, very fast.

Everyone began to dance.

Thirty-four

○○○○○○○○○○○○○○○○○○○

Night in the City

Blaze felt to Verity light as a feather beneath her circling arm, drifty, as he walked down the street, staring straight ahead. His hair was longer than it ever had been and the warm summer wind kept pushing it in front of his eyes; Verity pushed it back several times, just to touch it. Sphere was supporting his other side as the three of them headed north on a street that ran along the river. Every few steps Blaze tripped over something or other but his body always seemed to elastically adjust to the imbalance and stumble forward.

After they walked a block they were free of the crowd pouring from the music hall, and the breeze felt a bit cooler on Verity's hot face.

"He was arrested," said Sphere. "That's about all he'll say. I found him in a little club, playing like some kind of jazz god. He can do anything—Joplin, Jelly Roll Morton; he can sound like Oscar Peterson or Bill Evans but he's beyond that, Verity, he's burned through the whole history of jazz and he's just *himself*." Sphere's voice was hushed. Fireworks blossomed in front of them and were reflected in his glasses, tiny green and gold spiders of light, as he and Verity looked at each other across Blaze's unregistering face.

"I was arrested," said Blaze, his voice flat and strange, his words slow. He looked at her. "Who are you?"

This is not Blaze, she told herself. This is not Blaze.

"Verity," she said, and bit her lip and tasted the metallic tang of blood. "What does he mean by that?"

"What was he doing in those sheets?"

Verity took a deep breath and wished she could make her voice more steady. "He was shot in the chest. We wrapped them in the sheets. Russ—the—"

"I know who Russ is. You told me," Sphere said. "In fact you told me a lot about yourself, but you didn't really tell me much about Blaze."

"Well, Russ just thought that maybe there would be something here in Cincinnati that could help him, since the sheets came from here."

"Good guess," said Sphere, a note of sarcasm in his voice.

"Besides," she said, "Blaze and I always planned to come here, ever since we were little."

"Hungry," said Blaze.

"He says that," said Sphere, "But he won't eat anything. But he sure can play like hell."

"I heard him," said Verity. "Good for him. That's just grand."

"You have no idea what it's like to want to be able to be like that, do you?" Sphere asked.

"Be like what?"

"To be inside the music. To use the music. To *create*."

"I don't think he's creating, Sphere. I think he's replaying."

Sphere shook his head, and his face went stubborn. "Maybe that's true at one stage. But that's a learning process. Then he can move on. This is a place where you can truly learn things, if you're part of it." He sighed and looked wistful again. "Very, very quickly. Charlie Parker had this great breakthrough, you know. He was thrown off the stage one time when he was just a kid and then he was absolutely determined to show them. So he went home and played all the records that he could find, over and over, like a maniac. He learned all that and then tossed it aside. He broke through. He *created*. I think that here you can do that quickly. Learn all the masters that way, then break out into *yourself*, your true self, and still use all that stuff."

"Maybe that's what was supposed to happen," said Verity. But I think everyone here is stuck. They're all stuck in one little piece of it, and it's horrible, Sphere, I can't see how you could think it's wonderful. I just can't. They're not creating anything *new*, don't you see? They're just reliving whatever Durancy thought was important! He had no respect for them. He used everyone—he's *still* using everyone—and they can't grow or learn. They can only repeat. As far as I can tell. It's not like playing all the records—like your spheres, right?—and learning them and throwing them away. It's never being able to take the record off."

Sphere's face went stubborn. Finally he said, "Maybe you're right, Verity. But don't you think that if I could experience being all of these great musicians, that would help me do what *I* want to do?"

Verity said, "If you ever could, Sphere. That's the problem. I don't think these people ever can. They have nothing of themselves to bring to it. But right now I'm just worried about Blaze. What do you think arrested *means*?"

"You really don't know?" asked Sphere.

"I really don't know," she said, beginning to feel very weary. "Could you possibly give me a clue?"

"I don't know either. But, obviously, he had a plague," said Sphere.

"Hungry," said Blaze.

"Yes, obviously, of course," said Verity.

"Well, did he?"

"Yes," she said. "He did."

"Well," Sphere said, "the sheets worked. They arrested the plague. He would have stayed in that state forever but I put him into that activation cell, in the station. But plagues change the brain structure. They change it to something new, of course, but obviously the process Blaze was in was stopped in the middle. Arrested. Look, there's a coffee shop. He won't eat anything, but I will."

Verity pulled open the door and they went in.

There was no one in the place except a tired-looking blond waitress. She walked over to the booth they sat in and pulled a pencil and paper from her pocket. "What'll ya have?"

Sphere said, "Three eggs over easy with hash browns, grits, biscuits, and fried apples. And coffee. And a beer."

The woman glared at Verity. "Honey?" she asked.

"Same as him," Verity said.

"What about your friend?" she asked. Blaze was sitting next to Verity, staring at the silverware and grinning. "He sick or something?"

"He's fine," said Verity. "Just a little tired. He'll have the same thing too."

"Heck of an imagination you guys got," the waitress said. She turned and went behind the counter and yelled the order out. When she came back with the coffee, Blaze had dumped the salt on the table and was drawing lines in it, a look of absorption on his face.

"I'd say he needs something more than sleep," she said. "Got a cocoon in the back if he wants."

"No thanks," said Verity and took a sip of coffee and put it down. "This is pretty weak," she said.

"This ain't the Ritz," said the waitress. "And besides I've been having trouble with the voicecook tonight. I don't think it's reading my messages the right way. It seems to be messing up a lot. Had a big crowd in here before the show and it was all fucked up, a royal snarl. Dollars to doughnuts your order don't come out right either. Best I can do. And whaddaya want, it's free, ain't it?" She glared at Blaze, then went away.

"Maybe a cocoon is what he needs," said Sphere.

"The hell you say," Verity replied sharply. Next to her, Blaze shivered. A fine sweat broke out on his forehead.

"Look, Verity," said Sphere. "If he showed up like this in Edgetown he'd be killed on the spot. He's unmistakably a plaguer. And he's not going to get any better. He might stay the same, but he's been arrested, and that means the little nanomachines have put a hold on a lot of bodily functions—hormones and enzymes and stuff like that."

"What do you suggest?" asked Verity, her voice very small.

The waitress marched down the aisle, her arms full of plates, which she smacked down in front of them. "What did I tell you? Waffles, every one of you. And don't complain. Just eat them. I'll be glad when all this ruckus and upset is over."

Verity looked out the window at the fireworks coloring the night sky and shimmering on the river. "This is different?" she asked.

"You bet, honey. I haven't been hiding out in that cocoon forever you know, like some of you. I keep my ear to the ground. I pay attention to the signs. There ain't anything we can do about it, mind you," she said. "Not a damned thing. Like a tornado, like a storm. Sweeps through the place ever so often. God knows why, but you know how you can tell when your period's going to start?

All those little signs? This is kinda like that. I remember, yesirree, or at least,'' her eyes went sad and she looked a bit lost, "I *think* I remember. . . .'' She walked off, muttering, and went over to the door and turned the sign over to closed, then sat at a far table, opened a notebook, and began to write.

Blaze stared at his waffle, then he tore a corner off, stuffed it in his mouth, and began to chew.

"Could we have some milk?'' Verity yelled to the woman and she yelled back, "I doubt it. I told you the damned cafe's broke.'' She didn't budge; she didn't even look up.

"Why doesn't everyone in here have the plague?'' asked Verity.

"Oh, it seems to me as if they have *some* sort of plague, Verity,'' Sphere said. "I haven't exactly figured it out. It comes from the Flowers, from the buildings, from the walls. Except it doesn't affect me. I'm always the same. Normal. I'll never change. This is it for me.'' He looked morose. Blaze finished his waffle and started on Sphere's.

"I thought you said he wouldn't eat.''

Sphere shrugged. "It's a good sign. I guess we don't get any syrup either.''

"Do you think these people here are happy?'' she asked Sphere. Sphere pushed his plate in front of Blaze and took Verity's, which she hadn't touched.

"What's happy?'' asked Sphere. "You didn't want any of this, did you? Are people in Edgetown happy? Were people in Shaker Hill happy? Were people ever happy?''

Verity thought of Abe Durancy, of his mad wild visions, which were now spilling and growing and metamorphosing and mutating all around her, and thought, he was happy. Boy was he happy.

But he was pretty unhappy too.

"It's too bad half of them die,'' she said.

"Half of who?'' asked Sphere. Blaze wiped his mouth with the back of his hand and slumped back, closed his eyes, his head leaning at an unnatural angle over the back of his seat, and began to breathe deeply.

"Half of the people who get the plague.''

"They don't,'' said Sphere. "Whatever gave you that idea?''

"That's what Russ told me. And I saw three plaguers pushed off a raft,'' she said, then realized that one hadn't died and she had no real reason to believe that the other two had actually been dead. Maybe the woman who kicked them off had just been terrified of them.

"Well," said Sphere, "there are an awful lot of plagues. It's possible that the ones he saw killed half the people, but that's probably because some sort of faulty cure was released, or maybe something in the assemblers went bad for some reason. Or maybe somebody *wanted* people to die; that wouldn't surprise me either. I never saw anyone die of the Territory plague, but of course anyone I ever saw with it couldn't wait to get on the river. They were all gone pretty quick. There was my Aunt Ginny. One of my brothers, a long time ago. Even if they hadn't been itching to go they would have, I'm sure, to keep from getting killed. People in Edgetown are pretty happy with the way things are, to tell you the truth. They're tickled that they weren't Converted, that they live seminormal lives. They're much happier than the people in here, that's for sure. Yet I'm very glad I'm here. I'll never leave."

He looked at Verity, tilted his head, and said plaintively, "What are you going to *do*, Verity? What was that dance in the dance hall all about?"

Verity got up and walked back to the waitress.

Looking over the woman's shoulder, she was not surprised to see her notebook pages filled with small, fine print. The woman glanced up at her and seemed a bit confused. "Who are you?" she asked.

All vestiges of the waitress had worn off. The woman took a deep breath. Her face cleared, and she smiled to herself.

"I have someone here who was arrested," said Verity, "and I was wondering if maybe the cocoon could help."

Sphere had followed her. "Verity," he said, very quietly, "Do you know what you're doing?"

The woman got up, her eyes filled with keen, deep intelligence.

"Whatever you say will be done," she said, and bowed. She walked down the aisle to Blaze. Verity and Sphere followed. The woman looked at Blaze very closely. She shook her head. She looked back at Verity.

"You know about the strictures?" she asked.

"I know," said Verity.

And she did. She knew every arcane twist of this religion, she realized, not with fear, but with satisfaction. She knew just what to say. "I repeal them."

"As you wish," said the woman. "You take his legs." She leaned over Blaze.

"Damn," said Sphere, pushed past them, put his arms underneath Blaze, hoisted him, and stood. He looked at Verity. "All right, miss whoever-you-are High Commander. Where do we go now?"

"Do not mock her," said the waitress, and her voice had a dangerous edge.

"Hell, I'm not mocking Her Wonderfulship," said Sphere. "I'm not even questioning her judgment, or anything remotely like that. I love her and that's the truth. I was just wondering if she had enough to eat today."

"Probably not," said Verity. "But Blaze looks like he's going to die and I came here to save him and that's all I want to do and then we'll leave. I don't know how, but that's what I want to do. You come with us, all right?"

"Hmmm," said Sphere. "I just got in here, remember? I'm having a heck of a time. Kind of."

"You think it over," said Verity. She reached up and touched his cheek. "I'd really like you to come with us. I think it will be pretty dangerous to stay." She looked back at the woman. "Where's the cocoon? Do you know how to program it?"

The woman led them through a swinging door to a small room filled with light. Sphere settled Blaze in the clear, blinking cocoon in the back room. Verity sighed. "He always hated these," she said.

"I can see why," said Sphere. "These people are loony as peahens."

"I thought you liked it here," Verity said, kneeling at Blaze's side. He stirred a bit and the cocoon shrank a bit to hold him.

"That's what I like," said Sphere.

"Now what do we do?" asked Verity.

"We let it work," said the woman.

"No," said Verity. "I don't think that will really be enough."

"It will," said the woman. "You'll see."

The tiny lights began to blink. RESUME, said the side of the cocoon in large violet letters. Some numbers flashed next to the word, fluxing, then settled at 11:44:28.

And then it began counting down.

There was a huge commotion outside, in the restaurant. The woman ran to the swinging door and looked through the high round window.

"Oh my God," she said.

Verity looked out.

Five men had kicked the door in and surged inside. They were busting up the benches with sticks, shouting. The woman shot a heavy bolt through a hasp. "This is metal," she said doubtfully, and touched off the light. "I don't think they saw us."

"Where is she?" one of the men shouted. "Look," he said. "She was here." He shone a beam around the restaurant and a trail of flickering lights danced in the air like dust motes.

"She must have left," said the other one. "There's nobody here. The plates are empty."

The first man looked doubtful, but he followed the second out the door, and the other three men followed silently. Verity saw guns in their hands. She felt Sphere's hand on her shoulder.

"Why are they after you, Verity?" he asked.

"It's the old Queen that wants her," said the woman. "The new Queen always has to kill the old Queen. If she can. But usually the old Queen kills the new ones. She knows more."

Sphere looked at Verity. "You?" he asked, astonishment on his face for a second before he nodded once, and said, softly, "Of course."

Many things coalesced within Verity, then.

Azure and her prayer book, with her certainty that Verity was the *one*.

The way she was drawn to the Hive, and the way it had accepted her, and the subsequent menace she had felt once the Queen stirred and became aware of her presence.

Dennis's obscure hints, his questions.

The ravings of the Lion Woman in Edgetown, promised a savior who had never manifested Herself in the City.

Because each one had been killed. Killed by the old Queen.

Verity's eyes filled with brief tears for her lost sisters. Had that old woman with the nubs who bartered the dead Bees been one, her mission lost or twisted within her to simple hatred of all Bees?

"How often do new Queens come along?" Verity asked.

The woman shrugged. "Who knows? Depends."

"Fine," said Sphere. "Great. Well, New Queen, you got yourself into this somehow. What are you going to *do?* I'd say the safest thing to do is to stay here."

Sphere seemed wonderfully unimpressed, not at all likely to drop to his knees. Verity was immensely relieved. She hadn't chosen this, and she didn't intend to play this game. No matter how glorious it might be to be the Queen, Verity longed with all her heart for the normalcy of Shaker Hill.

Well, that was gone forever. But there could be a new life beyond the City, out in the Territory, with whatever wonders and terrors that might hold, so long as they were *real.*

First Blaze had to be restored. Then they had to get away. And quickly, for as the woman had said, the signs were there. A conversion was at hand. How easy it would be to wipe a new Queen away with a surge. Only a few islands, like the apothecary shop, remained intact, apparently. Yes, they had to get away, and soon.

Then Verity thought again of Azure, and the others like her who were depending on the victory of a new Queen. But how and why, Verity wondered, would a new Queen do things any differently?

Well, she thought, I would if I could, and of course I could; power is what the Queen is all about, isn't it? But what if I was so changed that I couldn't do anything different? What if I forgot who I was?

She thought of her young sisters, sleeping in the Hive. They too would be sent forth, she supposed. But by who? Did Dennis—Abe—continually re-manifest? Did the Hive remain intact during a surge? How would the young ones fare, set out in the world as she had been? Would one of them be able to kill the old Queen? Or would they too perish? What if, next time, even the memory of them, or the memory of Abe, was wiped out forever? Then there would never be any change here. She shuddered.

She took a deep breath and thought, this woman here *trusts* me to do something.

But what? How? Should she transform herself for *them?* She wished Russ were here. And then she was glad that he wasn't.

Somehow she knew what he would expect her to do.

"Those hoodlums will be back," said Verity. "And if they find me, they'll probably kill whoever is with me. I know where I have to go. You watch Blaze for me, all right?" she asked.

"Anything for a Queen," said Sphere and bowed.

"I *told* you don't get smart," said the woman.

"He can't help it," said Verity, and slipped out the back door into the warm summer night. The streets were filled with shouting. A map flashed in her head and she turned right, and took off running.

Thirty-five

○○○○○○○○○○○○○○○○○○○○

Vine Street Redux

The street was long and dark, and for the first time since being inside Cincinnati, Verity was deeply frightened.

She did not feel that she was heading toward some safe place, some refuge. Instead the long triple shadows cast by the street lamps looked menacing. Dark clouds raced across the face of the full moon to which she tried to cling in thought, as she hurried across empty intersections, as something real, nonconverted. A place free of nan, and Queens, and Flower Cities.

Oh, what do you know, she told herself wearily. No doubt they sent City-seeds to the moon too. Cities we can't even see from here. And then, as she ran, Verity recalled plans for them, burned into her head during one vagrant eyeblink, the nan-Cities that were to have been on the moon. ALL THINGS ARE POSSIBLE NOW! she saw, suddenly, the headline juxtaposed with a newspaper article in which a white-haired lady, apparently a famous scientist, said, "I think both the best and the worst will happen. All the very bad and all the very good scenarios will come true, only we won't know which is which until later."

This must be one of the bad scenarios, Verity thought, but laughed when she thought that it was entirely possible that worse ones had occurred.

Or might occur, and soon.

She heard footsteps behind her and turned, but saw nothing

except the dark shapes of townhouses falling away behind her, studded by an occasional lighted window which stopped her heart with possible reality. For some reason most of the corner pubs she passed were dark and deserted, fiction unmaintained this particular night, and that had been frightening too. It was as if the City was waking, not to light but to twisted darkness. Below, in the City's bowl, she could see that many Flowers were open even though it was night, bathed in light against the night sky through which stars glimmered in the gaps between clouds, and she even thought she could make out Bees moving between them on some dark and urgent mission. But she didn't want to pause long enough to make sure.

The footsteps came louder, a buffing sound against pavement, but not particularly hurried.

She began to run.

Not as fast as she possibly could; she paced herself. She did not want to become winded. The air was filled with the clean scent of the river.

She paused at a corner, trying to make out the sign, when a map that had remained hidden since that first night blazed once more in her mind. The fitful connections seemed to be getting stronger, more reliable.

After six blocks of steady running, she leaned against a lamp post, breathing hard. She wiped sweat from her forehead and pulled her light sweater off over her head, looked up, and saw the man at the foot of the hill staring up at her, his face white in the lamplight.

Dennis.

Don't go back to India's.

Was he trying to stop her?

She turned and ran with all her speed for a block, but stopped dead when the picture of her destination flashed into her mind. From his mind, she wondered, or from India's? They were both close enough now, for India's house was just a block ahead, the house for which she had searched so long, and the porch light was on.

She began to tremble.

Dennis was still resting against a lamp, tiny at the bottom of the big hill, several minutes away. Well, at least she had tired him. Apparently he felt no haste, which bothered her.

She wanted to leave, then. She wanted to go back to Shaker Hill, not the Shaker Hill where everyone was lying dead on the ground, but the Shaker Hill of her childhood where all the rules were known, and obedience was something that pulled the energies of life a certain way, polarized them so that they were arrows leading both in and out so that the self disappeared, so that being could actually dance.

She tried in vain to call another map. One with a passageway leading out. Blaze was being tended to—in one way or another. She was not very pleased with that, but saw no other choice. He was himself no longer, but only some sort of rarefied musical instrument. She shuddered. But she was not necessary for his redemption, was she? Maybe she should just go back, wait till the time ticked down, and flee with him and Sphere—down the river, through the tunnels, somewhere, somehow.

And as all her certainties were dissolving, there on the dark nan-street, a woman came out on the front porch of India's house.

Her hair was brilliant blond in the lamplight, piled atop her head and decorated with a pink crescent hat worn at an angle. Her thin print dress stopped midcalf and fluttered in the warm breeze.

She saw Verity, but did not wave, or call.

She just looked at Verity, and Verity could tell by the straightness of her body, by the lift of her chin, that she would not demand or even ask that Verity do anything she did not want to do. She would not assess her pheromone pattern and manipulate her with the correct mix, and neither would her house. They were both filled for Verity with a non-nan light, though part of her mind said *fool!* She can make you think whatever she wants. She can make you think *Fear Not*, but she is not at all an angel.

But still, this was the house. This was the house, and she must go in, or else fail forever. Why did she think so? Dennis said *help us*, then would tell her nothing. He tampered with her very being, then thought she would listen to whatever he said. She was sure that whatever she needed to know to make the pieces finally fit must be here, in Durancy's childhood house. And it would be foolish to go back to the Hive without as much information as she could possibly get. Anything would help. Anything. And this was where the mystery had begun.

Verity looked back, but Dennis had vanished, and she felt a

chill. Had he just been herding her here? Why did she think not, why did she think that now that she was in sight of the house he was more afraid than she had been?

She turned up the walk and walked between two large bushes. The front yard was fringed by flat-faced zinnias washed in moonlight. That light picked out the tiny lilies of the valley hanging from their stems in white rows, their scent strong as perfume in the night air. The familiar wide steps waited. Ferns hung between fat pillars, swaying in gusts of wind before the storm which the gathering clouds were bringing. The woman on the porch stood watching Verity as the wind blew loosened tendrils of hair across her grave face.

Verity took a deep breath, and climbed the front steps.

The woman opened her arms wide and enfolded Verity in a hug. Verity felt the ribs of the woman's back beneath the thin dress, and stepped back.

The woman's wide brown eyes were full of tears, which glimmered in the porch light but which did not spill over, and Verity realized, with enormous surprise, that she was India. But a younger India. The eyes were the same, and the nose. Her beautiful hair was held with pearled combs, and there was a pearl at the end of her hatpin. She wore long dangling silver earrings that caught the light from the foyer.

What are the limits of nan? Verity had asked Tai Tai. The core India was presumably stored in the Hive, so there could be more than one copy at the same time, at the whim of the City. Why not? Just like me, Verity thought wryly. It just didn't seem right. But then, nothing here seemed right.

"I'm so glad you came," this new, young India said. "Come inside. Quickly," she urged, and Verity was happy to comply. Dennis was not far behind, and maybe he wanted to stop her. Maybe he didn't want her to hear whatever India had to say. But Verity had to *know.*

An overwhelming sense of being home enveloped Verity as she stepped inside the house. Yet there was also an unsettling feeling of being displaced in time. It was not only that India was young this time. It was not only that. She could feel a different essence within this woman, vibrant and ready for action, steeled for something both necessary and dreadful, but Verity did not know what.

She followed India into the living room. India looked around anxiously, then went to the front window, grabbed the long, heavy green velvet drapes, and pulled them shut with a scrape of wooden rings along the curtain rod. She turned back to Verity and Verity saw that her hands shook, just a bit, before she clasped them together.

"I can't do this by myself," she said. "It's impossible." Tears spilled over and slid down her face.

"What?" asked Verity.

"Sit," she said, and sank down on the edge of the horsehair sofa.

Verity remained standing. "I want you to tell me what you're talking about. Something strange is happening in the City and I need to know what it is. It's night and the Bees are out. Why? This is a terrible place, India. Don't you know that? It's terrible outside, too, I suppose, in a lot of ways—everything deserted, people living on their own in the wilderness, but at least they're *free*. You've lived here since—" She had been going to say since you were born, but stopped.

"I've lived here, my dear, since before the Conversion. Since before the plague, the quake. I was born—the first time—in the year of the Millennium." She stood and walked around the room, slim and lovely in her long, flower-print dress, her fingers entwined behind her back.

"I think that I alone have kept my true identity and my *place* (the word was fierce) in the City. Because of my son. Because of Durancy." Her eyes were sharp as bird's eyes then, staring at Verity, and Verity stared back. You won't get into my soul, woman, she thought.

"It's a very nice place," Verity said, "but what does it have to do with anything?"

"Don't be silly," said India. "You know exactly what this place is. You're one of *them*. You're not the only one. Your heart and soul are mine, if I want, because the child inside your mind—Durancy—is my child. You can't help it. The ties between mother and child are the strongest and deepest there are." Yet as she spoke, Verity knew that this woman did not think of her in that way, as her child. She realized that India felt, instead, fear and hatred. She wondered if India knew who *she* really was, and what she did, eternally.

"What if the ties are that strong?—which I doubt," replied Verity. Then she said, "Does Dennis *look* like the real Abe?"

"Yes," muttered India, her head bent. "Frightfully so. And I look quite like his mother—"

"At various ages. Perhaps you choose your appearance according to how you would like him to feel? Is that a good way to treat your son?"

"What do you know about it?" she asked, whirling. "Do you have any idea how he treated *me?*"

"I know that he loved you very much," said Verity. "I've felt flashes of that now and then, you know."

"Presumably not now," said India.

"Not now," Verity agreed. Only when he's in my mind. Or, perhaps, on that first night. When you were an old woman, and seemed kind. Where was that old, kind woman now? Flung into the back of a truck, stuffed into some sort of rejuvenation cell? Why was she so *different* from this India? Dennis had muttered something about her young personality being saved, which lacked the socializing overlays of maturity. And Abe had been distraught, had he not, when Kay told him that the copy had been imperfect. . . .

Verity walked over to the glass cabinet and unlocked it. She pulled out the picture of Rose's graduation party, toppling a china bird. She turned, holding the picture out. "Tell me," she said. "Why do I look like *her?*"

India looked at the picture, looked at Verity, and blinked. "Yes," she said slowly. "You *are* her. Rose. I don't know." She rubbed her forehead with her hand and closed her eyes tightly. "I've always wanted to tell her that I was sorry—you know, my husband's sister was always so cold to me—"

"I don't *care* about all that. Really," said Verity. "I'm not her. I just want to know why I look like her. Don't you know?"

"No," said India, her voice a whisper. She looked frightened. "I really don't," she said, and Verity believed her.

"Damn!" she said, and threw the picture down on the couch. "*Somebody* must know!"

Then Verity heard the Bell.

The wind was kicking up, and the branches of a tree scraped the roof in front. The windows were open, and the heavy drapes billowed. Verity wondered where Dennis was.

She turned and walked through the dining room. India was behind her.

"Where are you going?" she demanded. "I'm not finished

talking to you." Her voice rose as Verity continued walking. "I have something very important to tell you. Dennis and I—we've tried to tell you before. We've tried many times. We've tried all your life, but the barriers are so powerful."

"What barriers?" asked Verity.

India looked puzzled. Then she spoke rapidly. "That's the problem, you see; neither of us know what they are. It seems to be . . . beyond our *capacity* to know. But I'm not who you think I am. I want to help you. I want you to help *me*. Really I do. You have to believe me! You must! Please don't hate me! I can't stand it anymore. I don't know what's wrong. It's not my fault." India was sobbing as she followed Verity, pulling on her arm from time to time. Verity ignored her.

Verity walked through the once-dear kitchen, remembering when the marble table was eye-level and she—*he*—had eaten a chocolate cake resting there and had been spanked. She pulled open the back door and stepped out onto the back porch.

Below, a lovely garden was wild in the moonlight, thin shoots with flowers she had never seen like long slim fingers reaching upward, looped with frail viny tendrils. Low bushy plants bordered brick walks, small white flowers pale. The walk wound into a central core hidden from her. A controlled wilderness, with a secret at the center.

India grabbed her arm and said, "No, you can't go down there, not yet, you have to listen to me. Oh, why did you take so long to come? I've been trying so very hard you see, this time. I *can* change, you know. You think that I can't grow but you're wrong, I do know how, I *have*." There was a desperation in her voice that Verity could not ignore.

She turned and said, "All right, what is it?"

But when India began to speak her words were nonsense, because Verity could hear only one thing.

The wind chimes hung next to the porch were long hollow pipes, and their sonorous tolling echoed and matched the sounds that had drawn her all her life.

This was the core memory. The Bell. That which had called her to the Dayton Library so these parasites who preyed on her very being could fill her full of her *role*, her *duty*, her *fate*. And then use her, suck her dry, throw her away. India clung to her, but Verity shook her off.

She raised her arm and swung it around as if pitching. Pitching with as much fury and cool, precise intent as she had put into pitching the radio stone. At John's head. To kill him.

As she must now kill this awful insistent past moored within her like an inescapable dream.

She caught the Bell, ripped it from its mooring with a light, springing twang of snapped translucent filament. She held the Bell for an instant, and the mottled metal tubes seemed to burn her hand.

She flung it to the ground, hard. The full tones of the Bell resonated for a few seconds as it settled, fifteen feet below, glinting in the moonlight.

Verity descended the steps as if wholly awake for the first time in her life. The dew from the garden brushed her hands as she passed the outreaching plants. Somehow she knew who she would find, curled up and cowering on the metal chair, in the center of the maze—a difficult one, but it took only minutes, for she had the map. She rounded the last turn and saw him, curled upon an ornamental iron chair, head down.

She knelt in front of him.

"Dennis," she said, and took his hand.

It was limp, and he glanced at her briefly from beneath lowered eyelids. "You didn't help," he said.

"Why were you chasing me?"

"I wasn't," he said, his voice dull. "It was too late. I just—it seems to be time, again . . . but I'm so very tired of it. It is always horrible. I told you not to come back. But that was a mistake, I think. It probably only made you want to do so. I forgot my resolve, lost control. Panicked. I just hoped that *something* would be different, just once, it seems that might be all it takes, but it may be impossible. Impossible. It's all so tightly woven. Everything just repeats and repeats. The loop is endless. There's no escape. There never will be." His voice was bleak with despair, low and flat.

"You have to tell me what's going to happen," Verity said, gripping his shoulders and shaking him. "What can I do? Now's your chance to really help, Dennis. Talk!"

He didn't respond. He just sat silently, staring into the night, as tears crept down his face. "It's all my fault," he said, finally. "All my fault."

"What's all your fault?" she asked. "The games? The murders? The Dance? Death that isn't death, life that isn't life, that's all your fault? If it's all *your* fault, why has the *rest* of the world been ruined? Do you know how I grew up? You didn't invent Enlivenment. You used it. You used it to try and give pleasure to people, only it was what you saw as pleasure, and they were helpless and couldn't disobey if they wanted to. There are no adults here, Dennis, *Abe*," she said, and was rewarded by open eyes and a stare of self to self which only made her more angry.

"I don't know what's going to happen now, but I don't like the feel of it. I don't like the feel of anything that's happened since I got here. I'm tired of you being in my head—" She broke off and stood up straight, stared at the sky. "What's the use?" she said to the garden, to Dennis, to India. "You're no more *him* than *I* am. And why do I look like Rose?" She would have shaken Dennis, but he looked so tired and defeated that she was afraid.

India said from behind her, "No, no, I don't think it's time. It can't be. Not yet." Her voice was odd, muted, resigned despite her words. "*I've* tried . . . something . . ." she looked around distractedly. "But what was it? I *know* I tried something to make it *change* this time. Oh, I can't remember." Her hands clenched into fists and she looked quite as helpless as Dennis.

"What's the difference?" Dennis replied, and Verity felt herself invisible as their words volleyed through the crystal air of night. "Every time I think that this time there will be a difference. But there never is. This web is so tight. The way it all falls into place. All my fault. All my fault. I *made* it that way."

"I wanted *you* to do something," India said. "But as usual you were too frightened, or the time wasn't right, whatever it was . . . you were always such a timid child."

Dennis sat up and stared straight ahead. His face became less fluid, more stiff with anger. "Why is it always my responsibility? What more could a person do than what I did?"

As they spoke, it was as if clouds were blowing away from the face of a mountain range previously hidden. Stunned by what she was seeing, by what she *would* see, Verity gasped, then looked from one to the other to see if they had noticed. They knew that she had to realize, at some point, the truth of what was happening. Or perhaps not. She gradually backed into the shadows as their argument escalated, paralyzed by some force she didn't understand.

"It wasn't right of you to do this, Abraham," said India, her voice severe. "You never listened to your father. You thought you knew everything about the world, about life. All those people out there, in the City—" Her arm swept widely, and she punched her fist at the sky at the gesture's conclusion. "They never *were* real. They don't know the difference. They're all your toys. Fine. But to play with your own mother like this . . ."

He was weeping, his head in his hands. "I didn't mean to. You never seem to understand. I did this because I love you. I love you, Mother. I wanted to give you *life.*"

As far as Verity could tell, they had completely forgotten their surroundings. Their voices faded as she remembered.

He restored the beauty of his childhood days, of course, but did not stop there.

He had seen his parents' life as perfect. Until he meddled in it. Until he allied himself with the new technology that had absorbed his mother, killed her.

So perfect did that life seem to Abe, and so terrible did he feel about his mother's death and his role in it that he felt no compunction about causing it to be relived an infinite amount of times, only pride and relief. He had brought her back from the dead. Except that as a gift, or perhaps a way to avoid thinking about what he'd done, he always left out India's last days, and gave her instead the visions from the books she had so loved.

Disaster—like earthquakes, for instance, and the nan-plagues—had twisted the telling, of course, but the fitful programs valiantly replayed themselves, however flawed, without fail, filling the new participants with grief and joy, with sweet, fleeting memory that seemed not memory but actual life unfolding anew. Each overlay, each new life when returned to the Hive, had an unexpected result.

Each new life had more information. Each new life was a bit more aware of the real situation, glimpsed unexpectedly as one might see the stars between a gap in the night clouds that had been there so long the real sky had been almost forgotten. Each new life was more keenly aware of the pain, the futility, the absurdity. Yet each was loathe to end itself. The next brief reliving—not child to adult to old age, but a season's life only—the next fragment, might bring the information that would lead to a sort of redemption, peace, the cessation of suffering while still in life. A bitter paradoxical idea, yet the one at the heart of most religions.

A natural beehive was beautifully balanced. Each bee rotated through a series of tasks. Each bee tended her sister embryos after she was born, and cleaned the hive. Then, she would graduate to guard. Finally, she might become a scout, dancing and singing directions to her sisters about exactly where to find food. If one tier was completely removed from a hive, it had been found that the others matured much more rapidly and filled the gap.

Cincinnati was simply an extension of this Hive. Durancy had taken that basic Flower-City model and caused these new humans to cycle through histories and experiences of his own mad construction. Experiences which his mother had loved, which had been her life. India—a new, partial India, one with the power of a goddess and the moral constructs of a young child—could drink these, again and again. Drink their distillation collected by the Bees, the emotional distillation which she craved, which all humans needed. The system had worked correctly during the Years of the Flowers, as an optional sideshow, a tribute to India that one could visit as people used to go to the movies. Verity knew this. Knew it too late, she thought bitterly. But now, here, the system was crazed. Perhaps a crucial tier, an essential regulatory interlay, had been removed, maybe by the earthquake, and part of the cycle had expanded crazily into that gap. The City had healed— but with a scar.

India could drink, and never be satiated.

But's not the whole of it, Verity thought desperately. Rose was somehow involved. But how?

"I don't think that there's any other way," Dennis was saying in a low, desperate voice. "You're not *her* . . . and I'm not *him*. We're both imperfect, incomplete, insane."

He stood, his face wild and pale, and pulled a gun from his jacket pocket.

He leveled it straight at India.

"*Do* it," she said. "It will give *her* time, at least. *Do it!*" she screamed.

But with a cry, Dennis turned it on himself, at his head, and pulled the trigger.

Verity whirled at the gun's report, and stared at the brightly lit City beyond the wall. The wind was picking up, and the trees and the garden thrashed wildly beneath the gathering clouds.

How can this be happening again? She sank down, face in her hands. No wonder I responded as I did to Blaze's death. No wonder I killed John without a thought, saving them all, of course, but leaving me still with guilt. That's in me too. Murder. But at least in me it turned outward.

India had stopped screaming. Verity looked up.

She was kneeling next to the chair, and Verity was glad that she shielded Dennis from view. Then India swung round, and was holding the gun. Pointing it at her.

"Every time. He thinks that you will save him. Who are you anyway? A nobody, a nothing."

Verity jumped and ran, stumbling, wondering why her information stopped at this point, like a street that was blank and dark. India was blocking the way she had come in. Was there another way out? How many of her sisters had met their death here?

Fear made her breath ragged in her throat as the hedges tore at her clothing and ripped at her face. And then, like a blessing, like a miracle, the maze map dawned once more, and the boy Abe opened to her with a whisper of "Here. Run quickly. Turn *now*."

Verity heard a thump on the other side of the hedge, and hoped that India had tripped and fallen. She ran faster, passing some turns, entering others, marveling at how complex a pattern could be pressed into a half-acre plot of land. A few rows over, India screamed, "You're useless, selfish, like all the rest; you're always useless, you never meant to help us."

As Verity ran never turning toward the center but instead toward the gate, bullets sang past her and she knew that at this moment India did not know that Abe would live again, in another body, with perhaps a different name—

But *why?* she wondered as she ran. She still did not know.

But at this moment the only thing India knew was black rage because her son had died, and because she blamed herself, as he had blamed himself. There was only so much the human brain could stand. Only so much information that it could hold.

That's why the new mind had to be invented. The intensity and grief involved in simply being conscious, in living and gathering guilt, was often too much. When that was combined with the simple explosion of information, of things-it-was-possible-to-know . . .

And then Verity was at the tall, white picket gate, higher than her head. Verity felt a sting of pain on her upper arm as she fumbled with the latch, seeing in her mind's eye, as she did so, a tiny van driving up, a team jumping out, removing the data sponges, returning her to the bank . . . the damned thing wouldn't open. It was locked! She shook it with all her might, and was trying to find a foothold to boost herself up when it swung open with a creak.

There was the old India, with white hair and sagging breasts, quietly standing in the shadows outside the gate, calm and so normal-seeming. Stunned, Verity stood stock-still. Of course, more than one manifestation of India could exist simultaneously, but—

As Verity stood, old India gripped her arm with a surprisingly strong grasp and pulled Verity through the open gate. Then she slammed it shut.

This was new. Utterly new. The death the other helpless emissaries had suffered slipped from her, shattered about her. Abe and Dennis and the Bell-invested memories receded. She was herself now, Verity only, and felt strange and raw and oddly light, as if she had lived her life under a heavy stone that had just been lifted. When her sisters' memories had been dutifully returned to the Hive, if any of them had reached this juncture, none of them had passed it.

"She locked it from the outside," the old woman said. "She always does. But she has grown, this time. She's grown to be me." Her voice was filled with yearning and, at the same time, valiant conviction, reminding Verity of the way she wished she felt right now. The old woman continued, speaking with haste, looking deep into Verity's eyes. "Each time I try and stay out longer. Just a bit. To grow, to forge a way beyond this horror. How long it has taken just to get this far! And *she* knows nothing of me. No one knows better how to keep her from knowing than I. Child, I *am* your mother, at last. In a way."

Verity stared at her, mouth open, wondering what to say.

After a few seconds, which seemed infinitely long, Verity demanded, "But do you know—what happens at the end—just now—when Abe—"

India shook her head, her eyes dark and puzzled. "A bit at a time, my dear," she said sadly. "I stay outside of her as much as possible, away from the dreadful thing that makes her insane. Someday—one *time*—I—*one* of us—will be able to understand—to *heal*—"

Verity heard footsteps approaching on the other side of the gate, and the gun was fired once more. The sweet, heavy scent of lilies of the valley rose up around them, and Verity stared in horror as blood blossomed on the dress of the old lady, in the middle of her chest.

"Go," she said, gasping. "You have very little time."

Verity fled.

The life that opened before her, the damp streets sloping away beneath the fireworks relentlessly flowering the sky, was absolutely new.

And, for the first time, and maybe just for this moment, absolutely hers.

Thirty-six

○○○○○○○○○○○○○○○○○

Some Enchanted Evening

Verity didn't begin shaking until she had gone two blocks. Because she had gone two blocks *north*. Toward the Zoo, the Hive.

Why?

The City seemed to breath in on her, as if it—as if *she*—generated the very wind, wrathfully. Verity was inundated with *fear* and *strangeness* and *wonder*, as if she had fallen into the completely alive paranoid informational world of Pynchon, Dick, and every religious mystic who ever lived.

As I think, so it will be.

This was the vision of India. *It has all come alive, don't you see?* India's voice whispered from somewhere. *The finest distillation of thought.*

"But it all serves just one being," gasped Verity, gripping a cool low wrought iron fence while catching her breath, refusing to play India's game. "Don't you see that it all serves *you*? India?"

She felt a moment's puzzlement, a shrug, and then, *Of course! Who else?*

Verity took off running again, losing her certainty, not knowing if she was fulfilling India's final vision by going to the Hive or whether she was embarking on a new course. She was far too weary to tell the difference.

Mother and son were two of a kind, she thought, passing many broad-porched dark houses. Only his pain had turned him toward fantasy. Hers, reduced to the basic instincts of childhood, of the untamed and completely selfish child-personality before she entered the net just before her death, had taken this dark turn toward revenge, one unsuspected and always unseen by her adoring son, the shadow self balancing the generous garden that always faced the sun, grown perhaps in desperation to keep this terrible inner darkness at bay.

Verity had been lifted beyond the wall to Edgetown—by Dennis, according to her memory of the implantation, or by an earlier version. Why? And why was Dennis different from Abe?

The streetlights dimmed around her and she stumbled on a curb, twisting her ankle. She stood, took a step, and gasped with pain.

India, she knew, would return to the Hive. Verity still was not sure of how the interface took place, but it seemed as if an ever-fresh intelligence, a collection of stored human matrices, as if they were truly mothers needing no fathers, informed the nan-preserved, or nan-engendered bodies. Apparently they grew quickly, or in the case of important ones, there were several to spare, lacking only the final animation. What would be difficult about that?

But Verity knew that India always returned. She had to. She had to complete her Bee-like cycle, renew and revitalize this dream-City.

And India always made Abe live again. He was her child. She had to. The purity and innocence of new birth—of a new *adult* birth—would for a time wash away the memory and the pain of what age—the peculiar age of nangrowth unlinked from time—would soon repeat.

And why should Verity care?

She paused, and reached down to feel her ankle. It was hot and puffy. Damn! Where was that nan-stuff when you needed it?

She realized, as she stood, that she cared what happened to these people—these *beings*—because of her life with the Shakers, because of Russ. She laughed, and the sound was bitter as the wind took it from her. She was filled with some crazy notion of responsibility to her fellow humans, which obviously did not come from the City. A notion that autonomy was important. So what, she thought impatiently. Who do you think you are, Mother Ann, providing a private conduit to Heaven for everyone here? As if that were possible, as if you could. Go! Forget the Hive, forget India. Find Sphere and Blaze, and leave!

Verity limped down the street, feeling the City shiver.

A new Conversion was at hand.

Escape, before it's too late, and you are folded back into it! She tried to go faster, clenching her teeth. She would figure out *some* way for them to leave. She had to!

A cab pulled up next to Verity on the dark street. She turned and cut across some yards, hearing the car roar away. She continued, led by the glow on the horizon, by the growing hum of Bees beneath the fitful light of the moon between clouds as the Flowers unfurled against all nature, moved by artifice. By India.

Soon, perhaps, too soon, India's Conversion would sweep through the City, through her very molecules, and wash her clean of all the information she had gleaned in the course of this life. She had very little time. Yes, that was certainly true!

Her breath was burning in her throat. Her legs felt like lead. Her mind was exploding with light and pain.

Blaze was down there somewhere, a half-person. Sphere, too, the only real human here and he longed to be like them!

A Bee flew over her head and Verity wondered if that was the Bee carrying the directions of India back to the Hive, or returning *this* particular Durancy, with his subtle new overlays, to the Hive, his little nubs extracted and stuffed into the pollen pouches. She shivered with anger. To be dissolved! And yet, in some ways, it did seem better than death. Different.

Except that it seemed to give them such enormous pain.

Because their reality was suffocated. Because they lived like John inside stubborn prisons, except that John believed his opened into light and they—

They did have a certain kind of heaven. Sideways in time, eternally returning. To be, again and again. In a different mode than humans had ever existed, their experiences prefashioned.

But was it that much different than Shaker Hill? Of course. At Shaker Hill you were free to leave, however much fear of Enlivenment and familiarity might keep you there. There would be no censure, only help in preparations.

Here, your perceptions were entirely in the service of the Hive. You could not even *choose* to leave.

She stopped running, on the last hill above the City proper, and hunched down. One last time, the beauty. One last time, Durancy's stunning vision.

And wasn't this what it was supposed to be like, after all? The

Bees serving the needs of the Flowers, agents of the humans, twenty-four hours a day, staggered by type atop buildings: morning, noon, and night bloomers. A City where one did not have to labor for food, clothing, and shelter. A City where *humanity's* promise could finally unfurl. Somehow she knew this.

Lightning shot across the sky, illuminating in a flash the brilliant scene. What did this swift activity presage?

It was less than a mile to the Zoo.

She paused at the corner for a long moment. She didn't have to go.

Then, with a sigh, remembering the eyes of Russ, she turned toward it.

She went down into a steep, narrow valley of dark sidewalks and looming buildings. Fear pounded through her but anger was stronger, and cleared her mind. All was silent, the sound of distant fireworks hidden by hills, and only the sounds of her own footsteps echoed about her until she heard a single word:

"Verity!"

The voice was urgent, male, and familiar.

Sphere.

She stopped and looked around.

Ahead, an interstice glowed, alone, even though it was difficult to make out the building that it fed in the darkness.

Was it some sort of trick?

"Verity, I *know* you're there. Come closer. Hurry. It's about Blaze. Toward the light. We—*I* can really speak to you wherever you are, but . . ."

She hobbled the last twenty yards and stopped, amazed.

A tiny picture of Sphere's face was lit, in a small oval next to the interstice, at the same level as her face. He smiled.

"This is," he said, panting, then catching his breath. "This is *exciting,* Verity."

"What are you *doing?*" she asked. "Where is Blaze?"

"I—" He looked over his shoulder, then looked back. "Verity, I'm using the City as it's *meant* to be used. You have no *idea.* . . ."

"I have *some* idea," she said, trying to stay calm. "I guess that crazy waitress woman—"

"She's not crazy," said Sphere. "But Blaze is gone."

"*What?*" she shouted, forgetting caution. "Where did he go? How did he get away? I thought the timer said—"

"Everything's going haywire," said Sphere. "We were just sit-

ting in that room and talking and suddenly Blaze stood up and
started singing those songs—you know, those river songs—"

"I know," she said, feeling distant from it all, as if nothing
mattered. "Didn't you try and stop him?"

"He was out the door in a flash. We chased him, of course, and
I was going to try and find you somehow, but I had no idea how
to do it, and that woman—Dezaray is her name, don't you think
that's lovely? Dezaray . . . *initiated* me, you might say . . . she gave
me a little vial of things . . . Verity, I never *knew* . . . Verity, I'm
more *free* than these people. I'm the same, but I'm different because I'm from *outside*. I know how to *use* all this. I'm not like the
rest of them here. I can truly *create!* Create something entirely
new! Listen . . ."

"Sphere," she interrupted, and he stopped talking. "Thank
you—thank you for telling me. I've got to go now. I've really got
to go." Her voice shook. "I have a lot of work to do, I think." And
then she was off toward the Zoo again, running even faster, ignoring the pain, her head echoing one word with each harsh breath:
Blaze. Blaze. Blaze.

Then she stopped.

Beneath the roar of the wind, she heard barking. She turned.
Yes.

"*Cairo!*" she yelled. "*Cairo!*"

She stood still, so very still, and the barking was closer this
time. It had an odd, slowed sound, but it was Cairo's bark.

Get Cairo, she thought. Find Blaze. Get out of here. Now.

She yelled some more, again and again; the wind pulled the
name away from her, but the barking became louder. She moved
toward it, cautiously, afraid to lose it.

Was that her? The stumbling, dark shape down the street?

Verity ran, suddenly terrified, for she felt a horrible darkness
coming from Cairo. In the streetlight, as she got closer, pictures
wavered, and they were like nightmares, worse than she had ever
had, even here, filled with loss and terror.

"Where have you been?" gasped Verity, kneeling beside Cairo
and hugging her as the dog collapsed in her arms. "No," she
whispered. "Don't think. I'm here now. I'm here."

Cairo was twitching uncontrollably. Verity looked into her
eyes and tried to ignore the pictures. Explosions, wars, people
running as they burned. Cairo's wounds had been healed, but
what had the sheets done? Something terrible. Something impos-

sible. "Cairo," she whispered, and the pictures changed, became simple again, and glad. Verity saw Russ. Blaze. Herself. Food.

Then, the waking, with Blaze. Then Cities, Bees. The desire to know more and more, the desperate desire to find Verity, the searing, twisted *knowledge*; human knowledge, Verity realized, which Cairo's brain could not assimilate; the dizzy sickness . . .

Cairo's tongue lolled out. Verity stroked her head, helplessly, again and again, and whispered her name. Cairo relaxed. Verity could feel her happiness, her satisfaction: she had found Verity. That was all she wanted. Now she could rest. She shuddered once, and stopped breathing.

Verity held her for a moment, then stood tiredly, laying Cairo gently on the grass next to the pavement. She felt immense, aching loss.

And deep anger. At who? At Sphere, who had activated the sheets? At Russ, who had bought the sheets? At herself, who had insisted on wrapping Cairo in the sheets, instead of letting her die? The sheets were not meant for dogs; Cairo's brain could not handle that information though her body had been healed. But how could I have known? Verity thought. It didn't matter. Cairo's suffering was her fault. She had done the best she could, and it had been wrong. Yet that was all she could have done. How could she have done less?

Verity looked down the street and saw that she was at the Zoo. She took a deep breath.

She had no time to mourn, not now. Cairo was now just one more mistake of the City, and she and Blaze would be too, if she couldn't figure out what to do. I'll be just like Cairo once I'm in there, she thought. But it didn't matter. She had to go.

The boy Enoch was still there, cradling new jesus as he sat on the park bench, watching the spectacular sky. He waved at Verity as she strode past, chilled with drying sweat. She looked straight into his eyes and fancied she saw pleading there. Release me.

Release him to what? What did he know? What could he do? In this fine City, in this crazy place, he had food and shelter and this odd repetitive mission, this role comprised of pure music. Was it any different than her life at Shaker Hill—hoe the corn, wash the dishes, and . . .

Dance.

Dance.

Could she call forth the Virgin Queen with dance?

Dance was a grammar. Dance told stories. Dance told the story of food, whether it be sweet summer nectar to be stored for the winter or the relived, pheromonally translated everlasting stories that fed a voracious India with the helpless lives of the people who lived and died, lived and died, in her service.

Verity gritted her teeth.

She had the Gift of Dance. And she had a new story for them. A new direction.

A direction, she realized, pausing as she did, toward Nothingness, for it was all new, and completely unknown even to her. She forced herself to start walking again.

The summer air was sweet in Verity's lungs as she approached the Museum of the Bees.

It was much different this time than in early spring. Was there a Verity each season, she wondered, like the ancient Corn Kings and Spring Queens, one of her favorite books from the burned library, with those figures of fertility becoming, to their own surprise, quite human? How many times had this happened? How many times had Durancy's foredoomed creation approached this apex?

The hell with those times, all of them.

One could possibly fear the Bees that faced her—how many? Thirty, forty, a hundred? Black and golden in the dim light, their hum embraced her and entered her bones like Enlivenment; their beautiful complex eyes stared at her in multiplied splendor, knowing an alien world. Verity recognized the guard Bees, to the far right and far left, poised for killing, yet puzzled at the sisterly pheromones, which Verity knew were a part of her being, absorbed by her DNA during that green and luminous handpress that seemed so very long ago.

Verity let go into the Light, as she had countless times at Meetings: the Light of Dance, of Motion as Grammar, as Story, as Redemption. Her own Light.

She stood well back from the Bees on the dance platform, where directions were signaled by running precise distances which reported as clearly as a map here is the food! This way! And oh what bizarre food you carry, my lovely cousins, she thought, watching them in their golden beauty, feeling their crazy pictures press upon her mind without allowing them to enter and change her. No, she gave them back the picture, no, then: This:

The map of the Queen Bee pheromones.

"I accept my conversion," she said.

A wave of scent instantly enveloped her, for there was no time here, not as she knew it. It was only a microsecond for the determining mind between the last time she had been here, and refused this gift, this responsibility, and now.

She shivered, and began to sweat. Perspiration beaded on her forehead, ran down her face, broke out all over her body and soaked her clothing. The throbbing in her ankle lessened, vanished. Glands that were a part of her City-created body awoke, circulating the necessary hormones. This one Story was essential, now, to her survival. And to her plan.

The guard Bees, rather than attacking, fell back.

The core of her thought could not falter now. And oddly, she thought of Shaker Hill, the truth of her being when living there, and baseball, and running very fast. And of Blaze, her very fine, very real friend.

This, she realized, as she set foot on the first step, was why no City-*raised* person could change anything. For the Bees knew how to mold the behavior of anyone who had lived here all their "life," short as a life might be here. A complete infant-to-adult brainpattern was alien to their way of knowing, except for those few children, such as she must have been, trained in school to continue a vestigial almost meaningless charade of human involvement in all of this.

She had to call out the Virgin Queen.

When a natural hive swarmed, each new queen called out, from within her hexagonal chamber, in a series of buzzes answered from outside. There were usually several virgin queens inside cells, unhatched but fully formed, as backups. Each new queen got the all clear and emerged to lead a swarm away from the overpopulated hive.

When only the two were left, there was often a fight.

The buzz signals could verify that there was still a queen who could repopulate and control the hive when the next-to-last one swarmed.

But if there was no other place to go (and where is the nearest Flower City, wondered Verity. Columbus, perhaps?), no good hiving site ascertained by the scouts, the next-to-last Queen had a choice.

She could call out the message to the Queen who had not yet emerged. That Queen would answer, within her cell.

Then she could go and destroy her.

India was, even now, she supposed, complete in the mind and mission of the new Virgin Queen.

Within Durancy's plan, Verity sensed a planned flaw, or perhaps a fluke of some kind, but within that seed was also the program that had called the surge into being. Insanity, but controlled insanity. *My* City. I can wipe it clean if I like. I can start from scratch if it doesn't work out.

The conversions that had swept through Cincinnati before had been no accident.

The hell you can wipe it clean India Durancy. The hell you can. It's my turn now.

She approached the cell that held the next India, and began to dance.

She made up the story as she went along, transmitting through motion the Grammar, the Story, of a New Cincinnati.

The air was heavy with pure thought, with the broadcasting, as she whirled, of metapheromones that were electric, and powerful. She released them with absolute precision, assembled them with newly awakened glands that responded to pictures in her mind, pictures filled with detail and shadings, with sound and thought and deep humanity.

They spoke of the outside world, of a life washed clean of the stories of others. Something that humans had really never had before, for the story of their culture were absorbed by infants before they could even speak.

Then she heard the voice of India, speaking throughout the Hive, yet addressing only her. It was powerful, sharp as a holo, cutting her metapheromone projections to shreds, pushing her hard against the yielding wall of the Hive, a voice dry as desert air:

"You are trying to steal from us eternal life. We will wake from the stories when we are ready. Until then, we learn, more and more, about consequence, about decision, about what it means to be fully human. It is all stored here, in the Hive, for all of us, to sample again and again, learning always more and more."

You can't stay a child forever, danced Verity. *Eventually you have to set out for the Territory.* She danced ever harder, sweating, her limbs like lead, dancing for the life of Cincinnati, pushing with each burning motion against the monstrous energy of the Hive, seeking to dismantle it, to supersede it. If but the other Bees would imitate her, take the new directions and disperse them through the system . . . *It's not learning,* she danced, *if there are no consequences. It's not life for anyone, not even you. Oedipa said it. You're all quite dead. It's possible, actually possible, to be alive. Take this opportunity! Take it! Live!*

"I want to live," said a voice from beyond the golden wall.

And then a pale white arm broke through.

Thirty-seven

◇◇◇◇◇◇◇◇◇◇◇◇◇◇◇◇◇◇

Wake Up and Dream

India stood before Verity, naked and very young. Maybe fifteen, thought Verity, as she looked at the Boticelli face, slightly puffy, and sleepy, with half-lowered lids. India blinked, and pushed back waist-long blond hair with one arm.

But as Verity watched, the woman's brown eyes sharpened. She took a deep breath, as if filling her lungs with air for the first time. As her eyes focussed she looked at Verity, and with her second breath she smiled slightly, as if that breath had filled her with knowledge.

"Ah, she said. "You have succeeded. None of the others have."

Now I have to kill you, thought Verity, and was upset when her words seemed to echo in the close, sweet air. She glanced around, wondering how she was to accomplish this, when the guard Bees flanked the ends of the tunnels and she had never even wanted to kill rabbits and foxes? And if she did, what then?

But India just smiled. "See if you can *stand* it first," she said.

The visions that racked Verity, then, were unlike any others she had seen so far, and they flickered swiftly and fully. Maps lit in her mind wildly, and they were more complex than any she'd ever seen. They were maps of books, charts of emotional matrices, information she tried to turn from, so burning was it in its relentless torrent, but she could not and so she turned to face it—

And it slowed.

She took a deep breath. This was more rich, more full, more powerful, than anything she could have dreamed of. She turned, looking for India, and did not see her, and wondered if she had just been an apparition.

See? said India's voice within her mind. *This is how it truly is, inside. Now all is yours, ours, as it has always been. You have gained the citadel. I offer you My entire being, the Hive.*

Verity knew then, that India, as she had known her, was absorbed here into some different state. A state she too could enter.

And she too could go back and forth between the worlds. As— India.

Yes, the voice continued. *We are all as one. Absolutely and forever, my new self who will soon join us. They may try and destroy us, but with each new addition we gain in strength. This is our City. Our beautiful realm, infinite, where we feed. We know of love, and pain, and joy, and peace, and harmony. Each bar of jazz, each wondrously sharp, precise poem, each model of reality is ours, the human essence ours. You've had a taste of it. You've felt the power. Bless you for joining us. Now we shall begin to instruct you, finally.*

Verity struggled in mind against this flood of information. There was no place to rest. There could be only going forward, into infinite information, more deeply satisfying than anything that she had ever experienced. And now, in just a moment, she would be a part of the Hive, in control, all-powerful. And when Dennis attempted to make another like her—

She frowned. Another *like* her?

The force of the question she had lived with all her life struck her like a blow. Who *was* she? Who was she really?

Don't worry about that. Soon you will know everything. Soon you will be able to do anything. Surrender.

Anything, she wondered? Save Blaze? Restore the City?

A storm of anger swept through her at that last thought. And laughter. So that she knew that her idea was mocked.

She wanted to remain herself, achingly. She did not want to learn anything, suddenly. She wished she could just flee with Blaze, somehow, in the conversion confusion.

Imperfect, arrested Blaze. And all the others like him, their being somehow stripped from them like Azure's.

Suddenly she realized: this was the battle. Not a physical battle, but a battle of thought that each of her predecessors had lost. Surrender to the Hive, *become the Queen!*

Or die.

There must be a third option, she thought frantically, and Dance surged through her once again as if she were already half-converted, and each step was an argument with the City, with the Hive, with India, a plea for freedom, a *demand* for freedom.

Don't you remember Huckleberry Finn? she danced. *Don't you remember Jim? What of the personal struggle of each musician, then, each artist, each poet—*

She felt India's laughter.

And finally Verity could dance no more. She faltered and collapsed to the soft warm floor, unable to continue. It seemed that she had been dancing for days, years. She could call forth no more stories; she could not even move. She wished for food, for some sort of energy, but there was none—not now, not ever again. As honeybees simply wore out after a certain number of forages midflight and fell to earth and died, Verity found only emptiness and lost connections when she tried to bend her legs and rise again; her face was wet with tears. Three sister Bees came forward, beautiful, limned with golden light, and pushed her into a cell despite her feeble struggle.

And there, she began to change.

She melted, she coalesced. Every memory she ever had flashed through her. The musing face of Russ washed by firelight on a winter night. Sare, yanking her hair so tight into braids that tears came to her eyes. Blaze, his green eyes gentle and unfocussed as he brushed a sweat-darkened horse in a barn filled with shafts of light in which danced motes of dust. John, blue and certain as death and the swirl of the New Ohio River, sweeping her onward toward the City.

But as memories washed outward she reached for them, caught them, the instant before they effervesced to lodge in the Hive's memory. Some tough faculty, some core of self that everyone else here lacked, roused, and focussed, a gentle, yet powerful light, smothered always before by the Bell, insisted on keeping those memories.

Herself. Verity.

Lying in the dark, she realized that it was true: she had complete access.

But access did her no good, she realized with frustration. She could *see*. But she could not *do*. She could not do anything different, anything new. She had no true power; she had won nothing. The only actions she could *execute* were those within certain parameters.

Those which would not harm the City.

There *must* be some way out. Why did one memory tug at her?

She searched for it. Something about when Abe was at the Big Lake. Wintertime. Something important had happened there . . . she *knew* it.

The memories were numbered, were they not? Yes, ah yes. And there . . . there it was!

Abe was frantically working—

Then she lost that one, overwhelmed by a myriad, swirling flock of memories, one called up by the other, swiftly, so that the one she wanted was buried.

She had no time to trace it back. Her very presence in this cell triggered the complex metapheromonal reaction that would eventually, within a day or two, lead to Conversion. The final failsafe of Abe's City. That which would start it anew, once someone like her got into the works. That which would swallow her as well.

She had to set the people free, get them away from the City. That she *could* do, and realized with grim elation that no one, no *entity*, had ever thought of doing this before. And she could find only one way to do it, only one thing that might be stronger than the City's hold.

Thinking here was much swifter, much more powerful, than anything she had ever experienced before.

Her plan had to do with history and desire and common denominators and all was changed to flashing graphs and charts that she did not really understand and yet she did, more deeply than she had ever before understood anything.

But there was one important missing piece which she needed.

When she emerged stumbling from her cell after a dark, timeless spell weirder than any previous dream, she had changed.

Was that what she wanted? Was her real body stored, or just the DNA, or her memories, or both together, waiting to manifest her again and again? She was not sure.

No Bee challenged her. They all stood back with what could only be reverence. She staggered down the corridor on hardening legs, then used them to grip and climb clumsily upward on the soft golden walls.

In the faint pink of dawn, on the roof of the Parthenon-shaped Hive, as the warm summer wind blew, she awakened into a new and brilliant world.

Fat trees glowed, summer-full, between the buildings and in dawn-empty parks wet with dew. The buildings were faint washes of power, the lines glistened and led upward to Food for which she longed with enormous passion.

Her wings hooked, and a powerful hum surged through her. She felt as bright as the sun that gave her new direction, for light was polarized now and all was so precise, even more precise than the maps.

She leapt into the beautiful clear air, among the unfurling Flowers, searching for the One who could save Cincinnati, wondering, as she flew, at the stubborn intactness of that overwhelmingly imperative Story.

Her new, and her own, Story.

Thirty-eight
○○○○○○○○○○○○○○○○○○○○○○

I Don't Care if I Never
Get Back

Verity didn't like being so fat. It was hot and her clothes were tight and she was very uncomfortable. She looked down at herself once again, confused. She didn't look fat. She just felt fat. And distant. And strange. As if she was wearing glasses that were not quite right. She had a terrible headache.

She sat back in her hard small chair, feeling not only the crowd press against her but the chair as well, squeezing her.

She was stunned at the number of people here. Of course, the entire crowd across from her, the Atlanta fans, here to cheer their team, the Atlanta Bees, were all holos, but they were satisfying enough. Their cheers and boos were just as loud, their fist-shaking quite lifelike, and she didn't have to worry about feeding them. She was pretty sure that she'd not created them, anyway.

Her crew now—that was another matter.

In the historical stratum she had decided—though deciding was a word that belonged *here,* and not *there*—to invoke, a fellow named Pete had just been run out of town on a rail. She'd put out a call for a new coach and it had been pretty easy to predict who would turn up, in the rush and roar of the newly filled city, where everyone had awakened at once. Who cared more about baseball than Blaze?

Verity was sweating in her red dress. The sun angled in beneath the overhang, catching her full in the face, and she squinted. When would the team get out here? When would the game begin?

It was wonderful to see the crowd. All that had been necessary was a few old-fashioned posters with the time, appearing just a few hours for the event.

The sorting she initiated in the Hive had shuffled down to a common interest swiftly. Everyone, no matter what Cincinnati timeframe they were living, seemed to remember baseball, the one constant core element that could draw them all together. The river swept along the south side of Riverfront Stadium, but stubborn nans had kept it pretty much intact.

She had been afraid to see if the new coach would recognize her—afraid that he would not, or afraid that he would, and shake her resolve. So she had not seen him, so far, but only *knew*, with her many new ways of knowing, that it was Blaze.

She blinked against the bright sun, which to human eyes washed the color away and gave but vague direction. She missed the amazing polarization that she had experienced as a Bee. Restlessly, she longed to get back to the Hive.

Blaze. She remembered sweeping down upon him, when she finally found him, wandering through the heart of the City. His pheromonal pattern, which she saw from above, told her that he was weeping.

She had tried to dance for him and ask for his help, but he only shrieked in terror and ran. So she had to buzz, and feint, and drive him to an interstice, one on the corner of Fourth and Race, of 1880 vintage, with the glowing purple line pulsing between old-fashioned cornices of gray stone.

Gasping, he had cowered into it, and she had been satisfied. With her new eyes she could *see* the information pulsing upward, changing to an analog of pollen. It only took seconds, and she rose into the air, collected it, and returned to the Hive to do her work.

Shielding her eyes with her hand, Verity wished she had a hat, and tried not to be startled when a boy with a box of Cincinnati Reds hats hung round his neck stopped at the end of her aisle and began passing them out. She jammed one on her head after it was handed to her and could see the green field better. A tractor with a drag attached was smoothing the baselines, kicking up dust, and she applauded the touch, remembering how Blaze had hooked a drag behind the plow horse and groomed the field after games so religiously. Had she put the tractor there? She didn't even know anymore, what she had and hadn't done, what she could and couldn't do. No wonder India was so arrogant.

It had taken Blaze two days to choose a team among those who tried out. He rejected several hundred, and Hemingway in particular had been very angry and threatened to kill himself but Verity saw that he was here too, several rows down from her, demanding gin instead of beer and why not? Give it to him she thought, thought a metapheromone instead of a verbal command, and soon a young man rushed up to him with an icy quart bottle in which olives floated. The old man's bearded face broke out in a grin.

Verity wondered a bit at the lineup. She studied her program once again. Billie Holiday pitching? Dizzy Gillespie in the outfield? Shouldn't these people be in the band? What in the world was Blaze thinking about? She worried. It might not work if the game didn't last long enough. She hoped his team was up to a fight.

She closed the program and fanned herself with it. It sure was hot. The woman next to her yelled out, "Hey, over here, more beer," and Verity felt enormously happy. Beat down harder, sun. Die down, wind. Let's go, Cincinnati Reds. But let everybody eat and drink first.

She did remember finding a match for Blaze's plague, the Territory Plague, with the glowing icon-wall she accessed in the Hive, and commanding it to replicate, and to go forth and find a way past the City's immunities. Those immunities had to be wiped out and she had chosen the medium of food and drink: assemble the multitudes, and give them loaves and fishes. Or beer and hot dogs, it didn't really matter. And you didn't have to understand. That was the glory of being a Queen. You didn't have to know how. You simply gave the commands. Durancy had fixed all that: there were shells and layers and vast convoluted *shapes* of information that expressed flavors, smells, feelings, events that linked to other events in a new, spherical geometry. She wanted to reach into these, to spend lives exploring them, but she had no time, she had to be brief, because they could all be wiped away, washed, the architecture grown from new clean seed . . . if she wasn't quick enough. The City would not be harmed, but at least these people would have the choice of leaving.

If it all worked.

The woman next to her glanced at her and said, "Hey, I know who you are, you're the Fat Lady," and Verity said, "I know you too, Zelda, nice to meet you," and the woman blinked and stuck her nose in the air and took a good swig of beer, which simply warmed Verity's heart. "Weren't you a dancer too?" she asked the pale woman, but Zelda only looked away, her face suddenly wistful.

Didn't do to think too much about things at this point. As if she could. It all seemed so fuzzy. Verity yelled herself, "Hey, another beer," and the people were just scurrying up and down the cement stairs passing paper cups of beer down the aisles, and hot dogs, that's right, thought Verity, more hot dogs, more beer.

And then it was enough and a tiny green light blinked in her lower left field of vision and the band, hammered dulcimers, began to play and the team ran out onto the field and Zelda looked at her and said, "Isn't it time for the national anthem? Aren't you going to sing?"

"Not yet, honey," said Verity, and yanked her tight dress down and sat once more and watched.

She hoped that Blaze wouldn't be too disappointed in his team. She could hardly believe that he could do much with them on such short notice.

She settled back. It was going to be a long game. At least she hoped it would be.

It would take time for everything to take effect.

She stared across the field. *That's him.*

How *is* he, she wondered. And then, with a shock, she *knew.*

It's a gift to be simple, was the thought that flashed through Blaze as he stepped up to bat. The home plate pulsed with color and he was inordinately glad to be able to wallop it a few times with the bat, making satisfying thumps. He'd gotten much too complicated. And what was causing this complexity? He shouldn't have drunk so much beer, but it had been so good. And was it right that he, the coach, had decided to put himself up to bat? But why not? He was the best player he had, that was certain. But maybe he should save himself for later?

The band began to play something . . . a Scott Joplin tune. What was it? The pitcher kicked at the mound and feinted. Blaze jumped.

That heavy woman whose stern face was hidden behind the

umps mask was making him nervous. What was her name? Stein, that was it. She insisted on the job. An arbiter of taste, she called herself, and I can certainly arbit baseball quite as well as taste. She had fought bitterly against the inclusion of that burly, bearded old man, Hemingway. She called him rude and ungrateful, as if that had anything to do with baseball, and they spat at each other for a while. Blaze broke it up by simply telling him that he didn't seem much like a team player. That had made him *really* mad, especially when he found himself agreeing wholeheartedly.

Something—the damned, pulsing home plate?—made him turn and look up in the stands.

He saw her, then, saw her seeing him seeing her—*her!*

Verity! The cry rose in his throat! He remembered! He remembered so *much*—

Then, suddenly dizzy as though someone had released a hold on him, he staggered. "Strike one!" yelled the umpire.

His head cleared. What had made him so giddy?

He turned to glare at Stein. He readied himself, hefted the bat, hit the next pitch with a resounding crack.

Yes! Verity jumped to her feet, cheering madly with the rest of them as he ran, very fast, around the bases. The Blaze Verity knew would have put himself up to bat when the bases were loaded. But—yes, that was it. He wanted to set the tone. Make them proud. Get their blood pumping.

Verity sweated through eight innings, ever more anxious and disturbed. They had eaten and drunk enough! Two innings ago, at least. Everything was ready. What if this window passed? What might happen then? Maybe she had done something not exactly right. And who was that blond woman pitching, wearing a print dress hiked up above her knees? Why was she wearing that funny straw hat? The Atlanta Bees were not doing too badly. In fact they were ahead by two runs. A hot wind rushed through the stadium and Verity held onto her hat brim. The woman pitched. The batter swung and missed . . .

"Strike two!" yelled the umpire.

Behind the scoreboard a row of yellow-tinged pink Tea Roses began to bloom. Round Riverfront Stadium had reminded Verity of the center of Black-eyed Susans, so they waved in the wind, fifty feet high, rising majestically from the top of the stands, their interstices running to the ground every hundred feet. Now those lines began to glow as the Flowers stretched and unfurled, slowly, each petal like a wave, curving convexly against the sun. At last! "That's right," yelled Verity. "Go! Go!"

Everyone was on their feet, screaming. "Fuck the umpire," yelled Zelda, both fists punching the air. "That was a ball! Don't you have eyes in your head?"

That's right, everyone, thought Verity. Yell. Take deep breaths. Take real deep breaths. Breath those nans that the Flowers are releasing. Take in the Territory Plague I replicated from Blaze. Then you'll *have* to leave. You'll escape the Conversion, and India. Once you get to Norleans, you'll be free.

Maybe.

Darkness swept through her. It's the only way, she reminded herself, not being able just at the moment to remember exactly why.

How long is this going to take? she wondered, wiping her forehead with a paper napkin. She sat down again. The Atlanta Bees were very good. Wise, somehow. They had a very quirky way of playing, but always followed the rules. At least it *seemed* so—would she really know if they didn't? Shaking, she realized that she needed to get back to the Hive before too long.

Finally they were at the bottom of the ninth inning. Verity was afraid Blaze would be very disappointed if the Atlanta team won. He'd chew that team out up one side and down the other. But wasn't there more to this game than that? She tensed, looking around at the vast crowd, remembering and forgetting in waves, and resolved to drink no more beer. What if the Atlanta team won? What if—

Verity looked over and saw that Zelda was getting a faint golden sheen.

Relief swept through her and changed to tears, yet she had never been so happy in her life. Her joy expanded and she felt, once more, like dancing but there was no room in the press of the crowd.

At that moment Charlie Parker hit the ball with a sharp crack. Verity watched it sail, white, in a huge arc, into the stands while one of the Atlanta Bees slammed into the wall trying to catch it. People dove for it in a frenzy while all four Reds jogged around the bases, waving their hands in the air. Parker kept stopping to bow to waves of deafening cheers. Halfway between third and home, he stopped suddenly. He looked around, clearly bewildered.

In the wild fray the band, the hundred hammered dulcimers, began to play. Verity stepped up to the microphone, yanked at her dress, and sang.

Looking enormously surprised, Zelda opened her mouth and sang with her.

And then they all were singing, and the team stopped on the field and they sang as well, adding their voices to the vast swell of music. The holograms across the stadium representing the Atlanta fans vanished and the words were simple as a hymn:

> Some rows up
> But we floats down,
> Way down the Ohio to Shawneetown.

I had to be here, Verity thought she was saying to Zelda, I had to be human again for this last time, but Zelda wasn't even Zelda anymore; her whole face had changed because the thoughts that informed facial musculature had changed and then Verity realized that it wasn't really *her* there either but only a great wide white blankness and the loneliness of a brand-new Heaven and the filling up of that Heaven with a new season of Bees.

Thirty-nine

○○○○○○○○○○○○○○○○○○

After Many a Summer Dies the Queen

It's not so bad, Verity thought. It all seemed to go quite well, and besides I can be human again, sometimes, and play with my little memories of Blaze and Sphere and Durancy, push them around like dolls. Can't I?

It was hot and there was a great rushing crowd, and they all rushed one way, riverward, and she went the other, stumbling up the concrete steps and down to the street, trying to keep focussed on her goal, hoping she would make it, sick as she felt. She had to make it. She had to get back. She had to give them time, hold back India, who was incredibly strong. There were so many of her! That would be very hard. Maybe they would kill Verity. Probably. But right now, what seemed worse than that was that it was *such* a long walk, and these two legs were awkward. And now it was much harder to walk, since she was heavier.

No, it would be good to do things in a different way, so hard being human, so goddamned stupid and it seemed to go on for hours and hours, like walking on molasses instead of on hard sidewalks and she laughed: command yourself a car, fair Queen, but she found that she didn't know *how,* she was much too tired. Maybe she was done for. Maybe she was dying. She didn't care.

But Verity was still, now, the acting Queen, Queen for a day, Queen of the City of Cincinnati. Now she would go back and try and do battle again. Call the waiting Indias out, one after another.

They were there, waiting for rebirth, forever and ever. An infinite line of them. But she felt so *tired*. She tried to think of how to send a new Story to each India cell, but could not. Being a Queen meant that avenue was closed to her, a programming impossibility. She could not *destroy* the Hive. Yet there had to be *some* way . . . some way to free Cincinnati, to break through the Seam, to smash the loop. To begin to use it as the Flower Cities had been meant to be used.

She was partly an architect, was she not? But every bit of architectural knowledge she had was bound up with Durancy's memories, his twisted dream. It would take cycles and cycles of work to unravel that. The emotional energy was dense and dark and filled with pain almost to death. But now she had time. Lots of time.

As she struggled on, up Third Street, and people rushed past her toward the river, their faces eager and yearning, thought became more and more to her like patches of color, blending into vision after vision, falling with kaleidoscopic regularity to new information with her steps, then losing that constriction and gaining flow, turning to a river of scent. Yet it was all distant, so she was protected from worry and guilt. She forgot how she had come to the Territory Plague solution. It had seemed all wrong for such a long time, as she projected solution after solution. But finally she had realized that it was the only thing strong enough to wrench them away from the City.

For the Territory Plague was filled with assemblers that infected people with Hope and the future possibility of Choice, duplicating those complex bodily chemicals hormonally, configuring the victims with the emotional maps of what America had meant to so many. The City hated it. Like a new band of Pilgrims, like Mother Ann's followers from England escaping persecution, like Huck Finn and Jim, those infected would fly—*could fly*—from the known to the unknown with the only vehicles at hand: rafts on the New Ohio River. They all had one story now, but that story had once been programmed to evaporate, after its purpose had been served. Verity did not know whether that part of it, where it ended, was still untwisted. But she would stay, and hold off the Conversion for as long as she could, and give them a chance to prepare, and leave. Even here she could feel India trembling with rage, eager to unleash Herself, rebuilding her power, growing herself once more.

And then—Verity would become a part of the new City. She had to remain so that everyone else could get away. She only hoped that she had stored enough of her own Story to break the cycle the next time around, to break it more fully, to renew the City, to give it back to the humans. That was her plan. She went over it again, seeing it all in pictures, deciding how to sharpen a detail here and there with a fillip of metascent, trying to forget Durancy and his endless loop, hoping that she had expelled him from herself but fearing that she had not, that he was a part of her very cells forever, through endless incarnations. But maybe, at the least, *this* story would repeat, and that would be some small triumph. She was sure that this was the first time people had been able to leave Cincinnati.

She had done the best she could. Now it was over and she still wasn't sure if it would work, and it was hot, extremely hot.

Verity had long since ceased to pay any attention at all to what her body was doing. It trudged on without her conscious direction, while at times, to her right, between buildings, she glimpsed the crowd assembling down at the landing, beneath the shadow of the suspension bridge, the New Ohio River as green in the summer sun as Blaze's lovely eyes. "The beautiful, beautiful river," she sang, "that flows by the throne of God," and then stopped, shaking with laughter that turned crazy and wild and brought tears to her eyes before she turned away.

Only a few blocks more. She continued to trudge, lost more and more in color and scent, turning and climbing and pushing though doors until she looked around and saw that she had somehow made it back to the Queen Cell.

She stood in front of the soft gold hexagon, part of a vast wall of hexagons. She wondered, now just what am I supposed to do now, why isn't my body telling me, where are the directions? Then she collapsed on the dance floor, spinning into a great warm sweet-smelling place while many small hard arms touched her all over as if trying to figure out what she was, and then all their sharp tongues licked her; that was how they got information, and she felt herself being rolled and shoved somewhere soft and sweet-smelling and she couldn't move, she felt languorous and warm and lazy and perfectly all right as the cap was busily sealed, and all was bright and golden.

Only a few more directions to release . . . have to trigger the

Conversion . . . can't help it any more than breathing—it's *like* breathing—with the next breath—

No!

But . . . why not? She relaxed. That was what the Queen did, forever and ever. Eternally. How lovely it would be . . . closed and predictable, yet full of passion . . . especially if she didn't know how it ended . . . she could forget the endings if she wanted . . . she could live, again and again.

Forever.

No, she said again, from somewhere back inside herself, somewhere far back, as far back as Bear Creek, and Russ, and Mother Ann, who commanded people to follow their own conscience and to trust that they had one. Verity felt as if she were being pulled right through herself, then, as if she were being turned inside out, literally, and it was not good, it was deeply sickening, for a long moment, and she simply wanted to die.

Surrender, whispered a voice, and at first she did not know how, and then, suddenly, she did.

The stored energy of the Hive rushed into her, and she into it, all her mind, all her being, nothing except glowing brilliance. India, Abe, all the Stories, all the Pictures, all the Music—she was them and they were her, and she had to do nothing except perpetuate them, forever, to make sure her minions could feed on them always, and it was bright, and dancing, and bright, and dancing like—

The brilliant and repeating Dance of Meetings.

Both within and without her, she was Verity dancing, and she watched Verity dance. Verity's dance merged with the dance of the Hive, as no other emissary's dance had been able to do.

India had been right, said the Dance, said Verity's movements. She could do anything now.

All of the stories.

All of the memories.

Every single one was hers now. All that was hidden was revealed.

No other emissary, she knew, had ever gotten this far. No other challenger to the Queen ever had this access. The glory of it suffused her, the power—infinite.

But . . . now she could find that which she had sought before. The thing that teased her mind.

The thing that might take from you this glory, warned the Hive with darkness, fear, entreaties.

She pulled herself from those thoughts. Dance, she thought, dance. You are a dancer of a new grammar of hope.

A new direction kicked in as she pirouetted and whirled. That memory she had asked for before. The numbers of it. But she didn't even need them now. She seized it this time, one of the times, as it slipped by, for she had infinite time now. It all fell open before her.

And then she was walking down Vine Street again, and it was long ago.

Forty

○○○○○○○○○○○○○○○○○○○

Redemption and Release

The day was brilliant and smelled of deep summer: a smell of green trees rustling, faintly, in the wind, a smell of heavy white peonies propped up with sticks, a smell of hot asphalt that left her as she turned off Vine Street and walked toward the house.

She paused in front of the broad steps and looked up at the screen door. It would be locked with a hook, and besides, she should just go around back. She walked around the side of the house, where the cool damp stones that were the girdle of the basement rimmed a narrow bed of lilies of the valley, their thick pointed leaves darkly glossy in the shade of large maples.

"Rosie!" called a thin boy from far back in the yard where he read in a hammock. "There you are."

"Yes," she said. "Here I am."

"Mother left," he said. "She was upset that you were late, but I told her I was too old to need a baby sitter anyway. I'm twelve!" His eyes flashed briefly with resentment. "And next year I'm even going to be in your school."

Rose was fifteen, and in a special architecture and technical school that had just accepted Abe as its youngest student ever. It rankled a bit, but India's preening had been the hardest thing about it. And she and Abe *did* have fun—until the last year or so anyway, it seemed.

"Well, that's six months from now," she said. "And I'll be able to help you a lot."

"Maybe," he said. "I guess."

"Damned right I will," she said.

"Oh?" he said. He rolled out of his hammock, beside which was scattered a pile of books. "Well, you're always asking me about architectural history," he said. "I guess you're all right with a lot of the more dull subjects. Vectors and stress and whatnot. But I know how to make things *beautiful*."

"Right," she said. "You couldn't even design a one-story house without those dull subjects. I know they're hard for you, but you'll get better at that, eventually. Takes a lot of math, but if you try hard you can probably get the hang of it." She reached up and touched the knot holding up the hammock. "Who did this?"

"Me," Abe said.

She made an impatient sound, gave the hammock a rough sideways jerk, and the whole thing came undone.

"Come on, Rose," he said.

"Oh, you're always so careless," she said. "Just don't want to take the time to do it right. But if you break your butt, who do you think your mother will blame?" With a quick motion she jumped and caught the lowest branch, walked her feet up the rough trunk, and pushed herself over the top of the branch so that she was lying on top of it. "Toss me that rope," she said.

He watched as she quickly, yet precisely, looped the rope around itself several times and then pushed the end down through the rope corridor she'd created. "There," she said. She turned a skin the cat on the branch and dropped to the ground.

"Showoff," he said.

She grinned.

Everything froze then. As if behind a clear membrane. She tried to make it continue, somehow, frustrated, wondering how long it would take to master these things.

No, said a voice, *there is another. You seem to have a name.*

Verity.

An address, as it were. Unlike all the others. Such a sameness about them! But I can show you. I'm not sure . . . but I think I've been waiting quite a while to show someone.

The voice was filled with quiet elation.

It was a woman's voice.

*   *   *

She shook her head abruptly as she entered the warm, dark coat room at the side of the cabin, and water drops whipped into her face. She yanked ice-crusted gloves from her hands and pulled caked ice from the ends of her hair.

"Who's there?" she heard from the living room.

"Just me," she yelled.

"What the hell are you *doing* here, Rose?" Abe, tall and lanky, entered the room and flicked the light on. Glancing in a small mirror hanging crooked on the wall, Verity was shocked to see that Rose was—

Herself.

"Your ears are so red! They must be frozen." Abe reached over and rubbed her ears and she laughed even though they burned. "Why didn't you wear a hat?" he demanded. "How did you get here? I haven't seen you in ages, and you turn up *here.*" His laugh was one of sheer delight.

The cedar planks that lined the wall in a herringbone pattern seemed to enfold her. *Winter,* they whispered. *Winter, and the Big Lake.*

"I got stuck at the end of the drive," Verity heard, and felt, the woman who looked like her say. "I smashed the mailbox, I think. The snow was a lot deeper than I thought once I got off the solar road. Never thought forty miles could take so long! I'm exhausted."

"I guess," Abe said, sounding angry. "So you walked two miles in a raging blizzard at two in the morning. It's a wonder you're alive."

"Give me a break, Abe," she said. "I have a flashlight. The road is wide. The trees are big. It's easy to follow. Besides, the storm has died down some. Got any brandy?"

They sat by the fire. He stretched out in a worn green chair, she lay on her back on the couch, her head resting on the arm, staring at the eyes of the ceiling planks.

"So what are you doing here?" he asked. "Decide to take a little winter vacation?"

"I knew that you would come here during the vote, Abe," she said. "I was worried about you. I've been worried about you ever since India—"

"What *about* India?" he asked, his voice sharp.

"Sorry," she said. "But I am. Worried."

"Well, you really showed it. Where have you been? Boston?"

"Denver," she said. "They hired me to solidify their failsafes. It was a damned big job. Lots of things can go wrong once a city converts, Abe."

"I know that," he said. "Anyway, as you can see, I'm just fine. So tomorrow I'll help you dig out your car, and you can head on back to Cincinnati." Then his voice softened. "Even though I've missed you dreadfully. Sorry. Stay. Please."

She shifted on the couch to face him.

"I don't know, if that's what you're thinking," she said. "I don't know how the vote went."

He shrugged. "I do. Really, I have no doubt. But that wasn't what I was thinking."

"Abe, I'm scared," she said. She sat up and put her snifter on the low table, a large slab of slate balanced on four stubby logs. Firelight licked the corners of the room, rich with wood and faded red curtains and rows and rows of books. Wind rattled the shingles as it gusted and whined in the eaves. The dull pounding of waves was an undertone to the crackling of the fire.

"Don't be," he said with odd suddenness, and rose, and knelt next to her. He took her hands and looked up at her, eyes intense. "There's a perfect city there. In Cincinnati, I mean. One that I've been working on. No—don't pull your hands away. You would like it. I'm sure of it. I designed it with you in mind, Rose. Perfect truth and integrity. Full of wisdom, freedom, and art. Living there, each individual will flower to their fullest extent. Ah—it's so different. It's like the cities we used to talk about when we were young—remember? I wish I'd brought it with me, actually. It's a different variation on the Flower Cities." He let go of her hands and sat back on his heels. "You're right, Rose, I guess—you always knew me so well. I've been working on something tonight that's—oh, I guess it's just crazy, in a way. I just ought to scrap it." He laughed shortly.

She leaned forward and took hold of his shoulder, shook it gently. "Don't worry, Abe. You've been under a lot of strain. You blame yourself for everything. It's not your fault." She took a deep breath. "Abe, I've seen your plan. That's what scares me. I think it could get started very easily. And I also think that it could spiral out of control just as easily. And it's very tight."

He stood abruptly. "Oh, you've seen it, have you?" he asked. "That's pretty nosy of you, don't you think? And where the hell have you been in the past year when I needed you? I felt like I was going crazy. I needed *somebody*—some dose of *reality*—Rose! I missed you so!"

"Abe," she said quietly, gazing past him into the fire, "Don't you remember what happened the last time I saw you?" Her eyes shifted to his. She was quiet for a second. "Maybe you don't. It was right after India . . . You were pretty upset—about everything. You screamed at me." She shivered. "You said that India had always told you that I was too flirty—that I'd try to—" she laughed sharply "—sink my *claws* into you—as if I *had* claws—" She laughed again and held out her hands and looked at them thoughtfully. "It rather confused me."

Abe leaned back on his heels. His face was sad. "No. To tell you the truth, I don't remember that at all. I'm terribly sorry, Rose. I can't believe that I would say things like that to you. I guess I am going nuts. It's true, she used to tell me that, every once in a while. And it was really strange—when you opted out of the design team, it only made her more angry—like you shouldn't have that choice. I guess she was always jealous of how close we were." He reached over and touched her cheek.

"I guess," said Rose. She abruptly scooted down to the other end of the couch. "Oh, well. I guess I was kind of stunned. I should have known that you were just upset." She took a deep breath. "Anyway, that's not why I came. I have been working hard, and not just on Denver. I have a—now, what should I call it that won't hurt your feelings—a bug-free Queen City."

He frowned and stood. "What do you mean, bug-free?"

"You know exactly what I mean."

"I'd like to look at it."

"I don't know," she said. "I'm keeping it in a safe place, for now. In a special medium. Where it will be safe no matter what happens—I think. If I understand *your* parameters correctly. Ready to spring into action! Yes, Rose will save the day! Responsible, plodding, careful Rose. Abe, sometimes I'm afraid that you don't have a conscience anymore. I mean, when I look at what you're doing—ah, now, don't get mad, I have my ways of finding out."

His voice was low when he spoke. "Sometimes I think I don't either. But of course I do—it's somewhere inside. You know that. I'm just trying to work this out. I'm just playing, Rose. Just dreaming. It's therapy. That's all. So beautiful, like her mind. Tell me where these plans are, Rose. Are they on the city net? I'd like to look at them. They might help me . . . solidify things."

She smiled. "Right. Oh, Abe, just think of it as a game. Remember how we used to play cards for hours and hours on end? When your city plays one card, mine will play another. And . . . it's not quite perfected yet either. I love you dearly, Abe, but—no. The plans are stored in a safe place now." She yawned and stretched. "When I go back, I'll work on them some more. Tell you what. When they're really finished, maybe we can work together on something more sensible. All right?"

"You have a lot of nerve to call *me* crazy," said Abe. "Tell me, Rose. Please. You know how you've always balanced me—"

"Well," said Rose, and sat up. "It would be irresponsible of me not to. You'd laugh if you knew where it was stored. But I don't know—"

A perturbation, like a wave passing through a thick, clear medium, blurred the scene. Then it vanished.

Verity felt herself coalescing, stirring, within her cell. She found that she was being drawn back into her body as if she had been asleep, and dreaming, and was now waking.

Put me back where I was! Verity thought, and *tried,* but could not move, could not return to the point where Rose might *say* where that City-seed was—

She heard India's voice then, and stirred. She found that she was able to sit up. Young India was there, sitting cross-legged on the soft, golden dance floor in a long print dress. Verity saw that she was no longer fat, and was wearing the clothes she had entered the City in.

India smiled.

"Yes," she said. "How did you *suppose* we pass our time here. So many options! A shame that we can't know Rose's answer, don't you think? But no one ever has. No one has ever been able to. That memory is lost. And personally, I don't think she told him. She was that kind of a person, you know. A tease." She looked around, and Verity saw that the comb walls were shining, brilliant. "It won't be long now," said India. "And then, my dear, we can begin again. You and I will truly be as one. We're sisters now. Equals. Heavenly!" She clapped her hands in delight.

Verity narrowed her eyes. She held out her hands and looked at them. She wondered if the receptors were still there. Her hands felt . . . different. She felt terribly ineffective, entirely superfluous to the workings of the Hive, Queen though she might be. She was only one Queen, and seemed to rule nothing. Though she *was* getting the people out of the City, while she dreamed in here, she had failed, ultimately, to change it. The City could grow more people and do it all again. Except—

"What happened to Rose?" she asked.

"She died on the way back to Cincinnati," said India, without a trace of emotion on her face. "She damaged the solar road linking device when she ran into the mailbox, and once she got back on the solar road, her car went out of control going around a curve." India frowned. "It upset Abe quite a bit. The car sheeted her, of course, and sent out a distress signal, and they brought her back to Cincinnati and stored her. But her memories had deteriorated quite a bit by then. The sheets didn't work just right in the cold."

"How do you know?" asked Verity. "You were dead then, weren't you?"

"My dear," India said almost sadly, "Don't you understand yet? I've never been dead. And Abe was so sensitive, he blamed himself."

"As *usual*," Verity said.

India's face changed. Suddenly she looked more mature. A bit older. And somewhat confused.

"I'm sorry," she said hesitantly, looking at Verity as if for the first time. "I always liked you, Rose. You were so bright, and you thought about the same things Abe did, and I just hated sharing that part of him." She sighed, blinked, looked away. "I don't know why I never see Abe anymore. There's always only Dennis. He's not quite the same . . . and I don't know why Dennis chose *you* to do this to. He kept making all these Roses, and I had to keep . . . killing them. They never could get to the end of things. But you—you're very strong." Her face looked even older. She nodded her head absently. "Yes. Even though Rose's memories weren't saved, I suppose he thought that someone *like* her might put it all together one day . . ."

Verity was shaking with this new knowledge. It was true, and immense, and there *was* a reason—*must* be!

She forced her mind to reel back, wondering if it took centuries or seconds. Back to the place where Rose was going to tell Abe where the City was. A City that was sane, a Flower City where the Bees were in service to the humans, not the other way around. An engineer's City. Safe, sane, functional. With art, but not *for* art. Where the children she had seen at Jane's school, or their successors, after this final Conversion, could truly be architects, engineers, physicists. Where they could learn about the Information Wars, the plagues . . . and maybe change things . . .

Darkness squeezed her. *I am the Queen,* she thought, and realized that she needed all the power, all the *will* she could muster to do what she wanted to do, what she had to do.

Less is more, said Miles.

She *had* to destroy the Queen.

That meant she had to destroy herself.

India was laughing once again. "Oh, I know what you're thinking. You see, poor child, it is impossible. An unsolvable dilemma."

Verity ignored India. She forced herself through the immense library of emotions once again. There were metapheromones for this, powerful ones. She gathered them to her and began to sweat. Though that avenue seemed dark and airless, she tried again and again. The secret was hidden here in the Hive. The Hive had always known—and so now, *she* could know. Because she was the first to know that there was *something to know.*

The answer burst through her with a sudden and painful light.

Rose, unbeknownst to anyone, had quietly kept herself fully updated in the City archives, as had Durancy. Her datapaths had become twisted, folded away, but now—

Verity cried out in triumph. She jumped to her feet. Not far! Not far! But she had had to go through all *this,* to know it, because Abe's program countered every move Rose's program made with one of its own. It was endlessly inventive, after all! It fought to live! Dennis—a Durancy with a conscience—was Rose's creation. But Abe's program—perhaps his living intelligence, hiding deep within the Hive, so deep that it no longer had any vestige of humanity—had been able to keep Durancy's understanding limited. And each time the whole sad mess began again.

Would begin again, if she didn't hurry. Abe's plan and Rose's plan had intertwined with the intimacy of children growing up together, playing, making their own games, their own rules, fighting, reconciling,

Having a soda fight in the drug store . . . shaking up the bottles, releasing fizzy streams of sticky soda in arcs across the store while the old man yelled and they laughed, and laughed, and laughed—

The very walls began to close in on Verity, trying to stop her, but she pushed her way through with a power she had not known that she possessed.

The power came from a small white room, where beneath her pillow lay the radio stone, where everyone she loved was close at hand. She was *not* Rose. She was *Verity*. She was *alive.*

And then she was running again, down a corridor, and the corridor became quickly more narrow. She came to the end of it, a golden membrane.

Panting, she burst from the Hive into the Bee Museum. It was hard to get a purchase on the slippery floor, but she ran like a madwoman, certain that at any moment the walls would crumble, the floor open up—

"Stop!" she heard India call out behind her. "Wait!"

But she ran more quickly, pushed open the tall, padded door to the outside. Warm summer air hit her face. On the wide white marble platform she paused between the tall columns.

A wild crowd filled the streets, rushing down to the river. The air was filled with their jubilant shouts, with Rafter songs.

Verity looked to the right, saw the awning of the apothecary shop—the old drug store—glowing through the tall wrought-iron fence, beneath the blossoming apple trees that lined the boulevard. "Yes!" she whispered and leaped down the shallow steps, made her stride long, as long as Blaze's; India could never catch her, never! and pushed through the crowd frantically against their current.

"Let me in!" she yelled, and raised her arm as she approached to pound on the door, but the old man opened it just as she reached it and he wept and trembled and wiped his eyes as she whooped with delight, smashed a fifty, a *hundred* jars from the shelf to find this *one,* dusty and hidden and precious at just the place Rose had stored it, and hands bleeding rushed out into the bright summer sun.

She raised the vial to the sun and it winked and glittered, many colors. India was dashing toward her, face twisted, her long blond hair loose and flowing behind her.

Verity tilted back her head and laughed, as she struggled to undo the lid but could not. "You wanted me to help you!" she shouted. "Well, *here!*"

She dashed the vial to the ground and knelt next to the replicators, scooped them into a pile, and cupped them in her hand, ignoring the fragments of glass that cut into her.

The replicators warmed within her hands. She jumped up and shouted, "This is Rose's trump card! The Queen can activate the seeds of Rose's City!" She shook her clenched hands in India's face. "You didn't want to know! Of course not!"

Then she loosed the activated replicators, which had only to meet the receptors that were embedded in the very fabric of the matter of Durancy's City for the change to begin.

The change to Rose's sane City.

If it was still viable.

Verity watched as a spatter of them fell to the street, and where they fell, black lightened to gray in circles that grew . . .

And then, hands bleeding, gasping for breath, she turned and looked at India.

Though the glowing plague crowd still trampled past, it seemed to Verity as though time had stopped.

And then it rushed forward.

She watched an amazing change come over India's face. Terror, sorrow, grief, anguish, and then joy suffused her features in quick succession, and then a puzzled wonder as a smile appeared and tears began to flow. Sobbing, she approached Verity, and Verity could not move.

India embraced her.

"Thank you," she whispered. Her face was growing old, into the face Verity had found so dear. "I thought I never could be free."

Then she clutched her chest.

She fell to the street, and the crowd parted and flowed around her. "It hurts," she said.

To her right, Verity saw the apothecary shop shiver, just slightly. Then it seemed as though the awning receded, and the shape of the windows changed subtly, as though she was seeing an earlier incarnation. A sign arched across the window—SODAS.

Rose's City was very powerful. It would wipe out even this place, unchanged through India's rule. Its usefulness was over now.

Verity knelt and cradled India. Then she was pushed aside by a woman in a white medic uniform.

"How did you know?" asked Verity, and the woman looked at her, astonished.

"How could we *not* know?" she asked impatiently. Two men next to her knelt and one man began pulling clear, blinking sheets from a large square case.

"It's all right," whispered India. "Please. Please, no."

The man paused for a moment, then continued arranging the sheets.

Verity looked out over the mad City, trembling now on the verge of change. She knew that she had to get back to the Hive, and hold the fabric of change together.

Rose's game might still be countered with moves from Durancy's.

In some part of her, she knew that she would then die.

She knelt next to India. "Don't worry," she said. "It will be all right, this time."

"I don't want to live," said India. "Please. I don't know anyone anymore. This world is too strange for me. Please."

"Are you sure?" asked Verity, as India lay amid the rush of people fleeing the City.

"Yes," said India. "I'm very sure." She gazed at Verity with deep, sure quietude. "I'm just so glad it's over."

Verity fought the impulse to give India no choice. She stood. "Leave her," she said to the medics. "And leave the City too, unless you want to be caught in the Conversion."

The woman looked at the man. "I was just thinking how wonderful it would be to see Norleans," she said, and threw down the sheets.

"That's funny," said the man. "I was too."

Verity turned and crossed the street. She walked back up the steps of the Hive, sweating. She thought about all the people she had met who claimed that they did not sleep during the winter—the apothecary, Oedipa Mass, Azure—and knew that they were part of Rose's plan too, her attempt to create a critical mass, even a religion, with which to combat India's dreadful recycling, one that might understand the predicament the City was in and try to help change it. She had tried to play all the angles. Each new Dennis and India grew a bit older, knew a bit more, before the City realized it, and swept them away.

At the door of the Bee Museum, she heard someone shouting

behind her, but she resolutely walked through the tall columns one last time.

She walked down the golden corridor and felt again the tickling touch of many tiny arms as her sister Bees drew her back into the cell.

She thought she heard a dog barking, and smiled, eyes closed, caught in a powerful dream of Heaven. Everyone she loved was there. John, and Russ, Evangeline and Sare, Tai Tai and even Blaze . . . Blaze was here too! And Cairo. They were all shouting and barking and making a racket, and . . . they wanted her to *leave* . . .

"I can't leave," she said in her dream. "I am the New Queen now. We're all going to die, all the Queens, we're going to die at last, we must—"

She felt the dream slip from her with a sickening, painful wrench. She was back in the Hive. Cairo was dead. She opened her eyes and was amazed.

Several Bees lay still on the floor, dead or stunned—yes, stunned by the *music* as they had begun to cap her cell, she knew in an instant.

For Sphere was there, playing a saxophone. The music was intense, stinging, yet oddly joyful, as if welling from some deep place in him, a place free and strong and filled with understanding, rage, love, and power.

He frowned in concentration; his entire body bore the notes upward and released them as his arms moved, as he arched his back and then bent over. Bits of color emanated from him and flew through the air to lodge in the walls of the Hive around her, making it glow too with some sort of organized vision of incandescent, glowing, changing light. She saw that it was a pattern where bits of color danced in an oddly lucid pattern, one which she could almost *understand* as she might understand print on a page. It had deep, precise meaning. This was one way in which the Hive could *think*.

With each change she herself felt lightened; restored, renewed, released from heaviness and pain and death. *Give the City to Rose*, the music said. *You can let go now. It will be all right. All right. All right.*

"No," she murmured, but Sphere would not stop, and she stirred inside the cell, wanting to return to the final metamorphosis, the final bonding of power that he had interrupted.

She knew now, with every atom of her body, the terrible desire of the City for *her*. To redo it, renew it. She wanted to stay. The buildings, the molecules, enlivened for so long by Abe's plan, called out to her in anguish. She knew at last that India's dilemma had gone deeper than the most intense and searing passion, and forgave her.

And there was still time for her to do it again. All was not lost. *Abe,* she whispered. *Help me.*

Her wanting to return to the Hive was Abe's last card. She did not have to hold the City together.

To release it, she had to leave it.

Impossible. She closed her eyes and tried to close her ears.

But relentlessly, Sphere played on.

The music and colors flowed through her mind like a river, torrentially, washing her from those moorings.

Sphere let the saxophone drop. He looked at the pattern on the Hive wall as if it meant something to him as sweat rolled down his face and he tried to catch his breath. He nodded. "There," he said. "Let's see if that worked. I hope—" His voice caught. "I *hope* that was something new. A true improvisation. It felt like it. Verity, see, people *can* learn here. I took off from the theme of the City, then made something new. It *has* to work. For you. It *is* you. A new, *free* you. So the City can be free."

"Sphere?" she said, as waves of awakening washed through her. "Is that really you?"

She opened her eyes and looked into his. Tears glittered in his dark brown eyes behind his glasses. They were filled with deep compassion.

He nodded at Blaze. "Now."

Blaze held out some flowers for her. His eyes were clear, though his face was wan even in the dim gold light of Hive. "Forget-me-nots," he said. "Sphere said they would work. He said that they would—oh, it sounds crazy—" His voice broke with despair, then he looked at Sphere, who frowned.

Blaze continued, "He said their smell would *cement* you in yourself. And help you to leave. He said that even then it might not work. Anyway, Verity, take a deep breath. It can't hurt, can it? Please! Hurry!"

Because Blaze and Sphere wanted her to, she pushed herself from the cell and buried her face in the flowers.

Forty-one

○○○○○○○○○○○○○○○○○○○

Bright Shining as the Sun

Verity stood on Roebling's Bridge, below one of the grand towers, leaning over the rush and roar of the Ohio Confluence, the two Ohio Rivers, old and new.

Verity realized as if she were a radio stone distilling the ever-present essence of the air that the City was shouting at her.

Shouting with all its might, telling her something, something very precise, and absolutely true, something she was born to know, something she was meant to know, as if it were her friend, her lover, her grandmother, Mother Ann. As if it were John and Blaze and a magnificent library and she infinity, knowing all that it was impossible for one human to know in one lifetime except that she did, and each bit of information lit each other bit in new ways, constantly, so that she was a function of time.

The Plague woman John had killed had been right. She had stood there, on the bank of Bear Creek, in the cold, and laughed. "The Plague is a *cure,* and *change,*" she had said. "The Plague makes you truly *alive.*"

Verity realized that it was true. It was all quite glorious, this force that had driven Russ's mother to create a new religion. She was glad that it had taken her differently, though, brought out something else in her. She was helping to lead people as in-nocent as children to a new land. The necessity to do so was powerful, inevitable, and somewhat frightening. She and Blaze were the only ones who had not lived their whole lives in the City.

Looking west, Verity could see where the rivers wove back into one, where they reformed into the water highway that would take them down to Cairo, New Bethlehem, the places beyond. Where the people who had created the Territory Plague lived.

Where, maybe, Norleans still lived. It shone in her mind, like a celestial City made of sunlit clouds, radiating a strange music of accordions and jazz and crazy rhythms. Blaze wanted to go there, he was wild for that new music. Norleans *might* be populated by humans. Real humans.

At least, that had once been true. Norleans had never converted, but there was no way of knowing if Norleans was even still there. The radio stone may have picked up a station simply programmed to broadcast endlessly despite the quasar, in the hope that occasionally something might get through; a station long since abandoned by living people. Verity absently touched the radio stone in her pocket—a large violet crystal with sharp-edged facets—but heard nothing.

But the roar of the falls was strong here, at any rate, too strong to hear it even if it was an exceedingly rare moment clear for radio transmission.

She thanked Roebling for the strong design of his towers, which held the glittering suspension cables still, through earthquake and flood. She could feel how the forces played against one another in amazing and delicate balance with some new part of her mind—Rose? Both towers were still firmly footed, though the land had cracked off just past the Kentucky tower, where water swirled into a vast and dangerous basin, so that the bridge ended in midair. Verity did not wonder anymore why no one had tried to drop a raft, rappel down the bridge, and take advantage of what looked like a narrow clear channel just below the tower nearest the City. A force stronger than the Seam had held them here, a force like love. A force that *was* love, love's chemistry, that which sparked whatever emotions were. She glanced at her hands, holding tight to the railing, and smiled.

Everything looked so hazy, so wonderful. The Territory, pristine and bright, lay ahead of them, beckoning. And who was that walking toward her?

"Blaze?" She was afraid, for an instant, remembering that for a while he had been very odd, but when he was closer, she saw his restored green eyes, filled once again with *himself*, his own true being, and was relieved.

He looked down at the arm she was admiring and sighed. "Ah, yes," he said. He looked up at her, so intently, so *gravely*, when everything was so wonderful! and bent toward her, brushed her cheek with a kiss, then clasped her hand fiercely.

"Come on, Demon," he said. "The raft is waiting. Everything's just about loaded, I think. Warm clothes, sleeping bags, food, guns, ammunition. The nan seeds. The amplifier for the radio stones is sealed against water; we can maybe set it up once we're out on smooth water. We've got a long trip ahead of us."

The spray of the falls dampened her face and the sun made rainbows jump from the white rush. Now she remembered. She had set all this in motion—when? Before the baseball game? During it, when the Plague was released? Some part of her had thought to make sure that the newly made Norleaners would be provisioned.

"Sphere's still not coming?" she asked, unable to believe that anyone could resist.

"No," Blaze said gently. "He's—he's changed a bit you know," he said, and looked quite sad. "He's quite fallen in love with someone . . . or something. Remember? I already told you how you wouldn't leave, there at the Hive after we found you, after *he* found you, and then he figured out what to do?"

She shook her head without thinking and Blaze's face crumpled for a moment, but he didn't cry like she thought he would. He was terribly upset each time she couldn't recall something, but she understood that well enough. Maybe he was just remembering how *he* had felt.

"That's all right," he said quickly. "Don't worry. I mean, I'm not worried. Sphere said it would take time for the Plague to—kick in, that's what he called it. I begged him to come. There's music in Norleans too! And what will I do on the raft without him to jam with? How can I play *alone*, now?" Blaze's eyes glittered then, and Verity knew he was remembering, somehow, the evening in the hall, when he and Sphere had played so ethereally. He said, "It was so strange. He found me in that huge, rushing crowd, I don't know how. I didn't even know who he was, but he said he knew you and knew me too and that we had to help you. While we ran to the Zoo he just kept chanting, 'Miles always said less is more,' and 'The City is a work of art, like a piece of music, *less is more,'* and when we got there he was real thoughtful, then said, 'I'll just take *this* metapheromone away—' then he'd play a bit more and the colors would change '—and *this* too and Verity will be *simple* again, she'll be herself, she'll be human.' I'll tell you again and again, Verity, I'll never stop telling you, no matter how many times you forget. But now Sphere won't leave. He wants everything he thinks the City will have, after . . .'' Blaze's voice faltered.

"I think it will be all right," Verity said, remembering in the sharpness of the moment that she *had* done something to heal the City, if it worked, knowing that she would forget again in a minute or two, as if seeing an island far off while lifted on the crest of a wave, then falling to the trough where it was hidden. It was almost like when the Durancy assemblers had activated her, but this was not alien, foreign, like him. This was more *herself*. "After this Conversion, it should be all right. I would have liked to see it. I think there was something I should have done to help it along. You should have left me." But even as she spoke, she felt no compulsion to return. She felt only one strong thing and that was all she had room for now. Norleans.

"You didn't leave me," said Blaze. He looked at her quite directly with his beautiful green eyes, the exact shade of the clean, pure, New Ohio River. "Verity. My love. You don't have to do *everything*. It's not your responsibility to sacrifice yourself because of whatever these people did to you. I'm not sure what that was . . . but maybe that's over now. Sphere said it would be."

"Come back and get me when everything's ready," she said. "It doesn't look ready to me." She squinted at him. How bright he looked, standing in the sun! "Are you better?" she asked, suddenly rememebering. "Do you still have the Plague?" Then she was puzzled. Had he told her?

Blaze gave her a sharp, sad look. "Half an hour, Verity. Then we have to get out of here. Our raft is ready. I don't care if all of them are ready or not. Most of them are angry, to tell you the truth. You should hear them whining. They act like it's the end of the world, when it's just the beginning. I bet half of them chicken out and stay here."

"Perhaps," she said, unperturbed. "They have a choice."

"Sure they do, Verity."

You don't understand, she thought, they really *do*, at least for a brief time, I *know* I gave them that . . . however simple . . . stay and be Converted . . . go, toward I know not what . . . perhaps just your own Selves.

She tried to tell him but forgot what to say, and he turned and she watched him walk toward the end of the bridge.

There was silence then, only it was not silence but a rush, the constant welling of the river, which could carry her to something entirely and absolutely new, something wholly herself. And that was something stronger, and more real, than anything she'd ever known before. Herself, the person beneath her name, stubborn, young, and glowing. Her Self, her pre-Durancy Core, like a strong, cool stone, radiated from some beautiful center, wiping away all that was past, and the way she had been used by Rose, Durancy, India, and the City. She felt relieved and whole, for a second, exactly like the sun, pure and hot yet at the same time cool and lifegiving with distance and essential energy. Could she ever approach and merge with that center, that sun?

But she was also Rose. Part of her was a person she didn't even know. She wondered if she would carry Rose within her forever, and Durancy. Well, that might not be so bad, if there was some kind of distance, some kind of control. There was a lot of information there. But she didn't know, yet, how that would be. How or what or who *she* would be.

Below, past the falls, people were loading what looked like hundreds of rafts and the great showboats with provisions. The showboats, two of them, had hosted plays for who knows how long, but they were working vessels as well. A few volunteers were going to try and pilot them through the confluence.

She remembered the Hive, now, and how she had thought it all out. Maybe the Rose part of her had done that. She had found the seeds for the rafts. They had not taken long to grow. Most of the things being loaded were knives, ropes, axes—the most simple survival tools.

But other things were more complex. The seeds for houses, vehicles, libraries. She no longer feared nan unreasonably. She understood it, deeply, knew its limits and dangers. This information was partly from the Hive, but the confidence had another source. She had, herself, changed.

She had come to the City only to save Blaze and Cairo. She had failed to save Cairo, and her heart twisted, for a moment, at the needless anguish Cairo had gone through because she, Verity, had tried to save her from death. She had tried. She had done her best, and failed, and in the process had caused an innocent being much pain. Maybe that was what Abe Durancy had felt. The scope had been different, but after all, one human could only feel so much pain and remorse. And now, she hoped, he would be able to rest, knowing some sort of resolution, some sort of absolution, when this Conversion took place.

And Blaze was living, was he not? And he was *himself* again. That was joy itself.

She studied the river. She had to concentrate on the rapids. She was pretty sure she knew the way around them, but could only be positive when she was out in the river, raft shifting beneath her feet as she leaned on the steering oar. She could hardly wait!

Yes, at least that map was in her. Was the map in all of them? All those maps, there in her cells; how wondrous were her and her kind, the humans. Made of knowing stuff, as knowing as the stuff of the City, and gathered together in such a way that light burst upon her and she knew it. The City, it seemed to her, knew it dimly, with a yearning faint as dawn's forelight, which grew stronger with each passing hour, inevitably. She knew she could not be here when that energy coalesced into a new and very different way of knowing, because she would be inexorably drawn into it and *changed*. She would dance in its streets and rejoice. Blaze would not let her stay. She remembered now. In the last day they had argued several times about her staying, but now it seemed that something else was taking hold. The Plague, pulling her to Norleans. Now *she* wanted to go too, she realized. Whatever she was supposed to do here was finished. Blaze was right.

Yet part of her wanted to see it, just to see it. The Conversion. Like Anselm's name of God that John had been so fond of stuffing down their throat at the dinner table on those timeless green summer evenings, the unknowable merging with and changing the known so that someone like John might drop to his knees and think angels.

Then those thoughts and memory as well were swept from her like smoke from the chimneytop on a windy day. A new City took shape in her mind, one that called to her with images of an exciting adventure: a raft, a mad river, escape from hypocrisy and slavery. A shimmering path to the truly new.

She held out her hand so that it was over the green rushing river and frowned. It looked normal. The wind caught her hair and pulled it out behind her. She turned out of the sun and looked at her hand once more in the shadow of a thick cable. She smiled: Yes. How oddly happy this made her feel.

She was truly human at last. Her immunities were gone. In the dark, it was unmistakable.

Already, she was beginning to glow.

She felt a touch on her shoulder, jumped, and turned.

"Sphere!" said Verity, and hugged him, then stepped back to look at him. "How are you?" she asked.

His saxophone was attached to a strap and hung at his back. His face looked beatific.

Where she had become more human, she realized, he had become *less* human, and more . . . something else. She was reminded of the words of a hymn as she watched the joy in his face and eyes. Changed from glory into glory. Sphere had become what he wanted to become.

He was music.

He frowned a bit. When he spoke, his voice was hushed and husky and very difficult to hear. "It's . . . very hard to *tell* you how I feel."

Before Verity could say anything, he shifted his saxophone and began to play.

The first notes were searching, tentative. Verity was reminded of the time she had first heard him play, that evening in moon-washed Union Station, the notes spiraling toward Heaven. Verity stood very close, and bent her head toward the saxophone, because the falls were so loud. She realized that Sphere was using the sound of the falls as a part of the music he was creating.

Though Sphere's eyes were squeezed shut, Verity's were open. She saw how his music seemed to bind together the huge green river with rafts hugging its bank, the people rushing back and forth, and the City, washed by wild fluxes of color and trembling on the verge of Conversion. The music even knew of Cairo's death, for when he played that, he opened his eyes and looked into Verity's and she knew that was what it was, those keening notes, that brief ecstatic staccato of Cairo's final joy at finding her at last. As he played on and on, she learned with each note why he could not leave. He was suffused with pure beauty. But it was *conscious* beauty, a beauty he was choosing.

She closed her eyes and allowed herself to be drawn into it. It was a true improvisation, and pulled her into herself, then out of herself once again. Herself. Not Durancy, not Rose, not the Queen of the Queen City. Verity, who had grown, changed, released a city from a nightmare.

When Sphere stopped playing, suddenly, it was jarring. She heard just the roar of the falls, the rough shouts and bits of rafter songs of the Norleaners below on the banks. She knew she would not hear such purity, such beauty, again. Sphere was a unique synthesis. He was what Durancy had dreamed humans could be.

Verity opened her eyes and looked into his. "Goodbye, Sphere," she said. She saw Blaze waiting at the end of the bridge. It was time.

She reached out and took Sphere's hand, and he bent briefly and pressed his cheek against hers.

She wished for a moment that he would just stay here, on the bridge, forever, playing, and that she could listen, and not plunge toward the fearful and beckoning unknown. She held Sphere tightly for a last moment, thinking that.

Then she let go.

He began playing once again as she walked toward the end of the bridge. Toward Blaze. The Territory.

And herself.